Mary's Boys

Sandra Shakespeare

*AuthorHouse™
1663 Liberty Drive
Bloomington, IN 47403
www.authorhouse.com
Phone: 1-800-839-8640*

Published by AuthorHouse 5/1/2013

*ISBN: 978-1-4817-8868-7 (sc)
ISBN: 978-1-4817-8869-4 (e)*

PENK

"Mary's Boys"

by

Sandra Shakespeare

Queen Victoria Ruled England.

The story begins in the 1880's, Harry loses his parents and sister Ena, to consumption.

He walks miles daily working on a stud farm, whilst looking after his ailing younger brother.

Mary is the daughter of the owner of the Stud Farm, where Harry works.

The death of Harry's brother throws them together. On her 18th birthday she proclaims her love for Harry.

Mary's father disowns her and throws her out pregnant, penniless and destitute.

Mary's journey begins:

She marries Harry, and over the following 18 months they have two sons, Joseph and Samuel.

In the years leading up to WWI, they have another 10 children.

Harry and Joe leave to serve their country. Joe joins the Army Veterinary Corps and is subsequently posted to Belgium.

Sam joins up, following an argument, and becomes a gunner. He is also sent to Belgium, despite being under age.

Mary is distraught with the deaths of her brother and cousins, whilst in active service in Belgium.

Harry is badly wounded, Joe is gassed and there is no word from Sam.

This is a story of a Victorian family, torn apart by WWI and a mother's love for her "*boys*", whilst they are away from home in a place where lives are lost in their 1,000's daily.

"***Mary's Boys***", is a story of love, heroism, loyalty and comradship, during the very difficult years leading up to and including WWI.

This book is dedicated to my dear mother, Ena Victoria Price (deceased). I promised her I would put this story to paper 22 years ago. I did not realise how difficult it would be to keep this promise and what a journey I would go on to complete this task.

Thanks also to my husband, David, without your help "***Mary's Boys***" would not have been completed.

DEDICATION

This book is dedicated to my dear mother, Ena Victoria Price, who passed away in April 1991. She constantly talked of her brothers' and sisters' and their difficult lives, whilst I was growing up.

I promised my mother in 1991 that I would put her story to paper, at that time I did not realise how difficult it would be and what a journey I would go on to complete this task.

She had an equally hard life and struggled, as did her mother, for a better life for her children. This will be outlined in *Mary's Boy's II.*

I would also like to thank my beloved husband, David, who has painstakingly stood by me through this very difficult journey, without him I would never have completed *Mary's Boys.*

Thank you David for all your support and making this possible.

BOOK ONE

CHAPTER 1

Harry, Henry and Mary

It was the 1890's, Queen Victoria reigned.

Henry sat on the oak window seat, where many orphans had sat before him. He looked at the scribbles and carvings on the old wooden sill, where those orphans had scraped their names whilst staring out of this very window. Henry took out his penknife and added his and his brother's name to the others. He stared blankly out of the leaded window, tears streaming down his young face, the grief that he felt was too much to bear.

Henry was quite short for his age, blonde with large green eyes and particularly high cheekbones, and beautiful long fingers just like his mother. He wiped away his tears on the rough woollen sleeve of his jumper, his face was tingling from his salted tears and the roughness of the coarse wool of his old jumper.

Tomorrow his brother, Harry, would be leaving the sanctuary of the orphanage; he would be left alone until he was old enough to leave and make his own way in the cruel world. So many orphaned young men had walked through those giant wrought iron gates into the unfriendly world beyond and, now it was the turn of his big brother to leave without him.

It had been almost two years since his family had been wiped out by consumption, little Ena first, then his father, and lastly his poor mother, dying trembling in his young arms.

Henry had climbed into his parent's feather bed to try and console his ailing mother. He cuddled up to her, hoping and praying she would not die whilst he was alone with her, waiting watching the seconds go by on the Grandmother clock. The chimes seemed so loud he covered his ears with his hands. He hated the dark, the fire had almost gone out and the embers just twinkled occasionally throwing shadows across the room. His mother was so wet and cold and a strange noise came out of her mouth, it sounded like a rasping noise. He had been alone for what seemed an eternity wondering where his brother and the doctor were afraid to get out of bed because of the dark.

Harry had gone for the doctor that dreadful night, torrential rain beating down stabbing anyone in it's midst. The horse Molly, who was very skittish at the best of times, had shied following a thunderbolt and thrown him off into the ford, which was well over three feet deep and becoming quite treacherous. He pulled himself up onto the bank and tried desperately to ring out the water from his trousers and coat. He looked for his cap, but could not see it in the dark. He focused his eyes in the darkness and looked for the horse for a few moments, he shouted her, but decided the animal would find her own way back to the cottage. It was more important for him to hurry to the doctors for the help his mother so desperately needed and still some 4 miles away.

In the pitch black of the night he struggled through the pot holes and puddles of mud with his Tillie lamp, which hardly had any kerosene left. Fortunately he had tied it to his belt when he left the cottage. It was only pure luck that he hadn't been injured and his gallant effort to get to the doctor's that night for help came far too late for his poor mother, she had died, despite her struggle to hang onto life.

How sad those terrible days had been for the boys and

now, again, the heartbreaking sadness had returned echoing through his mind, he was to lose the only person left in the world, his brother, to that world outside those gates only a short walk away from the window where he now sat.

Ena, his little sister, was only 8 with beautiful auburn curly hair and highlights of gold and red, like the autumn forest. A tall, skinny child, with big green/hazel tantalizing eyes and freckles all over her button nose. She constantly laughed and giggled for no reason and danced around the living room in front of the fire tormenting the boys and begging them to watch her. Ena wanted to be a ballet dancer and had mastered walking on her tiptoes lifting her thin little arms high above her head. Mother would take her tiny shoes off and rub her toes and reprimand her for the lumps forming on her big toes, but she didn't care about that. She would smile up at her mother, her second teeth sticking out like rabbits teeth, and say

"Mommy all ballerinas have broken big toes, I'm lucky, mine are only bent funny".

Henry could see her dancing in front of him, he reached out with his hand and realised it was just another memory from his past. He looked about him embarrassed at the thought of someone seeing him.

The boys had loved their little sister and doted on her, always giving in to her temper tantrums. Dying that way, withering away, delirious, her big eyes sunk back into her little head, her hair soaking dripping wet with sweat from the consumption, so early in life, without experiencing her dreams, was too sad and a complete waste of a talented young life. Henry thumped at the bench and turned to the window. The memories of her death still so clear in his young mind. He had laid in bed with her that night, just like the night his mother had been taken. Harry had climbed in one side and him the other, with mother at the bottom of the bed, all willing her to survive. She just closed her beautiful sad eyes and went to sleep peacefully and faded away. Her little torso had become just flesh and bones. Henry turned to look at the stairs he could hear something or someone, after a few seconds he realised it was just the building aching as it always did at night.

Henry had held his mother for hours after she had died the night Harry had gone for the doctor, he had finally fallen asleep crying into his mother's nightgown. They had to pull him away from her sobbing and screaming. He was so angry that his brother had taken such a long time to get the doctor. "Why"? he kept shouting "Why"?

Harry hugged him and rocked him like a small child that night. It took a long time for him to calm down. He sobbed throughout the night into his brother's shoulder and would not leave his mother's bedside. The boys sat waiting for the vicar and their aunt to arrive and take her away to the chapel. Every moment seemed unreal, like a terrible nightmare.

His mother had died in his young arms and he was so terribly afraid in that dark cold room. He had felt so alone, death and loneliness deeply frightened him now. The experience had made him very insecure and he had become even more afraid of the dark.

An aunt had taken the boys in following the deaths of those they had all loved so dearly, but fate was cruel, she had survived the consumption, but it had left her frail, with a terrible chesty cough. Her own loved ones were taken before their time following the death of her beloved sister and brother-in-law and little Ena. She was a kind sole, loving and gentle, just like their mother had been. The boys found solace in her unconditional love, they became the family she had lost, but it was only a matter of time before she would be taken from them too in a dreadful twist of fate.

She realised it was only a matter of time before she joined her loved ones and had taken the necessary precautions to secure the boys future and had put her house in order before dying. Her cottage had been assigned to the boys, as there were no other surviving relatives.

The boys were now just a statistic, two more orphaned young boys awaiting the day when they could make their mark in the cruel world that had already taken everyone from them.

Their mother had been deeply religious and took them to the local parish church every week. The vicar had been made appointee and had intervened, following the death of their aunt, he placed the boys into the church orphanage, until such time as they were old enough to look after themselves and take on the responsibility of their aunt's cottage and small free holding.

The vicar was a kindly old man, he was lanky and over 6' tall, with very sharp features, a pointed nose, which was always red and he sniffed all the time and constantly wiped it, which probably accounted for it always being red. He had wispy flyaway grey hair, which was becoming very thin on top. It reminded Harry of a horse's main. He was very conscious of his thinning hair and placed it precariously across the top of his head.

The boys would laugh at it sticking up in the air like a peacocks tail when they sat in the pews listening to him give his weekly sermon on sin and debauchery. He would look down on them and frown and they would hide their shame by turning their heads sideways. Mother would look at them sternly and they knew they had gone too far. Father would shuffle and fidget with his hands and Ena would giggle and look across at them. The vicar would pat his hair down and continue his sermon, which invariably made it look more funny to his parishioners, but his heart was good and he looked after his flock.

He had visited the boys regularly throughout their stay in the orphanage and he took it upon himself to rent their cottage to a young couple with a small child until such time as the boys were able to support themselves. The minimal rent paid by their tenants was kept in a trust fund. The vicar was very conscientious with the boys money and had appointed a solicitor to handle their finances for them, without any charge to thcm, who incidentally was also a member of his flock.

He made sure that the boys had a little money each month for the bare necessities, but made it blatantly obvious that wasting money was not an option.

Two years had now passed by since they had all been

happily living with their parents on the smallholding leased from the local estate. They had assisted their father ploughing the fields with the two old shire mares, Molly and Tillie. Little Ena regularly danced in the corn, her hair blowing in the wind, following them around like a puppy, mother at home baking awaiting their daily return tired and hungry.

Harry was a natural farmer, he loved the land and thrived on it's challenges. Henry was too young to understand the fundamentals of farming and his brother's love for the land and what it had to offer, he preferred to go swimming in the lake, or fishing with his pals. He had never thought of what he was going to do when he left school.

Harry had a natural ability with horses and learnt to plough the fields with his father and uncle from a very young age. He had also worked at the manor house stables on Sundays after church, mucking out and helping looking after his favourite gelding, Mickey. These had been such happy times, the long summer nights, riding with his pals at the stables, after their chores were completed, galloping and racing each other without fear of the consequences, if they fell or stumbled. Harry had glue on his pants, he rarely fell off, when his mount fell he grabbed onto the horses mane, or breastplate and, held on for dear life.

The boys would take Ena with them during holidays to the manor house and stables, the cook would pop out and give them muffins, or just a loaf of bread, to take home for their tea. Ena skipped along the bridle path and invariably got tired, the boys taking it in turns to sit her on their shoulders' and, more importantly, give her a piggy back home.

How sad it had been to lose such a pretty sister, too good for this world aunt Hilda would say. She believed Ena was a special child and that the angels had only loaned her to their little family. It helped the boys to overcome their grief thinking Ena was with the angels.

It had become so dark in the orphanage hallway, Henry had been sitting on the oak window seat for several hours drifting in and out of the past. He had lost track of time and felt so vulnerable and exhausted from the grief he felt, and finally stood up and climbed the old stairs, his shoulders hung over like a little old man, the weight of the world on his young mind.

One by one Henry climbed the oak stairs, creaking and groaning with a mind of their own, echoing shadows tantalising and dancing across the high stonewalls, the wind whistling through the corridors. He felt distraught and so very alone. How was he going to live alone in the orphanage without Harry?

Henry stood at the bottom of Harry's bed, his arms still drooped down his thin body, his head bent and turned sideways trying to hide his tears. Harry was awake, he too had been crying bitterly, pondering on his future and how his little brother would cope without him. So much sadness engrossed the young brothers, fate had dealt them such cruel cards.

Neither boy spoke, Henry crawled into his brother's bed, as he had done so many restless nights before, following that dreadful night their mother had died. This night they both knew was very different, this would be the last comfort from his brother for another two years, lying together side by side Harry's arms engulfing his brother's young frame. Harry clung to him so tightly, Henry could hardly breath, but he didn't mind, he had always sought solace in his brother's arms. As toddlers they had been inseparable and had never been very far apart, they were like identical twins, each knowing what the other was thinking.

Harry broke the long silence and whispered to his brother:

'I will come back every time I have a day off, I promise. It will pass quickly Henry, trust me'.

Henry nodded sadly and hid his face in the pillow, trying desperately to hide his tears. The sadness overpowered both boys.

Harry had continued working at the stables during his stay at the orphanage and had been promised employment as an apprentice groom looking after the working horses and other thoroughbred. He had already assisted the resident blacksmith during the past year and had become an excellent and willing student. The horses knew him and trusted him and stood amazingly still when he lifted their heavy hooves to take of the old shoes and replace them with ones he had lovingly forged and knocked into shape. He loved being around the stables, he could think of no better way of spending his life than this.

The tenants had vacated the cottage, he had been home several times in the past month getting the place ready for his final move from the orphanage. He would be walking to the manor house daily until such time as live-in quarters became available to him and maybe Henry, if employment was offered to him in the following year.

He had in the past slept in the hayloft above the horses, too tired to go home, but this time he would be working as a man, not boy, taking home a wage to support himself enabling him to save and make life easier for Henry.

The prospects of his future and new life on the estate excited him inwardly, but the thought of leaving his young brother at the orphanage to fend for himself made him feel guilty and selfish. Henry found it difficult to stand up to the bullies of the orphanage, he was small for his age and timid, inevitably Harry would get involved and sort the skirmishes out.

Both boys slept huddled together, exhaustion finally taking its' toll. When the morning came Harry gently moved his brother's arm from around his shoulders and climbed out of bed trying desperately not to wake him. He dressed and quietly tiptoed along the dormitory in the hope that Henry would not hear him leave, he could not face more tears and the sadness of his brother looking at him pleading with those sad green eyes. He only had a few belongings, which he had packed in his father's portmanteau.

Henry woke up startled, searching for his brother rubbing his eyes. He jumped out of bed and ran down the dorm, almost falling down the stairs, desperate for his brother.

Old Sarah came hobbling out of the kitchen,

"What's all this noise, you'll wake the other boys".

Henry ran over to Sarah burying his head in her soft breasts.

"Now! Now! Henry, stop all this crying, it's hard enough for Harry to leave, without you making it worse for him."

Sarah was a little over 5' tall, very heavily built, with a ruddy complexion, and wore a white starched cap and apron, long black skirt, her petticoats rustled when she walked, her lace petticoat always showed below the hemline of her skirt. She had long grey hair, with highlights of red, tied back in a bun under her cap. She had a big bottom that wobbled from side to side when she walked. The boys would mimic her behind her back, she would turn suddenly to find out why they were giggling, knowing what they were up to, but she rarely shouted at them. It had become a way of reaching the boys, she gained their trust by playing silly games with them.

Today, however, Sarah was weary and sad, trying desperately not to break into tears. She had loved the boys and consoled them in those dark hours in the early days, following the death of their family. They had become her extended family, she regularly took them home and had talked to her husband about fostering them, but money was so scarce and they both had to work to support their five children, all under the age of 12. Sarah had attended the same congregation as the boys parents.

Her husband was a kindly man, he worked in the mines, but his health was not good, he had a terrible cough from years of working in the deepest part of the mine. He did this to earn the extra coppers needed to feed his family. They had little money left after paying their rent and feeding the children. He had asked her not to take on any further burden, due to life being far too difficult with hardly a farthing to spare, but Sarah thought 2 more children would make little difference, and that they could manage. George had insisted that five children was enough for any man to feed.

Harry had spoken to Sarah about living with her and was grateful for the offer, but preferred to work and look after his brother himself. He had asked her to keep a special eye on

Henry and take him home as often as possible, so that he did not feel so isolated when he left. She had promised him and he knew she would not let him down.

She was still holding Henry and looking at Harry realised just how difficult it was for him to walk away from everything he cared about. He was carrying a heavy burden for one so young. He was beginning to weaken. Sarah gave him a kiss on his cheek and wiped away a tear with her big gentle hand, which had rocked him so many times in those early days when he first arrived at the orphanage.

"Go boy, I'll stay with him, go now before he starts bellowing again".

Sarah gave him a few coppers and a small parcel wrapped in brown paper.

"It's for your lunch dearie, there are a few worm bitten apples for the horses, give them a pat from me".

Sarah hugged both boys tightly, Harry looked up at her kindly wrinkly face and glanced guiltily at his brother and started walking away until he came to the large oak gothic double doors, he twisted and pulled at the cast iron doorknob, the door creaked eerily. The warden came out of his office and across the quarry floor and wished him well and shook his hand.

"Good luck son, work hard and be a man".

The tears welled up in his eyes again as he walked away from the orphanage. He did not turn back to look or wave for fear of running back. He quickened his step and just carried on walking until the orphanage was well out of sight, only then did he break down on his knees and sob uncontrollably.

It started to rain again and thunder. A strike of lightening flashed across the sky into the dark thunderous clouds. Harry had only walked a few miles and already his woollen clothing was sodden and sticking to his young body causing it to itch. He pushed himself on walking like a little old man to avoid the bellowing wind and rain, trying desperately not to think of his brother and the overpowering urge to scratch. He finally sheltered under a rambling hedge and the arms of a giant oak tree for a little while waiting for the rain to ease off. The water had dripped down the back of his collar and his back was now soaking wet and cold, he shuddered with the cold and stamped his wet feet and carried on walking, wishing the damn rain would ease for just a little while.

The journey to the manor house seemed an eternity, but he finally arrived at midday. He was very wet and picked up a clump of wheat straw from the stable and wiped his shoes and hands. His father's tweed cap and hair were sodden. He tried to part his hair in the middle with his hands and tidy himself up a little before seeing the Estate Manager. He popped his hat into his pocket, it was far too wet to wear for the interview. He had a hole in his shoe and his socks were so wet his feet squelched as he walked, his trousers were dripping wet, and his legs had become chaffed and so painful he could barely walk without discomfort.

The Gamekeeper came out of the Estate Office and bid him good day, he tipped his hat as he always did when he spoke to the employees.

The Estate Manager called him into his office.

"Well Harry, you know what your duties are.

I expect you to start in the morning at 6.30 a.m.

"The Head Groom will explain your duties to you, they will be slightly different now that you are an employee

Have you any questions"?

"No sir".

"See you tomorrow, lets hope the weather is a little better, aye!"

Harry nodded and water dripped from his hair down his nose, he turned quickly hoping he would not see and made a quick entrance out of the office.

The Estate Manager had always liked the boy and had watched him mature over the years, he had high hopes of him becoming Head Groom one day, when old Albert could no longer carry out his duties. He was proud of the way he handled himself despite the pain and heartache he had endured since the demise of his little family. He picked up the Hackney Stud diary and dragged his finger along the eligible studs that might suit his latest mare.

Albert, the Head Groom, had been in service on the estate all of his life. He was very short, with not an ounce of fat on his body and weighed around 9 stone, an excellent weight for a jockey. In his early career he had been one of the best, but had lost his mount on a steeplechase and broke his collarbone quite badly. The horse was shot and he opted to stay around the stable helping his master with the stud side of things following the accident. He was still an excellent teacher and rider and had coached Harry and many other young hopefuls. He realised Harry's potential right from the start. He was now grooming his young apprentice to take over his post when he retired in 3 years.

Harry had become a man over the past few years, he carried the responsibilities of his young life with pride and never complained at what fate had dealt him. Albert had been friends with the boys' father since childhood and watched Harry carefully guiding him, as a father would, in his duties at the stables. He had no children of his own, his wife had died with consumption 2 years previous, and had taken an active interest in the boys since the death of their parents.

Harry walked across the cobbled yard into the stable block, taking in the smell of the horses, which he loved so much, over into Mickey's stable. Mickey was a 17hh, ¾ bred, chestnut, with a black tail and mane and two white socks, with a white blaze down the middle of his face. The master had high hopes for this beautiful stallion. His eyes were kind and bright, his nose deep pink with black hairs sticking out. Mickey had his head stretched over the stable door, he was kicking and thrashing his head from side to side and neighing.

He had heard Harry speaking and wanted some attention.

"Shush, Mickey, you'll get me sacked, shush.

You'll have no shoes left if you keep kicking the door like that.

I'll ride you tomorrow, I promise.

Here eat this apple, old Sarah gave it to me for you, now hush."

The horse chobbled on the apple and carried on tugging

hay out of the wrought iron hayrack above his head, it was as if he understood every word that Harry had said and quickly quietened down. Harry felt more at ease now, he had confirmed his position and his clothes were beginning to dry out. He patted Mickey and told him he would see him early in the morning. He checked the other horses and bid Albert farewell.

He walked with a skip in his step towards his aunts' cottage. However, before he arrived he called in at a workers' cottage to see his fathers' two shires. He leaned over the fence and called the girls, they came cantering over to the gate, pushing and shoving each other, almost forgetting to stop, skidding to a dramatic halt in the mud. They pushed and shoved for attention rubbing their heads on Harry's coat, which had almost dried out. He tickled their noses and held their heads as he stroked the side of their cheeks, tears welled up in his eyes again, as his memories came flooding back of his childhood and his father. He had learnt to ride on Molly, his father had put him on her back at six months old, he couldn't remember a time when he hadn't been around horses, they were his life.

Molly was 19hh, with black tail and mane and had a dark brown silky coat, which glistened in the sunlight. She was as gentle as a kitten. He looked down at her big hooves, she had 3 white socks and one black. Her feathers needed thinning out.

"You need those brushing Molly, they're covered in mud, you also need shoeing. I'll come over the weekend and see to them." He promised.

She must be almost 18 years old, he thought. She had become a little fleabitten on her withers and hindquarters and her nose seemed much pinker now, but other than that she remained almost unchanged over the years. When she was younger Harry used to put cream on her nose to stop it becoming sunburnt, he had been knocked down so many times, or head butted, because she hated the cream.

Mother used to say: "You must watch Molly's eyes and ears, that's the quickest way of avoiding a bloody nose, Harry".

Tilly was Molly's first foal, she was almost identical in colouring, with the exception of having white on top of her tail, 2 white socks and 2 black and slightly shorter on her withers. Both horses were still gainfully employed in pulling the plough. Harry remembered with pride the girls gathering the golden grain, paired together to the harvester, being skilfully managed by his father and very occasionally by himself.

Harry was talking to the girls quietly and could see that they would hurt themselves if they continued to push at the bar gate.

"Now girls, steady, I've got a carrot for both of you"

Smiling at Molly as she nuzzled up to him he said,

"Don't let Albert know, aye!

I've taken them out of Mickey's sack"

He stood back and looked at his girls.

"You will always be my girls", he said. He patted them on the withers and turned away. Both horses neighed and kicked at the gate for more attention. When they realised there was no more food they turned and continued to graze.

When he arrived at the cottage he took off his coat and rolled up his sleeves, he still felt restless, so for several hours he worked on the little garden his aunt had so loved, her roses were now in full bloom. The recent downfall had given life to so many weeds and prickles it seemed to take him forever to pull them out of the black soft ground. Auntie would have been so proud of their vibrant colours, he had promised her he would look after them on the night she had died. It made him feel close to her and his mother when he worked in the cottage garden. His aunt and mother had sat on the porch when their men were in the fields, discussing the colour scheme for next spring and the roses they would plant. The men thought vegetables should be planted, but the girls giggled and took no notice and got their way by hook or crook.

Harry looked up at the sky and imagined she was looking down on him, he felt close to her here in this special place.

He had been to the cottage each month, staying when he could over the past months, awaiting the day he didn't have to return to the orphanage, finally he had his life back. Henry had also spent many happy hours helping him keep the garden tidy, they used to lie in the grass and discuss their future when both of them could be together again, Henry farming and Harry working at the stables.

Desperately tired he fell onto his bed without even undressing. Sleep came more easily that night, he was mentally and physically exhausted.

The morning came too quickly, light shone through the leaded paned window, Harry awoke startled and jumped up out of bed, he dressed quickly into his work clothes, without even washing and ran to the yard not stopping even for breakfast. He did not have a time piece to check the hour.

Tom was surprised to see him so early.

"You're early lad, it's only 5.00 a.m

Come have a drink before the others come"

Tom had befriended the boys, particularly Harry, he was only a year older than the Harry.

He was taller than Harry and had big brown eyes and thick red uncontrollable hair. His father's family were of Irish decent. He had come to England as a small child. His mother had also been taken from him at an early age, dying in the epidemic.

The boys had so much in common, a special bond had formed over the last few years, they had been through similar experiences and witnessed death in childhood.

"You'll get used to it", Tom said,

"As the weeks go by your body will become accustomed to waking at the right time".

Must go, I've me jobs to do you know".

The weeks turned to months, over a year passed by, Harry had become a valued member of staff, his riding and driving abilities were second to none. Harry was being groomed for the position his master had in mind for him, the lad was such a natural with the horses, they trusted him and were calm in his presence.

The master called Harry into his office one day, he asked him if he was happy. Harry quickly answered that he was.

"It has been mentioned by the Head Groom that you're a natural with horses and ride the thoroughbreds like a jockey, which, incidentally, is why I've asked you here today.

There's an opening at Ludlow Racecourse for an apprentice jockey, would you like to train and ride my mares for me? Harry you have the right build and height, you're a keen horseman and have all the capabilities of becoming the best. I can see you have the determination to succeed, you've shown this over the last few years, I have every confidence in you lad"

Harry didn't know what to say, he was honoured that they felt so highly of him. He was about to accept the offer, then thought of his brother, his happiness was short lived, realising he couldn't accept this once in a lifetime offer because of Henry, whose health had been declining since he left the orphanage.

Ludlow would mean living in during the week, weekends he may be able to come home, but Saturdays would be his busiest. It was impossible, how could he live away from the cottage when Henry came home, leaving him for weeks on end, so soon after leaving the orphanage. Harry pondered for a moment and replied without any more thought for his own happiness or promotion. "I'm sorry sir! It's Henry, sir.

I go to see him every chance I have, he's been quite ill lately. I would love to ride for you, but my responsibilities for my brother outweigh my own selfish needs".

The master admired his honesty and loyalty, and came around the desk and patted him on his back.

"Perhaps next year lad, you're still quite young.

If you change your mind, let me know. The Groom's job is still open to you when it becomes vacant, that shouldn't affect your responsibilities lad.

Good day".

Over a year had passed since Harry had left the orphanage, the last months had not been happy for the boys. Henry had become quite sickly. He pined to be with Harry. Henry had developed a terrible cough and had lost so much weight. During his last visit, his brother had been too ill to leave the orphanage and make the journey to the cottage.

Sarah had asked the doctor to keep an eye on the boy knowing how worried Harry was about his declining ill health. Harry had sat in the kitchen with Sarah and discussed his concerns. She assured him that she would look after him and take him home with her whatever the old man said if he showed signs of declining any further.

Everyone was talking about the forthcoming Derby, Steve Donoghue and Joe Childs, famous jockeys, were visiting the yard, the latter riding the master's mare.

Harry sat by the stables with a straw protruding from his mouth, thinking about the offer he had just turned down and wondered if he could ever become as famous as Joe Childs.

He hoped he hadn't offended the master in refusing this generous offer, and felt proud of the fact that he thought so highly of him. Then he stopped to think of his poor ailing brother, who was becoming increasingly more withdrawn following each visit.

Harry had requested that Henry be released into his care immediately offering to look after his brother himself with the help of Tom.

Sarah thought it a bad idea because he would probably have to give up work and look after Henry if he became too ill to be left alone, which in turn would cause even more problems for the boys. His trust fund would soon run out and without an income they would very quickly fall on hard times and end up as paupers.

Tom came across the yard and spoke to Harry.

"I would give me hind teeth for the opportunity of

becoming a jockey, wished I wasn't so bloody tall" Patting his stomach,

"Besides, I'm too damn fat and not such a good horseman as you, Harry".

The lads burst out laughing. They discussed the famous jockeys, they couldn't wait for their forthcoming visit, the excitement throughout the stables was infectious.

Harry rode Mickey almost daily and often saw young Mary in the meadow, the masters' daughter, riding her mare. They had been friends since childhood.

Mary was a pleasant girl, with flowing dark blond hair and dazzling ebony eyes. She was so pretty and everyone liked her, she was always laughing and flirting with the beaus who called to see her and her brother. Harry had watched her mature into a young lady and dreamt of riding side by side with her. Mary's riding skills were very good, she rode her grey mare carefully and thoughtfully, but her brother Michael rode his horses into the ground without a thought for their wellbeing. His horses often came back lame and broken winded, he was not liked by the stable lads. They had to work hard to get the horses back into good shape, only for him to undo all their hard work. Inevitably the horses would be sold on due to the damage he had caused them.

Because of his meeting the stable lads had already gone on exercise, it was a glorious summer day, Harry got his mount ready and decided to ride in the meadow, it always helped him think when he rode. He galloped across the stubble field, unable to see due to his eyes watering from the wind. He came over the brow of the hill and came down gently to a steady trot, he could see young Mary sitting by the lake. He kicked Mickey on into a steady canter and rode across to her.

"Hello, Mary".

"Oh! hello Harry, isn't it a beautiful day?"

Her mare was crazing by the lake, he jumped off Mickey and left him grazing, the horse instinctively went towards the mare.

Harry could hardly breath in her company, he admired her so much. They chatted about this and that and the famous jockeys visiting the yard. He told her of the offer he had just refused. Mary, was extremely sympathetic and assured him that things would get better when Henry came home. The time fled by and all his fears and worries disappeared whilst talking to Mary.

Reluctantly Harry decided it was time to go, Mickey and the other horses would need feeding and it was getting late.

"I'll have to go Mary".

He walked over to the grazing horses and grabbed their reigns and brought them over to where Mary was standing.

She put her hand out to Harry and he helped her onto her mare and popped her foot into the stirrup. She dusted the grass off her skirt she sat down into the saddle. She looked up at the sky and squinted, her eyes were almost shut, the sun was so bright: She looked down at Harry smiling, still holding her hand above her eyes.

"I would love to ride with you, Harry, but daddy wouldn't approve of us riding together".

She paused,

"I'll be here the same time next week, we can continue this conversation then".

He nodded and said,

"I would like that Mary, see you hopefully next week".

Harry took a different route back than Mary, he arrived at the stables nearly an hour earlier than Mary, she had obviously taken her time coming home to avoid a confrontation with her father. He wanted to ride back out in case she had fallen or worse. His imagination ran away with him.

He hardly slept that night, and the following nights, he could not stop thinking of Mary and those few precious minutes he'd spent with her in the meadow. His brothers' dilemma was becoming less of a priority because his vision was clouded with the thought of the day when he would speak to her again in the meadow. The day finally arrived.

Harry quickly finished his chores and got Mickey ready for his daily exercise, he paid particular attention to his mount by grooming his silky chestnut coat until it gleamed. Mickey's bridle and breastplate were immaculate, he had carefully oiled and cleaned the English leather the night before. Just as he was about to leave the yard Tom came out of the office and shouted to him.

"Go to the Estate Office Harry immediately, its very important".

He rushed across the yard wondering if his secret had become common knowledge, or what other crime he had committed. He gingerly knocked the office door.

"Come in Harry, sit down lad".

"I have some bad news for you, your brother has been taken into Bridgnorth hospital, he has influenza. Take the buggy, but you must pick up Mary when you leave the hospital, Tom will tell you the address. She's been visiting her aunt, she's been ill. Tom cannot go, the vet is coming over, one of the mares is due to foal today and is having a bad time".

Harry felt relieved that his secret was safe, and grateful he had not ridden into the meadow to meet Mary and waited disappointingly for her to arrive. He rushed over to the stable block and quickly untacked Mickey and fed him, the horse looked bewildered not going out for his daily exercise, but soon quietened down and ate the oats and chaff placed before him. Harry quickly got the buggy ready and asked Tom where he had to collect Mary from.

He pushed the horses dreading the thought of Henry leaving him without a final farewell. He felt so guilty. If only, he thought! He tethered the horse to the rail outside the hospital and put a nose bag filled with hay over the horses head and patted his neck. Harry ran across the grounds and onto the steps and gathered himself together.

As he came into Henry's ward he asked the sister where his brothers' bed was. His emotions were running away with him, he hated hospitals and the smell associated with them, he felt physically sick.

The closer he came to his brother the more afraid and frightened he became. He could hear his brother's chest rattling and wheezing, the noise was unmistakably the same, memories came flooding back. Panic overtook him. Standing at the bottom of his bed he whispered to himself.

"Please god, not Henry too".

All the thoughts that going through his head now were of guilt, selfishness and thoughtlessness, over the past week hardly taking time to think of his younger brother. He stood by the bed and felt totally helpless, he just looked down at his little brother, he had lost so much weight. He barely recognised this skeletal figure lying before him.

Henry opened his eyes and lifted his hand up to his brother. He was so weak even this small gesture was too much for him. Harry held his cold clammy hand in his and smiled at his gaunt brother. Henry had no strength left in his body. His eyes were black as coal and deep set in his skull. He looked like a little old man.

He asked the sister if he could lie on the bed and hold him, the sister was crying quietly and gently nodded, with trembling hands he unlaced his muddy boots, putting them together carefully under the bed, out of habit from being in the orphanage. Lying on the bed, he put his shaky arms around his brother, as he had done so many times before, Harry could not curtail his tears, he knew that this time it was different, this would be the last time he held his brother in this way.

Sarah and the warden had brought Henry to the hospital, she was afraid Harry would not get there in time. Tears were streaming down her sad face, she put her shaky hand onto Harry's shoulders, he turned and looked up at her. The warden took a few steps and put his arms around her broad frame looking at her knowingly. None spoke.

The doctor came over to the bed and pulled the curtains around to give the boys some privacy. The sister turned her head in an effort to hide her tears, trying to be brave for Harry's sake. The doctor put his arm around her trying to console her. Harry sensed from the sadness and bleak faces that it would only be a matter of time before his brother took his last breath and joined Ena and his parents. He hugged Henry and told him about the cottage and how his aunt's flowers were growing and that it would be only a matter of weeks before they would be together at home. Henry hardly moved, he was struggling to breath and hardly moved, each breath laboured.

It happened so suddenly, as if Henry had been waiting for his brother to arrive. He took a deep sigh, raised his head slightly, smiled feebly at Harry as he cradled him in his arms like a baby, and died.

Harry continued to cradle his brother for what seemed an eternity, not wanting to send him on his journey, or believing that he had gone from his life forever. He rocked him and talked to him about what they were going to do when he came home. Sarah cried pitifully into her pinny, the warden wiped away the salted tears from his own ruddy face.

The doctor closed Henry's eyes and gently patted Harry on his shoulder, not speaking, just acknowledging the sadness he also felt. The sister spoke to Harry gently in an effort to break the silence,

"I'm so sorry, it's a good thing that you managed to get here before he passed away".

Harry looked up at the sister, his eyes clouded with tears, he just nodded too broken hearted to speak.

All the anxiety and pain of the last few years flooded back, the deaths of his family and the sadness of losing his aunt, how much more could he bear? Why was he the only one left? Guilt and remorse overwhelmed him.

"We need to take your brother away now Harry", the sister said.

"Do you want us to send for anyone."

Harry lifted his head in a daze and just looked blankly at the sister. His heart was broken, he was unable to speak. Sarah came over to him and gently kissed his forehead.

"I'll come to the stables with Bill to discuss the arrangements that must be made, tomorrow"

The warden nodded the tears still flowing freely down his wrinkled face.

"Go lad, we'll stay with Henry"

Harry climbed out of the bed and gently kissed his brothers forehead and apologised for not looking after him better. He carried his shoes out of the ward and sat on a bench outside the ward and popped them on. He sat dazed at what he had just witnessed and could not believe that Henry had gone, forever.

He remembered Mary, waiting for him at her aunt's. There was obviously nothing more he could do, so slowly he walked down the two flights of stairs in a bewildered gaze. Bill stood by the buggy and assured him that they would look after Henry and sort things out for him. Harry looked down at Bill and nodded and tapped the horse on his rump with the reigns.

He pulled up outside Mary's aunts house, she came rushing down the path looking anxiously at Harry, she could see how solemn and distraught he was. The blankness in his grim face frightened her, his eyes were red and swollen.

"What has happened Harry, where's Tom?"

He looked at her tears welling in his sad eyes unable to speak he started to sob into his clenched fists.

"My brother's dead, I have no one now, absolutely no one"

Mary sat down in the buggy and put her arms around him.

"You have me, Harry".

He buried his head into her shoulder and sobbed like a little baby, all the sorrow from losing his family and, now his brother, came poring out in anger and frustration. Finally, he looked up at her and tried to hide his shame for crying in front of her. He grabbed the reigns and whacked the gelding on his rump, the horse went into an immediate trot obeying his young master. Harry never spoke another word to Mary, he was too sad to look at her let alone speak to her. She just sat there by his side not knowing what to say to reassure him everything would be alright.

Henry's funeral took place in the village of Pattingham, he was laid to rest with his little sister and parents. The church was full with his father's friends and people from the stables. Albert had stayed with him the night before and drove him to the church. Sarah and the Warden stood side by side next to Harry during the funeral, he was distraught. The lads had organised a collection and placed a beautiful wreath on Henry's coffin and the master sent a donation to the chapel as a gesture of good will. Mary had given Tom a single red rose to put in Harry's buttonhole.

The vicar asked for everyone to stand and go to page 32. The congregation commenced singing

"All things bright and beautiful" Henry had loved this hymn.

Harry couldn't sing, the memories came flooding back of days gone by when they had both sung this hymn, with their parents' and little Ena. He could see Henry looking at him smiling sitting on the bench where he now sat. He became inconsolable, the overwhelming grief of losing his brother, his best friend, the last and only member of his family, finally became too much to bear. He had been so brave the last few days, keeping himself busy not wanting to think of the funeral, but it was useless trying to subdue his grief, dropping down onto the church bench burying his head into his clenched fists he sobbed uncontrollably, he was inconsolable.

Harry, Joe, Albert, the warden and 3 stable lads carried the coffin to the open ground where he would be laid to rest. Sarah and the Warden stood by him as the coffin was lowered into the ground.

Harry threw Mary's single red rose onto Henry's coffin and glanced over at Tom, his eyes were transfixed on the open ground and his brothers' coffin. Harry could not get over how small his brother's coffin was. He turned and looked at the other graves by the side of this one, his whole family lay in this little churchyard. He wondered whether he would be joining them one day.

After the burial Tom drove the buggy to Harry's cottage, Sarah had made sandwiches and organised everything at the cottage. The Warden and Sarah sat quietly, both looking at Harry worrying how he would cope without Henry. Tom stayed on after the others left, but the silence between them was unbearable.

It was Harry who finally broke the silence.

"I need to ride and feel the wind in my face".

Tom knew how he felt and didn't argue with him. They both returned the buggy to the stables. Harry saddled Mickey whilst the buggy was being cleaned by Tom and the mare attended to.

Harry knew if the master came out he would forbid him to ride, so he quickly got Mickey ready. He trotted him out of the yard before anyone could stop him. He needed desperately to fly away on his mount into oblivion. He galloped along the bridlepath on the canal siding, then down the meadow where he had seen Mary and, sat by the lake wondering what he was going to do with his life now that he had only himself to think about. Thoughts were racing through his head so fast, should he take the apprentice job at Ludlow?

Was it too late?

What about Mary?

Was it useless folly thinking she would ever care for him?

He sat in the meadow for several hours thinking. He realised that dusk was almost upon him and that it was becoming to late for Mickey to be out. He had a long day ahead of him tomorrow. He put his right foot into the stirrup and his hand on the pommel, popping his left leg over the saddle and sat down gently. He felt a little better now, he had had time to think about his future.

It was strange how the animals knew when their masters' were sad, the lads had talked about horses' instincts so many times, Mickey was behaving perfectly today, normally he became restless when in the meadow and on grass, jumping about wanting to gallop off before the other horses, but today he was being a perfect gentleman.

He squeezed his legs and pushed Mickey on trotting him steadily through the meadow trying to avoid getting the horse into a sweat. After dismounting and taking off Mickey's bridle and saddle, Harry quickly fed the horse and waited by the stable in a semi-sitting position before giving the horse his water. Mickey had bouts of colic and Harry knew he had taken him out for far too long so he was waiting for a suitable time before leaving him. There were no signs of colic and Harry was just about to go when Mary popped her head around the stable door, checking that the stalls were all empty before doing so.

"I'm so sorry I could not be there today, daddy forbid me. I wanted to be by your side. How are you Harry?"

He looked up at her and smiled sadly, his heart pounding.

"I'm alright Mary, honest I am"

"Will you meet me tomorrow in the meadow by the lake, I need to talk to you Harry, 2.00 p.m. please".

"I'll try Mary, it depends on how many horses need attending to without Tom about the mare still hasn't foaled".

His sleep was disturbed that night the thought of his poor brother being buried alone in the dark cold soil. Henry had been afraid of the dark, Harry comforted him night after night following the death of their parents'. He tossed and turned tormented by dreams of his brother waking in his coffin frightened and alone. Harry could not sleep, his mind wondering about Mary and Henry, so he lit the fire. This night was the longest of his entire life.

Harry rushed through the mucking out, exercising and feeding, finishing a little after 2.00p.m. He left exercising Mickey till last and tacked him without grooming him because he knew he was late. He trotted through the courtyard standing high in his stirrups looking back to see that no one was watching, or following him. As soon as he was out of sight of the yard and house he galloped up the bridlepath and across the meadow, the wind blowing into his face, hardly able to see, hoping Mary would wait for him. He came to the top of the hill and stood up in his stirrups, he could see her standing waving at him in the meadow. How his heart pounded looking at her waiting for him.

He pushed Mickey on down the meadow to Mary and jumped off the horse and ran into her arms. They held each other tightly looking into each other's eyes searching for the first time, frightened the moment might end too quickly. Mary broke the silence of that first caress,

"I love you Harry, I love you with all my heart, please say you love me too?"

He held her at arms length and looked into those beautiful ebony eyes

"I do, love you, Mary, I've loved you all of my life"

Harry hugged her tightly again. He looked up at the sky and then kissed her head.

"Mary, what about your father, he will send me away if he finds out?"

"I will be 18 soon and able to make my own decisions about who I talk to and associate with"

Harry looked into her beautiful eyes and kissed her again and again, he hung onto her as though there were no tomorrow.

"Oh! Mary what are we going to do. We are from different worlds, you will grow tired of me and want the life you have always had, not a life living in poverty in a humble cottage. Love such as ours is forbidden".

"Harry, I will love you until the day I die. I've loved you ever since that very first time you came onto the yard with little Ena and Henry. We were all children at play, but I knew I loved you, even then. There has only every been you in my heart. I've dreamt about our first kiss and caress all these years"

"Oh! My darling I never guessed you felt the same way as I?"

They held each other frightened the moment would pass too quickly, then Harry kissed her so passionately his manhood stood erect pressing against her thigh. Gently they lay down in the meadow, buttercups and daisies all around them, the rustling of the trees and twittering of the birds made everything seem so perfect.

Harry's hands were shaking as he undressed his love, she was a trembling too, not out of fear, but love and excitement. She undid his breeches and looked down at his pounding chest admiring his young body, she could hardly breath.

They made love gently and cautiously the passion they both felt exploding into a realm neither knew existed. Afterwards he looked at Mary and sighed, remorse and guilt began to overtake him. He kissed her closed eyes. The sun was beating down on his bare shoulders, he felt a sharp tingling and climbed off her slowly, the realisation of what had just happened finally sank in, he felt ashamed. She started to get dressed and put her skirts straight. Harry put his shirt on and tidied himself up and looked at Mary, he held her tightly to him, his head buried in her hair.

"What have I done to you Mary? I've taken your innocence and you will never be the same again".

"Mary kissed his lips and looked into those grey saddened eyes"

She felt no remorse, or shame for this act, only love.

"Make love to me again before we go back Harry. I love you with all my heart, I never want this day to end"

He took her into his arms and she gave herself to him again. Mary felt as if she were flying, lifted out of herself into a realm she had only dreamt about.

The love she felt was relentless, this was the man she would marry and have children with, whatever her parents said, he was her destiny.

Dusk fast approached as they lay fulfilled in each other's arms in the meadow. Mary finally broke the silence.

"I'll go first Harry, daddy will be back from the race meeting soon. You follow me in about an hour so no one will know we've been out together. We will find a way my love, I promise"

They clung onto each other and kissed tenderly, both wondering when they would be able to hold each other again. He put his hands around her slim waste and lifted her onto her mare, she bent down across the neck of her horse and kissed him softly.

"I love you Harry, be brave my darling"

She squeezed her mare gently and rode away.

Harry couldn't take his eyes off her, he watched until she was a small dot on the horizon.

It was like a dream, he didn't won't to wake up, he wanted love and to be loved, he felt different somehow, he felt alive. Finally, his life was worth living. He had known nothing but sadness and heartache for so many years. He lived those precious moments over and over and thought about the stories and conquests the stable lads had talked about. This could not compare with the love he had shared so passionately this day with Mary, he never dreamt it could be like this.

After what seemed an eternity he mounted Mickey and slowly cantered up the meadow, his thoughts re-visiting the love they had shared this idealistic afternoon.

He trotted into the yard looking around guiltily hoping no one had seen Mary returning earlier. He quickly sponged Mickey down to get rid of the sweat marks under his saddle and girth and fed him putting his tack away in the tack room. His friend Joe popped his head over the stable door and made Harry jump.

"Harry, I'm not being nosy? The lads are starting to talk about you and Mary. I would hate you to get the sack, the gaffa has been looking for you mate"

Harry just turned and nodded, without saying a word, his heart saddened at the thought of idle chatter among the grooms.

Several weeks passed by, Mary had been staying at her aunts' and their meetings had become extremely difficult. It was too dark and late on her return to exercise her mare, weekends were the only time they had to sneak stolen seconds together, which were becoming few and far between. Mary's brother was always somewhere on the yard, or out riding with his sister, and her friends.

He felt frustrated and unwanted, the idle chatter was beginning to get on his nerves. A fight broke out in the yard and he hit one of the lads because of his cruel jibes and had been warned about fighting. Harry had become quite moody and frustrated not knowing whether he would be able to spend quality time with Mary again. He desperately wanted to hold her and feel her body next to his again. He ached for her caress and softness, these new feelings were driving him to despair.

Mary's 18th birthday finally came, her father held a grand party for her, all the beaus from the local villages came, her school friends, aunts and uncles. No expense was spared. Harry had bought her a silver locket, but he had not been able to pass her the present. All day she had been with her friends. He had given up hope of speaking to her.

He sat outside the stables looking at the manor house

wondering whether he would ever hold her again, jealous of the beaus putting their arms around her slender waste, waltzing!

"Hello! Harry"

Startled he looked up and there she was.

"I snuck off for a moment, I had to see you, even if it was only for a second. Be in the meadow tomorrow, I have to talk to you, it is very important"

She was gone as quickly as she appeared.

Sitting in the meadow the following day Mary looked up at Harry, with tears in her eyes, Harry felt a rush of panic.

"What is it Mary, for goodness sake tell me?

I haven't slept wondering if you have someone else, Mary?"

"Oh, Harry darling, that is not what is wrong. I think I may be pregnant"

Harry felt relief, the panic had subsided.

"Are you sure, Mary"

"I think so, but I will know for definite next week if I miss another period.

"What are we going to do, Mary"?

"We will marry, of course", she said smiling.

Harry, looked into her eyes and smiled, admiration overwhelming him.

"What about your father"?

Mary was quite adamant if she was pregnant, she would tell him and face the consequences of his wrath.

"I'm 18 now and I *do not* need his consent".

She smiled again at Harry cheekily and sat down with a bump on the ground. He laughed out loudly, this was one of the things he so loved about her. She was beautiful, stubborn, wilful and determined. Fine qualities he thought, for his wife to be.

Three weeks passed, Mary confirmed she was pregnant and Harry decided to seek alternative employment and then ask Mary's father for her hand in marriage.

He applied for two stable management jobs and was offered both places. After discussing this with Mary they decided he should accept the job in Kidderminster, a tied cottage went with the Head Grooms job.

He shook hands with his new employer and arranged to start on January 1st 1897, or sooner if he was released earlier from his present post.

On returning from his final interview he mulled his plans over in his head. He had already confided in Joe, who wanted to rent his cottage, he too planned to marry soon, his girlfriend was pregnant and marriage imminent. Both friends were relieved when they sat in Harry's cottage that evening, but the thought of Harry's impending confrontation with Mary's father was of great concern to both of them.

Joe and Harry got quite drunk that night on parsnip wine, Harry constantly bragged of his wine making skills at work. It was his grandmother's recipe and very very strong. Joe stood up to go home and fell over onto Harry, suppose I'd best stop tonight, I'm too bloody drunk to go home, or even find my way out of the door. Both laughed and Joe fell asleep where he dropped.

Harry sat thinking about everything, he had worked most things out. The money from the rent would help them live and buy baby clothes, the furniture in the cottage could be moved to Kidderminster, he would make the babies crib and any other accessories could be added later. His income was sufficient to keep them and they should be able to save, things would be hard to begin with, but he wasn't afraid of hard work or commitment. His father's shires could be sold, if it was absolutely necessary.

He was a man now and able to handle his own affairs, particularly if he was to become a father and also a husband. He smiled at the prospect of being a father and Mary's husband. He could think of no greater life than to be with the one he loved, the only person left in his world too love. All he had to do now was speak to Mary's father and give his notice.

The following morning both young men had tremendous headaches, but before departing for the stables they shook hands on the lease for the cottage. Harry picked up the courage and walked across the courtyard to the Head Groom's

Office. He felt emotionally drained and physically sick, his heart pounding, he just wanted to run and hide. Sadness overwhelmed him, he had been so happy here and owed so much to the Estate, but he had made his decision.

He knocked the door, a voice called him in. It was too late now to back down, he took a deep breath and began to speak. He had rehearsed what he would say and commenced talking.

"I have decided to seek employment elsewhere, I would like to give you notice"

Harry handed his notice to the Manager.

"I would like to leave after Christmas, if that's possible"

It came as a big shock to the Head Groom and the Manager, they had been discussing stud fees and their next purchases.

Harry was asked if there were any point in reconsidering his decision. He shook his head sadly, turned and walked out of the office with head bowed.

His next task was to see Mary's father, this would be the hardest thing he had ever done. His courage was dwindling and he felt it was now or never. The master had always treated him with respect, but had made it quite clear that he was a hired hand. He in turn repaid his gratitude by getting his only daughter pregnant. It was too late now to go back, things had taken their course and were now in motion.

Harry was sick just before reaching the manor, his stomach was rolling around. He wiped his mouth and proceeded to the manor and knocked on the door and entered.

"Yes Harry, what is it?"

Harry stood in the hallway of the big house and just blurted out what he had to say without even as much as a breath.

"Sir, I wish to ask for your daughters' hand in marriage"

Harry stood in front of his employer, his hands by his side, trying desperately not to be too intimidated by the look Mary's father was giving him. A strange calmness came over him, the shaking had stopped and surprisingly, his stomach had settled, his new found courage surprised him. The master was absolutely dumfounded and stumbled for words at first. Then he spoke;

"Harry what did you say? My daughter's hand in marriage"

"Yes sir, I love Mary. I want to spend the rest of my life with her"

"She's just a child Harry! Go back to work and we will forget this silly romance as long as you promise to go back to your duties right now"

"Sir, I am leaving your employ at the end of the month. I've found alternative employment, my notice has been handed to the Estate Manager already. I will not change my mind. This romance is not folly. I love your daughter and want to marry her"

Harry clenched his fists and put his hands behind his back in a desperate bid to stay calm and collected.

"No sir! you will not, I want you to leave my house, pack your belongings and leave immediately".

Harry could here footsteps on the stairs and looked up.

Mary had been listening on the landing and came running down the stairs and almost fell into Harry's arms.

"Daddy please! I love Harry. I want to be with him, daddy please!"

She was pleading now, pleading for Harry

"Go to your room immediately, I'll talk to you later"

"No daddy, I'm staying with Harry"

Mary was desperate and angry, she gritted her teeth, looked at Harry and then at her father.

"Daddy, I'm pregnant"

Her father looked hurt and surprised, he held his head down in shame and with his hands behind his back he walked across the hall and into the sitting room over to the open fireplace. They followed him into the room. The silence was unbearable, Mary gripped Harry's hand so hard her fingernails were sticking into the palm of his hands. Her father finally turned and spoke.

"You'll stay at your aunts' until the child is born, then you can come home after a suitable time, the child can be adopted and cared for by your aunt Amy in London. We can forget this terrible mess and get on with our life's and hopefully this shame will be forgotten in the coming years"

Tears were streaming down Mary's face as she looked at her father,

"No daddy, I will not. I want this baby and I want to marry Harry"

Mary's mother came in from the kitchen.

"What is all the noise, Samuel?"

"Your daughter is pregnant mam! that's what the noise is about!"

"Is this true Mary, are you pregnant? "

"Yes mother, I am"

Mary's mother sat down on the chaise lounge her hands cradling her forehead. Looking up at Mary she said:

"My dear you are just a child, listen to your father, you have your whole life in front of you. Mary, listen to your father".

Mary looked at both parents in turn, and then at Harry standing firmly by her side. Mary's father could see that his pleading was useless, she had always been a wilful and stubborn child. He turned to look at her, his face solemn.

"Go from my home now and never come back. You will be disinherited, your brother will get everything."

Mary was calm now, she had made her decision. She walked over to her mother and kissed her gently on her forehead.

"Mother I'm so terribly sorry. I never wanted to hurt you or daddy.

I love Harry with all my heart, I know I can be happy with him, please understand mother!"

Mary turned away from her mother, held her head high, looped her arm into Harry's and walked out of the house without looking back. She left the house with the clothes on her back.

They walked across to the stables, Mary stood by her stable and whispered to her mare,

"Be a good girl for Joe, I will not be riding you again sweetheart. I will miss you so much".

Joe came across the stables and stood by her side and assured her that he would look after the horse and keep her informed if anything happened to her. She was one of the estates best breading mares.

The horse seemed to know what was being said to her. She reached her head over the stable door and lifted her top lip as if to talk to her. Mary walked away and the horse neighed and barged the door until her mistress had gone out of sight.

Mary stood outside the stales and leant against the wall waiting for Harry to finish his farewells.

Harry bid farewell to Mickey, he had no heart to look at the other horses he was too concerned about Mary. Her courage had now dispersed, she looked very pale and subdued. He quickly left the stable and walked over to her.

"My darling if you have regrets it is not too late? I will understand. You are leaving everything for me. Do you want to change your mind"?

"Harry please let us leave this place before my courage leaves me"

Mary finally broke down and cried bitterly when they reached the cottage. It had all been too much for her.

"Oh! Harry, what is to become of us now".

Harry looked down at her and said:

"We will marry, have our baby and live in Kidderminster. I have a new job to go to. We have plans to fulfil Mary, a wedding to organise, we have our whole lives together darling.

Your father will come round when he realises how we feel about each other and sees how determined we are to make a life together. Joe will look after Mags, she'll be alright sweetheart, your father likes the mare".

Mary gave birth to a boy and named him Joseph after their closest friend. He was a beautiful bonny baby, he had dark blond hair and deep brown eyes.

Joe, Harry's friend, had a daughter and called her Mary Elizabeth. He kept his promise and looked after Mickey and Mags and visited Kidderminster on his weekend off each month. Both families were happy and remained best friends.

CHAPTER 2

Harry, Joseph and Samuel

On 1st August 1914, Germany declared war on Russia and mobilised Russia's alloy France on the same day. On August 3 at 6.45 p.m., Germany declared war on France, the following day Germany invaded Belgium, which was a neutral country since the Treaty of London in 1839. Now the British had been drawn in. They sent Germany an ultimatum asking her to withdraw from Belgium. With no reply Britain and Germany were at war, on 4 August.

Mary now had a large family, her brood consisted of:

Joseph 16.1/2, Samuel Henry 15.1/2, Elsie, 14, Susan 13, Bernard 12, Dorothy 11, Leonard 10, Nancy 9, David 8, and heavily pregnant with her tenth child. Five boys and 4 girls.

Harry had a pet name for Mary now, it was 'Polly' because she was always putting the kettle on.*(for the rest of this book Mary will be affectionately known as either Polly or Mary)*

Joe had grown up to be his father's equal on the stud farm and happily worked side by side with him at the yard. He was an apprentice blacksmith and an accomplished rider and his future secured.

He was well respected within the yard and liked by all. Joe was a lot taller than his father, which ruled him out becoming a jockey, he loved being around horses and was his father's son. He lived to become a qualified blacksmith, was sensible and had ambition.

Samuel, however, had no interest in farming, or horses, he had one dream he wanted to join the armed forces and make it his career. He counted the days when he could join up, travel the world and fight for his country.

He was different to Joe, he had black hair, hazel eyes, 6ft tall, well built and handsome. He worked on the land to please his mother, realising it would only be a matter of time before he flew the nest and fulfilled his dreams. In the meantime, however, he had to help support his family, his mother had given him little choice in his career?

The arguments with his parents during meals regarding his future were constant. Harry thought it would be best for his son to follow his dreams, but Mary dreaded the thought of him going away, never to return to her, dying in some distant land for a lost cause. She prayed every night that her boys would not be brought into the war hoping this terrible nightmare would cease.

The girls would be reaching the age soon when they could be taken into service, it was Mary's intention that Elsie be taken to Birmingham, where she had been promised a place working for a rich family in Kings Norton.

Elsie was a lovely girl, with long auburn hair and hazel eyes like her brother Sam. She worked very hard for her mother and helped with her young siblings. Elsie also had her dreams, she wanted to be a midwife, or nurse. She would only be going into service for a few years to help her mother, after which she would follow her dreams and go into nursing.

A place would be sought for Susie nearer to her birthday. Susie was a selfish child with a spiteful nature and Mary constantly reminded her she was like her brother. Susie thought she was too good to do chores in the house and look after her brothers' and sisters' and, constantly caused trouble between the boys. The girl thrived on mischief and skulduggery.

Mary was looking forward to Susie going away and learning some respect for her elders' and oh! the peace she hoped for in her home again.

Harry came home with the boys, saddened by the news of war and flatly refused to discuss it during tea. He could see how desperately upset Mary was his heart went out to her. She had been restless at night for weeks worrying about the possibility of war and now the nightmare had become a reality, her boys, when old enough, would be needed to fight for their country. It was only a matter of time.

They sat at the table eating their food, Polly finally spoke of the war, she had a calm about her and looked over to her boys and then to Harry.

"Harry will you be called up?"

"Polly, dear it's too early to say. The banners are already up in the streets asking for volunteers. There's a picture of a soldier with a gun held high, with comrades walking by his side, in the town centre already.

The Banner says":

Think!
Are you content for him to fight for YOU?
Wont you do your bit?
We shall win but YOU must help
JOIN TODAY

"The lads are all talking about joining up and doing their bit at the stables. There's going to be a meeting tomorrow with the management, decisions will need to be made on the estate and in the yard, jobs will be delegated to the other lads until they too are called up. Everything is happening so quickly, everyone is talking about the war, all other matters seem to be forgotten".

"I suppose if the male members' of the families are called

up into the services, the females will have to learn to work the land and do factory work?"

Susie was not happy at this latest statement, the thought of her doing manual labour disgusted her, she jumped up from the table and stamped out of the kitchen. All she ever dreamt about was to meet someone rich and leave the poverty behind her, she had no interest in her mothers' forthcoming birth, or her father working at the stables. She had no interest in anyone other than herself and her own desires.

"I will never work in a factory, or clean out filthy horses, never! Never, I tell you", she shouted and ran up to her room sobbing and stamping her feet and, as always, slammed the bedroom door then threw herself onto the bed.

Mary was relieved than she had finally left the room.

"That girl will be the death of me, Harry. You'll have to have a word with her, or I will take a strap to her myself, I swear"

Harry was too wound up to go into Susie's tantrums.

"Everything is in a turmoil Polly. I do not know when, or whether, I will be called up, but I am sure that I will be asked to volunteer my services. People such as myself will be needed to teach the young recruits how to ride and not forgetting horse management. The army need experienced horseman in the Cavalry and Veterinary Corps. The horses are needed to pull the guns, distribute food, clothing and ammunition, they will be an integral part of the war. They will be needed to pull the ambulances and take the wounded to the Field Hospitals and trains.

"Hundreds of thousands of horses will be shipped to France, already discussions are taking place regarding the heavy horses from the yard being shipped to St James's Park in London by rail. Donkeys will be used for the heavy work, pulling the gun carriages and the like. Only the mares in foal, fillies and colts and the horses too old to work will be safe, Polly. I expect anyone with skills such as mine will be needed, despite being in my thirties, this I am sure of"

The boys decided to go for a walk and discuss the war together rather than upset their mother further. She was so distressed, Joe felt his heart breaking when he looked at his mother, he adored her. Being the eldest he felt the responsibility more than his brother. He was gentle and thoughtful, and had his mother's kind temperament.

Sam on the other hand was so different to his brother, he was arrogant, a little selfish and stubborn. He had made his mind up, even before war was declared, that he would leave home and join HM Forces. The lads walked for some considerable way, then Sam looked at his brother and said:

"As soon as I am old enough I will run away if mom and dad try to stop me joining up. I am going to join the army and go to Africa. I want to be in the Artillery Corps"

Sam had made his decision on his future and, no one, not even his mother, would change his mind.

Joe loved Sam dearly, he hugged him and told him that boys of 15 were joining up and saying they were older. He made Sam promise that if he decided to run away before he was 17, he must first discuss it with him, so that he could break the news to their parents. Sam reluctantly agreed and they shook hands.

Joe thought he would have to join the army on his 17th or 18th birthday, he wondered if it best to volunteer for the Veterinary Corps, it was only in London. There had been discussions at work about camps being opened in Aldershot and surrounding areas for training purposes. He thought at worst he could come home regularly and make sure his mother and the children were safe if he volunteered. His wages would be sent home, he didn't need much money.

So many decisions for such a youngster, his head was pounding thinking of the way his life would change, his ambitions of becoming a blacksmith would not be threatened, but the turmoil the war would bring to his young life worried him immensely.

Maybe his skills would be more valuable here in England, than in France, or elsewhere, in some distant land. He had been told only that morning that the army were asking for Shoesmiths' to volunteer and report to St James's Park, where they would be needed in the Cavalry Regiment. He realised he had not qualified yet, but his experience over the past few years would account for a lot.

Some of his friends had already joined the forces and were at this very moment telling their parents' of the decisions they had made without consulting them.

A silence had come over the boys as they walked solemnly back to the cottage, each thinking of what the future held for them, Sam excited and Joe full of remorse and concern for his mother, pregnant again and, his young brothers' and sisters', how would she manage without them and their father?

He knew how selfish Susie was, not wanting to help, only under duress, he had lost his temper so many times with her, she was enough to make a saint swear. Elsie on the other hand was willing, but she too would be called to work in some factory, or household, if she didn't go to Kings Norton. How would his mother manage without the support of her loved ones, with six children to look after. He had always played arbitrator when the arguments started. So many things to think about! He was the thinker and the shepherd of the family. He turned to Sam before they entered the cottage and hugged him.

"Sam our lives will never be the same again, our world as we know it will cease and from here on, there will be nothing but sadness and remorse. So many of our friends will die in this war. I pray that you and I, and father, will survive, and come home safely into mother's arms".

Sam had tears in his eyes. He loved his big brother and nodded and turned away too ashamed of his tears. Still thinking to himself.

"Nothing you say will change my mind, I will go to war and fight for my country. I am willing to die"

The boys entered the cottage and sat down by the fire on the two brass seats either side of the range.

With tears in her eyes, Polly turned and looked into the fire. Harry walked over to her, and lifted her head gently and turned her face towards him. He loved his wife and did not want to be separated from her. Having all these children suddenly became a burden, how would she manage and what would happen to her if he were killed. It was so hard for Harry he had the world on his shoulders and realised that there was nothing he could do to help his wife overcome her sadness.

"My dear heart. I expect they will call for Joe when he is 18, we will not need to worry about this immediately. I may be able to talk to the gaffa and see if he can be put in charge of the stables in my place, if I have to go. He knows my job well. He is a valuable member of our team and could take my place at the yard"

Joe walked over to his mother and hugged her.

"Mother, wild horses will have to drag me away from you if father is sent away, I promise"

She smiled and kissed his cheek. Sam jumped up and lifted her up in the air.

"What about a kiss for your big son, aye"

"Put me down you big oaf!"

Sam put her down and asked if she was alright.

Harry noticed that she looked quite ill, he realised immediately that this evening had been too much for her. She sat in the chair and asked for a cuppa. Joe offered, and she tried to get up out of the chair then suddenly fell back down, she grabbed her stomach and cried out in pain.

"Harry the child is coming, take me to my bed and fetch the midwife", she shouted.

Harry turned to Joe.

"Fetch the midwife, get the girls to boil water and put the little ones to bed", Joe.

"I'll take your mother to bed. Find Elsie and send her up to me, please. Hurry lad. The baby!"

Elsie was outside talking to the horses, distraught and bewildered at the prospect of being taken away from everyone she loved and her dreams being shattered.

Joe got the buggy ready and raced off the yard for the midwife.

All he had ever wanted since boyhood was to follow in his father's footsteps and work with horses, it was in his blood. He had ambition, he wanted to be a blacksmith, breed horses so that he could further his career and become known throughout England and Ireland for his horse stock.

His dreams could be fulfilled, the wages earned for shoeing were quite good, building up a round during evenings, weekends and holidays. There was a shed out the back he could turn into a smithy, the castings for the shoes could be purchased and paid for at work. He had it all worked out in his head. This was his dream.

He hadn't spoken to anyone about the way he felt, only his girlfriend Mary knew what he wanted out of life, she was Joe senior's daughter, they had grown up together and had become inseparable.

He did not want to be branded a coward by waiting for his enlistment and thought it best to volunteer when the time came and join the Veterinary Corps as long as his duties included working with horses. He would talk to Mary tomorrow. He too had made his decision on his future that night, but how would he tell his mother? He had made that silly promise only minutes earlier.

Henry lifted Polly into his arms and carried her up the stairs to their bedroom. He was covered in blood and becoming increasingly concerned about his wife's wellbeing. All the worry had caused her to go into premature labour, he was frightened that she may lose this baby. He tried to calm her and kissed her gently on the lips as he helped her into her nightdress; he then lifted her into bed, she was such a dainty sole. She was distressed and very frightened for her unborn baby.

Harry tried to console his wife.

"We will make this our last child, you cannot keep having babies like this Mary, we will never have any time for ourselves at this rate".

"It seems to me that I only have to take my bracers off and you become pregnant?"

Mary gently put her index finger to his lips and smiled sympathetically, then grimaced in pain. Harry gripped her hand. She asked whether Joe had gone for the midwife.

Harry sat on the bed waiting for the midwife to arrive,

trying to remain calm for the sake of his wife. He had been present during many of the births, but the blood loss frightened him. This delivery seemed different!

The bleeding finally subsided, after what seemed a lifetime, she was now well into labour. Elsie sat on her mother's bed with her father holding her hand, they were becoming increasingly concerned at the length of time she had been in labour, Mary was so very tired.

Elsie was a natural nurse, rarely panicked and took everything in her stride, but she too was alarmed at her mother's labour, the midwife had still not arrived, it seemed hours since her brother had gone with the buggy. Elsie was experienced with childbirth and had been present during the delivery of her siblings, but did not want to delivery this child on her own without professional help.

"Father, do you think you should send Sam to see where Joe and the midwife are"?

Harry went downstairs and had a quiet word with Sam. He was about to go out the door when the midwife arrived. It was about midnight, she had already delivered 2 babies that day and was exhausted. The outbreak of war had obviously caused these women to go into premature labour, she hoped this would be the last delivery this day.

Joe came onto the yard in his buggy shortly afterwards. He quickly put the buggy away and settled the horse in, he rushed into the kitchen.

"How's mother Sam", he asked (out of breath).

Sam held his brother's arm and sat him down.

"Joe, I'm not sure whether the baby will be alive or not, she's lost so much blood and is physically exhausted from the long labour"

The midwife had left on her bicycle and took the shortcut through the woods, which was roughly 5 miles to the cottage, she had left her apprentice with her previous patient until the birth.

Harry and Elsie were relieved that she had finally arrived, Elsie popped the kettle and took a cuppa up to her mother.

Elsie sat down with the midwife patiently waiting for the crowning.

"Push Mary, push. I can see the head, your almost there, push" shouted the midwife.

"Push"

"Mary screamed at the crowning and turned her head towards Elsie"

Harry grimaced at the sound of his wife's scream, he was downstairs with the boys ready to carry the water upstairs and do any other tasks demanded of him.

"You'd better put the kettle back on Joe, it'll be needed soon", Joe jumped up and popped the kettle onto the range.

The birth had been very difficult, labour had lasted over 18 hours and Mary was very weak from the blood loss and long labour.

Phyliss was born on 5 August, the day after war was declared, she was premature and very small. The midwife suggested putting her down the bottom of the bed to keep warm.

"Prem's grow better down there, she chided".

Mary named her daughter after her mother, whom she missed so, she had not seen her since the day she left the manor house over 18 years ago.

Joe, their life long friend, was still employed at the Manor House stables, he was Head Groom now and kept her in touch with events, but it was her deepest wish to be able to go to her mother and take her children, so that they could meet her and know their grandparents and also meet their twin cousins, who were only a little younger than Joe.

Her brother William had married and had three boys, they were of similar ages to her own children. Mary had been informed that her brother had joined the Cavalry and would be leaving quite soon. Her father was also doing his bit he was travelling around the country with the RSPCA under the supervision of the War Office, recruiting suitable mounts for the war effort. Her father had pined for Mary secretly, he worried for her well being particularly if Harry were to go to war, but he was far too proud to admit to his wife how he felt.

So the loneliness continued between the two families as they drifted further apart, but fate would make their paths cross sooner than both families realised.

Over nine months passed by, the friction in the Price household was becoming unbearable, Sam was brooding, he desperately wanted to join the army and Joe had become withdrawn and silent during meals. He rarely spoke at work or at home.

Harry carried the world on his shoulders, he knew it was only a matter of time before his boys were in the armed forces and that he would be needed to train the young recruits to ride and teach them stable management. He had already been to St James's Park to discuss his enrolment and had not told Mary or the boys, Harry had intended breaking the news later that evening.

Harry and the boys returned from work, it was June 1915. There journeys home were not happy any more. So many of their friends were fighting in the trenches, the lists of the dead were a constant reminder of the perils of war. Sam was his normal self boasting, when he was old enough, Joe was quiet and secretly dreading his forthcoming birthday. He had decided that on that day he was going to join the army and try to get into the Army Veterinary Corps, he did not know of his father's recent visit to London and that he would be leaving very soon to fulfil his duty to his country.

Everyone was sitting at the table when Sam started going on about the fighting again, Joe jumped up from the table and stormed out. It was so unlike him to display such outrage.

Harry went to find his son. Joe was sobbing in the stable.

"Father I do not want to leave you or mother, I want to carry on with life as it is, but this damn war is tearing me apart. I am going to join up soon and try to get into the Veterinary Corps in Aldershot, in the hope that I can be stationed in London, so that I can come home and help mother the best way I can during leave, whenever that may be".

"There are several veterinary hospitals in France that are being built by the RSPCA, albeit I'm not a surgeon, but I know enough about horses and ailments to be of service. My shoeing skills will be needed, they need shoesmiths".

Harry hugged his son, he was so proud of him.

"Son, I will be going in the next few weeks myself. I did not know how to tell you, please wait a while before you join up, at least be here for your mother in the first instance so that she can become accustomed to me being away".

"Will you do that for me, Joe?"

He was shocked at his father's news and nodded vaguely at him.

"Joe, subscription will be brought into force soon, could you wait until then, please?"

"But father, I want to work with horses, if I wait for subscription I could end up anywhere. I do not want to kill people, I want to save lives, I do not believe in killing"

They shook hands and, Joe agreed to wait at least a few months, until his father's routine was established.

Walking back into the kitchen, neither party wanting to discuss the war, but Sam started to talk about what he had heard, about the heavy guns and artillery being used in the war, the thousands being killed daily and how he wanted to be part of the killing, he thought it was exciting.

He said he may join the Royal Flying Corps, but thought there would not be enough action for him, aeroplanes would never become popular. Aeroplanes had not yet become fully realised, they were for observation purposes only he chided.

Mary jumped up from the table and banged it with her fists.

"I do not care if you join the forces Sam, just stop going on about it every meal and every moment you are awake. Give me some peace, dear god"

She ran out up the stairs. Harry also jumped up from the table and stormed across to where Sam was sitting. He caught hold of his collar and dragged him outside throwing him to the ground. Sam was shocked, jumped up, and turned on his father punching him on the nose.

Harry retorted and knocked Sam to the ground again, dived on top of his son and continued to punch him in the stomach and head. They were fighting like animals. Joe tried to intervene, but it was useless, he was punched in the face and landed up underneath both of them. He scrambled to his feet dusting himself down. He just stared at his father and brother fighting like hooligans.

Nothing would stop this brawl it had been coming for almost a year.

Mary heard the commotion from the bedroom and looked down at her men fighting like common criminals, this was too much. She turned to the washstand behind her picked up the large jug of water and tipped it out of the window on top of the pair of them. Harry caught the full jug of water over his head. He looked up at the window just as Sam punched him in the eye. Harry fell to the floor and was just about to get up again and punch his son in the stomach when Polly came storming out of the cottage. She had a broom in her hand and whacked Sam straight across the head so hard he fell to the ground. He had a gash across his forehead, which was bleeding profusely. She shouted at him,

"You will honour your father in my house, or you will leave"

"Do I make myself understood, young man"

Sam was ashamed, he loved his mother and realised he had gone too far this time. He lowered his head and turned away from her piercing eyes, which were black as coal. She dusted Harry's clothes and they went back into the cottage.

"I do not want you brawling like hooligans in my yard, if that boy wants to live under my roof he will have to behave himself and stop talking about this damn war". I have had enough, Harry! Do you hear me? Enough"

Joe followed Sam into the barn. He wiped his head with his handkerchief.

"You've done it this time Sam".

Both boys were astounded at the strength of their mother. She had never lost her temper with them before, neither had she raised her hand to them.

Sam was feeling quite stupid. He never wanted to hit his

father, he just lashed out in a blind rage. With all his faults he respected his father and mother and would not hurt them intentionally.

Joe sighed,

"Now what are you going to do"?

Sam would not go back into the house whilst his parents were in the sitting room, he was still shaking and sat on the fence trying to calm down and wondering what he should do now.

Joe went back into the house and asked if there was anything he could do. Both parents shook their heads together. He kissed his mother on the cheek. Joe apologised for his brother's behaviour.

"Sweetheart, it's not your fault, he's just very highly strong"

"Go to bed Joe, leave this to me and your father"

Elsie had already tucked in the children and was sitting on the bed wondering whether it was safe to go back downstairs yet. She heard Joe and went into his room and sat on the bed. They chatted about what had happened, Elsie wanted to go and hit her brother and tell him what an idiot he was, but Joe calmed her down and thought it best that they left Sam and their parents alone.

He knew that this night his father would tell their mother of his forthcoming post into the Veterinary Corps. He told Elsie about what his father had discussed earlier with him and she wept pitifully into Joe's shoulder, he stroked her auburn hair until the crying subsided.

Meantime downstairs Harry told Mary of his post in the Army Veterinary Corps. She was so angry with him she lashed out and slapped his face and stormed across the room and went to bed without uttering another word.

Harry filled his pipe with old shag tobacco and stoked the fire with the poker. He hoped she would come back down and discuss it with him, but in his heart he knew she would not.

Sam came into the sitting room and spoke to his father.

"I'm sorry for hitting you dad, I get so frustrated at being too young to join up. There I go again. I need to get this out of my system, I want to join up so badly"

Harry looked up at his son still smoking his pipe.

"What can I say to you to make you realise that 20,000 young men, like yourself, were killed in the trenches in a few days this month. All of them probably with the thought that they were going to make a difference, all with their futures ahead of them. The Germans are using some sort of mustard gas to kill, men are dying in the trenches, their lunges are collapsing."

"This war is like no other, people are being maimed and blinded, soldiers' and horses' in their thousands are drowning in mud in giant craters and in the trenches. Young men are being blown apart in their thousands in the fields. The craters these bombs are making are wider than our field"

"Son, do you understand what I am saying to you"

Sam looked down at his father, he had heard what he had to say, but none of it mattered to him.

"Dad whatever is going on, I want to be part of it"

Harry stood up tapped his pipe on the grate and walked away. He was too distraught, Sam did not know that his father would be leaving soon, or of the argument with his mother.

Harry climbed the stairs with the world on his shoulders. He knew that this night would change his world, and that his boys would soon be leaving the safety of their home to fight in this dreadful war.

Harry opened the latch in the bedroom, Polly was breastfeeding Phyliss, her nightgown lowered to her waste, she was sitting in the oak nursing chair that had been used for all of his children. He looked down at her breasts, they were firm and white, he envied the children having the freedom to suckle her.

She looked up at him and popped Phyliss onto her other breast squeezing her nipple gently, she then placed it in her daughter's mouth.

He continued to stare at her, he loved her so much. He dropped his bracers from his shoulders and started to undo the rubber buttons on his shirt. He became aware that he had an erection and turned sideways so that his wife would not see the bulge in his pants, but she had eyes like a hawk, she missed nothing.

Polly put the child into the pine crib that Harry had carved so lovingly for Joe, all her babies had slept in it. She gently rocked the cradle.

She turned and looked at Harry realising her husband had needs and lifted Phyliss out of the crib and took the baby into Elsie, who was still crying and lying awake.

"I need to talk to your father Elsie, look after her till morning will you?"

Elsie lifted her baby sister off her mother and lay her down on the bed next to her. Susie moaned and moved over away from the child.

Harry lay under the white cotton newly starched sheets waiting for his wife to come to bed. She climbed into bed and lay beside him and buried her head in his chest, she was crying.

"Harry, my love, how am I going to live without you. I love you more than life itself, without you, I have no life. I am nothing, my darling"

Harry kissed her and held her in his arms, he wanted her so much, but he also knew that he didn't want her to have any more children following the difficult birth of Phyliss.

She made the first move, searching his body she found his erect penis and climbed skilfully on top of him. They started to make love and Harry stopped abruptly and pulled out of her.

He desperately wanted her, it had been months since they had made love. Harry turned and spoke to her.

"My love what about our promise"

He held her closely to him and kissed her gently on the forehead.

"My darling, I can wait"

Mary was determined to fulfil his needs, she kissed his chest and caressed him searching his body with her tongue and lips, she slid down the bed and straddled him, she looked at him cheekily and put his erect penis into her mouth. This was the first time she had done this to him.

Where had she learnt to do this, he wondered?

He closed his eyes in wonderment, how beautiful this was, he was on another plain. Up and down she went, searching with her tongue, he stroked her hair and held onto her shoulders gritting his teeth for fear of climaxing in her mouth. He was in heaven, everything that had happened that night forgotten. He groaned at her gently and lifted her head.

"My darling, it will be all over if you carry on like this"

She smiled wickedly at him.

"That's why I'm doing it, Sweetheart"

"He dropped his head onto the pillow, it was all over"

He sighed and kissed her hair.

She came up from under the bedclothes with a strange expression on her face and promptly popped out of bed and went across to the water jug and pored a glass of water, gargled and spit the water out. She washed herself and popped back into bed.

She still had a mischievous grin on her face and a look of satisfaction. Harry was bewildered and surprised at what had just happened.

"Where on earth did you learn that trick, Polly?"

"Well if I tell you, promise not to discuss it with the other men on the yard or down the pub".

"I certainly *will not* discuss it on the yard, I promise" Harry said sternly.

"Well I was at the Bruce today doing my washing with Elsie, as you know it is my day for the bedclothes, the other women were laughing and joking about how they satisfied their husbands' without having sex. They always seem to get onto the subject of sex, anyway, Elsie was listening so I sent her over to swill the bedclothes in the cold water, while I discussed this act of mischief with Annie Parker. Apparently they were all doing it to avoid pregnancy, their husbands have all been sworn to secrecy. So now you know".

"What do you think Harry?"

He laughed out loudly, she put her hand over his mouth for fear of the children listening.

"Polly, you never cease to amaze me. It was wickedly lovely, but what about you my love"

She smiled again and whispered in his ear that it could be done to her as well and why didn't they try to fulfil her needs that way too.

Harry was quite willing, but Phyliss decided otherwise. She was crying and keeping everyone awake. Mary climbed out of bed and fetched her daughter back into the bedroom. She changed her and fed her again, by which time Harry had fallen asleep.

CHAPTER 3

St James's Park

Joe wiped his eyes and smiled at his father, he had taken a morning off work and drove him to the railway station in Kidderminster. He carried his bags and crossed over the railway bridge to the other side, neither spoke a word.

The train came into the station on time, as she slowed down the steam out of her chimney puffed into the air, making it almost impossible to breath, her big wheels clanking and slowing down, finally coming to halt. The noise from the steam and wheels made it difficult to hear anything.

Joe could hardly see his father climb onto the train. He coughed and wiped his eyes. Harry opened the carriage door and threw his luggage onto the rack above his seat. He turned and lifted the leather strap and the window dropped down, he pulled the strap towards him tightly and window stopped dropping. He released the leather strap and popped his head out of the window. Joe was standing looking up towards the engine. So many young men were getting on the train, their wives sobbing desperately into their shoulders.

He tried to make his father hear him above the noise of the train and the crowds saying their goodbyes. He sobbed uncontrollably as he looked into his fathers' eyes. Harry could only reach out and hug his son, words would not help. He tried to smile at Joe, but a lump came into his throat.

"Son go now, or you will be stuck behind all these weeping ladies", again he tried to make light of the situation.

So many young men littered the station, each kissing their loved ones. The train started to move slowly, its' big wheels turning, steam filling the station again. Joe tried to hide his tears, he loved his father, there had never been a day in his life that he had not looked up to him for encouragement. He could not imagine life without him by his side.

Joe shouted to his father

"I will look after mother and the children, I promise".

Harry put his hand to his ear in a gesture to hear his son, he shook his head and leaned further out of the window waving until Joe was just one of hundreds left standing on the platform.

Harry fought his way along the corridors looking for a better place to sit, he was always sick if he sat with his back to the engine. The seats had been taken when he was so busy saying goodbye to Joe. The smoke from the fags and pipes was almost unbearable, it was like walking through a foggy street. So many young men were in the isles chatting about the war. War for them was an exciting adventure, only when it came to saying goodbye as the troop-train drew out of the station, did the grim reality that this might be a final parting loom large.

Harry finally came to a carriage with seats available and popped his head through the door to see if there was a seat for him. Arthur, from the neighbouring stables, looked up from reading his paper and moved over for him to sit down. They hardly spoke during their journey each acknowledging the sorrow the other felt. Arthur was going to Salisbury.

Harry embarked from the train in Paddington and walked along the platform in a daze, it was so busy, soldiers' where everywhere, loved ones sobbing as the new recruits climbed onto the troop-trains heading for France. The Salvation Army were making tea on the station and offering it to the soldiers' and their families. He was glad he had forbidden Mary seeing him off that morning, he glanced at the women and children distraught as they left the station.

He was surprised at the women porters and ticket inspectors on the station, this obviously released the men for more vital work. Polly and the children were in his thoughts, they'd cried bitterly when he left the cottage that morning. Elsie had taken the little ones for a walk so that they would not see him leave. Mary had buried her head in Sam's shoulder trying to hide the heartbreak she felt.

Harry arrived at St James's Park and stood in awe looking at the hundreds of marquees and tents erected as makeshift barracks. Horses were turned out in roped paddocks and training was taking place. Numbers of enthusiastic recruits had joined up and were attached to units, where riding skills were required, but they had not the least idea of horsemanship. Full-sized dummy horses were scattered about employed to teach the rudiments of riding.

He stood and watched in amazement, as a loud clatter of hoofs and the physical power and mechanical efficiency, of a mass of artillery horses, and guns under review paraded past him, the lancers in full military uniform. The awe of the regiment made him stand to attention, he was so proud of his fellow countrymen. Harry reported for duty and was shown to his bell-tent, which was basically a house under canvas shared with three others.

The following months went by quickly, he was so busy with the horses and training the new recruits, he hardly had time to think of his loved ones. He was normally too exhausted, as soon as his head hit the pillow he would fall into a deep sleep.

Teaching the young men how to ride was a difficult task for him he had always been able to ride and could not see why it was so hard. When he was not too tired he wrote to Mary and the children and tried not to fill his letters with the heartache of the young lives lost in this terrible war and the maimed soldiers filling the hospitals to bursting point.

The horses that came back were the lucky ones, thousands of our four footed warriors were shot by the AVC, without being given the chance to return to England's shores. The ones that came home were normally officers' mounts, their master's critically wounded.

He had assisted the horse dentist that day, rasping off some very uncomfortable wolf teeth on a 4 year old, when he heard a commotion in the stalls block, where the horses were kept, following their return from the front line. All too often they were so far gone, it was better to shoot them and be done with their suffering.

He picked up his pistol and popped it into his bag and strolled over to see if he could be assistance. He was shocked to see a poor horse with shrapnel wounds in his neck and rear quarters, absolutely covered in dried blood and mud. The horse was snorting and stamping his hooves and ready to kick out at his intruders', he was obviously very frightened and had been through hell.

The vet had decided to put him down, he hadn't got time to mess, the animal was too traumatised, he thought it more humane to shoot the poor thing. He asked Harry to pass him his gun, he was distraught at having to put this beautiful thoroughbred down.

"The kindest thing would be to put him out of his misery Sergeant as quickly as possible".

Harry stood in front of the horse and shook his head in disgust.

"The humane thing would have been to put him down in France", Harry said.

"Your probably right, but his master was a captain in the cavalry and had asked for him to be brought home and sent to his father's estate for retirement. His master had been taken to hospital earlier that day mortally wounded".

The vet shook his head and spoke to Harry.

"Why did they put this poor horse through the pain of shipping him back to England"?

"It's so senseless?"

Harry shook his head not knowing what to say.

However, he thought if the horse belonged to him he would want him home if there were a chance that he may have a future, rather than be shot for his gallant efforts in a strange land. He turned quickly and threw his bag containing the gun behind a bale of hay.

The vet had destroyed so many beautiful animals since the war started he thought the losses of both men and beast to be senseless.

Harry carried out the pretence of fetching the Officer's gun and on his return the team had all moved on. He sighed with relief and opened the stall and walked into the stable stepping very carefully to avoid stressing the horse further.

He was saddened by the sight of this graceful chestnut gelding, covered in mud and obviously suffering from battle fatigue. As he came closer to the horse he could not help but notice the resemblance to his old mount Mickey, he checked his flanks and ran his hand along the horses back and withers, picking up his feet to check them. The horse turned his head and dropped his ears back, but Harry assured him he would not harm him. The horse dropped his guard and stood quite still.

He had so many injuries that had not been attended to, the horse was obviously traumatized and in a great deal of pain. As he continued to examine him he noticed an old injury on his flank, gradually he began to realise, this was Mickey. He stepped back and looked at him, the horse seemed to recognise him as well, he started to ninny and pushed Harry with head almost knocking him over. Harry said to Mickey,

"What have they done to you lad, if only you could talk?. You should not have gone to war at your age old boy?"

Harry calculated that he would be nearly 21 now, which was quite old for a veteran of war, but not unusual. Mickey was of exceptional blood, Mary's brother had kept him all these years. He stood staring at Mickey in amazement. Harry had known horses live over 35 years and still carry their master's into the hunt. He had delivered a foal back home to a mare believed to be over 20. He stood there shaking his head, tears welled in his eyes for the plight of his old friend.

Harry gently stroked his old friend searching for shrapnel

wounds. He stood back again and looked at him thinking to himself, if only his injuries were not so bad?

He had just started to clean Mickey, when the vet and his assistants came back into the stall. The vet stroked his walrus moustache, he was quite surprised at how calm the horse had become.

Harry quickly explained that he knew this horse and, also his master. He also reiterated that they could not shoot him without at least giving him a fighting chance, or shipping him back to where he belonged, on his father-in-law's estate. They owed the old fellow that much.

He explained to the officer that his master and his father were influential and integral officers' with regard to the supply of horse stock and, that the least they could do was wait until a member of the officer's family came to look at him.

Harry pleaded with his commanding officer to let him have a few days with Mickey to see what could be done to improve his wounds. The vet was reluctant, but Harry pleaded that they owed him. The vet scratched at his face and took a long look at Mickey.

"He had calmed down and does seem to know you Price"

Finally he agreed. He was a fair man who was sick of all the death and useless slaughter, he didn't want to put another beast down unnecessarily, particularly if he could be saved.

Harry sighed, relieved that his pleas had been heard.

He was concerned as to what hospital his master had been taken and asked if the officer knew where he was. The vet suggested he go to Charing Cross Hospital, he understood he had been crucially wounded and had only arrived earlier that day.

Harry felt sick, he realised it was probably Mary's brother, William and asked if he could be relieved duties for a few hours and explained that it was probably his brother-in-law who had been wounded.

The Captain agreed he could go and make enquiries. He admired Harry and valued his commitment and knowledge, he had become a respected member of his team.

"Take the day off Price, report back on duty tomorrow"

Harry saluted the Captain and thanked him for allowing him to go to the hospital.

Before Harry left he bathed Mickey's wounds with surgical spirit and wiped the stale sweat from his neck and girth. He quickly groomed him and wiped some of the caked mud from his wounds. The horse seemed at ease with his old master and stood quietly whilst his wounds were tended to. Harry plastered Vaseline over the back of his fetlocks, frog and inner hooves, he had very bad mud fever, which had caused him to go lame, Harry never noticed the abscess in his foot. He put the last of the used engine oil over his badly cracked hooves, which he had scavenged from the MT Section. He also put a hot poultice on his knee.

Harry needed to get some Sanfrazan powder from a midwife, if he was going to save Mickey, his wounds were obviously very deep and infected. The wound that concerned him most was a large piece of shrapnel, which had penetrated the frog on his right forefront. There was a hole through the back of his heel in the soft part of the frog, he could put three fingers into the wound. Mickey could not put weight onto the foot. If the horse was to survive he had to do something about this particular wound, Harry had never seen such an injury, he felt sickened at the state of Mickey and his terrible injuries.

He thought it a good idea, whilst at the hospital, to make enquiries about the powder in the maternity ward. *(It was generally used by old midwifes on babies belly buttons to stop the bleeding)* The powder worked on wounds and healed inside first and then outside. It was a remedy used by jockeys with deep wounds to their mounts. Polly always had this at home if the children were cut and when they were first born.

"Well lad that's it for now, I'll do my best, but you have to try as well. I'll be back later. Must go and see if William!" He stopped for a moment and patted Mickey.

"Never mind that lad, eat your hay and I'll be back as soon as possible".

Harry hurried to the hospital and made enquiries at the information desk. They had so many injured soldiers' brought in that day, the administration assistant was having difficulties finding William Wakelam.

She dragged her finger down the long list of casualties admitted that day and looked up at him.

"Ah, yes! He's on the Surgical Ward"

Harry's suspicions were correct it was William.

She quickly gave him directions to the ward.

He climbed several flights of the stairs and wondered endlessly through the long corridors, so many young men lay in beds, strewn everywhere, with arms and legs missing. Some with their bodies covered in bandages. He could not help but stare at the injuries sustained during the recent fighting in France. So many of the soldiers had severe burns. They stared at him blankly.

He thanked God his boys were safe at home.

He finally came to William and stood at the bottom of his bed. He was covered in bandages, it was impossible to see his face fully, he had been burnt and disfigured terribly. Harry felt so sad, he was such a good looking young man when he last saw him all those years ago.

Harry spoke gently to William and asked him if he wanted anything. William was very weak and didn't answer. The sister came over to him and asked if he was family, Harry nodded, she asked if she could have a quiet word with him.

He realised that William was critically wounded and asked what he could do?

The sister suggested he contact his family before it was too late. The wards were full of young officers' and injured soldiers', it was becoming increasingly more difficult to notify the families immediately the injured came into the wards.

She told Harry that soldiers', with no identification tags on them, were strewn across the hospital with no possible way of notifying their loved ones, they were often in a state of shock from months of shelling and lying in sodden trenches. Many were dying without seeing their family and loved ones one last time. Some soldiers cowered in corners their hands over their heads, obviously afraid of some terrible nightmare they had endured. She was obviously a very experienced nurse, but she too was terribly shocked with the injuries sustained by the wounded.

William was lucky insomuch as Harry had heard of his dilemma. He went back to his bed again tried to speak to William.

Harry bent down to listen to William, he was speaking so quietly it was difficult to hear him with the bandages on his face.

"How is Mickey"?

"I'm looking after him, William, I will attend to his injuries".

William nodded painfully.

"I would not have survived without him, he carried me without question despite being injured by flying shrapnel".

Harry assured William that he would look after Mickey and get him home safely into retirement as soon as he was well enough to travel. William seemed relieved and nodded off again into oblivion.

Harry left him and returned to speak to the sister.

"I will notify his next of kin today"

The sister smiled at Harry.

"It's a miracle he's lasted this long, he still has shrapnel in his leg, the doctor is afraid of gangrene setting in, we must amputate the leg, but the doctors would like to wait for his relatives before performing the operation. He may not survive surgery, the surgeons are operating none stop, we have so many amputees awaiting surgery.

Harry tried to smile but felt an overwhelming sadness, the loss of so many brave soldiers was too much to take in.

"I will send a telegram immediately, hopefully his family will be here tomorrow"

The sister shook Harry's hand and asked where he was billeted in case things changed for the worse.

Harry rushed back to St James's Park, his thoughts were of his wife and her critically injured brother. He knew he should inform William's wife and family, but he wanted to give his wife that last opportunity of seeing her brother and making peace with him.

He sent a telegram to Mary and returned a little later to send the second telegraph to William's wife and parents.

The telegram read:
Polly, leave the children.
Catch 8.30am train to Paddington tomorrow.
I will be waiting for you at the Exit gate.
Harry.

She received the telegram late that evening, she was frightened to open it. There had been so many bombings in London recently. She realised that something dreadful had happened and sat throughout the night worrying about what terrible thing lay ahead. The children were left with Elsie and a neighbour. Joe and Sam went with her to London, neither had been further than Wolverhampton in their lives.

Harry was waiting for her at the gateway. There was so much commotion on the station he almost missed her. It was Joe who saw him and rushed over to his father, they shook hands and hugged each other. Harry kissed his wife and quickly told her about William. He also told her he had sent two telegrams and that her parents would probably be arriving on a later train.

They hurried across London to the hospital. Mary was apprehensive about seeing William after all these years, particularly knowing that he had made no attempt to contact her these past years. All she could think about was their childhood and the happy memories they shared as children, she had always loved him and felt no ill feelings towards him. She realised that her father had always influenced him.

The boys were either side of her as she walked down the ward. William had a fever and was in and out of consciousness. Mary sat down and gently sponged his brow with a wet flannel, he finally opened his eyes and looked up at her. Tears welled in both their eyes, she stared at her brother's injuries and held his bandaged hand and kissed him gently on the forehead.

"Oh! my dear what has happened to you".

He had realised who she was and smiled at her and

continued to hold her shaking hand. She could not hear what he was saying to her and leaned closer to him. He told her he had missed her so much and was glad she had come to see him. She introduced him to her boys.

William looked at the boys and said how like his twin boys they were. She sat beside him for a while talking about her children and life in general.

Her thoughts drifted back to when they were children again riding in the meadow and playing hide and seek. They had been so close as children it saddened her to see him this way.

He asked if she would look after Mickey, she nodded. Harry had forgotten to tell her about the horse. She looked up at Harry, he generally acknowledged what William had told her and whispered that Mickey was in one of the stalls at St James's Park.

The sister came over to the bed and tapped her on the shoulder.

"William has other visitors', we only allow a few visitors at one time. Would you like to wait outside the ward. He will be having surgery in a couple of hours"

She was surprised that her family had arrived so promptly and nodded to the sister, she kissed her brother on the forehead.

"William, I will come back tomorrow after your operation, be brave my darling".

Joe and Sam both gently touched their uncle's hand and smiled at him neither spoke. They had nothing to say, this was their first sight of the war and what it could do to a human being. They were shocked at what they had witnessed whilst walking through the corridors of the hospital.

The boys again walked either side of their mother as they left the ward each boy holding her hand. Harry followed them closely behind. He was so proud of his boys to display their feelings in public without a care in the world.

Mary's father and mother were standing in the corridor, William's twin sons and their mother were sat down on a bench. She walked over to her father, but he turned his head away.

Mary's mother just looked at her pleading with her not to cause a scene. She held her head high and walked over to William's wife and said how sorry she was that he had been injured. The boys shook hands with their cousins and introduced themselves. The family then rushed into the ward to see William.

She was distraught, the only consolation she had was that she had made peace with her brother at long last. The hurt she felt at being shunned by her father was still unbearable. After all these years he still would not accept her marriage to Harry and her family.

Harry was waiting along the corridor, he had seen the reception she received from her parents, they had ignored him too.

He had made a reservation for his family in a boarding house around the corner from the hospital and had been granted 48 hours compassionate leave. Harry took Mary to the lodging house and they walked back over to the stable quarters together to check on Mickey. Harry had put the powder into Mickey's wounds and above his coronet band, which had been ripped open by barbed wire, a large piece had been left in the wound and wrapped itself around his shoe.

Harry had been unable to stitch the wounds around his hoof, or lower leg, so he wrapped them with gauze bandages, taken off his sock and put it over the hoof to stop the horse from pulling off the dressing. Mary looked at Mickey's foot and then at Harry's trousers and lifted his trouser leg up, he was till walking around with only one sock on. She smiled at her husband and kissed him.

"Harry, thank you for rescuing Mickey"

He had carefully taken out the shrapnel from his neck and stitched his neck and flank. Mary hugged him and thanked him for saving his life again. This horse had been an integral part of their early lives and bringing them together.

The horse was very weak from losing so much blood, he put up little resistance to the surgery. He seemed to know that

Harry would not hurt him and responded to his kindness. Joe had assisted his father in changing some of the dressings and offered to sleep in the stable overnight to keep an eye on him. Harry would have slept there himself if Mary had not been in London, he was still concerned that the vet might shoot Mickey if he saw the wound in his frog.

Harry and the boys left to pick up the hay and straw for the night. Mary stayed in the stall with the Mickey. It seemed strange to her after all this time to be back with her old friend.

Mickey nudged her with his head, he obviously remembered her.

She stroked him tenderly and walked all around his body, she too checked his wounds and ran her hands gently over his body to make sure none had been missed. She had been so busy with the children she had rarely had time to go out with Harry and the boys riding. It had been far too long.

She began to talk to him as she had done so when he was just a 2 year old.

"I haven't forgotten you lad. Thank you for bringing my William home to me"

The horse seemed to know what she was saying, he ninnied and rubbed his head up and down her coat, she was covered in chestnut hairs, but she didn't mind. She was relieved that he was responding to her kindness and his care programme.

She took off her coat and started to brush him tenderly. There was a bale of straw in the corner of his stall, she gently turned it towards him and climbed onto it and pushed herself up onto his back to enable her to brush his mane, the way she did when she was just a child.

She was very careful not to knock his wounds, Mickey never faltered, he just stood there, he turned his head to look at his mistress sitting on his back, he carried on nibbling at the straw in his net.

She had sat on him for hours when he was first broken, her father often caught her on his prize stallion, grooming him and spoiling him. She smiled to herself and felt proud that she could still hop onto a horse despite having 10 children. She hadn't lost any of her skills, it came so easily to her.

As she sat on Mickey she reminisced and thought of her father and the way he was always reprimanding her for her lack of discipline around his horses. She smiled and wondered what he would think of her now sitting on Mickey.

Harry and Joe walked across the park to see his commanding officer, he asked if Joe could sleep in the stable with the horse, explaining that he was Head Groom at the stables where he had worked and, that he was hoping to become a shoe smith in the AVC. It was agreed that he could stay as long as he remained in the area designated for the sick and wounded horses and reported to the duty officer.

Joe discussed the Veterinary Corps with Harry's Commanding Officer and the fact that he wanted to join the Corps, when he was old enough, if the war was still being fought. The officer complimented Harry on his son and hoped he would become a member of his team.

Harry and Mary took a long walk that night and discussed Joe and Sam and subscription, which was to become law soon. They talked about the conversation he had with his commanding officer and thought, if Joe could be stationed here with him, he could watch over him. Harry realised that he would not necessarily be posted into his regiment, but he did not want to worry her any more than he had to. He had every intention of talking to Joe later and possibly discussing with his commanding officer the possibility of him becoming part of the AVC team at St James's Park.

They talked about Sam, Harry asked whether she had experienced any further problems with their wayward son. Polly looked at Harry and said,

"He had become very quiet"

She feared he would just leave one day and join his beloved forces. They talked throughout the night. Polly lay in Harry's arms, too frightened to sleep and miss valuable minutes with her husband. They both knew they could be called out at any time, their time together was so precious. She wanted to cherish every second with her husband, she missed him so much.

Sam slept on a settee in the lounge, there were no rooms available for him, and he wanted his parents to spend what time they could together without his encumbrance. He was finally beginning to grow up and realised how much his parents loved each other and needed this time together, it could be a year before they were together again. He was so sorry for all the hurt he had caused and rarely stepped out of line now. He lay on the settee thinking about what he had seen at the hospital, it did not deter him, he still wanted to see the world and join active service. He decided that night, that on the following day he was going to enquire at the Recruiting Station about joining up, despite being under age.

Joe lay in the stable next to Mickey, he felt at home with the horse. He couldn't sleep, his mind was on joining the Army Veterinary Corps as a Blacksmith (*Shoe-smith as they called them*). He was restless and decided to rasp off the excess horn on Mickey's hooves and try to tidy his feet up a little. He was unable to finish the job off and wondered up the stalls block looking for someone with the relevant tools for the job, when he came across a young solider having problems with a mare. Joe popped his head over the stall and asked if he could help. The lad smiled and said:

"Any help is better than none. This mare is foaling, I think it's going to be a long job. It's a bloody surprise to me, we never noticed she was pregnant. I just thought she was fat"

Joe smiled at the lad, there was an instant rapport between them, they were the same age and both had been brought up with horses.

"Hi my name's Joe"

"What's yours"

"Fred, pleased to meet you"

They shook hands and turned to look at the mare.

"Just joined us have you. We need experienced horsemen desperately. Not enough of us you know. She'll be a bit yet, I hope"

The lads sat down and chatted for a while. Joe told him

about his poor uncle and his father in the Corps. Joe asked if he had any blacksmith tools so that he could sort Mickey's feet out. The lad went out of the stable and came back with another pal.

"I'm Bill, pleased to meet you.

"You can borrow my tools if you want"

"Thanks, I'll leave them outside this stall when I've finished",

Joe said

"Not so fast Joe, remember the mare"

Joe smiled and plonked himself down on the straw next to Fred and Bill.

He asked the lads what life was like in the Corps and they both looked at each other.

"It's a good life, I love horses and feel that they get a rough deal, only now are they opening up hospitals in France to treat them. So many have been shot needlessly. I will probably be shipped out some time soon, I've volunteered to go and assist in one of the Veterinary Hospitals being opened to care for the injured Trojans"

"Bill's going too, I do hope we're posted together"

Joe was overwhelmed with the commitment the lads had for the horses they chatted well into the night.

Fred nudged Joe.

"Well I think it's time"

The lads kept out of the mare's way until she lay down, the mare was bearing down now and Joe could just see the foal's feet showing during contractions. He had been present during foaling several times before, it always amazed him, today was even more special with all the death and heartache of the war.

Fred was edging her on:

"Another push girl, almost there"

There were no complications and the mare gave birth to a filly, she had a white blaze and three white socks, she was a pretty little thing. She was so unsteady the lads could not stop laughing at her. Finally, they held her up and wiped her with straw, rubbing the circulation into her. They popped her under her mother and went outside for a fag.

"Joe , if you don't mind, I'm going to call her Josephine after you", Fred said.

He had a big smirk on his face. Joe nodded in acknowledgement.

"I love it when everything goes alright. We've lost a lot of foals at the yard, particularly if it's been twins".

Fred nodded.

"Aye! Joe it is a lovely feeling, birth"

Bill just looked at the two and acknowledged nodding his head.

The night was almost over, when Joe finally said goodnight, after exchanging addresses with the lads, he went back to attend to Mickey's hooves.

He cut the excess hoof back and did his best to repair the damage caused from not being properly shod for so long. Mickey had bits of nails sticking uncomfortably out of his hooves, which had caused an abscess. Joe lanced it, the smell was awful, the puss oozed out onto the dry straw. Joe put a milk poultice on the wound to stop any further infection in the hoof. After almost two hours he was finally happy with his work, Mickey seemed to be standing a little better and walked about the stable without a limp. The pressure from the build of puss in the abscess had now subsided.

He pared off the foot with the gaping hole in his frog. Joe cut back the infected frog and cleaned the wound again and popped his father's sock back over the new dressing. He felt quite pleased with his work, Mickey looked a thousand times better than when he first saw him. His coat was gleaming, he pulled his mane and tail and platted them. He looked fit for a race meeting when his father came early in the morning.

"Joe you've done a lovely job on him, I'm sure he'll be spared now"

Mickey shoved both of them with his head, he wanted some attention too.

Harry went back to Mary at the Boarding house and they walked to the hospital together to see William, who had now come out of surgery. The sister assured them that the surgery had gone as well as could be expected, but William was in a very poorly condition. They sat by his bed waiting for him to wake up. Polly held his hand and talked to him the whole time she sat by his side. She told him about Mickey and the fact that he would probably recover fully and how Joe had slept with him and drained the abscess in his foot and made a joke about Harry's sock and the fact he walked round all day the previous day without a sock on.

William opened his eyes and turned slowly and looked at his sister.

"Thank you Mary, thank you"

He then went back to sleep.

The sister came over to them and asked them to leave because her father and mother were waiting outside. She stood up, kissed him and walked out of the ward with Harry,

As they left the ward Mary spoke to Helen and the boys and kissed her mother's cheek. Harry was so proud of her at that moment she made her stand and left without causing a scene. She also informed everyone that she would be back later that day to see her brother.

They both walked for a while before Harry finally broke the silence,

"I'm so proud of you darling, I wish things were different for our families. At least you have been given a second chance with William and his boys"

She gripped his hand with tears in her eyes.

"My darling, I love you so much, my life is with you and our children. My father and mother are the losers. We have so much together"

Harry took her in his arms and kissed her. He loved this woman as much now as that very first time in the meadow. Their love was so powerful, but they both knew, that their boys would be going to war soon and there was nothing either could do to avoid it?

When they eventually got to Mickey's stall Mary's father was at the stables with the twins. She decided to go back to the digs and leave Harry to speak to him.

"We'll be shipping him back to Pattingham as soon as he is fit. I've spoken to your commanding officer, he will be notifying me by telegram when he feels the horse is strong enough to make the journey. I understand from William that he asked Mary to take care of him"

Harry nodded.

"If you don't mind Harry, I'd rather take him home with me, William is not going to make it. The horse means so much to me and the boys, they both ride Mickey. I think they should have his horse, it will ease the pain of losing their father, I'm so sorry things turned out this way, but I can't change now". He shook Harry's hand and opened the stable loose box and left with the twins. The boys turned and smiled at Harry before the stall was closed. The boys could not understand the animosity that their grandfather held for their uncle and aunt. Both boys were almost old enough for service in the war, Harry felt sad that they may also be lost in battle?

Harry put more straw on the floor for Mickey, checked him over and went in search of Mary.

She was sat on a bench outside the boarding house crying. She knew her brother would die, but hoped that her father would come round and heal the rift that had separated their families for almost 2 decades.

They went to the hospital, both optimistic that William would survive the surgery and his terrible injuries. When they got to the ward, Mary's mother was sitting by his bed crying holding Helen's hand. Her father was cradling the twins. Mary knew instinctively that William was dead. She turned to Harry, he held her close to him. Her mother looked up at her and nodded acknowledging the sad loss of her only son.

CHAPTER 4

Joseph and Young Mary

Joe stepped off the train at Victoria Station, a contingent of British Infantry was entraining for the field of war, whilst on his platform young men were disembarking, mostly new recruits, only a few days out of basic training.

Jim shouted to Joe from the train and threw his rucksack at him almost knocking him to the floor.

"Sorry Joe" , he shouted.

Jim jumped off the step onto the platform and caught Jack's luggage. The three recruits stood looking at each other, it was Jim who spoke first.

"Well I suppose this is it, Joe".

They shook hands and patted each other, they all turned together looking for the exit.

"We'll have to go Joe, otherwise we'll miss our connection".

They were going to the front and were due to be shipped out later that day. The lads shook hands again and pushed their way through the crowds to *'The gate of goodbye'* in the forecourt of the station. The gate had been adequately named, the families kissed their loved ones goodbye as they walked through the heavy iron gateway often never to be seen again.

Joe stood at the bottom of the stairs and waved goodbye,

he felt terribly sad. The three had been constant companions throughout their induction and basic training. He paused for some time wondering whether he would ever see his pals again.

A trainload of British wounded drew up on another platform, the sight of those carrying home the wounds of battle inspired and aroused all kinship of a common cause. Cheer after cheer was sent across the platform.

Joe's uniform was still extremely uncomfortable. Throughout his young life he had been used to wearing open shirts, comfortable pants and his father's old jockey cap. He felt overdressed and irritated by his khaki uniform. It made his skin crawl, his new hair cut annoyed him, his ears felt cold and the stubble was beginning to rub on the back of his neck. His hair had been shoulder length prior to joining the army, now he was almost bald, with a circle of hair perched on his head. His pals disappeared out of sight, he straightened his belt and popped his beret back on and threw his rucksack over his shoulder, he stepped up the stairs two at a time. Excitement overwhelmed him with the thought of seeing his father and the lads at St James's Park again. They had kept in touch during his training, he would now be serving in the same regiment as his father.

When he arrived at St James's Park it was late afternoon, he was not due to report for duty until the following day, he desperately wanted to find his father. He booked in and left his luggage and arranged to collect it later and, proceeded to the stable block. He couldn't find his father and had so much to talk about. He was about to give up when Fred sprung out of one of the stable doors, Joe jumped, Fred laughed out loud.

"Bloody hell Fred, you scared the crap out of me"

"Sorry Joe, couldn't resist. I'll be finished in half hour if you want to wait for me. Give us a hand with this mare, she's very nervous. Poor thing's petrified of her own shadow. So many are like this, their eyes are full of terror, if only she could talk?"

"I expect her mount has been killed, or lying mortally wounded in hospital. Most of the ones coming home belong to wounded officers. It makes me wonder how many are left in the battlefields dying and wounded?"

Joe, nodded and stared at her sadly.

"Oh! Joe, I'm so sorry, you lost your uncle recently didn't you? Me and my big mouth, I'm always opening it without thinking. By the way how's that lovely chestnut gelding? I never thought for one moment he would survive"

Joe, smiled at Fred, and said:

"He's fine, they've retired him following my uncle's death. Last I heard he was in a paddock with several prize mares"

"I'd like to be turned out with some prized mares when I retire" Fred jested.

As soon as they settled the mare, the pals walked over to their bell tent. Joe fetched his rucksack and unpacked his few belongings and placed Mary's picture by his palyass and one he had recently had taken of his parents, he had every intention of taking the children to the photographer's on his first leave.

"Poor thing lost her foal last week", Fred said.

"They shouldn't send them into combat if they're carrying"

"I agree", Joe said.

"Fancy a drink Joe".

"No thanks, I want to find my father".

"I think I know where he may be, hang on a minute, I'll take you over, he's normally in the cookhouse with the other sergeants and officers', they have a meeting daily to discuss the animals and what course of action is to be taken the following day".

Joe finally found his father tending an injured gelding, he poked his head over the stall.

"I've been looking for you dad for hours".

Harry was so happy to see his son, it seemed an eternity since Joe informed him that he was going to join the AVC and not wait for conscription to become law, he hugged him and patted him on the shoulders. He then pushed him back a little and looked at Joe in his uniform, pulled him back to him and held him close to his chest. Harry was overwhelmed.

Fred could see they needed to be alone, said goodnight and left.

Harry sat down on a bale of straw and listened to Joe's tales of basic training and his new comrades. He asked how his mother had been during his leave, Joe said she'd been distraught last time he went home. There was still no word from Sam.

Joe would be working in close proximity with his father and was relieved that they would be together again. It was far too late to eat so they decided to go back to the cookhouse and have a cuppa. They talked for hours, Joe looked at his watch, it was 2.00 a.m. and decided to call it a day and go to bed.

"See you tomorrow dad"

Harry picked his son up about calling him dad.

"Joe, when officers' are about you must call me Sergeant or Sarg"

Joe smiled, saluted and jumped to attention.

"Yes sir, Sergeant Price"

They hugged each other laughing, Joe marched quickly whistling happily back to his bell tent. The lads were still awake and brewing up. They chatted until the early hours of the morning. Joe finally managed to get a little sleep. He woke at 5.30 a.m. and felt as if he had only just nodded off, rubbing his eyes and yawning he shook the other two. He quickly dressed and brewed a cuppa. He was raring to start work and longed to get back into the routine of mucking out and riding again. He wanted to strip off his khaki jacket and start his new career. Uniform was still a necessity, but working in and around the stables you were allowed to lose the tie and jacket and wear a shirt and bracers, as long as the Senior Officers' were not on the war path.

His first day was hard, many horses were injured and maimed, three were shot, it seemed so cruel, none of the Trojans were above five years old. Joe knew that if he had more time to care for these wounded animals he could undoubtedly have saved two of them, but they had been so traumatized and battle weary that it was kinder, in the short term, to put them out of their misery. The horses belonged to wounded officer's, shipped home with their mounts. Joe had been told that thousands of horses were being killed in the battlefields never to return home, it was only the lucky few that were being shipped home with their injured masters. Joe wanted to forget his first day and unwind so he agreed to have a drink with Fred and the lads. They hardly spoke of the horses and what cruel fate awaited them, they needed to forget the misery and have a sing along and discuss their sweethearts.

Five months passed by, Joe fitted in well with his team, he now had the rank of corporal and carried his responsibilities well, although he still had problems accepting the slaughter and suffering of the horses.

Joe often joined his mates after work for a drink, it was difficult to socialise with his father due to his rank.

One evening the lads were discussing the notice on the Cookhouse notice board, asking for volunteers for the new field hospitals for injured horses in France and Belgium, with the AVC.

Fred looked at his pals across the table and spoke:

"I understand that there is one officer and 26 other ranks with each mobile veterinary station, they are manned by the Army Veterinary Corps, each is assigned to a regiment on the front line. Bill and me are thinking of volunteering for active service. Will you be joining us Joe?"

Joe wanted to, but he was torn between his loyalties for his family and young Mary. He'd been battling with his feelings for months.

"I've thought about it Fred, it seems awful that the horses are dying and being shot due to lack of experienced personnel to tend to the injuries sustained during battle. I'm going home this weekend with dad, we have a 72 hour pass, I have every intention of discussing this with him and Mary before I make any decisions".

"This is my first leave since I joined H.M. forces. Will you guys wait until I get back before volunteering without me?"

They both nodded and agreed they would wait for him. They had become such good mates, it seemed they were meant to be together working side by side. They all had different skills and helped each other whatever the situation.

Joe was the expert with hooves and leg injuries, following his apprenticeship as shoe smith, he had a calming influence over the horses he tended. If they had injuries to their feet or hooves, they called for Joe. The lads joked about his babies doing everything but dance for him.

Fred was an excellent midwife and dealt with the most difficult horses without showing any fear, he had endless patience with them. And sat up night after night and spent hours picking names for his newcomers.

Bill had so many remedies up his sleeve for every ailment, he inevitably persuaded the commanding officer in charge not to shoot the horse until he'd at least tried one of his concoctions. He had slings and harnesses for almost every injury, his bran mashes cured even the worst case of colic. He would walk round for hours on end with his charges trying desperately to save them from a painful death.

He had so many odd socks in his kit due to using them for foot injuries. He nearly always only had one sock on. Joe often wished he had not told him of his father using his old socks instead of bandages. The lads laughed all the time about how funny they looked with green socks up to their knees.

Joe looked at his father, they were travelling home on their 72 hour pass, and told him he was thinking of volunteering for the Field Hospitals with Fred and Bill.

Harry was not surprised, he had walked in on conversations with other soldiers', discussing the Army Veterinary Corps Field Hospitals being established on the front line.

"Joe, I can only say, I understand why you want to volunteer. Do you realise that you would be in mortal danger, you will be open to shelling and the battlefields? I've been told that the Germans are using mustard gas. It must be a terrible way to die, or live, if you manage to survive an attack"

"Dad, I know what's happening, but I feel I am letting our 4 legged warriors down. So many are being shot unnecessarily and abused through lack of knowledge, shoeing and the conditions they are forced to live and work in. Father, thousands of horses are just drowning in the mud. The horses will receive, for the first time in war, the same medical attention and care accorded to our troops. I'm going to volunteer as a shoe smith, I think I can make a difference"

"Dad look at Mickey, he's retired and safe at home turned-out with his mares. If you hadn't intervened that day he would certainly have been shot"

Harry knew he was fighting a losing battle. How could he argue with his son, if he was younger, without responsibilities, he would be the first to volunteer for active service.

He was distraught at the thought of his eldest son going to the frontline, but he had never been so proud, his emotions overwhelmed him.

"Son, you will have to follow your heart, I know the others are waiting for you to join them. I cannot go, I need to be here for your mother and the children"

"Dad, I know, but it just seems right for me to go"

Harry felt tears welling in his eyes and took his handkerchief out of his pocket and blew his nose. He was too choked to talk anymore, he looked out of the window watching the landscape disappear as the wheels clattered along the tracks taking him closer to Mary.

Joe realised how his father felt, he had a lump in his own throat also, leaning back into his seat he shut his eyes. Neither spoke another word.

The children were all at the station, they were so excited jumping up and down waving. Joe ran to his mother and lifted her off her feet and kissed her. He then picked up Nancy and swung her around until she was so giddy she couldn't stand up. He put her down, looked up, young Mary was standing behind his mother smiling and holding out her arms. She ran to him and hugged him, tears streaming down her lovely young face, Joe gently wiped away her tears and kissed her tenderly.

Harry threw his arms around his children and kissed his

wife. They were all so happy, being together as a family again, everything was so perfect. Everyone was talking at once going home and were so excited. Joe talked of his training and life at St James's, making sure the children didn't hear of the terrible injuries and losses sustained by both man and beast on the battlefields of Europe. No news had been heard of Sam, everyone avoided talking about him for fear of spoiling the reunion.

After tea, Joe and young Mary went for a walk. They had missed each other desperately and were so in love, this had been the longest they had been parted.

Joe held her in his arms, kissed her passionately over and over, his tongue searching her tender young mouth. He knew this might be the last time he held her in his arms for months, or even years, if he went to war. He longed for her, his manhood stood erect and pressed hard against her thigh.

She wanted him too, they instinctively knew that this night would change their lives forever, no longer would they be innocent. They were about to give themselves to each other for the first time. They walked across the yard hand-in-hand and into the barn. Joe pulled the wooden doors shut.

He climbed onto the donkey cart and helped Mary up. She put her arms around his neck and kissed him as she stepped onto the wooden floor of the wagon. Joe made her feel as small as a young child, she was helpless in his embrace. He took off his grey coat and laid it onto the wooden floor, Mary started to undress and looked at Joe as he stood in front of her. Joe lowered his bracers and took off his shirt, his body was pale, she could just make out his shape as the moon shone through the gaps in the barn doors. His young body and his manhood stood proud, she whispered gently:

"I love you Joe, I always have".

He kissed her tenderly and said:

"I love you too, my sweetheart.

"You will be in my heart until the day I die"

They lay down on the floor of the wagon and Mary took him in her hand, he was as hard as if he had been carved from ivory, her nipples ached from wanting him.

"Oh how I need you, my darling", Joe whispered.

He came astride her and lowered his young body on top of hers, he was shaking with passion and need. He stared at the cluster of curls in the fork of her thighs and put his hand between her legs, she opened them for him, he lowered his young body on top of her again. He gently entered her with his fingers. She was moist and ready for him, he separated her lips and entered her very carefully at first. Mary sighed and pulled away from him, he lifted his body from her and started to pull away, but Mary put her arms around his neck and pulled him down on top of her. Don't stop my darling, its just! I'll tell you later. Joe thrust forward and Mary put her hands on his firm buttocks and writhed in unison with him. She whispered in his ear,

"My darling, I am yours and will be forever"

She could feel the full length of him inside her now, the pain of him taking her virginity had subsided, the pleasure of their unity overtook them. Joe groaned and Mary gripped him as his manhood convulsed into her most sacred part, Joe shuddered and rolled over onto his back.

Mary rolled with him onto her side and stared into his glazed eyes, his pupils were like ebony balls of glass. He smiled shyly and kissed her forehead and stroked her hair.

Remorse and sorrow at what had happened overtook Joe and he started to apologise for taking her innocence.

"Mary, I'm so sorry"

She put her finger on his lips and kissed him.

They lay together and stared out of the hay hatch, it was a full moon, the stars shone brightly piercing through the barn, dazzling tantalising rays of light. Mary finally stood up and started to get dressed. She looked down at him reassuringly.

"If there wasn't a war Joe, we would have to wait, but there is and, we have so little time together"

"My darling, all I ask is that you come back to me"

He nodded and kissed her gently. Guilt overtook him again, he looked into her lovely young face and wondered how he was going to tell her that he would be volunteering for active duty on his return to camp.

Mary lay down again by his side and kissed him tenderly and whispered in his ear.

"Darling lets stay here for a little while longer, I don't want to go back in just yet. The children will not give us a minute tomorrow."

Joe hugged her and rolled over again on top of her. They both laughed and started to take each others' clothes off again.

Harry was poking the fire in the cottage when Joe and Mary finally walked into the living room holding hands. He had guessed Mary had lost her innocence and, she sensed he knew her guilty secret. She looked radiant and so in love.

"I'm going to bed now Mr Price, thank you for letting me stay,"

She kissed him tenderly on the cheek and turned and kissed Joe and proceeded up the stairs looking back at Joe and smiling shyly.

Elsie was eagerly waiting in her bedroom for young Mary. The girls chatted throughout the night. Mary kept her little secret well, despite wanting to tell the world of her love for Joe.

Joe and Mary left the following day to visit her parents and as soon as they had gone Harry grabbed Polly's hand and suggested having a picnic in the meadow. She told the children, they were so excited. Elsie, Nancy and their mother hurriedly baked cakes and bread and packed the picnic hamper.

Harry sat in the meadow content looking at his children collecting daisies and wall flowers, jumping happily about, the boys fishing in the stream. He turned to Polly and held her hand and searched her eyes as he kissed her tenderly. She realised he was hiding something from her, and asked about Joe and how he was coping back at camp.

Harry put his arms onto her shoulders and told her that Joe was going to volunteer for active service in France with the AVC. He explained about the new field hospitals and the stable lads who were waiting back at camp for Joe's decision. She tried to turn away from him and Harry turned her head gently so that he maintained eye contact.

"Mary, Joe is a man now, despite his young years, not a child"

(He only called her Mary when he was angry or serious)

"I am that proud of our boy it hurts. I've watched him over the last few years grow into a fine young man. He is well liked by all who know him. We must both let him go without pressurising him to stay and just be there for young Mary".

"Our boy will be in mortal danger whilst in the battlefields".

"My darling, my life would be so empty without my son by my side, he is our first born. He is officer material and the lads listen to him, but Joe is as he has always been; he's a plodder, a worker and has no real ambition to become anything other than the rank he is. He has only one true ambition sweetheart and, that is to have his own round and smithy and hopefully, if permitted, a stud yard. His life revolves around horses, the same as mine"

"Joe thinks he can make a difference, he's going to volunteer as a shoe smith, hopefully he will not be fighting in combat. At least we can thank God for this small blessing. Joe is in some control of his destiny, hundreds and thousands of our young men are dying, shot as they leave the trenches, they have no choice in their destinies"

Mary buried her head in her husband's shoulder and promised she would be brave, she knew how desperately sad Harry was. Her heart was breaking, her boys and her husband were all in mortal danger and all their destinies were at stake!

"My darling!, we will make this weekend a weekend to remember. Lets have a party tonight and invite all my mates from the stable and, Sam and Joe's friends over".

Little did Harry know, many of the lads had died, or were now fighting for their lives in the muddy trenches of Europe.

Mary had cried with so many of the wives and mothers following the deaths of their husbands and in some instances, their sons too. She was so tired of this bloody war.

Harry lifted her up from the blanket and said:

"We must hurry my love otherwise we will not be able to let everyone know of the party. Joe will be back around 4.00 p.m. with young Mary. He's so much in love, they make a lovely couple. I think our son will soon be flying the nest and starting his own family my love".

Mary smiled and said:

"I think you are probably right Harry, let's hope he's a little more sensible than us and wait a few years and not have quite so many children?"

He patted her on the bottom and laughed out loud.

Harry shouted to the children and they quickly packed the picnic basket and gathered up their belongings. Leonard had caught a nice young trout and planned to cook it for tea. Harry told them about the surprise party, they jumped in the air and shouted *Yipee, Yipee.*

The ride back in the cart was lovely, the sun was shining, the children sang 'Oh McDonald had a farm' all the way home. They were so excited about the party.

Harry and Polly tried desperately not to get upset during their journey back to the cottage, they were both subdued and put on a brave face for their children.

Joe pondered all day and found it so difficult to talk about going to the front. He finally plucked up the courage to tell young Mary of his decision to join the AVC. She looked at him with those piercing eyes and turned her head away and sat on the porch with her head lowered. She was crying bitterly. She looked up and asked him why he was volunteering, he did not have to go? He had never seen her so angry and upset.

"Why did you wait until today, after what happened yesterday, Joe?"

He tried his best to explain his feelings and asked her to try and understand why he felt he needed to do this. His protests made no difference to her. She was upset and hysterical.

All his pleading made no difference whatsoever. She finally

stood up, slapped him hard across the face and ran back into her parents cottage, slamming the front door shut in his face.

He tried to talk to her through the letter box, but she was not listening. Mary had retreated to her bedroom, she threw herself onto her bed and sobbed into her pillow.

Mary's mother came out of the cottage and asked Joe to leave. He apologised for the upset he had caused, she held his hand and told him things would be ok as soon as her daughter had calmed down.

After Joe had left she went to Mary and held her in her arms. Her daughter was broken hearted. Mary's mother talked to her daughter and told her she would have to let him go if she ever wanted to marry and settle down. Mary listened quietly and sobbed into her mothers shoulder. She rocked her daughter like a little child.

All the way home Joe wondered if he was making the right decision. He loved Mary, but he had a duty to his country and his family, Mary must realise this. I am man not boy, he thought!

Whatever his feelings were, his duty to King and country came first. His mind was made up, Mary must accept this.

He arrived home early, his parents were surprised that he was alone. His mother sensed Joe had told Mary of his intentions to go into active service. She walked across to him and reassured him that Mary would calm down and understand why he had to go. Joe was surprised at how calm his mother was and smiled and hugged her gently.

Elsie came running over to him and told him of the surprise party. He looked down at her and smiled and looked up at his mother.

"That's nice, Elsie" , he said.

He was in no mood for a party, but he didn't want to spoil their plans, they had so little time together as a family. Joe walked across to the barn, with his father, who was about to tack up Flannigan.

"Dad I'll do that".

Harry sensed how sad his son was and handed him the

bridle and walked out of the barn over the yard back to the cottage.

Polly had been standing outside the door staring at her men walking together side by side. They both had the same mannerisms, anyone could see that they were both out of the same pod. She smiled to herself and turned trying not to cry.

Harry came over to her.

"Our boy has the world on his shoulders, I wished there was something I could do to ease his burden".

Polly nodded, she was crying again and did not want the children to see her. Harry stopped Nancy and the other boys outside the cottage and told them to gather some wood for the fire. He followed her into the kitchen and put his arms round her.

"Oh! Harry, what are we going to do, if we loose *our boys?"*.

Joe popped the saddle and bridle onto Flannigan, the horse was very restless and Joe was becoming frustrated with him fidgeting , the bridle fell to the floor and got covered in dust. The horse sensed Joe was in a bad mood and stepped backwards onto his foot. Joe punched him in the neck frustrated at dropping the bridle. The horse settled down and Joe finally managed to pop onto the saddle. He stepped into the stirrup and cocked his leg over the horse. He squeezed him with both legs, the horse responded immediately to his master and walked out into the yard.

Nancy came running out of nowhere and caused the horse to shy and buck at the same time, Joe almost fell off. He was up around his neck and just managed to grab his mane as the horse turned again and fly bucked so high his head hit the oak beam above the barn doors. He had lost both his stirrups.

"Nancy, you should know better than to do that, you silly girl", he shouted.

She looked up at her brother, she was not used to Joe shouting at her and began to cry. Wiping her face on her apron she again looked up at him and asked still sobbing:

"Can I come Joe, please?"

Joe felt so guilty that he had shouted at his little sister, she was not to blame for him being in a temper. He looked down at her sad little face and took her arm and pulled her up onto Flannigan. She was still crying a little and put her arms around Joe's waist and rested her head on his shoulder.

He turned around to her and jested.

"Don't wet my shirt, will you?"

She shook her head shyly and smiled at him and buried her head again into his shoulder.

Nancy had piggy backed most of her young life, she felt elated being behind her big brother on Flannigan.

"Hold on tight, Nancy"

Joe kicked the horse on and put his arm behind him to check that she was seated correctly and sitting deep, he put the horse into a fast trot and Nancy began to laugh out loud.

"Do you want to canter Nancy"

"Oh! please Joe, I'll not slip off I promise"

He squeezed the horse again and he stepped into a nice steady canter. Nancy hugged Joe even harder and laughed out loud.

"It's like daddies arm chair, Joe", she shouted.

The party was a huge success, everyone had become slightly inebriated, on the parsnip and nettle wine, even the children were slightly drunk.

Leonard had sneaked into the cellar and helped himself to 2 bottles of parsnip wine. David couldn't stop giggling as they sipped the wine straight from the bottle. Bernard (*bunny as he was now known*) fell over backwards off the cart laughing at the top of his voice, then fell asleep sitting up, Leonard couldn't wake him up and fell over his legs. He stumbled about trying desperately to stand up. He took his coat off and placed it over Bunny's shoulders. He was giggling that much he fell over again and landed on top of David. He helped him up and they both staggered out of the barn doors. They staggered around the back of the barn and fall onto the grass and went to sleep.

Joe missed his Mary so much, he moped about not wanting

to socialise. So many faces were missing, he was frightened to ask whether his friends were dead, or just could not make the party. He was about to go to bed when someone tapped him on his shoulder, he turned around and young Mary was there.

"Mother and father are here, they're talking to your parents".

She was crying and also smiling at Joe, he just held her by her shoulders, and tried to speak to her, he had a lump in his throat, trying hard not to cry in front of his true love.

"Oh my darling, I thought I would never see you again, please forgive me" Joe sobbed.

"Does this mean that you will love me the rest of my life?" Mary said.

He looked at her, emotions overtaking him,

"No my darling", he paused.

"I will love you the rest of my life"

He kissed her over and over again, grabbed her hand and they snuck away from the party and sealed their love again away from prying eyes.

CHAPTER 5

Army Veterinary Corps

Joe hugged his father, he didn't want to leave the safety of his loving arms. He turned and started to walk away fighting his way through the hoards of soldiers' boarding the ship at the quayside. Fred and Bill had already embarked and were standing at the top of the gangway waiting for him.

Joe grabbed hold of the rope on the steps and started to climb up the steep gangway, he could not turn round because he was crying and did not want his father to see him.

Harry shouted to Joe, he turned to look at his father again, wiping away his tears before turning. He could hardly hear what he was saying, Joe turned and pushed through the soldiers embarking the ship.

"Son, I almost forgot, I have a letter from young Mary and a pair of mittens Elsie knit for you"

Joe could hardly hear with everyone shouting in the crowd, he pushed his way back to his father. He took the letter from him and popped the mittens in his greycoat. Harry hugged him again.

"God bless and keep you son, until we meet again, Mary will be looked after, I promise"

Harry was fighting the tears, his heart was breaking, he did not want to let Joe go. Finally, he let go and patted his son on the shoulders. Neither could speak, Joe turned, the world was on his shoulder's, he climbed the stairs up to the deck of the ship.

Joe stood on the deck of the troop ship searching for his father in the crowd, panic overcame him, he could not see him anywhere. He searched up and down the crowds, then he saw him standing at the very back leaning on the iron railings at the back of the dock, he had lit his pipe. They found each other at the exact same moment, Harry and Joe lifted their hands together and then he was gone again. Joe turned and walked away too sad to watch England shores disappear.

The old steam troopship began to pull away out of the Southampton's harbour, heavily laden with it's 13,000 passengers, its big funnel hooting and filling the skies with dark smoke. The crowd began to sing *"Abide With Me"*, troops and families sang, young and old, their hearts breaking, hankies waving as the big ship chugged away from the dock. Fred and Bill waved frantically leaning over the railing until their loved ones were just dots in the distance. Joe could not wave or even look back, he was too sad, he sat down hiding away from the heartbreak of leaving his beloved home and country.

Harry started to walk away from the docks, first quite slowly then he quickened his pace until he was marching. His head held high, swinging his arms proudly, he could not comprehend what was happening to his world, it was falling apart at the seams.

Joe was still so young, drawn from the safety of his family, Sam not yet 18 away in a distant land. He had no way of knowing where destiny would take them. Sam could be dead and buried in an unmarked grave in France, or Belgium, abandoned, wounded or dying on the battlefields of war, buried in the craters of mud.

He had read about the way the young men were dying in the deep mud and vast craters, drowned unable to crawl out, in the newspapers. He could not stop thinking of the plight of his boys and his family at home.

So much was happening, his whole family was being torn apart, this war affected every aspect of his whole life. Elsie was due to leave and go into service in Northfield, Birmingham in a few days. She still wanted to go into nursing and resented being sent away, but she had been promised long before the war, her indenture had been signed and sealed, it was her duty to go.

She had sobbed uncontrollably before he went back to camp, begging him to go to Northfield and make them wait until after the war. He reluctantly refused and shouted at her. She would not say goodbye to him when he left the cottage. It saddened him to see her so unhappy.

Susie was working in the fields because there were no men available to farm the land, she hated every minute she worked. She washed and scrubbed her hands repeatedly each evening following work and moaned incessantly about her nails and hair.

Mary was so fed up of her daughter moaning night after night. Her life had become a complete nightmare, she was ageing before her time. Her letters were full of what the children were doing, nothing nice was ever written anymore.

Bernard, who at 13, was becoming the man of the family, he worked at the stud yard and had become the man of the house. He had become almost as qualified in horsemanship as his older brother. He now smoked a pipe, Harry smiled at the thought of Bernard smoking a pipe. David and Nancy helped their mother at home, where possible, with the other children.

Harry climbed onto the train and sat down in a carriage filled with young soldiers. He was still deep in thought when a young solider passed him a newspaper. The headlines shocked him, HMS Hampshire the ship carrying Lord Kitchener to the battlefields, had been torpedoed and all lost at sea, he checked the date 5 June 1916, the nation was in shock. He looked out of the window of the train and sighed. No one was safe in this war, where was it all going to end?

Harry had omitted to tell Joe that he had been promoted to Staff Sergeant and would be moving to Aldershot later that month. So many things had been unsaid. He wanted so much to reassure Joe that everything would be alright, but he had left it too late. His son had gone away, maybe to his death, without knowing how much he loved him. He looked out of the window and watched vacantly wondering when he would be together again with his boys.

Back on the boat, the tommies were sitting and standing on the crowded deck, discussing the prospects of this new adventure. Fred and Bill found Joe sitting in a corner by the chimney stack reading Mary's letter. Both of them sat down beside him, they lit up and offered Joe a woodbine. He looked up and thanked them. He continued to read his letter.

4 June 1916

My dear heart,

Come back to me my love for I am with child.

Will you write to your parents for me and tell them they will be grandparents early next year.

I know we planned to marry on your return.

I do not want you to think that I am trying to trick you into marrying me. I think our child will be born January/early February 1917. Lets hope this terrible war will be finished by then and that you will be home for the birth.

My darling our lives are in such a turmoil right now. I am sure that as soon as this war is over, and you come back into my arms, we will find peace and happiness together with our child.

Please write to me soon my dear, I am so sorry for breaking the news in this way.

I tried to tell you my darling, but the words would not

come out. I have been so tormented and after discussing this with Elsie, I decided to write to you and let you know.

Elsie sends her love, Nancy is seeing a boy at school. Bunny, Len and David are into all sorts of mischief. Susie is still moaning and Phyliss is now talking.

Your ever loving Mary.

Hope you like the new photograph, I had it taken especially for you sweetheart.

I love you with all my heart and always will.

Joe took the photograph and kissed it and put it back into his wallet with the one of his parents and siblings. He took out the gold hunter watch his father had given him the last night they were together before leaving England. Joe had admired the watch throughout his young life and, felt honoured that his father had given it to him, knowing that this was all he possessed from his own father. He closed the watch and popped it back into his pocket and checked the chain and fob were secure.

Joe looked at Fred and told him about the baby.

Fred smiled and said:

"Snap, Mavis is pregnant too, shall we make it a double wedding when we get back?"

"That would be nice Fred, shall we write to the girls and suggest they organise everything for us on our return from the front, whenever that is?"

Bill shook hands with his pals and asked if he could be best man, they smiled and nodded together.

"We'll have to cut you in half Bill, or you stand in the middle, aye"!

Bill took out 2 silk handkerchiefs his grandmother had given him before he left England. They were beautifully embroidered, one had Union Jacks around the outside and other was red, white and blue. Bill showed them to his pals and they remarked on how beautiful they were.

Bill had been granny reared, following the death of his

father in a mining accident and, his mother dying in childbirth before his father's sad death.

His nan had taken him in, together with his two sisters. She was the love of his life and he worried how she would manage without him to support her. The girls were only 13 and 14, his grandfather worked in the mines, but had a very bad chest, it was only a matter of time before he retired and the money stopped coming in.

The lads lay back on their kitbags and lit another cigarette, each was battling with their own feelings and worries for their loved ones back home and what would happen when they finally arrived at the front line.

The excitement on board had now subsided and the reality of war imminent, there was a strange silence around the ship now, each individual battling with his own inner feelings.

CHAPTER 6

Sam

It was September 1916, the battle of the Somme had been ongoing for some months, a bloody stalemate had developed, where neither side could do much. Soldiers' would go over the top and be killed in their thousands daily and, even if a soldier reached the enemy line, it was almost certain he would be killed or injured.

The front line consisted of several trenches, which zig-zagged from Belgium to the British Channel and to the north, this was known as the Western Front.

The first trench was protected by barbed wire, next front-line trench, where the soldiers' spent most of their time, with camouflaged machine guns to stop German spy planes seeing them, then behind the front-line, running parallel with it approximately 40 yards back, was the Command trench and 100 yards behind lay the Support Trench, which was extremely important holding the support infantry in readiness to rush out to the front line. Supplies were also kept here.

A further 500 yards back lay the reserve trench, housing soldiers who were not on the front-line and a last resort for the troops should the enemy capture the other trenches. Communication trenches were joined up to the other trenches allowing movement in and out undetected.

Over 25 miles of British and French soldiers' were attacking the German positions on the Western Front.

The Germans had tactically picked the best locations and dug their trenches on higher ground, the allied trenches were only fractionally above sea level and inevitably, whilst being dug , hit water only a few feet down. Even during the summer the allied trenches were very rarely dry, they were constantly muddy and filled with water.

This battle was supposed to be one of the great offensives of the war continuing for a further three months, killing in excess of 430,000 young infantrymen and officers', needlessly, but the Battle of the Somme, along with other battles beforehand, failed.

The Commander in Chief was General Haig, he realised that a change in tactics would need to be made if this war was to be won. He introduced the tank, however, little impact was made by these monsters, out of the 40 ordered, 13 broke down before reaching the Western Front, the giant craters of mud brought them to a standstill, the Germans would bomb them before they could recover from the craters, caused by the constant shelling from both sides.

Gas had become an integral part of modern warfare, measures had been taken to counteract the effects of this weapon, declared illegal by the International Convention, to which Germany was a signatory.

The soldiers were becoming immune from the poison by virtue of the box respirator, which was much more effective than the handkerchiefs soaked in ammoniated water and chemically impregnated wool and flannelette, which had been held over the face.

Sam was waiting for orders to go over the top, he was in the front-line trench. He stepped onto the first step allowing him to look over the trench, starring out across *no-mans* land, stretching desolate and barren, littered with human waste and mangled flesh.

The wire looked like ghostly gossamer in the glare of the search lights. He stepped down and opened his tobacco tin and rolled a fag, licking the edge of the paper he popped it into his mouth and lit it. He took a deep breath and leant back up against the sandbags, piled 8 high, which were scattered everywhere along the trenches, playing a paramount part in their safety.

It was a daily routine to fill them and he had won the raffle for the job everyone hated, together with two other soldiers, they were constantly riddled with bullet holes. He patted the one he now leant on, it felt much firmer.

Sam looked up at the stars, wondering about his family. He worried about his father, there was talk in the trenches of bombs dropping over London and thousands of fatalities, including a direct hit on a hospital in London.

He also wondered whether Joe had joined the AVC, before conscription came into force in March of that year, and, if so, whether he was in the trenches a mile or so down the line. He couldn't help but wonder if his father and brother were even still alive?

He missed his mother most of all, many times he had tried to write and say how sorry he was for leaving without a bye your leave, but he had now written, that long overdue letter, and would send it home when next at the Rest Camp. He regretted his rash decision to join the army and wished he had listened to his father and waited until he was a little older.

Sam had witnessed too much misery and death for his young years, he had become dispirited. Initially he entered the war opened minded as an excited teenager looking for adventure in fighting for one's country, but life in the trenches had very quickly destroyed his passion for adventure and his dream of war!

The first weeks in battle very quickly disillusioned his dreams and lulled his passion for adventure.

Life in the trenches was a daily regime and began at 5.0'clock most mornings, when light grew and would finish, unless one had been on guard duty, during the night. Soldiers' would have to "*stand to*", fully armed, bayonets fixed, silent and waiting, rifles would be checked regularly during this time and, if they were dirty, you'd get Field Punishment.

They were kept busy by carrying ammunition about, strengthening the wire, resetting the duck boards and rebuilding the trenches, these were just a few of their daily duties. Constant bombardment and water inevitably made the trenches collapse.

"*Stand-to*" would take place again at dusk in case the Hun decided to launch a surprise attack. Sentries would be sent out to scour "*No Man's Land*" for movement in case of a surprise raiding party.

Looking along the trench he stared at the other lads awaiting the order to advance over the top, their expressions all the same each battling his own inner demons.

A huge mine exploded, hurling heavenwards it's tons of earth and stones. Sam instinctively ducked and threw himself on the ground to avoid being hit by the downfall and storm of fragments flying overhead, he covered his head and face with his hands and waited. His mates cowered and watched the bellowing earth go upwards. He had become accustomed to the shell fire and the sounds of battle, a whistling willy flew over, the pals looked up and smiled at each other, they were relieved the shells had missed them.

Sam dusted himself off and spoke to Len.

"The Germans seem to be hitting their targets well, obviously their spy planes were marking the ammunition dumps. Not for us, though, aye lad?"

Sam felt edgy, it wasn't fear, it was a feeling of sadness and remorse, he was so tired of all the death and squalor that they were forced to live in day after day.

The trenches were rarely dry, new duck boards had been placed higher than ground level to keep feet a little dryer.

Over 20,000 men had been diagnosed with trench foot during the first years' of the war, and finally precautions were now being taken, soldiers were issued with three pair of socks standard issue and also whale-oil grease . The soldiers' covered their feet in the grease to stop the water getting to the skin. Thousands of soldiers' had lost feet due to gangrene and frostbite, following months of standing in icy muddy water. Bathing was also a problem, lice infestation was rife along the line. They were in the soldier's clothing, 95% of soldiers' were infested by lice. During the night they would endure, not only being bitten by rats as big as cats, but cold and extremely damp conditions. Sores developed, following the bites, and once the lice had their fill of blood the area became sore and itchy.

Sam looked at Len and spoke to him again:

"Len I think there is going to be heavy bombardment tonight"

He nodded and passed Sam a fag.

"Lets hope the orders to go over the top are cancelled"

"I have a bad feeling, Len"

Sam tried to smile at his mate, but turned his head away sadly. He had been thinking of his family a lot lately and felt overwhelmed at the thought of losing contact forever with them, never to see any of their faces again. Sam reminisced more and more lately, the days were often far too long to endure. He thought of the happy days spent in the fields with his father and Joe, tending the horses after work, walking home chatting about this and that. He would give anything just to sit around the old pine farmhouse table with his parents and siblings, discussing simple things, again.

Len had promised Sam, if he were to be killed in battle, he would make sure his letter got back home and, Sam had made the same promise to Len. He looked in his pocket to check his letter was still there and patted his pocket.

Four stretcher bearers pushed past Sam at that very moment, they were going to a wounded soldier, obviously injured by the flying shrapnel. No one seemed particularly interested in what was happening, or who had been injured. Sam looked down the trench, thinking to himself, he was one of the lucky ones, if he survived the Dressing Station, he would be sent home, or at least he was out of it for a while.

He turned and looked the other way and saw a heap of mangled flesh, which only a few moments ago was a man.

Len nudged Sam,

"Fancy some bully beef, Sam"

"Why not, aye"

"Mine or yours"?

They chewed on the beef and Sam popped a biscuit into his mouth. He winched as he bit into the biscuit, his teeth ached, they had become very sensitive from months of living on bully and biscuits, which were far too hard and caused his gums to bleed.

"When I get home, I'm going to the bloody dentist. My flaming teeth ache like the devil"

He opened his mouth and pointed at his sore gums. Len leant forward and looked into Sam's mouth.

"They look really sore, Sam. Perhaps a gargle of salt water might help, before you end up with no teeth at all."

Sam pulled his lips together and mimicked.

"You mean like your old grandma"

Len pushed him and he almost stabbed himself on his bayonet.

"Watch it Len, you might cut me vitals off"

The lads burst out laughing and carried on eating their bullied beef.

It was almost nightfall and curving flares of the star shells lit up the battlefield, the incessant bombardment seemed endless tonight.

Sam moved over to his "funk hole" and folded his arms around his chest, he brought his knees up under his arms.

It was better than his feet being in the mud all night, at least this way they dried out a little. Inevitably when he woke and stood up his back ached, he wondered what was the better evil 'bad back or wet feet'

His feet had begun to ache, he knew he had trench foot, (footsore weary mickey, the lads called them), caused by not taking his puttees and boots off. His feet were cold, pale, mottled and his lower legs and feet, had become painful and swollen. He was concerned because they were beginning to go numb and, it was common knowledge, that numbness could develop into frostbite.

He had seen a young soldier with frostbite some weeks earlier, his toes had to be amputated, he assumed he had been sent home. He remembered so vividly the sight of his black toes, the lad had taken off his socks to rub his feet, one of his toes came off in his hand. Sam put him over his shoulder and carried him to the First Aid Post, he had become hysterical. He had not seem him since that day.

The gaiters recently introduced helped keep the lower leg dry, but inevitably became damp with the wet conditions endured in the trenches. His uniform was heavy from the damp weather and he itched because he was infested with lice again.

The conditions in the bloody trenches were hideous and inhuman, the stagnant water caused an eerie mist to form, the stench of rotting flesh was repugnant.

Thankfully he only had one more day, if he survived going over the top, before taking some rest. He hoped he could have a proper wash and maybe a change of clothing and warm his poor feet. He washed his feet and dried them, where possible, but lately it had become increasingly more difficult to carry out the simplest of tasks, following weeks in the trenches.

He had heard that de-lousing machines had been introduced to combat the lice and additional uniforms were being issued, enabling everyone to have two sets of clothing.

Sam asked Len if he would be going to the de-lousing section, he nodded.

"Too right Sam, they're eating me a bloody live"

"Now look what you've done, thinking about the little bastards has starting me scratching again"

He put his hand down his trousers and started scratching at his crutch.

Rats carried a disease called pyrexia, which was commonly known as "*Trench Fever*", causing pain to the shins and very high temperatures. If caught, the soldier would inevitably be taken off duty.

The buggers would scamper across you when sleeping, decomposing bodies, which were in abundance, and scraps of food scattered about, attracted them into the trenches.

The weather had been so bad lately, the incessant rain had no let-up. They were ankle and, sometimes knee deep with water and mud, they stood for days in the sodden earth. The pumps, recently introduced in the trenches, were only marginally successful. Cave-ins were becoming a common occurrence and carried dreadful consequences. Often the soldiers were buried alive and died under tons of mud and soil, despite desperate efforts to dig them out.

Sam had been buried alive, following a terrible cave-in, some months earlier, he thought his time had come to meet his maker. He had given up all hope of being saved, almost unconsciousness, oblivion had overcome him, then a hand grabbed him and heaved him up and out of his tomb of mud into the daylight. Only two survived the cave-in, seven soldiers' died that day, buried alive in that mud slide.

The soldier who saved his life had become his best friend, they were always together now, Len was a little older than Sam, he was 19 years old. He was 6' 3" tall, had dark auburn hair and freckles all over his face, but were more prominent on his nose. He had lost one of his front teeth through fighting at school and often got caught up in scraps when they had a few days away from the trenches. Len was a happy sole, with a girlfriend at home called Edna, the lads had hit it off immediately.

Len came from Accrington, he almost joined the Accrington Lads, sadly almost all had been lost and killed in a battle, many of whom had been his friends from school. He joined up after a blazing row with his father and, he too regretted not making peace at home. They had so much in common.

Len had worked down the pits since leaving school and suffered from claustrophobia, he understood exactly how Sam felt. Often when he woke up, more so since the cave-in, sweating and shouting, fighting for his life. Sam would nudge him and assure him that it was only a dreadful bad dream.

Len had fears of being buried alive, he rarely spoke to anyone of his phobia, but he had confided to Sam one night. The nights were so long in the trenches, particularly when nothing was happening, the lads would sit or stand around, talking and discussing home, unable to sleep. They knew almost everything there was to know about each other, the lads had submitted their most intimate secrets from childhood to the present day.

Sam had nightmares following the cave-in, his dream was always the same. He would wake up suffocating, buried in tons of earth, fighting to get out, clawing at the mud, his fingernails bleeding from digging with his bear hands. Some nights he'd stay awake waiting for dawn to appear too afraid to go to sleep.

Continuous sleep was almost impossible with all the noise from the enemy, only when he was totally exhausted did he manage to fall asleep for a little while, but the silence in the trenches was even worse, it was eerie and daunting and put everyone on edge, it was far more intimidating than the droning of the shells.

George, another young recruit, shook Sam, he woke up with a start. He didn't know where he was at first. He could see the rockets and the thunder of the gun swells breaking into separate explosions, the heavies hoarse with a distinctive distant bellow. He turned and looked at George in a distant gaze.

"Price it's your turn, to keep watch"

Sam felt as if he had only been asleep for a few moments. He rubbed his eyes and stamped his feet to try and bring the circulation back into them. They ached terribly, he patted his arms about his body to bring the circulation back and jumped up and down.

"George, I'm ok now, you go and have some rest"

He looked at his pals huddled together trying to catch a little sleep, utterly exhausted, they looked like orphaned children out of a Charles Dickens novel. He popped his head carefully over the parapet, avoiding any sudden movements, which may cause his helmet to sparkle in the moonlight and give a trigger happy sniper the opportunity of shooting him. The dank dark mist crept eerily across the inky darkness, it surely was a creepy night.

Suddenly there was a whir and a brilliant light shining over the scene for a few seconds illuminating the trenches and '*no mans land*'. In the space of those few seconds snipers from both sides marked their targets and bullets whistled from the trenches. Ever few moments this was repeated with alternate light and darkness as the star shells burst and went out.

Sam steadied himself and leaned against the sandbags, balancing on the third rung of the trench ladder, he dropped his chin on the sandbag and lowered his head and looked through the sight of his rifle. He fired a few short bursts at the enemy, marking his target carefully, he heard a ghastly scream and turned away. He had hit his target well. Sam rarely missed, he was saddened and ashamed at killing his fellow man. The only consolation he had was that it was his duty and the job must be done. It was kill or be killed. He would answer to God after the war.

He stepped down and leaned against the trench wall, it was starting to rain again, he lifted his collar up under his chin and stamped his feet again. The wet soaked through his trench coat, making it even heavier than before. He stepped back up and kept guard, making sure the enemy were not advancing the trenches.

Sam had become quite an expert with the rifle, he

was considered an excellent marksman by all his mates, his commanding officer had also commented on his keen eye, sadly he had been killed when a direct hit shattered a command post two days earlier.

He had learnt to shoot at home, his father had spent hours walking the fields weekends, shooting rabbits and vermin, Sam and Joe by his side. He would stand behind the boys coaxing them, steadying their hands, moments before shooting their game. The memories of those happy hours helped him when he fired the rifle, it was as if his father was behind him prompting him, talking to him.

"Mark your target, son, steady now, steady and fire"

He felt his presence somehow when he fired his rifle.

After a while everything went ghostly silent again, it was like this some nights, he had become quite accustomed to the habits of the snipers firing at each other night after night. The rain had turned into a drizzle and it dripped off his helmet down the front of his coat, he took it off and shook the excess water off and popped it back on. He was absolutely soaked through to the skin again. He checked his watch to see how much longer he had to stand watch.

Sam took everything so matter of fact now, initially everything excited him, he loved the action, but all he wanted to do lately was to get himself clean and have some sleep. He was exhausted, both mentally and physically. He had survived, by some miracle, going over the top several times.

On one occasion he was hit on his helmet by a bullet, knocking him senseless. Len dragged him into a deep crater and waited till nightfall, with several other lads. It was the most frightening few hours of his life. Crawling along the sodden land, eerie with fog and dead mutilated bodies, touching the severed limbs and heads as he crawled back to friendly ground, each shell fired above their heads highlighting their bodies trying desperately to get back to the trenches. He wanted to cry out and stand up, but he knew if he did some trigger happy *Hun* would shoot him.

Len had poked his finger into the hole in his helmet and commented Sam must have someone looking after him *'up there'*. Fortunately, he was only stunned by the stray bullet, but nevertheless it gave him a nasty headache.

Sam stared out across *no mans land* again, mist and smoke from the guns lay breast high over the killing fields of the Somme, he was unable to light the much needed cigarette for fear of being shot by a sniper. He shot a few more rounds at the Hun, this time he missed his target.

He started thinking about his family again and the arguments he had caused at home and that dreadful fight! Smiling to himself at the thought of his mother hitting him with the yard brush. He desperately wanted to make peace with his father.

Sam never had parcels or letters from home, they arrived periodically through the goods office of the Red Cross, he watched sadly his many friends open their parcels and read letters from home. He did not have a loved one writing him and waiting for his homecoming. He longed to hear news from home and was determined to post his letter, he could not tell his mother what was happening at the front and had been extremely careful over his wording, in case his letter was intercepted by the enemy. He had asked her to let Joe and his father know the address allocated to his squadron enabling them to write to him.

Most of the lads in the trenches were older than Sam, he had never really confided his actual age to anyone, other than to Len. He had lied to the Enlistment Officer in London. Fortunately, he was tall for his age and well built, the officer in charge was not really interested, due to hundreds of new enlistments standing in the queue behind him on that day.

Sam was still day dreaming when someone shouted across the lines

"Gas attack",

He reached for his mask in the satchel hanging around his neck. He hated wearing it, it made him feel claustrophobic and brought back memories of the cave-in. The smell overpowered him and inevitably made him sick.

He looked along the line, the lads were alert and were putting their masks on, they made a petrifying scene. It gave them an alien appearance. Sam breathed heavily into the mask inhaling the stale air. He looked out over *no mans land*, searching for the yellow-grey smoke to appear in the distance, but there was no vapour to be seen. After what seemed an eternity the order was given to take off the masks. Sam pulled his mask off and put it back into the satchel, breathing in deeply, he leaned over and put his head between his knees trying not to be sick.

This sort of thing happened all the time, someone would panic and shout "*gas*" and a few moments later "*false alarm*" would be shouted and everyone took off the hideous masks. He had not experienced a full gas attack, but had no illusions about the deadly suffocating effects rendering one into a comatose condition.

Len had witnessed an attack the year before, which had killed thousands of French and English soldiers' in Ypres at Gavenstafel Ridge. He told Sam how a green cloud dissipated towards their lines, soldiers' fell to the ground holding their throats, blood oozing from their mouths, staggering across the fields, being shot at by the Germans, with ashen purple faces. Fortunately, for Len he had been a long way behind the lines, he only had sore eyes and a tender throat following the attack.

Preliminary bombardment had commenced again, the trenches shook, clouds of drifting shell-smoke obscured the German lines. Shells flew over their heads in a steady stream; it died down a little after almost 2 hours. It was now 9.00 a.m., brigade had called off the attack again to go over the top, the orders were passed down the line to hold ourselves in readiness to go over at dawn.

There was a northerly breeze, Sam could smell a pungent, nauseating smell that tickled his throat and made his eyes smart. A rotting corpse a few yards from the trench lay in the mud, it's smell was overpowering, he vomited. The wall of the soldier's stomach had collapsed due to a bullet wound. Sam looked over the parapet, he could see the soldier's face it was green and turning black, his eyes had been eaten by the rats, they had chewed off his nose and lips, hoards of the buggers were all over him like flies on shit. They were eating his intestines and one disappeared into the soldier's stomach.

Sam fired a single shot just a little above the decomposing corpse, the rats scattered, but returned within seconds.

Sam turned to Len saddened by how cheap life had become in the battlefields, no-one had bothered to pick him up and bring him home. He looked at Len and said:

"That soldier could be my brother, or my father"

Len could see Sam's distress and spoke to him:

"Suppose we'd best move him tonight, the rats will be in the trenches in their swarms if we don't. Don't want the buggers in here again tonight, do we? One bit me leg the other night, Sam"

Len loosened his gaiter and rolled his trouser leg up and showed Sam the bite, the rat had pierced the skin just below his knee. It had become quite reddened. Sam leaned closer and smelt the wound.

"Len, it looks inflamed and I don't like the redness around the bite, perhaps we ought to lance it. I'll do it, I helped my brother Joe when the horses were bit back home. If you trust me, that is?"

Len nodded and Sam suggested going to the Nursing Post when they went to the Rest Station the following day.

He was obviously distressed, soldiers' had lost their legs through rat bites, the trenches were infested by the buggers and, they weren't afraid of humans, they'd just stand their ground and stare at you with piercing eyes.

Len spoke to Sam again:

"Big bugger it was, big as a bloody cat, the bastard made me jump. He pinched food out of my pocket. I felt him run down my body"

He shook himself as he explained to Sam what had happened and shuddered at the thought of rats crawling over him while he was asleep.

"I was dreaming of Edna and I felt this sharp sting, I smacked him with me helmet and stamped on him. I'm the last bugger he'll bite, anyway"

He smiled at Sam and reached for his haversack.

"Think I'll boil up a Dixie, you want one Sam?"

"Please, Len", Sam said.

Sam took out his bowie knife and searched in his kit bag for his mentholated spirits, he tipped the spirit on the knife and held it over the primus stove. Looking over at Len he smiled shyly and turned the knife over. The smell of the mentholated spirits was overpowering, it made Sam's eyes water and his throat dry again. He checked both sides of the knife, which had now begun to glow.

Sam asked Len one last time:

"Len if you would rather I didn't do this?"

Sam was hoping Len would stop him, but he knew deep down that if this wound was not cleaned and cauterized it would undoubtedly go septic. The bite was quite deep. It wasn't worth taking any chances.

If only the rat had bit him just a fraction lower, Sam thought!

Len shook his head and sat down in his funk hole. He took off his boot and gaiter and rolled his socks down again.

Sam took a deep breath and passed Len a piece of wood to bite on, Len turned his head away, not wanting to see the knife.

"Ready or not Len, here we go"

He pushed the point of his knife into Len's leg and waited for a second. The smell of burnt flesh and mentholated spirit mixed was awful, it made him feel nauseous again, he turned away to avoid looking at the wound and throwing up.

Len gripped onto Sam's arm and bit down hard on the piece of wood as the knife sizzled the flesh on his leg, he bit down so hard the wood broke in two in his mouth. He spit the splinters out and looked up to the sky. He was afraid Sam would see the tears welling in his eyes.

After a few moments Sam tapped Len on the shoulder and asked if he was o.k., Len nodded and looked down at his leg.

It was burning like hell Sam, but strangely enough it feels better. It was obviously a physiological reaction, but nevertheless, Len felt relieved it was all over.

A lot of the lads did this to the bites, rather than suffer the excruciating discomfort, caused whilst festering took place. Better to nip it in the bud, so to speak.

"Thanks Sam, you should have been a vet"

He smiled sarcastically at Sam

"I may take it up Len, if ever I get out of this bloody mess"

The lads laughed, Sam tipped a little of his rum over the wound, then gauze and wrapped a field bandage around Len's leg.

"Waste of good rum Len", Sam said.

He smiled at his friend and offered to dry his socks over his primus, Len pushed him over and he fell in the mud landing on his bottom.

"Next time I have some rum I'll drink it, you bugger. Thanks a lot Len, that's gratitude for you" , Sam said

George had watched the whole thing, he was keeping watch for them. He admired Len for being so brave and smiled at the two lads fooling around now that the worst was over.

Len offered Sam and George a roll-up, they all smoked the much needed fag.

With everything going on Sam had completely forgotten the rotting corpse. He turned and noticed a young NCO orderly soldier, he was climbing the trench ladder, he leaned on the riveting frame for a moment and looked over at Sam, obviously he was composing himself for the next moments would be life or death to him. He had a white handkerchief on the end of his bayonet, he held it high above his head and commenced waving it above the parapet. He looked down at Len and Sam again, smiled sadly and continued to climb the ladder. Sam jumped up in readiness to give the orderly gun support.

He watched as the soldier bravely strolled over to the dead body, whacked the rats with his rifle and dragged the body back to the trench. Two other stretcher bearers pulled the body over the parapet into the trench, the right arm came off in the hand of the NCO. He gave the arm a cursory glance and popped it onto the stretcher on top of the soldier's body. The three men lifted the stretcher and carried the dead solider away. The lads watched as they disappeared with the stretcher down the trench.

Sam and Len couldn't believe how stupid the young NCO behaved, walking out like that, but the soldier could see how the body was distressing everyone close by in the trenches.

This sort of thing was common practice on both sides, the Germans would wave a white flag so that they could retrieve an injured soldier(s) and so did the tommies. Then other times some bugger would take a pot shot and not respect the flag. There was no rhyme or reason why?

Len and Sam went to the rest station with several of the other lads, relieved that they had finally been excused duties for a few hours.

A draft of new recruits, heavily equipped, had just arrived and were unloading boxes of ammunition into the firing line. They were replacements for the officers' and soldiers' killed in action, here to fill in those gaps left by the dead and wounded. A burst of enemy shrapnel shells exploded around them, it was becoming quite perilous. A spy plane had just flown over and obviously notified the Germans of his findings.

Sam looked at Len and said:

"I think it may have been safer in the trenches?"

Len smiled and nodded.

Finally after what seemed a lifetime the ammunition was unloaded and moved away from the cookhouse. No-one was hurt by the shell fire, this time. A little way from the cookhouse a ruined house had been commandeered by Brigade Headquarters, a Regiment Aid Post had been set up in an abandoned building next to it. Not a single house in the small village had a roof tile left on it, the roof struts were still in situ, evidence of fierce fighting. The village had been under the fire of guns from both sides during battle and now received constant bombardment from the Huns.

Sam took off his trench coat and held it around a large barrel with a fire in it, the steam from his coat drifted over his head. The lads had taken their socks off and put them on sticks and were holding them near to the side of the barrel, someone had knocked tree stumps into the ground to sit on.

They brewed up and watched 2 soldiers boxing having fisticuffs, it was a friendly sparring match to keep themselves fit.

George took out a pack of cards and started playing poker with Albert, Sam never learnt how to play poker and declined to play. He was quite warm for a change and felt refreshed, following his wash and full change of clothes. He hoped the flees had gone following the de-lousing and checked the cuffs to see if their were any eggs present. He smiled to himself and leaned against the cookhouse wall and smoked a fag, finally it had stopped raining.

He could hear a ruckus behind the aid post, it was coming from over by the road, it sounded like a horse. He strolled over to where the noise was coming from and stubbed his fag out on the floor.

A beautiful black shire horse was stuck in the mud up to her chest, getting more and more stressed by the minute. She was in a large crater and sinking deeper and deeper into the mud, the gun carriage she had been pulling was dragging her down, causing her to panic and thrash about. A young soldier had taken a crop to her. Sam hated cruelty, he stormed over to him and took it off him and threw it to the ground. The young lad turned in shame and walked away.

Sam took off his coat and stripped to his bracers, checking his laces were tied tightly and his trousers were tucked into his socks, he walked over to the distressed animal and sunk into the mud. Stroking her face he began to talk to her, reassuring her, stroking her warm silky coat, whilst he checked her over. He held the reigns and tried pulling and coaxing her out of the mud with no avail.

Len was in the mud now with Sam, he pushed his shoulder tight against the wheel of the gun carriage. A few more lads came over to help. They were getting nowhere.

Sam asked them to stop for a moment and bent down feeling for injuries on the horses legs, she appeared to be unhurt, just fretting. She was obviously very tired, unable to help herself. She became very quiet when Sam started to put his hands down her lower legs. He was amazed how she just stood for him, despite being buried up to her belly in thick mud. Sam continued to reassure her and stroked her neck and flanks as he checked her over.

"There now girl, we'll get you out, you've got to help us though, I won't leave you sweetheart, I promise".

The horse seemed to know that Sam was trying to help her. She was a beautiful shire, almost 18 hh with wall eyes, one eye was a shade bluer than the other. The fear in her seemed to subside with Sam by her side, she looked down at him, he could not get over how blue her eyes were. He had never seen a horse with two wall eyes before.

She had lovely markings, a white blaze, black feathery mane and tail, typical of a shire and obviously from good stock. She was caked in mud from head to tail.

Captain Scott came out of Headquarters with Lieutenant Green to see what the commotion was. They stood looking at Sam still submerged in the mud. Scott walked over towards them, he had a crop in his hand and tapped it against his leg, he played with his walrus moustache with the other hand. The captain took out his revolver and offered it to Sam. He looked up at the officer and declined to shoot the animal.

"Sir, can I please try something before we take such drastic measures"

The captain turned and walked over to Lt. Green. He commented to him that he thought Sam was silly trying to get the animal out, it would be kinder to shoot her.

Sam took the harness off the mare and handed it to Len, it was obviously the weight of the gun carriage that was dragging her down deeper into the mud. He asked Len and George to push on her rump when he pulled the reigns. The others were to hold the gun carriage steady and keep it from sliding onto her back legs. The horse seemed to gain her footing almost immediately the harness was taken off her. Sam pulled the reigns willing her to help herself.

"Come on girl, they'll shoot you if I can't get you out of here"

Sam was at his wits end and beginning to think she would never get out of the hole and resigned himself to the fact that he would have to shoot her. He walked around her again and noticed he had forgotten the thong under her tail, and two leather straps on the gun carriage, he removed them, handing them to Len and went back around the front of her. Willing her on again.

"Now come on girl, there's nothing stopping you now, is there?"

She finally started to move her legs, getting a foot hold and beginning to pull herself out of the mud, she now realised that she could get out. After almost 2 hours she clambered up out of the crater shaking the mud all over Sam. He dropped to the ground and lay on his back, absolutely buggered. The horse dropped her head and nudged him. He smiled at her and patted her nose. He stood up and strolled around her checking for injuries. Amazingly, she had none, other than a few grazes, he was not too surprised, however, these horses were bred for brewers drays and heavy work, but not necessarily in these conditions. The horse rubbed against him and pushed him again, he almost fell over.

Sam was so happy he had saved her, she reminded him of a mare called Sally he had learnt to ride on at home. Sally pulled the plough, he rode her home after work, occasionally the two brothers' would pop on her back and their father would ride the other shire called Ada. He had spent many happy hours grooming them ready for shows, Joe and his father would take them in ploughing matches. His father was very proud of the first prizes he had won over the years, particularly when he showed Sally, she had a lovely nature for such a big horse.

He led the mare over to a battered oak tree and tethered her. He walked back over to the carriage in the mud and helped the lads get it out, with the help of another shire and a huge chain. They were all covered in mud, but happy for once. A loud cheer went out from everyone who had been watching the incident.

Captain Scott came over to Sam patting his leg with the crop again, fiddling with his moustache.

"Good work private"

"Where did you learn horse skills?"

Sam stood to attention, trying desperately to wipe his dirty hands on the back of his trousers.

"My father sir, he's serving in the AVC, he's a Sergeant. My brother is also a shoe smith, also serving in the AVC. I was brought up on a farm and have handled heavy work horses, like this one, most of my life"

The captain seemed taken with Sam.

"Private I could do with more men like you and those others over there, when you've cleaned up go over to Headquarters and speak to Staff Sergeant Jones, he'll arrange transfers to my company. I trust you would like a change from the trenches, private and be part of the Transport Corps?"

"Yes, Sir, I would and thank you, Sir"

Sam went over to Len and asked him if he fancied a change from the monotony of the trenches. He shook Sam's hand, George hugged them both and they all went over to the shire. She was chobbling hay, none the worse for wear.

Sam felt fulfilled and calm somehow, his anger had subsided, the shire had brought back memories of home and his childhood. At last he felt peace in this God Almighty Place.

The three privates went over to the Headquarters and registered with Staff Sergeant Jones, they were asked to come back the following day, but the sergeant asked Sam if he would go over to the shoe smith in the paddock, he was apparently struggling with so many horses needing attention.

Sam smiled at the sergeant and said:

"I'd be happy to help, Sarg"

He looked at Sam and said:

"Incidentally, private, you will be corporal from tomorrow, the job allocated for you carries NCO ranking. A little extra for the wife, aye"

Sam shook his head.

"No wife yet Sarg"

Sam smiled smugly, thinking to himself how shocked the sergeant would be if he knew his real age, he would be 18 years old in January 1917 and legally would then be of age to join HM Forces.

"You should get one lad, it helps", Jones said.

"I'll work on that", Sam said smiling.

Sam popped over to the paddock and met Archie, the shoe smith. He was in his late thirties and reminded him of his father, they hit it off immediately. Sam assisted Archie shoe several of the Corps horses and examined the latest batch, which had arrived that morning.

He noticed a young gelding limping, and following close examination by Archie, it was decided they should shoot him. He had injured his leg after stumbling quite badly in a pot hole. Archie was reluctant to shoot him, but thought the horse would not recover from the star fracture to his nearside lower leg. Sam held the horse whilst Archie shot him.

"We'll have our work cut out tomorrow, Sam", Archie said.

"See you tomorrow, lad, and try and get a little sleep, if you can"

Sam borrowed a few grooming brushes, and a rasp from Archie and returned to the shire, who was still quite happy by the oak tree. He spent the next few hours grooming the mare, rasping her teeth and shoeing her. She looked a treat when he'd finished. He was quite pleased with himself, it felt good to be around horses again.

Sam sat down admiring his work looking at his new prodigy. Len came over to him and patted the mare on the hind quarters, she looks lovely Sam, you've made a good job of her. Len leaned down and looked under her tummy, smiling sarcastically he said:

"You've missed a bit though, Sam"

He pointed to a chunk of mud stuck on her stomach, the horse seemed to know what they were talking about and popped her head between her legs to where Len was pointing. Sam said:

"She understands what your saying, we'll have to watch what we say in future".

Sam made a gesture and put his fingers across his throat and made a noise as if he were choking. The horse just carried on chomping her hay. The lads burst out laughing.

"I'm going to call her Gracie" Sam said to Len.

"That's a lovely name, Sam"

The lads sat down on a bale of hay, chewing straw and mulling over how beautiful Gracie looked despite the mud under her tummy.

"If it's in my power, I'm going to take her home with me following the war, she deserves to be looked after better than this. No horse deserves to be treated in this way, it's so cruel, Len"

CHAPTER 7

England late 1916

Mary looked at the letter, but couldn‘t open it. She realised it was from Sam, but was frightened it may contain bad news and popped it into her apron pocket and carried on making bread.

When Bernard came home she told him about the letter and asked if he would get the children to bed early so that they could read it later that evening.

She sat in Harry's chair by the fire and looked down at Bernard, who was sitting on the corner seat of the brass fender around the hearth, Len sat on the other side, with hands shaking she opened the envelope. Bernard looked up at his mother and asked if she wanted him to read the letter, she nodded and passed it to him, he smiled at her tenderly and took the letter out. Mary popped some wood on the fire and poked the ashes with the poker a cinder jumped out of the fire and landed on Len's trousers. He patted it quickly and smiled at his mother.

Bernard looked up at his mother.

"Mother it's o.k."

"It's from Sam"

Bernard started to read it aloud.

20 September 1916

Dear Mother,

I am so sorry for all the trouble I caused you and father. Will you forgive me?

I'll buy you a new broom when I come home, I promise.

I joined the army and have been fighting on the front for over six months. Things are quite bad here. The lessons father gave me with the rifle have been very useful to me it's earned me extra sixpence a week.

I cannot tell you exactly why or where I am, mother. I'll tell you all about it when I come home.

I have a few mates here, one is from Accrington, he saved my life and we have become great pals. We look after each other now and have become inseparable. Most of his village were killed over here, but he was too young and joined the army later. Good news for him really, but it is a terrible thing for his village to be whipped out like that. You've probably read about the massacre in the papers.

When I get home, I want to bring him to meet you all.

Could you let me have Joe's address, if he's joined the AVC and also father's. If not the address, his regiment so that I can write, or maybe even go find him if he's on the same front as me.

I'm sorry it's took so long for me to put pen to paper, but you know how stubborn I am? I didn't think you would want to associate with me after me running away the way I did without even a word.

I miss you all so much.

How is Phyliss? I bet she's grown?

I can't say too much, mother.

Please write to me soon. I love you all.

Your loving son, Sam.

P.S. I've just been promoted to Corporal, I've probably got a higher rank than Joe. Ha, Ha.

She hugged Bernard and popped the letter back into her apron. Len jumped up, smiled at his mother and hugged her too. They jumped up and down for a few moments.

"I think this is a good excuse boys for a tot of parsnip wine. Go fetch some Len and Bunny get the glasses please and could please get me my quill and ink from the writing bureau, I must tell your father Sam's ok"

The letter had taken well over a month to get to her, it passed through her mind that during this time he could have been killed. She shook her head and dismissed her thoughts.

"My boys are safe, I know they are safe"

She assured herself.

Joe, Sam, Elsie, Susie, Dolly and her beloved husband were all away. She worried constantly about whether her boys were safe and, most of all, alive.

She hadn't heard from Joe since entraining and was becoming increasingly concerned, the silence was unbearable. Harry had told her that it was not unusual for soldiers' to write home for several months due to them moving about and difficulties with the postal service and moreover security.

Young Mary was besides herself with worry too, the baby was due in a few months, she came over to see her future mother-in-law every weekend in the hope that Joe had written. She had become a welcomed guest weekends, and helped with Joe's siblings.

Harry was now stationed in Aldershot, he came home every six weeks or so, but it was becoming increasingly more dangerous for him, so many air raids and bombs were being dropped along the coast and surrounding areas. A German airship had been shot down a few weeks earlier near Enfield, the fire could be seen for over 20 miles, hundreds of people had been killed and maimed. Thousands of innocent bystanders' were being killed and children were being evacuated to the countryside, whole trains were being filled with the children, many orphaned in the raids over London and its' suburbs.

Mary's life was full of worry, 5 children away from home, her boys in life threatening situations in a foreign land and, her husband in such a vulnerable place coping alone with the worry for his whole family.

There seemed to be no end to this bloody war, already it had been ongoing for almost 3 years and no end in sight.

Mary couldn't feel excited about becoming a grandmother, she was frightened the baby would be born and Joe would not see his child come into the world.

She knew of all the thousands of young men dying everyday in the battlefields of the Somme and surrounding areas, and further a field in Europe and Africa, and the chaos and utter desolation felt by all. Whole villages were losing their young men after being annihilated on the battlefields. The notice boards throughout the land were besieged daily by women awaiting word of their men and loved ones. She visited her own little village and queued with other mothers' and wives' awaiting news every week, the relief she felt when her sons were not on the list was enormous and, then guilt because sons of her friends were taken at such a young age.

Women across England were working on the land, in garages, driving, on the railways, and in industry. Mary's best friend had become a chimney sweep and another a post women. She was unable to work herself due to her children being so young, but knitted gloves and jumpers and made bandages at home every evening, it helped take her mind away from the fighting and heartache of the war.

Leonard, despite his young years, was working at a local factory repairing boots for the RACD, re-building or re-soling. Many young wives and teenagers were having lessons in local village halls in boot repairing. A measure inspired by economy and patriotic desire to free men for service overseas.

She would knit until the early hours by candlelight sitting in Harry's fireside chair, her needles clicking away in rhythm with her grandfather clock . She had taught Len and Bernard how to knit, despite their protests at being men, knitting was for girls they would say to her, but they would all sit chatting in the evenings, her boys at her feet knitting or making rag rugs.

Many rooms in large mansions were turned into workrooms

for the manufacture of hospital requisites. The hospitals were at bursting point with the arrival of wounded men daily.

Mary wrote back to Sam and said, if he sent her the letters she would deliver them to his father when he came home on leave and gave him the contact addresses of Elsie, Sue, Dolly and the last known address for Joe.

Elsie was home that weekend and had written to her father and Sam, she popped her letters' into the respective envelopes. Mary told Sam of the Derby winner, Mr Hulton's "Fifinella", who also won the Oaks race and informed him that he would be an uncle in early 1917.

She also told him Joe hadn't written home since entraining and his last known station.

Elsie had pointed out to her younger brothers' where they both were in the Atlas, it was only an inch or so apart Leonard had commented. Bernard had worked it out on his scale ruler, it was about 30 miles from where Sam was stationed. Elsie looked at Ypres,

"See that big town, they could rendezvous there, that would be a mutual place to meet".

Little did she know at the time that a combination of over-ambitious aims, appalling weather conditions and, misguided persistence by Commander Haig, would lead to horrific casualties for both sides.

Mary, didn't know at this time that the boys were only 15 miles apart and that destiny was about to step in. She couldn't wait to speak to Harry, he was due home that weekend.

Bernard was growing so quickly, he was taller than his father now and carried his responsibilities on his young shoulder's like a man, despite being only 14 years old. He was gainfully employed at the stables, many of his school friends were also working there due to their fathers' being away at war. He was almost as good with horses as his big brother Joe and his reputation with the brood mares was becoming known at other stables. Bernard was quite happy working the land and hoped Joe would take him as his partner when he came home from war. He felt sure Joe would offer him employment when he set up his Smithy.

It was Friday evening, Mary couldn't wait for Harry to come home, she was busy tidying the house and baking when the post lady knocked at the door. She had a telegram in her hand.

Mary opened the door and held her hand out, she froze unable to take the letter from her friend, Annie. She handed the telegram to her and walked her back into the kitchen and sat her down. Mary couldn't open it, she looked up at Annie with tears in her eyes.

Annie asked if she could do anything.

Mary nodded.

"Get Leonard he's in the yard, he'll fetch Bernard from the stables"

Annie rushed out and sent Leonard for Bernard, she left when he arrived. Mary passed him the telegram and asked him to read it.

Len sat down with the little ones, who were very quiet for a change.

Bernard opened the telegram and read it to his mother.

"Harry injured in bomb attack.
His leg is badly broken.
He's in Charing Cross Hospital awaiting surgery.
Lt. Smith AVC Aldershot

Mary took the telegram from Bernard and read it again. Her head was buzzing, what could she do to help her husband.

She stood up and took off her apron and spoke to her son.

"Bernard, go fetch Mary she'll have to watch the children when Elsie goes back to Northfield. I'm going to London. I want you to stay here and take over at night"

Mary thought for a few moments of her uncle Bertie, he was a surgeon and had been stationed in London throughout the war. She knew he was working in London and decided to ask him for his help. He had always resented the way his brother had treated his favourite niece. It was her only hope.

There was a very slim chance that he may be at home, she thought!

"Bernard, go get the buggy ready. It's a chance in a million. I'm going to see if uncle Bertie is home"

She was shaking all over when she lifted the wrought iron heavy lion door knocker on the lodge house, the knocking echoed eerily.

Uncle Bertie had never married, he had written to her and sent her birthday cards over the years, she knew in her heart that if he was there he would help her without question. There was no answer to her repeated knocking.

She was just about to walk away when the door opened, her uncle was standing their in his dressing gown, he was obviously in the middle of shaving he had soap all over his face. She would have smiled at his father Christmas face if the situation had not been so dire.

"Mary is that you child", he said as he popped his glasses onto his nose, and wiped the soap away from his face with the towel around his neck.

"Oh Uncle Bertie, I need your help"

"Come inside and tell me about what ails you Mary"

Mary sat at the kitchen table sipping a cup of tea, Bertie had tipped whisky in it, it made her eyes water.

Bertie had only been home a few hours following almost six months working flat out in the operating theatres at Charing Cross Hospital.

Mary showed him the telegram and asked if he could help her. He asked her to wait a few moments and rushed upstairs. He quickly packed his portmanteau and came downstairs within a few minutes.

"Well I'm ready, you are so lucky to catch me, I've been to see your father, he's ill, he's never got over the death of your brother, you know?"

"Father and I still do not talk uncle, he's never forgiven me for marrying Harry"

Mary and Bertie returned to the cottage. He was surprised at how his nieces and nephews had grown. He sat them on his knee and talked about their mother when she was a child their age. Mary looked at her children with their doting uncle and wished with all her heart that her father would acknowledge his grandchildren and call to see them. She sighed and went up stairs to pack ready for the journey to London.

CHAPTER 8

Bertie, sat Mary down on the hospital bench and held her hands and gave her the sad news.

"Mary, dear, Harry's leg is badly broken, he may lose it.

I will do my utmost to save his leg, the surgeon in charge is a good friend of mine and has agreed I can assist in the operating theatre.

He couldn't be in better hands, Captain Drake is one of our best surgeons. If Harry's leg can be saved, it will mean months of nursing and painful splints Mary. His other injuries will heal, but you must realise that if things deteriorate we may have to amputate Harry's leg."

"Uncle Bertie, I know you will do your best, his life is in your hands now. Please do not amputate his leg, Harry's whole world revolves around his beloved horses."

Bertie kissed her on the cheek, hugged her and walked away. She watched him disappear and thought how much he reminded her of her father. He was the youngest and the gentlest of the brothers' and most understanding.

Mary felt lost, Harry was in the same ward that her brother had died in, the memories came rushing back. She started to cry and searched for her handkerchief in her pocket. Sensing someone else was now in her presence she looked up and saw Bernard and Leonard standing in front of her, they had listened to the conversation and where obviously very distressed. Their father had always been a strict taskmaster and handed out any punishment, but he had always been fair. She stood up and hugged her boys close to her.

"Uncle Bertie, paid for us to come mother, his batman met us on the station and brought us to the hospital, we caught the next train, he thought you would want us by your side", Bernard said.

"Your father is in surgery, it will be hours before he comes out"

Bernard held his mother's hand and Leonard held her other hand, they sat down together and waited for news of their father.

Mary looked at her boys in turn and smiled, she was happy they were with her. Her pride overwhelmed her.

Bertie shook Mary gently, it was 3.00 a.m. they had all fallen asleep on the bench. She woke up dazed. Bertie stooped down on his knees and held Mary's hands.

"Harry's out of surgery, dear. We've managed to save his leg, it may never be the same again, he'll probably limp the rest of his life. His army days are finished Mary. I will arrange for him to convalesce in a nursing home near to Kidderminster, but he will be in hospital for several months whilst the callous forms between the breaks in his leg. Better get the Guiness and cheese out, it helps form the callous and has all the right vitamins for Harry's recovery"

Mary started to cry, she was so relieved. He was alive and would recover, that was all she cared about.

"Thank you so much uncle Bertie, thank you from the bottom of my heart".

Bertie took the boys to one side and spoke to them.

"Your father is still in danger, there are many things that can happen. Stay with your mother for a few days and be by her side. Your father has been burnt and has other injures. Your mother needs your support".

"You can stay in my living quarters for the time you are here in London, I will take you there as soon as I can arrange transport"

The boys thanked their great uncle, he held them close and patted them.

"I am so proud to have such lovely great nephews"

"Your cousins have been posted to the front line, I will get their address from my brother. Perhaps you would like to write to them, I'm sure they would like to hear from you"

Bernard smiled and shook his hand.

"Have you heard from Joe or Sam yet", Bertie asked.

"No uncle, we haven't heard from Joe, but we have heard from Sam this weekend, he's in Belgium".

Bertie smiled,

"I'll see if I can get a message to him, I do still have friends, who may be able to help find news of Joe".

Bernard thanked his uncle again.

"I'll get their last addresses for you uncle and drop them off at your lodge when I get home. Mother and young Mary are desperate for news of Joe, since entraining we have heard nothing".

Bertie leaned down to the boys.

"Better not tell your mother what we've talked about, just in case, o.k"

They all nodded and turned round at the same time. Mary was standing at the entrance of the ward. She looked very tired. Bertie walked over to her and held her close.

"Oh! uncle Bertie, he's so pale and!!!!"

She just broke down and cried, all the pain and stress of the last few days catching up with her.

Bertie, patted her and held her.

"Mary, I'll keep an eye on him over the next few months whilst your at home and help with the costs of travelling to and from London, if you'll let me?"

"Thank you uncle, thank you"

"Now come on lets get you to my apartment, the boys must be tired out. By the way Mary, they are a credit to you. I cannot wait to meet Joe and Sam". She smiled at him and hooked her arm in his.

CHAPTER 9

Joe flung himself to the ground and waited for the burst of a high-explosive shell, such was the effect of the concussion that it lifted him clean off his feet and bowled him totally over. He sat up and put both hands to his forehead, he was badly shaken, blood was poring down his nose, he could barely see around of him. He wiped his eyes on his sleeve and stared at the carnage of brown earth and the shell hole he was now lying in, both veterinary assistants were dead and his commanding officer lay critically injured in the middle of the crater.

He was buried beneath the hailstones of mud, slime and barbed wire, his hand had been blown off, he lay a few feet from Joe, blood spurting into the air like a fountain where his wrist had been blown off. Joe crawled over to him and clumsily took off his belt and tried to stem the bleeding, he couldn't stand, he had no balance whatsoever and kneeled uncomfortably, but fell over. Joe's thumb was dislocated and it was very difficult to pull the belt tightly, he bit on the leather and pulled with his teeth. He could barely hear the words coming out of his commanding officer's mouth, the blast had affected his hearing. He could see he was critical and barely conscious. Joe spoke to him.

"Sir, you have been mortally wounded, I will have to crawl along the trench and try to get help" Pointing over to where the trench had been only moments earlier.

Joe pointed to his ears and shook his head,

"I can't hear you sir, the blast has affected my hearing".

He held his nose and blew as hard as he could, trying desperately to clear his ears, with no avail. Joe checked the tourniquet again, he could see the officer's lips moving, he motioned Joe to his tunic pocket. Joe lifted out a letter, but still could not hear what he was saying. His Commanding officer nodded feebly and spoke, despite Joe being unable to hear his dying words.

"Get this to my wife, I know I will not survive", blood was now coming from his mouth and his eyes were dying. Joe had seen this look many times.

"Tell my wife I love her, and kiss my boys for me"

Joe realised what he was saying and nodded and patted him on the shoulder.

"I will sir, I promise".

Joe started to crawl out of the crater, he struggled to get through the mud and slime, it held him down like a vice, it took all his strength to pull himself over the top and roll down the other side of the crater, almost immediately a second shell exploded. He automatically curled himself up into the foetal position and put his hands around his head, gripping with all his might. The ground shook beneath him and the hailstones of earth battered his young body almost burying him alive. After a few seconds he uncoiled his aching body and pushed away the black earth and debris, which now covered him. He turned his head away, only his friends upper torso was visible a few feet from where he was buried. Joe crawled and pulled himself across to him and took his few belongings from his jacket. He closed his eyes and said a prayer for his comrades.

Joe was still stunned by the power of the blast. He wiped the dirt from his eyes and turned to look behind him at the carnage in and around the crater. His commanding officer had disappeared entirely and also his team, only their helmets remained as a grim reminder that his comrades had been there only moments before. He turned and looked the other way, he was physically sick, one of his friends legs lay by his side, his shoe had been blown off in the blast.

A panic stricken beast lay a few yards from him, both it's legs had been blown off in the blast. Only 20 minutes earlier his Commanding Officer and his team had sedated the poor animal to take shrapnel out of a wound in his chest and now everyone was dead who had assisted in the operation, other than Joe. He pulled himself over to the horse and gently patted him on the neck.

"There, there, lad soon you will not have to endure any more pain"

The horse lifted his head up slightly, the fear in his eyes subsided slightly, Joe put his hand over his eyes and pulled out his pistol, he marked the spot well, he had executed so many horses now that it had become second nature to him, he pulled the trigger. Joe put the gun back in his holster and leaned up against the horse, he was past caring about who could see him and lit a cigarette and started to cry. He put his head on both his hands and rocked himself from side to side.

Joe sat in this position for a long time waiting for dusk to come, he felt nauseous and he was still experiencing difficulties with his hearing, his head ached and throbbed like a drum. He realised he had a serious head injury, and fought desperately to remain calm and awake, but tiredness and fatigue overtook his caution. He curled up into a ball and lay still and thought of home and his family. He had gone past the point of caring whether he lived or died.

Some time had passed, he had fallen asleep. He could see Mary, she was talking to him, she had a baby in her arms and held her out to him. Mary was smiling at him and told him they had a daughter and that he must be brave and wake up and come back to her, they needed him. He put his arm out to her, but she was gone.

He shook himself awake and looked around him checking to make sure the enemy had not seen him, he took his handkerchief out of his pocket, Mary had embroidered the union jack in the corner, he kissed it and wrapped it around his forehead and put his helmet back on.

He went in and out of consciousness over the following hours as he crawled back along the heavy mutilated ground, dragging his sodden body towards the sandbag barricade in the first line trench, the star shells continued to explode in the sky. As they exploded he kept perfectly still as the skies lit up, trying desperately to avoid a snipers bullet. Every inch he crawled he knocked his dislocated thumb. Silly as it was, his thumb caused him more pain than the head injury. He searched his pockets to find a field bandage just to hold it in a position where he wouldn't keep knocking it. He looked around him and saw a dead soldier. He checked his pockets and found a field bandage. He also took out his belongings and identity tags so that he could notify his family of his demise. Clumsily he put a splint on his thumb and used his mouth to tie off the bandage.

An eerie mist had formed across the ground, the wind blew into his face, it felt like someone was cutting into his skin with a razor, it was so bitterly cold and had started to rain, he was shivering and shaking uncontrollably from the effects of the cold and shell shock, the ground beneath him was soaking wet and muddy. His clothing had become so heavy it dragged him down, every movement was hell, he took off his trench coat, it had become too heavy and made it impossible to crawl along the sodden ground and left it.

Many soldiers had drowned in this mud, not having the strength to crawl out of the craters that entombed them, mud sucking them down into oblivion. Joe knew he only had a short time to get to safety before the dawn, or death, whichever came first.

He kept Mary's image in mind, she drove him on. He was so very cold, it would have been so easy to give in, but the thought of Mary and the baby drove him on. His fingers and knees were numb, they ached so much, but he carried on dragging at the dirt clawing himself along further and further, nearer and nearer to friendly ground. He stopped for a moment and tried to focus on his surroundings, when a hand grabbed his collar and pulled him over the top and into a trench behind him. Joe was startled by the force of the hand around his collar and tried to defend himself. Despair overtook him, he couldn't believe he had crawled all this way only to be killed by the enemy, or worse still, to be taken a prisoner of war, he lashed out in desperation.

Someone was shaking him, he tried to focus, but could not hear what they were saying, he could only see the movements of the sergeant's lips. Relief overtook him, he looked up, he was back, he had overcome the odds and crawled back behind his own line. He smiled at his captor and buried his face in his hands.

"Corporal, are their any survivors out there", the sergeant-major asked repeatedly.

One of the lads leaned over him and stared into his eyes and Joe pointed to his ears.

"Sarg, he can't hear you".

The soldier passed him a piece of paper and pencil.

Joe wrote on the paper, the commanding officer was killed with the second blast, the other lads were killed instantly on the first blast. I'm the only survivor. The sergeant called for first aid.

"Stretcher Bearers, take him to the First Aid Post, he has a nasty gash to his forehead", the sergeant ordered.

Joe, smiled bleakly and passed out.

The enemy had come from nowhere the previous day, the AVC were normally behind the lines and rarely came into firing range, the Germans were gaining ground and retreat was imminent. The Field Hospital would need to be moved yet again.

CHAPTER 10

"How you feeling Joe?", the doctor asked

"Can you hear me?"

Joe had been in the Clearing Station for over a week, he nodded his head and smiled at the Captain who was standing in front of him.

"Well Price, you gave us quite a scare, are you up to visitors yet"

Joe, smiled and nodded his head and tried to lift himself up on his bed.

"You have been quite ill Price, another few weeks and we'll have you back in the front line, or should I say behind the front line with the AVC. In the meantime, enjoy the rest son, you deserve some peace."

Joe looked around him, so many soldiers' lay dying or having lost limbs and arms, he felt a fraud somehow, with only a head injury. The smell of the dead and dying and stale blood was overpowering. He turned and wrenched into the bed pan and lay back onto his pillow. It was some time later, he had dozed off. He opened his eyes and looked up George was sitting on the corner of his bed. He tried to focus on who it was. Still dazed he realised where he was.

"Got a letter from home for you Joe, been keeping it until you woke up"

"How long have I been unconscious, George?" Joe said.

"Well I'm your first visitor, a little over a week"

"You were lucky Joe, everyone else was killed"

"I know", Joe answered, he lowered his head trying to avoid the tears welling in his eyes.

"I feel a little ashamed that I am here George. I tried to get help, but it was too late, I was nearly a gonna myself, but Mary came to me and helped me back to our lines".

"I'll tell you all about it one day George"

George nodded and smiled at his pal.

"I've heard other people say their loved ones have helped them through, sometimes even people who have passed on".

Joe nodded and they both sat silent for a few seconds.

"I have a letter in my tunic pocket, I want you to take it to Major Haughton and ask him to forward it to the wife of my Commanding Officer and ask him to pop this note in with it please, George. Also, check my jacket there are belongings from some poor sole killed in action. Someone should notify his family".

George took the letter and note from Joe, and the few belongings from the deceased soldier and shook Joe's hand,

"Glad you made it Joe, see you again in a few days".

Joe never saw George again, he was killed the next day on what was supposed to be a safe route behind the battlefield, a freak "Jack Johnson" hit the ammunition in the wagon he was transporting, throwing him off the wagon and killing him instantly and the four transport mules. Bill was thrown clear and only had minor cuts and bruises. Ironically they were doing a favour, whilst waiting to operate on a horse that had been injured by shrapnel.

Joe looked at the writing on the front of the envelope, his heart skipped a beat, he kissed her handwriting and opened the letter, he looked around him almost guiltily before he started to read it:

"My darling, you have a beautiful daughter, she weighed in at 6 lb 2 oz,

Your mother and Elsie delivered her at the cottage. I was out in the garden with Elsie and before I knew it I was giving birth to our baby girl.

I have called her Valerie Mary, after your mother. It is becoming increasingly more difficult with everyone in the house being called "Mary".

Joe smiled and wiped away a tear and continued to read his long awaited letter.

I have been staying with your mother for the past months, your father was sorely injured. He is now beginning to improve, he has taken a few steps this week and the doctors' think he will walk again without a stick, but he will probably never ride his beloved horses again.

He has been in Mr Joseph Chamberlain's Orchid House in Highbury for a little over a month. He almost lost his leg, but your uncle Bertie saved it, he performed the operation on him in London. Your mother, Bernard and Leonard were all their together waiting for him to recover from the operation. We would have been lost without uncle Bertie's help. He's a lovely fellow.

Your grandfather passed away last week, I'm not sure if your mother will be present at the funeral, there is still bad blood between the family. I thought following his death things would have changed?

I hope nothing ever comes between our two families, my parents have been wonderful about my pregnancy and your parents have made me so welcome.

Sam is well. He is fighting in Belgium.

Your mother sends her love, Elsie has been visiting your father daily and helping with the children when she can.

My darling, look after yourself, I miss you so much. Little Valerie Mary has your eyes and dark hair like the Price's, she is a bonny child and very good, she's sleeping through the night already. I'm breast feeding her.

We've popped her into your mother's bottom drawer until your father can make her a crib. She's almost too big now, her little feet look so funny over the top of the drawer. Your mother said you used to sleep in there when you were first born and too small for your crib.

Sweetheart, I have written you so many letters and have been worried sick, please write me soon.

I love you with all my heart, come back to us, we need you.

I have put your father's address on the back of this letter and the last contact address for Sam.

Your ever loving

Mary and daughter Valerie Mary Price

Enclosed is a letter from your mother.

Hope you like the photograph of your daughter, isn't she a stunner?

He smiled at the fact that his little girl had taken on his surname despite his pending marriage, he popped the letter back into the envelope and put it in his pyjama pocket. He patted his pocket and smiled remembering how Mary came to him whilst he was crawling to safety in his darkest hour.

It was no surprise that he had a daughter, in his heart he knew. Mary had always been his strength, his life. She would not let go!

He opened up the letter again and looked at the photograph of his daughter and put it under his pillow. He was tired and lay down. For the first time in, what seemed at decade, he felt peace and dropped off to sleep.

CHAPTER 11

Sam jumped off Gracie, walked around to her front, patted her neck on pulled his fingers through her thick forelock and mane.

"Must groom you young lady, your beginning to look a bit like me",

He chuckled to himself and tried to straighten his own thick locks with his fingers.

"Don't know who is the scruffiest out of us two, girl"

She looked him straight into his face with those lovely wall eyes of hers and he could not help but smile at her.

"I do declare you understand every word I say", he said smiling.

Gracie looked at Sam and nudged him with her "Roman nose". Sam almost fell over, she was so strong. He steadied himself and brushed the white hairs from her muzzle off his sleeve and pulled the neck strap open on her bridle. She was well over 17 hands and he had to stand on tip toe to pull the bridle over her ears, he dropped it down over her nose and shook the bridle so that he could loop the neck strap through the bridle to keep it from getting tangled up. The bit was covered in slobber and bits of grass, so he popped it into a bucket and washed it.

"You're a messy bugger, Gracie", he said
and continued to take her harness off.

"Suppose I'll need to clean these also while I'm at it girl, they're getting quite hard again".

He fussed her and pulled the lumps of mud from under her belly and turned her and the Rupert out into the paddock, well behind the Divisional Headquarters.

"You should be safe here".

Sub consciously he was trying to convince himself that they would be out of harms way, but he knew they would never be safe, wherever he turned them out. The German shells had no feeling for man nor beast. He shook his head saddened by the thought of his beauty being maimed and mortally wounded.

Sam had seen literally thousands of dead horses lying in the killing fields of Belgium, left on the side of roads, rat infested and covered in flies. He tried so hard not to think of the poor Trojans, who had given their lives to this war. They had no choice in their involvement, they just did as their master's wanted and perished on the battlefields. He felt the slaughter of these innocent creatures ludicrous, but necessary. He just wished that all the suffering and killing would cease and he could go home to his family.

He turned away from the paddock and Gracie neighed as he began to walk away. He felt a twinge of guilt, leaving her there vulnerable.

He turned around and stood looking at them again grazing, not a care in the world and reminisced about home. How many times had he sat on the fence with Joe and his father after they had worked all day in the fields, the sun dropping down over the Clent hills, so tired and hungry, barely able to walk home. The overpowering smell of his mother's cooking as they took their dirty boots off on the porch and popped their warmed slippers on ready for tea. His father tapping his Meascham pipe on the mantle piece and filling it with "old shag" tobacco.

He missed his father so much, being around the horses

made him realise just how good England and his life on the farm had been. Memories were so important in this God forsaken place, your life was worthless, just another number. So many of his mates had been killed, he was frightened to get too friendly for fear of them being killed or maimed. Thinking of home depressed him in a way, home meant security, love, a future. Here in this war zone you had no future, only today!

He shook his head trying to forget the heartache of war and looked over at Gracie grazing. She had become an excellent lead horse, and was an integral part of his daily life and routine, she was relentless and brave, worked well opposite Rupert his other acquisition.

Rupert was jet black with four white socks and long feathers, a wide white blaze and forelock, he too had a pink hairy nose, and much too pretty to be a gelding, Sam thought. He was bigger and taller than Gracie, almost 18 hh and as gentle as a lamb until turned out with Gracie. He protected her and would let no other horses near her and, dropped his ears to other members of Sam's team if they came too close.

Sam smiled to himself, strange how Rupert had taken to him, preferring Sam to handle him. It had become an understanding that only he handled Gracie and Rupert, rather than risking his staff being bitten on the bum or cow kicked.

It was a standing joke that any new member was told to tack Rupert up and everyone would wait for the poor sole to come running away with Rupert chasing afterwards with his ears far forward fly bucking. He looked so evil and powerful, not many even attempted to go near him, but Sam just sauntered over and took no notice of his moods. They understood each other. This was a marriage made in heaven they had instantly become friends, and were now inseparable, and a Team.

He left orders for the other livestock to be un-harnessed, fed and turned out.

Sam turned around and jumped, Len patted him on the shoulder and said:

"Joe will be o.k. Sam, if he's anything like his baby brother for surviving"

Sam smiled and patted his pal back.

"Thanks Len for coming with me"

They had both volunteered to deliver much needed ammunition and stores with the Munitions Column of convoy wagons to Passchendaele outside Ypres, where Joe was convalescing in an Advanced Dressing Station.

Both lads felt relieved that they had gotten through without any major problems. Many battles had been fought in this area and thousands of lives lost on both sides during the past two years.

Ypres suffered intermittent shelling daily, and despite the front line being only a few kilometres from the Eastern side of Ypres, 100's of inhabitants we still living in the historical medieval town and the surrounding villages.

Sam asked directions to the Advanced Dressing Station, he smiled to himself, the accent of the soldier was Australian, he belonged to the 1st or 2nd Division. Sam had met numerous nationalities over the months since joining the Transport Corps. He and Len had become friends with members of the New Zealand Divisions stationed on the Menin Road on the West-East route to Ypres. His new post delivering stores and much needed ammunition to the various Divisions was rewarding and he felt he was finally being of use to his country, instead of "gun fodder" in the trenches.

On his return journeys he joined the Red Cross Wagons and Horse Buses taking the injured and needy to the Clearing Station Hospitals and Field Ambulance HQ and the second stage of their long arduous journey to the Hospital train and eventually back to England so that the wounded could receive more specialist attention and urgent operations.

America had joined the war in April 1917, with battalions stationed throughout a 25 kilometre front around Ypres. He guessed there would be fierce fighting again soon in this area. Already there had been 2 major offensives at Ypres, he wondered what the third offensive would yield. Deep in thought he proceeded to the Dressing Station, but became apprehensive at the last minute and stood by the entrance and lit a badly needed fag.

A young nurse tapped him on the shoulder and asked if she could help in any way, he stared at her and, she asked if he was injured. Sam had not been in the company of a woman for so long and smiled shyly and shook his head.

"I'm here to see my brother, Corporal Joseph Price of the AVC, I believe he has been injured quite badly and is billeted in your hospital"

She smiled at him and offered to take him to Joe's bed. He felt shy in her presence and declined the offer and asked her to point the way.

He walked cautiously towards Joe's bed, he could not help but stare at the injured soldiers, the stench of sweat and death was overwhelming, it stank of stale blood, it reminded him of the slaughter house where they took the dead horses back home. Sam shook his head in despair as he walked towards Joe's bed.

Sam stood by his brother's bed, tears welled up in his eyes, he loved Joe so much, he looked so poorly and helpless lying there. He pulled up a chair and remained by his bed thinking of the times they had spent with their father shooting game in the stubble fields back home. He missed that life so much. After almost an hour, sitting watching his brother's slumber, and dreaming of the past, he decided to go outside and come back in when Joe had awakened. As Sam turned to go Joe caught hold of his hand and he turned to look at his brother.

"Sam is that you, or am I dreaming again", Joe said

Sam sat on the side of the bed and hugged his brother, both were now crying.

"How on earth did you find me?".

"Uncle Bertie has been waving his magic wand again, he has friends in high places, mother asked him to find you and as I was stationed so close, I volunteered to deliver the latest supply of ammunition and stores, and here I am".

Joe had so many questions to ask Sam, but all he could do was hug his brother and laugh uncontrollably.

Sam informed Joe that he had made Sergeant and told him of his exploits. He explained how he had been promoted and miraculously been moved out of the trenches, which had probably saved his life.

"I've got a very special lady I want you to meet tomorrow, Joe, so I am going to let you rest and I will come back later today and arrange the transport for you to go for a little walk with me".

"Incidentally Joe, the twins are serving with the 4th Cavalry Brigade of the Royal Horse Artillery. Uncle Bertie is trying to locate them, they are serving in Belgium, not too far from here, lets hope a reunion can be arranged for all of us. I know, if anyone can do it, he can".

Sam leaned over to his brother and kissed him on his cheek and told him he loved him. Joe smiled and hugged his brother, neither being ashamed of their deep love and devotion for each other.

Sam walked away from Joe with tears streaming down his cheeks, he did not notice the nurse following him outside. The smell of death and rotting flesh was overpowering, he felt as if he was going to throw up before he could get to the doorway.

"He'll be alright, you know"

Sam turned around, startled, he wiped his eyes on his coat sleeve. She popped her hand into her apron pocket and handed him a handkerchief, she smiled at him and hooked her arm in his.

"I'm off duty now, fancy a cuppa"

"I'd love one", he said.

They sat together on a bale of hay sipping tea from an enamel mug and nibbled on a ration biscuit. Sam was quite shy, he hadn't been this close to a young lady before, he could not count the schoolgirls behind the boiler room as encounters.

"Oh! By the way my name is Sam"

"Pleased to meet you Sam, I'm Hilda"

"I'll never get used to death and destruction, despite being in the trenches for almost a year" Sam blurted out.

She nodded and turned her head away hiding her feelings from Sam.

"I have always wanted to be a nurse since childhood, but the waste of human life in this war is too much to bear. I have nursed young men with no limbs, eyes missing, skulls caved in and so badly mutilated, that even their own families would not recognise them. The gas causes such devastation that I have nightmares gasping for my breath. I'm terrified of being gassed"

Sam held her and reassured her that the gas was only active on the front lines and thereabouts, and that you always had a warning, enabling you to protect yourself with the new masks now provided, which were much more effective than the old cloth ones.

"Yes, I know, we have to carry one with us on duty at all times, but they smell and I feel physically sick when my face is covered".

They continued to chat for another hour or so.

Sam was smitten with Hilda, she had a lovely broad northern accent, he felt immediately close to her. She had blond curly short hair cut in a bob, ebony eyes and a lovely smile, her front two teeth crossed, but nevertheless her smile was overpowering. He noticed a few freckles over her lovely button nose and dimples in her cheeks. She was only 5'4" tall, with a slender figure and, there was a radiance about her, he could not help looking at her beautiful slender hands, her fingers were long and her nails manicured. He looked at his own nails and popped them into his pocket. He had bitten his nails as a child and continued to do so throughout his life.

Sam introduced her to Len and they hit if off immediately. She had a cousin who lived in the same street as Len in Accrington, they had attended the same school, unfortunately he had been killed in the early days of the war.

Most of the young men enlisted from Accrington had been killed in battle, they were known as the "Accrington Pals", whole communities had died in this way, the young men enlisting together from their various communities and being put into battalions together and going over the top together. Friends, brothers, cousins and close relatives, all dying together in battle and devastating whole villages throughout

England. Changes had since taken place to stop the useless slaughter and devastation of the lost "Pals Regiments", but it was too late for many towns and villages, losing all their men in one battle or another.

Sam arranged to meet Hilda the following day so that they could take Joe for a stroll, if Hilda could find a suitable wheelchair. They said goodbye and Sam returned to his brother's bed.

He told Joe about Hilda and the little trip out of his hospital bed that had been arranged for the next day.

Joe could not believe his brother had found him, they had so many things to discuss, first Sam talked then Joe and so on until finally the sister in charge came over and asked Sam to leave.

"Your brother needs his rest still Sergeant, you'll have to come back tomorrow" she chided.

Sam winked at Joe and smiled, they hugged each other again, Joe's face ached from laughing and chatting to his little brother. He was so happy.

"See you tomorrow bro" they both said together and started to laugh again, so loud that the sister told them to be quiet.

Sam walked away from Joe's bed and turned to look at the sister, she was frowning at him.

"Goodnight sister, I'm sorry about the noise"

She nodded and smiled at Sam. He couldn't help but think about how different Hilda was to this old trout.

"I'm glad your brother's o.k., but we have to have rules, Sergeant"

"I know, I'm sorry, but I thought Joe was dead and to find him alive" , he paused for a moment, "well it's a miracle".

Sam strolled over to the paddock and fed the horses some hay and checked the other stock before retiring to his makeshift bed behind the paddock. He lay on the hay palliasse looking up at the stars, he could not get Hilda out of his mind. He decided there and then to ask her if he could write to her, and if he could arrange another field trip with the next batch of ammunition from H.Q., see her and hopefully Joe again if he was still in hospital.

He knew that deliveries to this region were a regular event and was happy to volunteer if it meant seeing his brother and Hilda again, despite the danger.

He did not sleep that night at all, despite this being the first night in months where he was warm and comfortable, Len told him off for being a fidget. They talked most of the night about this and that and, Len's first encounter with his girlfriend. He advised Sam to take it slowly, but not too slowly, otherwise the war would be over before their romance began.

Sam made a mental note of Len's comments and decided his course of action and turned over onto his side for the 100th time to try and get to sleep.

Hilda and Sam pushed Joe into the sunshine the next day, he blinked and put his hand over his eyes to shield them from the sun. He was still very weak and delicate.

Sam told him to shut his eyes as he was going to meet a very special young lady with beautiful blue eyes.

Joe laughed and shut his eyes, as ordered. Sam left Joe with Hilda and Len and walked over to Albert and took Gracie off him and walked her back to where Joe was sitting in his wheelchair.

Albert and Len had plaited her mane and tail and popped a red, white and blue, ribbon on her head, with a Union Jack embroidered on it. Albert had spent most of the previous day embroidering it for this special occasion. Albert was talented in embroidery and made beautiful birthday and commemorative cards for his comrades for them to send home to their sweetheart's and mother's. He normally charged them tobacco for his efforts. This time, however, there was no charge. The lads had oiled and cleaned Gracie's tack, she looked a picture.

"You can open your eyes now Joe, meet Gracie my female friend and love of my life" winking at Hilda in the process. She smiled at Sam and blushed profoundly.

Joe looked up at her and tried to stand, but fell backwards, Len stopped him from stumbling, he was still very weak after all the time he had spent in bed.

"Oh! Sam she's lovely. Where did you find her? 2 wall eyes, that's unusual, she's like dad's old shire"

Tears welled up in Joe's eyes again as he thought about his father. Since being injured he had cried a lot and felt a little ashamed of his emotions. Sam patted him and assured him lots of lads cried like babies, particularly after surviving going over the top. They both nodded and Hilda smiled. She admired the boys and how close they were and not afraid to show emotions and feelings, this was something very special and honourable. She was overwhelmed with her feelings for Sam. She had nursed hundreds of young men and somehow Sam had taken her heart from the moment she had seen him waiting to see Joe.

Sam sat down on a tree stump and told him the story of her being pulled down into the crater of mud and how he and his friends had been there and managed to get her out, just moments before she was to be shot by some idiot. Also, the promotion and lucky break they had when asked to join another regiment.

They chatted about how fate had dealt the cards and brought them all together again.

"She's my good luck, Joe," Sam said.

Unhappy with the lack of attention bestowed on her Gracie dropped her head and sniffed Joe and nuzzled at his pocket to see if he had anything to eat. Sam passed him a carrot and he fed it to her. In return she dropped all the chewed bits of carrot into his blanket and proceeded to eat them from his lap covering him in slobber. Her face was covered in bits of wool from his blanket, she looked as if she had grown a beard. They all burst out laughing, she looked so funny. Gracie curled her lip up, as if she was laughing with them. She looked hilarious.

"I want to take her home with me, if I can keep her alive. I take her everywhere, I try to keep her away from the shells and back as far as I can behind our lines when I'm off duty. She's a bloody good worker and leader, she shies at nothing Joe", Sam said.

"We have another shire, his name is Rupert. Len has taken

a shine to him and he wants to take him home also when the war's over, God willing, if ever he lets him near to him. He's in love with Gracie and thinks I'm his master. We'll have to sort it out who's boss at a later date. But, until then he's my lead horse and Gracie follows him like a lamb to slaughter, so to speak"

Albert put her back in the paddock and the three sat in the sunshine chatting. The day was over too quickly and they wheeled Joe back to his bed. Sam picked his brother up into his arms and lifted him onto his bed and tucked him in like a baby.

Sam had grown so much since joining the army, he was much stockier than Joe and 4" taller. He was now 6'2" tall.

Joe smiled at his brother,

"Sam, don't expect me to do that to you if ever you get hurt",

Sam grinned like a "Cheshire cat" and patted his brother's pillow for him.

"I'll see you early tomorrow, Joe, it looks as if the Ambulance Buses will be ready to go at about 10.30 am".

Hilda and Sam walked outside and Sam took the opportunity to kiss her on the cheek and thank her for the lovely day. She gave Sam an envelope and asked him for his address and promised to look after Joe personally.

"I'll see you in the morning before you leave Sam, I'm on duty first thing".

Sam hardly slept that night thinking of Hilda and Joe, the night dragged and the morning finally came. He stood by the paddock and waited for the morning light. Len tapped him on the shoulder and Albert stood the other side of him.

"We'll do all the loading Sam, go spend some time with your brother", Len said.

Sam smiled at them and nodded.

"Thanks guys, I owe you one", he said.

He proceeded to walk over to the First Aid Post, dreading the farewell he had to make. Hilda was standing at the entrance and hooked her arm into Sam's.

""I'll watch over him Sam, he's a survivor. You look after

yourself and come back to see me. I'll try and get some leave, I've worked none stop for six months, I'm sure I can get a few days off".

Sam turned and kissed her full on the lips and blurted out "I love you Hilda, I know if has only been 48 hours since we met, but in these times you realise quickly how you feel. If we get out of this bloody war alive, I want you to be my wife".

Sam could not believe what he'd said and just stood looking at Hilda nervously awaiting rejection. He looked into her eyes and became overwhelmed, her eyes were flirting with his she felt the same.

She wiped a tear from her cheek and tried to talk, but she was so choked the words would not come out right to start with. She coughed and touched his cheek and tried again.

"I've met hundreds of soldiers' over the time I've been nursing Sam, but you have taken my heart also. Lets hope you can come back to me quickly and our love can develop. Sweetheart please write to me and let me know you are safe and well and look after that blue eyed lady you love so much".

"I'll try to get messages to you via one of the lads, they have to come to take the injured away, Hilda".

They both smiled and Sam kissed her on the lips again and wiped a tear from Hilda's face and popped his finger onto his lips.

"Don't cry, my darling, I'll come back to you, no more tears, it's so difficult leaving you both".

Sam went back over to the paddock.

Hilda walked back into the hospital tent and along the injured soldiers where Joe was waiting in his wheelchair, she pushed Joe outside. The matron had her eye on what she was doing, but she was human too and smiled coyly at her. Joe waved to Sam and the others and turned his head away to hide his tears.

Sam turned only once to look at his loved ones as he left, he was crying like a baby, he could not turn round again for fear of Joe seeing how overwhelmed he was at leaving him so soon after finding him.

Hilda took Joe back to his bed and he too sobbed into his pillow punching and cursing this bloody war. Hilda shed her tears in the toilet and tried to compose herself as she went about nursing that day. She could not get Sam out of her head, she was in love.

CHAPTER 12

Back in Birmingham, Elsie stood in front of her master and fidgeted with her apron straps. She had always been afraid when in his presence and this time she knew exactly why she was there.

"Well, Elsie what are we going to do", her master said.

She smiled shyly and shook her head.

"I don't know, sir"

"Charles has told me about the baby and, this is what I wanted to discuss with you"

She nodded, her legs were shaking and she wanted to turn and run out of the room and never stop running.

"I do not blame you child for the predicament you are now in, nor do I apportion the blame on Charles, I want you to understand that before we proceed with our meeting. This sort of thing has been going on since the beginning of time. Sit down over there, Elsie".

She sat down by the fire and continued to fidget, she placed her hands on her lap and looked down on her fingers. She looked up surprised as her master spoke to her again.

"Have you told anyone that you are pregnant, my dear"

She shook her head and answered:

"No sir, I have told no-one".

"Good, I have a proposition for you and, I want you to listen and not interrupt me, do I make myself clear?"

Elsie nodded and sat on her hands, wishing with all her heart that this wasn't happening.

"You have placed the family in a very difficult situation. It is impossible for you and Charles to marry, he will be taking up his commission in the cavalry and going to war pretty soon. Besides you are a commoner, the marriage would never work. I know he loves you and does not want to leave you, but it is impossible. You would not be accepted in our society dear, the marriage would end in disaster. You are both from different worlds. Both of you will meet and fall in love with people of your own station sometime in the future, after this damn war is over".

He looked down at her pitifully and smiled. He could not help wonder whether he was making a terrible mistake stepping into their lives and playing God.

Elsie felt sick and wanted to argue with her master, but she just sat there and listened as she had been ordered. She felt absolutely drained and knew it was useless to even contemplate arguing her plight with her master.

He walked around the room with his hands behind his back. Elsie smiled and thought of her father when he reprimanded her as a child. She wondered if all men did this when they were in a serious mood. She was miles away in her thoughts and did not hear him speak to her again.

"Are you listening Elsie"

"Yes, sir I am"

"Well we have to sort this mess out and make sure that you are looked after and the child. Charles wants this and, I respect his wishes. I have arranged for my solicitor to be present later today and we will be drawing up an agreement for you and the child. Unfortunately the agreement must remain a secret and no one outside this family must know."

Elsie nodded and wondered what he was talking about. This is a terrible dream she thought, I'll wake up and everything will be ok. She looked up again and tried to listen to what was being said to her.

"The child will be supported financially until he is 21 years of age. A trust fund will be set up of 12 guineas a year following the birth and, 10 guineas for yourself immediately and a cost of living allowance thereafter increasing with inflation. These monies will be payable in advance throughout their term. If the child dies the fund ceases. Your child will have no claim on the family fortune and will have no inheritance from this estate. If you decided to try and bring this to light, the arrangement will cease".

Elsie did not understand everything that had been said and looked puzzled at her employer, her fingers were numb from sitting on them to avoid fidgeting. She moved her fingers to try and bring the blood back into them. She felt overwhelmed and wanted to run out the door and into the arms of Charles and out of this nightmare.

"Is there anything you are not sure about, Elsie"

Elsie stood up proudly and held her head high and commenced talking to her master, determined that she did not let herself down.

"No sir, I think I know what you are trying to say", Elsie said, trying hard to disguise her fear.

"This afternoon at 1.00 p.m. I want you to come back to my office and sign the agreement. Your indenture will be cancelled and no funds will be required from you parents. Also, I do not want you to think that you will be on your own in this situation, I, myself, and my good friend David Richards, who I have made executor, will follow your progress and that of the child periodically over the years."

"However, I will not acknowledge that he/she will be my grandchild, I will only be in the background organising the trust fund and making sure that it is administered correctly."

There will also be school fees to think of when the child becomes of age to attend school, this will be discussed with you at that time. Again, our family will remain anonymous. The child will have problems relating to these conditions, hopefully you will find a partner and marry in the future and bring the child up together. There will be literally hundreds of thousands of orphans following this terrible war and I am convinced that you will not be on your own in your plight, I promise."

Elsie could not comprehend what her master was saying totally, but she was determined not let herself down, her head ached and she felt physically drained, but she could not help think that none of her family, other than her mother, had attended private school.

"Right Elsie, do you understand the arrangements? I want you to interpret what I have said to you so far please." Her master looked away shamefully. He was overwhelmed by Elsie's composure and grace.

Elsie was relieved that the Rules and Regulations had finally come to an end and spoke slowly and methodically. She took a deep breath and started to recite her interpretation of what her master had spent the last two hours explaining to her.

"Sir, you are telling me that I will have a wage whilst my child is growing up and you will be setting up a trust fund for the child, on top of that you will pay school fees for my child's education in turn for my silence"

He admired her intelligence and understood why his son had fallen so deeply in love, she was beautiful, graceful and brave. He knew Elsie had obviously been brought up properly and in a loving environment and sensed breeding in her. Little did he know her mother's parents owned land and buildings almost as big as the one she was standing in and that her uncle owned properties in London and was an established surgeon and practiced medicine in London and Switzerland. He couldn't help wonder whether he was making a dreadful mistake forcing these conditions upon one so young.

He knew what this young woman was feeling and the hurt, yet despite all this he still carried out the fiasco, because when he was a young man of 21, a similar situation had arisen. He had fallen in love with a chamber maid, knowing the love was a forbidden love, and had been foolish enough to make her pregnant. She had died in childbirth in a work-house alone and frightened. His father had sent him away to York on business and turned her away into the night without his knowledge. He had tried desperately to find her, to no avail, until he found out from a groom in the stables, who proceeded to punch him for walking away from his responsibilities.

He swore this would never happen again, the guilt he had bore all these years was still as if it had happened yesterday. He could not help wonder whether this was history repeating itself. The difference being he was going to support this young girl and her child!

Elsie fidgeted with her apron again and he turned to look at her.

"I'm sorry, my dear, I was thinking!"

He paused for a moment, embarrassed and, stopped himself from saying anything further. He was on the verge of telling Elsie the story of his first love, but was too ashamed of his past and the way in which his parents had dealt with the whole scenario. He had never forgiven them, it had driven the whole family apart. He inherited the Estate and a title, but he had never found happiness, or true love and, had become a very bitter man living his life in total misery and remorse. His only happiness had been his son, Charles, his other son William was too much like his wife's family. He had never bonded with him and William knew and felt the resentment.

He felt somehow that he was being punished for his past, he did not want his son to bear the same guilt throughout his life, but still he proceeded to intervene with his future and force him to walk away from his responsibilities. Thinking money would solve the problems and that they would go away. He knew in his heart that what he was doing was wrong and that it would probably come back and haunt him.

"Elsie, Charles is waiting outside to see you. He will be leaving today to join his regiment. I will leave you two together child. I am so sorry, but you must understand our position. Charles's brother, William, would never allow your child to take his heritage away from him. "My wife!", he stopped himself again too embarrassed to carry on.

Elsie smiled at him sadly, thanked him and curtsied.

"I'm so sorry for all the trouble, Sir" she said.

He walked out of the room too afraid to show her his true feelings. He liked Elsie as a person and had high hopes for her being a valued member of staff in the future. He was saddened by the whole scenario. He went to his study and shut the door, walked over to his bureau and opened it and reached for the cut glass decanter and pored a large whisky. After poring a further two large glasses of whisky he slumped into his chair saddened. No amount of whisky would wash the guilt away.

Charles walked into the room, but could not look at Elsie. He had paced the hallway for well over an hour wondering how he was going to face his beloved. He was dressed in full cavalry dress, he looked so impressive, Elsie could not take her eyes off him, she had not seen him in full dress before. She thought to herself that this may be the last time she ever laid eyes on him, or even spent time with him. They had had so little time together, any time they had spent had been stolen during her duties when Charles's parents were away on business.

She watched him as he walked and her heart felt as if it was coming out of her chest.

He placed his scabbard over the chair and turned to face her. She turned away, he suddenly realised what she must be thinking.

"My dear, I have done too much damage to you already. I've joined the Royal Bucks Hussars, my appointment has come through today. I have to be with my Regiment by Monday".

He walked over to her and held her in his arms and kissed her on the lips. He was so distressed and broke away from her and turned away, tears were openly flowing down his cheeks.

Elsie looked up into those green eyes that she loved so much, she could hardly breath, and wondered whether their child would inherit his impressive looks, high cheek bones and eyes, she was overwhelmed with the love she felt for this man.

Charles was tall, dark and handsome and looked so

elegant in his cavalry uniform. How could she hate him for the situation that had arose following their stolen love. Despite her young years she was well aware of the consequences and the dangers of becoming pregnant, but all that seemed irrelevant now, the damage was done. All this seemed like a terrible nightmare, she just wanted to wake up.

She loved him and he loved her, never in her wildest dreams did she think that she would become pregnant from only one brief encounter in the library. Over the 18 months she had been in service she had resisted falling in love with Charles, but fate had dealt a cruel blow, their love had blossomed and there was nothing either of them could do to avoid falling in love.

"Elsie, maybe after the war we will be able to work something out, but in the meantime I want you to know that I care and will not let you carry this burden alone. Father will honour this agreement, he will look after you if I get killed, I have only agreed to this arrangement - Elsie, my darling, I just want you to wait until this terrible war is over. I will come back and we will sort things out, please believe me.

She clung to him and cried like a baby.

"Charles, darling I will wait for you forever, just come back to me. I do not care whether we marry or not, I will always be yours forever and ever".

He kissed her tenderly and took his gold watch and chain out of his pocket.

"Will you give this to our child and tell him that I am so sorry for not acknowledging him and making him my heir, if I don't come back, Elsie"

She smiled and looked into his eyes, and said:

"Are you sure it will be a boy, Charles"

"Yes, darling, I am sure. Tell him this watch was my grandfather's and he must pass it onto his first born boy child".

She took the watch from him and popped it into her apron pocket and looked back up into those irresistible green eyes.

He held her again and kissed her as though there were no

tomorrow. It was as if he knew that he would never see his child born, or Elsie again.

All this seemed so hopeless, time was running out for him and, he had to know that they were both being looked after and the child would have a future in these terrible times. He desperately hoped that things would change if he survived this damn war, but in the meantime this was the only way he could guarantee Elsie's future. He knew that if this arrangement was not made and, he was killed, the child would grow up a bastard without wealth and Elsie would be ruined. This was the only way for her to survive the ridicule of becoming pregnant out of wedlock. The world was so cruel and people would turn their backs on her.

Charles had talked with his father until the early hours of the morning sorting out the final details in case he was mortally wounded. He loved Elsie and did not want an arranged marriage with some pompous woman he could not stand to be in the same room with. He had decided that if he could not have her as his wife he would rather meet his maker.

He knew of his father's dreadful secret, he had listened outside the library door one evening when his parents were arguing and was tortured by the thought of the same thing happening to Elsie. Although, she had assured him that her parents would never turn them away.

Charles hugged Elsie again, kissed her, and asked her not to weep for him, he was unworthy of her tears. He held her at arms length and took a long look at her, freezing her image in his mind, then turned away, picked up his scabbard and walked over to the oak door, he turned once more and smiled at Elsie and walked out of the door. It banged shut with such force it made Elsie jump. She ran to the door and put her hand onto the brass handle, but did not open the door, she turned around and sat down in the arm chair by the fire and cried bitterly into her apron.

CHAPTER 13

Elsie sat on the bed and spoke to young Mary, she started to cry and was obviously very distressed. She could barely speak through her tears.

Young Mary went downstairs and made a cup of tea and checked Valerie Mary was asleep and returned to the bedroom.

"I don't know what to do," Elsie cried.

Mary hugged her friend and tried to reassure her everything would be alright, whatever was bothering her.

"Father will kill me. Mother has such a lot on her mind with father's injuries and the boys being at war, the last thing she needs is more trouble" Elsie cried out.

Young Mary held Elsie and asked her what was so terrible that her father would kill her.

"I'm pregnant", she cried out.

She threw herself onto the bed pounding her clenched fists into the pillow.

Mary walked over to the bedroom door and checked that the children were not eves-dropping and looked downstairs. She shut the door and walked back over to the bed and held Elsie tight.

As soon as she composed herself she sat up wiped her eyes on the sheet, sipping at her tea.

"Well, when are we going to meet your beloved", Mary jested.

"Joe and I sorted things out Elsie. I'm sure your parents will understand, they just get very angry in the beginning, but after their initial outburst they calm down and forgive you"

Elsie started to cry again and wrapped the sheet around her shoulders and started to rock herself backwards and forwards.

"I can't tell anyone who the father is, that is the arrangement. He will support the child until he is 21, as long as I keep his identity a secret. I cannot tell anyone who he is, not even you my dearest and best friend."

Young Mary looked at her friend, it had finally began to sink in what she was saying. She hugged her close.

"Elsie, you must tell us who the father is, you cannot have a child and never let the child know who his or her father is"

Elsie shook her head again.

"I cannot tell you, we've seen a solicitor and executor and, everything is agreed and legally binding, it's the way it must be."

Young Mary held her friend and agreed she would go downstairs with her and hold her hand whilst she told her parents.

Harry was home for the weekend, he had been convalescing in Birmingham for several months and this was his weekend at home before being discharged from hospital. He was sitting in his armchair smoking his pipe, the boys were outside seeing to the livestock and the youngsters were now tucked up in bed. Mary was busy washing up following teatime.

Elsie came down the stairs cautiously and sat on the hearth stool in front of her father, poked the fire and popped a log on.

"Thank you Elsie" Harry said and stroked her hair gently and smiled at her. He continued to puff on his pipe. Harry turned to see if Mary was watching him. He whispered into Elsie's ear.

"Pass my tobacco down please love, my pipe's run out again".

He then spoke in a load voice so that Mary could hear what he was saying and winked at Elsie.

"I'm trying to quit this filthy habit",

He winked again at Elsie. Smiling broadly and almost giggling he poked his pipe, tapping it on the copper spitoon, which he had been banned using by Mary, he turned and looked at his wife again and shook his head

"I wasn't going to spit, honest"

He filled his pipe up with Old Shag and took a deep breath, enjoying the aroma of the tobacco. Mary smiled to herself,

"Quit, she thought, never in a million years will you quit Harry Price, but at least you've stopped spitting"

Elsie looked to see if her mother was watching and cuddled up to her father and popped her head onto his lap. He patted her head and lifted her chin up and looked into his daughter's eyes.

"What is the matter Elsie, I'm alright, I'll be home soon"

She cried out ~

"Daddy, I'm pregnant"

Mary dropped a plate on the floor and turned to look at her daughter.

Harry turned and looked at Mary and then back at Elsie.

"Young lady I think you have a little explaining to do",

Harry shouted and dropped his pipe into his lap and almost set his trousers alight. Elsie looked at her father, shook her head and dropped her head into his lap again. Harry could smell burning and pushed her head off his lap.

"Elsie your hair is burning"

Harry wet his fingers and pulled them through the singed hair.

"Elsie, (he raised his voice), you'll have to move, your hair is on fire"

She moved away a little and sat down again frightened that her knew found courage would desert her oblivious to her singed hair. Harry lifted her chin up again.

"Well Elsie, did I hear right, that you are pregnant"

Harry looked deeply into those lovely green eyes of hers and knew without a shadow of a doubt that she was telling the truth. Mary was now sitting at the table looking out the door to make sure the children were not about.

"Well, what do you have to say for yourself, Elsie. You are barely 17 and in service. What are we going to tell the Manor where you work. And, who is the father young lady"?

Elsie looked up at her father tears dropping off her cheeks into her lap. She was frightened to move away from him for fear of what her mother would do. He wiped a tear from her cheek with his finger and felt all the pain that a father feels at the disappointment of dreams that he had for the future and then sorrow and despair for his daughter's plight.

"Well! I'm waiting"

Elsie took a deep breath and tried to compose herself and blurted everything out without taking a breath.

"Daddy I left my employ today, my indenture is finished. I cannot tell you who the father is, it's agreed. The child will be supported until he or she is 21 and the agreement I have signed today is final. I cannot tell, please do not ask me again, I will not tell you even if you never let me out of your site again, I will not tell you, I have sworn an oath. The father will deny all knowledge and, therefore, I will end up with nothing. I have the agreement upstairs, I had an appointed solicitor and I am happy with the finalities of the agreement"

She breathed and lifted her head shamefully and looked at her father adamantly. He pushed her off his lap and tried to stand up, but fell backwards and almost stumbled into the fire, but regained his balance and dropped down into his chair with a thud. Mary jumped up to help him, but he held his hand up and waved her away. She sat back down on her seat and dropped her head into her hands, trying to wipe out what was happening. It was like a terrible dream. She turned and looked again towards the door, the children were across the yard playing. Her father began to speak again, he had gained a little composure.

"You are but a child, how can you make such decisions without mother and myself present to guide you"

It was too much, Mary got out of her chair and crossed over to her daughter and slapped her across the face. She turned her back on her and shouted.

"Go to bed now, I need to talk to your father. You stupid,

stupid child, letting yourself get pregnant after all I have taught you. I'd a good mind to send you to!" She stopped herself from saying the word. One of her friends had been sent to a workhouse and died in labour. She felt ashamed at the thoughts she was having. Mary and Elsie stood opposite each other defiantly.

Elsie arrogantly looked into her mother's eyes, hurt and humiliated, full of pride and for just a moment she hated her mother. She turned and walked to the stairs with her head held high and climbed the stairs slowly, her legs trembling and almost crumbling beneath her. At the top of the stairs she turned and listened for a moment, she could hear her parents talking in almost a whisper. She lifted the catch on the bedroom door and threw herself on the bed and punched the pillows in anger.

She cried out the name of her lover into her pillow.

"Charles, why have you forsaken me, Oh! my darling why have you left me. What am I going to do, now?"

It was too much for one so young to bear.

Young Mary had been sitting quietly in the other room biting her nails, wondering whether she should go downstairs for moral support, but she knew better than interfere in family business. She came into the bedroom and sat on the bed and held her friend, rocking her in her arms.

She understood only too well the pain and anguish her friend felt, she had been through it with her own pregnancy. She tried to assure Elsie that everything would work out. She never mentioned that she had heard the name of the baby's father. They had discussed him before, Elsie had been besotted by her beau.

Downstairs Mary and Harry were going loggerheads at each other over the way Mary had struck Elsie across the face. Harry never struck the children, he used his belt across their backsides, but he rarely raised his voice. A look was normally enough to put the fear of god into his brood. He was always fair and just when the situation arose for him to show his authority.

Mary stormed across the kitchen and stood looking at

her children outside and she put her hands on her stomach and thought about the child she was carrying. Saddened she turned to Harry and weakened. She walked over to him and buried herself in his shoulder. She was crying now, frustrated and tired of all the heartache and worry about her boys, the pregnancy, Harry's injuries and now this. Her world was in tatters.

"Mary, you should not have hit her, that will only make her more futile towards us. You should know, dear?"

"I know Harry, I know. I feel so angry, she is only a baby with her whole life in front of her"

Harry lifted her chin up and looked into his wife's tired eyes.

"I wonder where she gets this stubborn streak from", Harry jibed.

She smiled at him,

"I know, I know, like mother like daughter. I'll apologise for hitting her tomorrow, I promise".

They talked into the night about the problem of another child and the shame, but were both sympathetic about Elsie's plight, they decided they would support her whatever happened. Mary emphasised the heartache they had endured following their own love affair and realised how vulnerable and helpless Elsie must feel. She got out of bed and walked over to the door paused and turned back and climbed back into bed.

"I'll leave her to sleep now and talk to her in the morning".

Harry looked at Mary saddened at how tired she looked, his love for her overwhelming him. He turned to blow the lantern out. He was a little more composed now.

"Elsie is our eldest daughter dear and has obviously made her mind up about the way things must be. If the father will not accept the responsibility of his child, we have no alternative but to support her through her hour of need".

"We will talk to her tomorrow, but in the meantime your husband needs some well deserved sleep".

Mary didn't sleep much, she tossed and turned throughout the night. She went downstairs at 5.30 a.m. and put the kettle onto the range. Elsie was already downstairs sitting at the table. They were both silent for a long time. Mary made her daughter a drink and sat down opposite her not knowing what to say or where to start. Finally, she spoke to her daughter.

"Well Elsie, we have to sort this mess out and, if you are adamant you want to stick to this agreement, there is nothing father and I can do to change the arrangements you've made with the father of your child and his family. He is obviously very rich and I can guess who he is, without even pressurising you any further".

Elsie stood up and went to turn away from her mother. Mary grabbed her arm and pushed her back down into the seat.

"Sit down Elsie, stop fighting me, lets sort this bloody mess out before your father and the children come downstairs".

"I will not tell you mother, I will deny it until the day I die. I will take my secret to the grave" Elsie blurted out.

"Elsie, stop being so dramatic. I know how desperate you are and the terrible heartache this child will bring to you, so I want you to listen to what I have to say"

Elsie reluctantly listened to her mother, fidgeting with her fingers in her lap the whole time she was speaking, trying desperately not to interrupt her mother's well rehearsed speech.

"Father and I will bring the child up as our own, one more little one will not cause too much grief in this household. The trust monies will be dealt with as per your agreement and a little must be put away for the unforeseeable future, in case something happens and the trust ceases.

You will have to stay away from here for a while until the child is born. The child can be brought back to us as soon as it is able to safely travel. I will tell people the child belonged to a second cousin who has been killed in a battle, his young wife too distraught to cope with the death of her husband and the birth of a child without family to support her.

I'm sure my cousin, Ada, would love to have you stay with her for a while, I'll write to her today. Her boys are both at war and the company will do her good. We will have to finalise the details nearer to the birth, but in the meantime young lady there is washing up to be done".

"But what about the children, what shall we tell them", Elsie asked.

"They will not know, because the baby will be born away from here and they will have to believe what I say, only the older children will know the truth, Elsie. You must promise me now otherwise it's a waste of time even contemplating putting this plan into action".

Mary walked around the table to her daughter and put her head into her tummy.

"I'm so sorry I slapped you last night, Elsie".

"I'm sorry too mother for being such a fool"

They were smiling now and started putting the dishes away from the previous night. Mary smiled at Elsie and popped a plate into the cupboard.

"Many young mothers will have children without father's to fend for them following this war. I'm sure we can overcome people talking. We'll invent a chivalrous cavalry officer killed in action as the lost husband of my cousin".

Elsie dropped the cup she was washing and flung her arms around her mother and burst into tears.

"Elsie, darling things are not going to be easy, the difficult part is telling us, things will start to get better now, I promise. We both love you and whatever happens in the future, you must always remember that your father and I will support you and your child throughout the difficult times come what may. Don't cry dear"

Elsie was on the brink of telling her mother that the father of her child was indeed a cavalry officer and was going to war, would probably be killed in action, but she stopped herself just as her father hobbled into the kitchen. He picked up his pipe and shag and smiled at his girls and limped out into the yard. He sat on his bench and looked out proudly at his cottage garden and vegetable patch, lit his pipe and pushed himself down into a more comfortable position. He patted the arm of his bench and smiled, had it been all those years ago that he had so lovingly planed and stained this old bench, he thought.

Back in the kitchen Mary was trying to make light of everything, but in her heart she felt her whole world falling apart.

"Now, Elsie I will not let you shirk your responsibilities, we must get the breakfast going, the children will be sitting at the table with nothing to eat in less than 30 minutes. This is not the end of the matter, father and I have a lot on our minds at the moment"

Mary paused for a moment, looked down at her swollen tummy and held Elsie's hand.

"I'm pregnant myself, Elsie. The child is due in September, so we will need your support more than ever. I do not want the children to know quite yet what I have just told you, it's a secret, do I make myself quite clear young lady"

"Yes mother, I understand".

"It'll be nice spending a little time together, I've missed you terribly over the last year", Mary put her hand to Elsie and patted her daughter gently on the shoulder. Elsie nodded, fighting back the tears.

"I've missed you too mother"

Elsie wiped her hands on her apron, turned hugged her mother. Mary wiped the tears from her daughter's cheeks with her apron.

"Elsie if you want to talk to me about anything, I'm here for you, I want you to know you are not alone"

"I know mother, I know" Elsie replied.

Elsie went to her bedroom and put her walking shoes on and coat and shouted to Young Mary. They went for a long walk with baby Valerie and talked about what had been said and agreed it was probably the best thing for both the child and Elsie.

Young Mary could not help but think of Elsie's cavalry officer away at war fighting a battle, with the worry of his beloved and never being able to acknowledge or see his offspring. She wanted so much to tell Elsie she was her friend and her secret safe, but thought this was not the time to reveal she had been eavesdropping throughout her discussions with her parents. She guessed he was the cavalry officer her mother had so unwittingly commented upon. She also believed that when Elsie was ready she would reveal her secrets, but in the meantime it was best left hidden away for another day.

They agreed they would write to each other and, possibly visit and spend some time together before the child came. Elsie was relieved she had Young Mary for a friend, at least she was not alone in her plight, but Charles had no-one.

Elsie shook her head, what was my Charles going to do and who would he talk too? She knew he was ashamed of his actions leaving her and doing what was right by his family? She also realised he had done this for her and the child in case he was killed in the battlefields.

Her love was stronger than ever, she wanted to write to him and tell him that everything was alright and that the future was not quite as bleak and hopeless. She looked across the fields oblivious to her friend.

"I love you Charles with all of my heart", she mouthed, holding her hands on her stomach and her unborn child moved. She looked down at the bump she now had and smiled.

"Yes my darling, I know", she muttered to the bump.

She decided there and then to try and find out which regiment he was in and where he was fighting, but it had to be discrete, otherwise!! She realised that she had not been listening to her friend and tried to make light of the situation and hooked her arm into Young Mary's.

"I know it is going to be a boy, I just know" Elsie said.

When they got back to the cottage Harry was just getting up off the oak monk bench in the kitchen. Elsie and Mary walked either side of him to avoid him falling over, each girl had their arms around him. He smiled and pushed them away.

"I'm not quite that old yet, you two" he said smiling, taking his pipe out of his mouth.

"This diddy needs filling, Elsie. Get my tobacco will you please".

He hobbled back into the living room without his stick, the girls both stood beaming they rushed over to him and they both kissed him on each cheek. Mary shook her finger at him, and smiled.

"And you wonder where our daughter gets her stubborn ways from, Harry Price?" , Mary jested.

He could still not make the stairs, his leg was far to painful to climb and hold his weight. The only way up the stairs was on his bottom with Mary taking the weight off his injured leg.

Harry dropped down onto his seat by the fire, exhausted from his little walk and smiled. He was absolutely buggered.

"Polly put the kettle on, please", Harry jested to Mary.

Mary smiled and came over to him.

"Well dear, what happened, is everything sorted? Did you tell Elsie about the child we are expecting?" Mary nodded.

"It's going to be pandemonium with 2 little ones screaming to be fed and, not forgetting Valerie Mary. Lets hope the war will be over soon and we can be a family again, all of us together"

Mary hugged Harry,

"I love you Harry Price, thank you for being so understanding".

"We may regret this Mary, I would not be too eager to thank me quite yet", Harry retorted looking out of the window into the fields beyond. His thoughts were of his two boys, he hadn't heard Mary.

CHAPTER 14

Joe stood at the entrance of the hospital looking about him. So many injured men lay scattered about on the ground awaiting attention and a bed, some dying before help was available, all so young and barely out of school. So many doomed, never to see home again. They had the same look of desolation and sadness, a look of despair and disbelief. Joe understood the distance he was witnessing. He had been there and was still captivated by the enormity of it all. What a waste of so many young lives and for what? He thought. He looked about him again wondering if any of his pals were waiting to be taken to the operating table.

He felt guilty and, at the same time relieved, to be going back to active duty. The smell of stale blood and the muffled moans of the injured and dying had been too much to bear, but what haunted him most was the surgeons sawing off limbs and carrying out operations without chloroform, or any form of pain relief for the poor soles lying on the blood soaked operating tables. Many died from shock during these protracted operations, rather than from their actual injuries. Looking about him he thought that maybe, it was kinder just to let them go, at least that way their pain would be over and they would not be subjected to the cruelty of the surgeon's knife or worse still the after effects of surgery.

Rats were always present, feeding off the blood and abandoned limbs lying on the floor waiting for some young nurse or orderly to take them away to be burnt. The buggers' weren't afraid of humans, throwing shoes at them made no difference, they just moved and stared back at you with those menacing sparkling luminous eyes, waiting for you to fall asleep, so that they could crawl up your body and forage for scraps of food or nibble at the blood on your fingers or clothes. It sickened him and frightened him, he hated rats, even as a child he wouldn't go near them. Sam was always the one to whack them with a shovel or rake. They were almost as big as cats daunting and unafraid, they had thrived on the battlefields from the decomposing flesh of dead animals and soldiers'. He shuddered and tried to be positive and think of home, but it was impossible, Joe was in his own kind of hell.

He now had nightmares of being covered in the filthy creatures eating his eyes and flesh. He would wake up throwing his hands about trying to get them off his face and chest, sweating and shouting. Always the same dream, he was on the battlefields, unable to move because of the sodden earth covering him from head to foot, his own warm blood all over his face and hands, unable to see to stop them eating his flesh. He rarely slept for long for fear of being bitten. He shook his head trying to change his thoughts.

He had been so lucky to receive such specialist attention without losing a limb or worse, his injuries had been minor compared to some. Hilda had looked after him like one of her own. They had become very close during the time he had been convalescing.

He had seen too much misery and destruction in Belgium, he couldn't help wondering whether the nightmares would ever go away and that normality was now a thing of the past.

He lit a much needed cigarette and offered one to a young soldier sitting propped against the wall, who had been injured in his leg. The soldier took it and broke it in half and gave the next injured soldier one. Joe passed his tin of roll ups and lighter around the soldiers', without speaking they all broke their cigarette in two and passed the other half to the next man. They smoked in silence, staring into oblivion, nodding acknowledgement at Joe.

Hilda tapped Joe on the shoulder.

"Hope you were not going before saying goodbye to me, Joe"

Joe turned and smiled at her.

"I've still to pack, what little belongings I have and be signed out Hilda. The doctor wants one last look at me. With all these newcomers' god knows when he will eventually see me. I just wanted some fresh air, it smells awful in there, I needed air". He was so overpowered with emotions and could not understand why he felt so tearful.

"I have problems myself Joe, I pop in and out all day. It makes me wrench and I have trouble keeping food down when I go on duty. Last night the wounded poured in, a lot of them were what we call 'head cases'. The doctors' were operating none stop throughout the night. It's terrible to see them wounded in the head. The lucky ones die, but the others become paralysed and helpless and some just keep screaming and they stare!! Joe, it's like they are in hell. When you look into their eyes you can see fear, their world has become one far away from this one.

We talk about the lads where we sleep in the marquee at night, during the day we just get on with our duties and nod to each other acknowledging each others' plight. We cannot sleep at night we huddle together on our camp beds and reassure each other that it will all end soon. A few of the nurses are talking of practising back in England. It's just too much Joe, it really is too much.

The doctors and padres are awfully good on the wards. At present we have over 100 critical and dangerously ill on the list, they are unable to make the journey home. We do what we can, some recover miraculously and make it and go home, but invariably these young men die needlessly without comfort of a loved one or a kind word, alone in a foreign country, fighting for what? What is freedom? I'm bloody sure it's not worth all this destruction and pain".

Hilda's eyes filled up with tears, shaking her head

desperately trying to hide the penned up emotions, she turned away from Joe.

It was Hilda's turn to look away and hide her shame of what one man could do to another. She composed herself and sniffed. Joe, lifted his hand to her face and wiped away a tear from below her eye. She tried to smile, but the emotion of it all was becoming too much for her.

"I heard from Sam today, he'll be coming over again, hopefully next week. How can I get in touch with you, Joe?", she said trying to be positive sniffing like a child in between words.

"I'll get a message to you, I promise, but I think you guys might want to be alone?" Joe retorted.

Hilda smiled and blushed,

"Oh Joe, you don't think"?

She pushed him and he almost fell over one of the injured soldiers.

They both laughed out loud forgetting for a brief moment their despair.

"I'll have to get back, Joe. Come and tell me when you are off, old misery guts is on duty today. I've already crossed swords with her this week, she's a right miserable old bat".

Hilda smiled at Joe and walk back into the field hospital.

Joe put on his new trench coat and went to fasten his 'Sam brown' (belt), memories came flooding back to the old belt from his grey coat and of those terrible minutes, trying to stem the flow of blood from his Commanding Officer's severed hand. He shuddered at the memory of the explosion that killed all his comrades and almost took his own life. He put his hands to the side of his head and shook, the memories so vivid and alive. He sat down on a bale of straw and tried to compose himself.

A stretcher bearer asked to come past, Joe jumped up startled. He moved over allowing them to put a young cavalry officer on the floor awaiting his turn to be admitted into hospital. The bearers, injected him with anti-titanic serum to prevent lock-jaw, which was the most dreaded plague of the wounded. He was obviously under the influence of morphia, he could scarcely focus his eyes. The stretcher bearer went to find his bed space and the other asked Joe if he had a cigarette. He shook his head and said he'd just given them all away.

"Shame that, I'm bosting for a fag. An't had a bugger all day", he said as he dropped onto his bottom and put his hands over his forehead.

"We've got hundreds of these officers' to bring in, God knows where they are going to be put". The stretcher bearer was totally exhausted. He looked about him at the injured already lying scattered about, shaking his head in disbelief.

Joe, went into the hospital and found Hilda.

"Have you got any tobacco Hilda, please".

She gave him a box of 10 Woodbines.

"I was given these this morning, Joe, that's all I've got. Save me one luvvy, please, the poor sole who gave them to me is over there".

He looked at where she was pointing. He turned back around and acknowledged her sadness. The dead were piled high ready to be taken away and buried in a mass grave. He pulled the rough dirty muslin over the window, a young soldier tried desperately to look out at the dead piled high outside his window. He was so weak, he could hardly lift his head off the pillow. Joe patted him on the arm and gave him one of Hilda's cigarettes.

Joe walked back out to the entrance and poked the stretcher bearer on the shoulder. He had fallen asleep. He stared at Joe in amazement.

"Oh! thanks mate", he said as he took the fag off Joe.

Joe looked down at the young officer and smiled sympathetically. He lifted his hand up to Joe feebly and asked him if he could post a letter to his father and his loved one. Joe nodded and the young man took the letters from his pocket and passed them to Joe. He promised to post them later that day. Joe turned around and wiped the blood from the envelopes with his glove and popped them into his pocket. Joe could not help feeling he knew the officer and had the strangest feeling of de ja vous.

The officer was mortally injured and covered in blood. Joe could not help wonder about his twin cousins fighting in the cavalry somewhere near Ypres where they now stood. He asked the officer if he knew whether his cousins were in his regiment. The officer shook his head.

"I've only been at the front a few weeks, but I do not recall anyone by the name of Wakelam. There are several cavalry regiments within the area, you should ask someone higher in rank, they may be able to help you".

His pain was quite evident, Joe tried to make him more comfortable. He took off his trench coat and popped the letters and his gloves into his uniform pocket and lifted the soldier's head gently and put his coat under his head.

"Where you from?" Joe asked.

"Birmingham. My whole regiment has been wiped out, it was senseless slaughter sending us in like that, absolute slaughter", he said. "Bloody slaughter I tell you".

Joe looked over at the other young men lying on makeshift beds, all crucially wounded, none of them looked much older than 20 years. It saddened him to think of such carnage.

Joe asked about his horse and the officer turned his head away.

"My mount was shot, many of the horses were maimed and mortally injured, it was the only thing that could be done, to put them out of their misery".

Joe nodded and thought about Sam's shires. He wondered how his brother would cope if he lost his beloved "Gracie".

"I'm in the AVC, I struggle with the slaughter of these beasts daily", Joe muttered, trying to avoid the stares of the soldiers lying scattered on the floor.

He shook his head and turned away, fighting off the emotions of all the misery, death and slaughter of these dumb creatures, sent into battle, taking their masters to uncertain death and destruction. He composed himself best as he could and felt a rush of guilt and emotion, shaking his head wondering how he could feel so much compassion for the animals and take the death of his fellow men in his stride.

"I feel more for the animals sometimes than the people.

They are just dumb creatures, Trojans, without any say. It's so cruel and pointless", Joe said to the young officer. He nodded and smiled meekly.

"What's your name, mine is Joe Price", he said trying to change the subject.

"Charles, Charles Monckton", he lifted his hand to shake Joe's hand, he hardly had the strength.

"Pleased to meet you, Charles, I would like to come back and see you, if that's ok. We live so close in England, perhaps after this bloody war is over we could meet and maybe become friends and have a pint of beer in your local and forget this damn war".

"I'd like that Joe, I have very few friends back in England"

"Please post my letters it's so very important to me".

Joe looked up, Hilda was standing behind the stretcher, she shook her head and turned away.

Thousands of young men were brought to the First Aid post each week to die, or be moved into hospitals more equipped to handle their injuries. Emergency treatment was carried out at the first port of call. The injured were made as comfortable as possible until the inevitable. Other wounded were despatched to more Advanced Dressing Stations and finally shipped by train and boat to England. The largest hospital catering for the injured being King George's Hospital in London, which was initially the HM Stationery Office and covered over 9 acres of floor space.

"I'll post these Charles, I promise. I'll come and see you before I leave for active duty. If you want?"

Charles smiled at Joe and shook his hand again and passed out.

Hilda came back over to Joe.

"Did you know him, Joe?"

"No Hilda I do not know him, but I feel that at sometime

our paths have crossed. There's something deep inside me telling me to come back and see him and talk to him"

Hilda put her arms around his neck.

"Joe, darling he will not make it, I have instructions to make him as comfortable as possible. He has shrapnel in his gut and bowel, there is no hope for him dear".

Joe looked at Hilda.

"I cannot understand what it is Hilda, I just have this feeling?"

"I'll have to go Joe, we have so many injured coming in today. Hundreds of young men have been killed in this latest battle. The cavalry have been wiped out, they charged into a slaughterhouse. Only a few have survived this carnage, our young men are just gun fodder. I'm so bloody fed up".

"This is just the beginning, we will be sending the injured back to the front before they are ready, we cannot cope with the daily intake of injured from the battlefields. They are dying before we can help them. The wounded men lie waiting on the battlefield drifting in and out of consciousness, dragging themselves to the rear, or if lucky, are found by someone and pulled back to safety. Doctors are crawling along the trenches and administering what help they can in terrible conditions and sometimes dragging their patients with rope around their ankles into the safety of our trenches".

"The ambulance workers' pick them up and bring them to us. I am so fed up of the unnecessary slaughter of our young men, a whole generation are dying and, for what?"

"The weather alone and exceptional heavy frosts try endurance to the limit. The bitter winds and cold make convalescing very difficult. The young men come to us with terrible injuries complicated by coughs and rheumatism, so many of them die from pneumonia and chest infections"

"I'm fed up of the waste, I feel absolutely bloody useless, and frustrated. Joe, it's too much, too much I say"

Joe held her to him.

"Perhaps you should go home and continue nursing back in England with the other nurses, you may feel more useful there, Hilda, your under too much stress here. I think you need a break, otherwise you will be the one in a hospital bed, dear."

"I've been thinking about going back home Joe, but since I've met Sam, all I can think about is when we will be together again. I think I'm in love, Joe"

They smiled and Joe kissed her on the cheek.

"I hope you are going to be my new sister-in-law, Hilda. You'll love Elsie and Nancy and my Mary. We are such a close family and love children. Mom and dad will love you, particularly knowing that you have clipped our Sam's wings, he's such a live wire", Joe smiled at Hilda and hugged her tightly.

Joe showed her a picture of Valerie Mary and passed the picture around to the injured shoulders. They all nodded and said "what a little corker she was".

"Isn't she a beauty Joe, you are so lucky", Hilda said.

"I just want to go home and be with my girls, all I can think about is when this bloody war is over and get back to the fields with dad and Bernard".

"Sam is taking risks coming to see me, I get so worried. Ypres and Passchendale, where he is, are such dangerous areas. So many battles have been fought there advancing and retreating as little as 50 yards. Thousands of our young men have died across this divide".

"Hilda, Sam is a survivor, he will make it through this damn war, I know it. He told me he wants to make a career in the army. Can you cope with this"?

"I think so Joe, I could always find work in the hospitals wherever he is stationed".

"I think you are both so suited, Hilda"

"Sam has mentioned marriage, but I think it is too soon" Hilda smiled at Joe.

Joe wondered if she knew how old Sam was, but decided against saying anything. He smiled to himself and wondered if Sam would need permission from their father to get married.

"Hilda, I think in these dire times you realise quite early in a relationship that life is so precious and being together, having someone to turn to, is the only thing that keeps you going and makes any sense. Having someone who cares for you helps you survive the carnage we are subjected to and the terrible conditions endured, not just by the individual, but by all."

"I have decided to say 'yes' to Sam, when we next meet", Hilda said.

"I'll try my best to see you both, I've been moved again, I'm only a few miles away. I've been put in charge of the rest camp for the injured horses, I will be probing for shrapnel and assisting in minor operations. My duties will be light until my injuries have totally healed, hopefully I wont end up too near the front. If I knew where the bloody front was?".

"Is your head injury still giving you pain, Joe" Hilda asked.

"I was asked if I wanted to be discharged and sent back to England, Hilda. I just could not walk away. So many of my friends are here, it wouldn't be right to walk away. My head aches like mad, the pain is continuous, but I would feel a fraud if I went home. My side still aches, my ribs are a problem, when I breath. I'm buggered Hilda, hope young Mary goes easy on me when I get home". They both chuckled and hugged each other again.

She smiled at Joe and jested,

"Careful young man people talk, don't want Sam hitting you with the lavatory brush, do we".

They both burst out laughing again.

"Hilda, shall we meet about 2.00pm before I go", Joe said.

"I think I can manage 30 minutes, Joe", she turned around startled at the new intake of injured they lay everywhere, there was hardly an inch between each of the young men, the silence amazed her, despite their injuries. She shuddered and turned back to Joe, trying desperately to hide here emotions.

"You should not go back to duty yet Joe, your injuries were very serious. You shouldn't think light of them. If your ribs are aching like that you may have a collapsed lower lobe of your lung or cracked ribs, working may only cause more problems for you in the long run."

Joe shrugged his shoulders.

"Hilda, I've made my decision, you must know how I feel?"

Joe held her hand for a moment and turned away and walked over to post the letters he had taken from Charles. He studied the address on the one and thought about Elsie. He recalled she worked somewhere in Northfields, Birmingham. He wrote the address down and popped it into his pocket. The other was addressed to a firm of Solicitors. He was saddened to see that such a young man, with his whole life in front of him, putting his house in order before he even had a chance to live.

He decided that if the cavalry officer died he would go to see his parents when he got back to England and if he survived he would take him for a drink. This was the least he could do. Little did he know at the time how fate had crossed his path. This was Elsie's young man, the father of her unborn child.

Charles died before he could see him again.

CHAPTER 15

With shells screaming over their heads, Sam threw himself to the ground and dug like fury throwing the sodden soil over his shoulder not stopping to look where it landed. Finally absolutely exhausted he flopped into what he thought was his dugout, he could barely breath, panting and soaking wet covered in sludge and muck, unaware of what lay beneath him, suddenly he realised that there was a much larger crater below him. He was now lying on top of a hole some 50' wide and god knows how deep, the mud trickled down the sides of the crater at first, quickening like a fast stream towards the bottom. Realising just how dangerous his situation had become he lay still desperately trying not to move. Unable now to crawl out, he had become embedded in the sludge which was sucking him down to certain death. Clinging to the sides he stared below him. He could not help wondering how long before this became his own tomb. He felt a sudden panic come over him, he desperately wanted to get out of the pit, but he knew it was certain death if he moved. He was dead if he lifted his head and dead if he moved. Frozen in time he just waited.

The mud threw up great geysers mutilating the ruined landscape. He crouched down in his plot of earth like a wild hog, his eyes searching backwards and forwards, up and down. Blinding flashes in a long and accurate line blazed and vanished, blazed and vanished, over and over again. The barrage multiplied, the inferno, the machine guns rattling like thousands of typewriters in a large typing pool. Looking around for higher and dryer, less dangerous ground, Sam realised he was in a helpless position, his fate was sealed?

They had become detached from the rest of the battalion, who would be compelled to follow. Sam watched in silence as a commanding officer shouted like a cavalry leader from Napoleon's army. Horror struck as the officer took a direct hit through his heart, he flung his arms into the sky and flopped to the ground like a sack of spuds. Sam buried his head in his arms and thumped the sodden earth.

Soldiers' were falling to the ground wounded writhing about like wasps crawling in and out of rotten apples fallen from a tree in late Autumn. Young men and officers' all crawling on hands and knees writhing and desperate like babies through a shelled bog. He put his hands to his forehead and buried his head into his knees, the ground began to give way and he pushed himself into the bank digging furiously to avoid the same fate as those he was watching.

He looked up to the heavens and swore. Why! do you let this happen, these are my countrymen and just boys!! Why? He cried and pounded the walls of the crater. He could not see for tears and mud on his face, he tried to wipe it off on his sleeve, but it burnt like crazy. He searched for his handkerchief, spitting on it he wiped the tears from his face, Sam shook it and smelt it, lavender perfume was still present, looking at the initials embroidered in the corner *"MP"*, (Mary Price), he smiled and kissed it gently. He realised how much he had hurt his mother and promised himself when he got home he would make up for all the heartache he had caused and would never argue again with her as long as he lived. It helped him somehow to think of her. She had given the handkerchief to him at the hospital when her brother was so ill. She had spit on it and wiped the tears from his face. He had pulled away from her in disgust, thinking he was too old to have her spit on a cloth and wipe his face. She just took it in her stride and offered the handkerchief to him and he put it into his pocket. He had felt so guilty at the time, but would not apologise to her, he shook his head and thought how stupid he had been. She was just doing what all mothers do.

He looked up to the sky again and tried to remember how long it had been since that terrible day, that had changed his whole life forever. He had regretted the hasty decision so many times, sneaking off in the night like a burglar, what an idiot I was to think that I could make a difference, shaking his head again he began to remember the last kiss from Hilda and how he yearned for the next. Strange that he thought, Hilda smelt of lavender that day, they must both use the same perfume. Mother would like that I'm sure, thinking out aloud! He took the handkerchief out of his pocket again and a few purple flakes dropped onto his lap. He picked up the tiny grains and smelt them. He realised that it was little seeds of lavender. How on earth have they survived all this time, he thought. He could feel his mother's presence somehow, as if she was by his side willing him to be brave. He suddenly felt calm.

His thoughts had carried him far away, he had forgotten where he was, then suddenly a star shell flashed him back into reality, he was lying on the ledge of the crater, he stared in horror, beneath him at the dirty smelly mud and water and a 15‘ gaping expanse below him, which was slowly opening up and would bury him alive if he did not get out of there.

The incessant rain had started to cause the crater to open up more and more. Sam looked down again and saw dead soldiers' beneath him, who had either drowned or had been killed by an enemies bullet. Shrapnel was bursting all around him and liquid mud was flying from the ground into the sky. Shells were flying up into the air forming clouds and then spitting down like rain bouncing off the sodden earth. All of this causing the sides of the crater to open up.

Sam looked about him, everywhere the dead and wounded were piled high on top of each other, the moans from the injured was unbearable, he put his hands over his ears. He rocked himself to and fro trying to control the fear and hurt he felt for his fellow man. The surviving soldiers' and injured clustered together like sheep. They stuck their bayonets into the ground leaving their rifles upright, the butts pointing upwards marking their places for the stretcher bearers. Dozens of rifles were sticking up out of the ground, Sam looked about him, so many soldiers' were injured, he wondered to himself whether he could crawl those few yards and pull at least one of the injured into his fox hole.

He turned around and looked at the forest of rifles sticking up out of the ground, as he looked they were uprooted by shells bursting around them. Sam couldn't help but think of skittles being knocked down in the 'Skittle Alley'. Again, he buried his head in his hands, there was too much distance between him and his nearest wounded comrade. He stared over the battlefield almost in a trance unable to lift a finger to help.

A stretcher bearer was dragging an injured soldier by his right foot to the safety of a trench. Sam wanted to run over and give him a hand, but a stray bullet flew over his head, making it impossible to move. He ducked back down trying not to slip further into the crater he was entombed in. He moved back up to the top, peering over, he could not see the stretcher bearer anymore. He hoped he'd made it back to safety. He continued to stare across what was once farm land and shook his head from side to side. There was so much destruction and desolation. He could not help wonder whether the landscape would ever return to normal and how would crops ever grow again on this land riddled with the dead.

The wounded unable to crawl were now doomed awaiting the inevitable stray bullet, or they were blown apart by a shell. The heart rendering cries pierced the din of the explosions.

Sam turned again looking over the other side of the crater and realised some of his crew were in the shell hole with him, all intact, clutching at the sides, with only minor injuries apparent. He smiled and put his thumb up wondering how he had missed them. He couldn't help wonder where the other lads were. He feared the worst. He was still wondering why he hadn't noticed the lads before, it still hadn't sunk into that thick skull, just how big the crater was that he could easily become entombed in, like the poor sods beneath him.

A Lewis gun commenced firing in bursts, Sam fumbled

for his rifle and looked at it, wiping away mud from the barrel on his coat. It was too thickly coated in mud and his attempt at cleaning it was useless, he knew if he had to use it he would only be able to use it as a bayonet, unless he could clean it quickly. He looked about him and found part of a soldier's jacket, he tore the piece in half with his teeth, it was so difficult to do this and remain on the ledge, putting one half onto the sodden earth he started to take the gun apart and clean it the best he could. He kept sliding and losing his balance. He cussed out loud and dug his heels into the ground in desperation. His mates watched him, they were having there own battles trying not to slide down into the hell hole below them.

The drone of the shells firing and the flashes made his eyes blurred and he found it difficult to focus. He rubbed his eyes with the back of his hand and could not see at all, his hands were covered in mud. He swore aloud again and frantically tried to clear the mud away from his face. He spit on the cloth and wiped his eyes, the material was so coarse it made his face sting and his eyes water. He looked at his pocket thinking of his mother's hanky, smiling he decided against using it again for fear of destroying it. Suppose this will have to do, he thought!

Sam crawled back up the muddy slope and watched in horror as our lads climbed up and over the parapets right out into 'No mans land' making easy targets for the German bullets. A tremendous explosion rocketed across the line. Mud and blood stained soldiers' fell like flies writhing in agony and falling into craters of mud, drowning one on top of the other. He could hear their muffled moans and groans. He hid his face in his hands desperately trying not to fall apart. He was determined that this would not be his fate, he would rather die from a German bullet than drown in the mud.

There was nothing anyone could do to help their fallen comrades. This carnage was common practice on the front line. He looked out again over the crater and could not tell the British from the Germans, both were smothered in mud, making it impossible to distinguish who was who. He studied for a moment and he tested his rifle. A German officer threw his arms in the air and slumped to the ground without a sound, Sam had hit him in the head and he died instantly. His helmet rolled off and lay just inches away from his bloodied body.

He thought how easy it was to take a life. This was like killing the pheasants and grouse at Christmas. He lowered his head in shame.

Sam continued cleaning the outside of his rifle and smiled across at Len. He looked so funny, all he could see were his eyes and that silly gap between his teeth.

"Still here Sam, that's lucky isn't it?" He jested.

Sam looked back at him and commented,

"You call this luck you stupid Northerner".

They both laughed nervously and carried on cleaning their rifles.

Funny how easy it was to laugh in the trenches when there was nothing to laugh about, Sam thought.

He tried to occupy his mind with other things and thought about Hilda and their last conversation:

"Why did you join the army Sam?", she had asked.

Oh! Why indeed, he thought looking around him.

He went over the conversation in his head trying hard to forget the death and destruction about him. His thoughts went back to that day when the sun was shining and they sat under the oak tree with Joe grooming Gracie.

"Sweetheart, I was so restless, excited, and eager to do something, desperate for the cause of England. The impulse to join the army sent tingles all over my body when I marched away to the dreams of glory, but found only carnage on an unimaginable scale" he had answered.

Shaking his head he remembered how she had kissed him on the lips. It was the first time he had been kissed like that. He didn't tell her, but kissed her back clumsily.

He pushed his tongue out and brought it across his lips remembering that kiss. The dream was quickly over, his lips were covered in mud, he spit it out and wiped his lips on his sleeve. Now both his eyes and lips stung.

Again he looked about him, and dropped back down thinking how impetuous and stupid he was running away like that. The heartache he must have caused his parents haunted him continuously.

Sam lit his pipe and thought about his father and the good old days. He preferred to smoke a pipe nowadays, it reminded him of his father, he felt close to him somehow. The smell of the 'old shag' tobacco brought back memories of stories told around the fire at night. He smiled to himself and took another long puff on the pipe. He curled himself into a ball trying hard not to be noticed above ground, curling his hands over the smoke from the pipe.

He had brought a carved ivory Meascham pipe from a young solider, who had no money, it was the lad's grandfather's, he didn't want to sell the pipe, but he had no option. Sam had promised if he survived the war he would return the pipe back to him, but unfortunately, the lad was killed within hours of Sam buying the pipe. Sam took a long deep breath sucking in and puffed the smoke out slowly through the side of his mouth down the crater. Sam tapped the pipe on his knee and decided when he got home, he would give it to his father. He knew he would treasure it and enjoy smoking it. He looked at the pipe and gently wiped the mud away from the ivory carving and popped it back into the brown leather case, shaped like a pipe, and put it into his lapel pocket.

His thoughts returned to Hilda.

She had told him that almost 1.1/2 million lives had been lost since the war had started and that was only our lads and God knows how many insurgents had been killed. He thought about the figure and tried to imagine that amount of people in a single area. It was impossible to imagine. He looked over at Len again, he was cuddled up trying to sleep. He thought how tired Hilda had looked on their last meeting. She had also commented,

"I am amazed my sanity is still intact, Sam"

He wondered if she'd be happy being the wife of a solider in peace time. He thought of how she had dedicated her life to saving others' and how concerned he was that she was in mortal danger working on the front line.

Sam smiled to himself and wondered whether she would be surprised at his age and promised himself that this would be discussed at their next meeting.

"The battles plumbed new depths of suffering, thousands are slaughtered and left out there with no one to nurse them back to health and send them home, or into the next world", she had commented.

He looked over at Len again and rubbed his eyes and glanced up at the sky, it was starting to get dark and the time was fast approaching to start moving back towards friendly territory.

He spoke to Len and lifted his rifle and in turn each of his mates looked over at Sam lifting their rifles in acknowledgment of their next move. It had now become quite dark.

"I think it's time we made a move lads, can't stay here all night, can we?", Sam whispered to them. They all nodded looking at each other in turn. They scampered out of the crater one by one, lying low to avoid being seen, crawling on their bellies.

Moving forward now apprehensively, the skies were black, the only light was the star shells firing into the sky periodically, it was deathly quiet, the mist was eerie crawling like a giant snake across the damp sodden ground. You could still hear the odd moan from the injured.

The craters' looked like giant monsters waiting to swallow you up. Sam, breathed heavily to compose himself and bury the cowardice thoughts.

A shell dropped amongst them, hurling heavenwards tons of earth and stone and, when he pulled himself together he realised he was lying in another shell hole. Two of his mates were lying a little way from him, both with their legs blown off. He crawled over to them, he could not hear, he shook his head and held his nose and blew desperately, he could see white thigh bones sticking out precariously. Then it went dark again. He felt a sudden panic overcome him, he realised he could not help them, all he could do was wait for them to die, he was afraid to touch them. He put his fingers over his nose again and blew hard, he was experiencing terrible pain in his ears and head. All his attempts were in vain, he could just hear echoing and distant thunder like sounds. He felt down the side of his face and looked at his fingers. He was relieved their was no blood coming from his ears. At least my eardrums are not damaged, he thought.

A few moments passed by and he heard a muffled voice. He leaned over to where the noise came from, it was so dark, the only light was the star shells and they seemed to have stopped firing. He crawled closer and touched a sharp object, at that moment the sky lit up lighting the battlefield with un-earthy gloom. He was confused and jumpy, realising he had touched what was left of his mates leg he felt sick to the stomach and threw up. He was really struggling to compose himself and then the voice spoke again, he could barely hear what the soldier was saying. He dropped his head down nearer to the voice.

"Pass me my wife's photograph out of my breast pocket, please, whoever you are".

Sam leaned over and put his hand into his pocket and gently placed the picture into his hands.

The soldier could not see the picture in the darkness, but it obviously comforted him. He could hardly move, but he managed to hold the photograph of his wife to his chest. He spoke to Sam again,

"Could you do me one last favour mate".

"Yes, anything" Sam retorted.

"Put my legs straight mate, I think I may have broken my ankle".

Sam stared at the stubs that were once legs and gently touched the top of his hips and pretended to put his legs straight. He felt sick again and looked up at the sky and breathed deeply trying desperately not to throw up. He had now become accustomed to the darkness and realised the enormity of the situation.

"Thank you mate, that feels better".

He took a long deep sigh and died.

Sam emptied his own belongings out of his pocket and put them into his trousers and took the photograph from George's hand and popped the contents from his top pocket into his trench coat. He crawled over to Fred and took what little belongings he had and put them in his pocket with the other contents. He closed Fred's eyes gently and was relieved that he had died instantly and hadn't suffered like George.

He patted his pocket and thought how little they had between them, considering they were both probably at least 30 years old. He knew he was alone now and wondered where Len and the others were.

The silence was frightening. He felt relief that George had passed on, but also frightened to be alone again. The black night surrounded him, the dark was terrible, booby traps had been planted everywhere, he had talked to fellow soldiers' about the way they killed and maimed, constant fear overpowered him of sudden death. He was entrenched in another great hole made by the enemies shells, his foothold gave way, and he was powerless to stop himself from falling.

Sam fell further into the shell hole, legs and arms were everywhere. He touched a hand and lifted it, the smell was awful. Maggots fell onto his trouser leg. He dropped it and shuffled away, but there was nowhere to go only deeper into the pit from hell. A shell flew over the crater and he saw the remains of fallen comrades left in pieces for the rats. He looked at the arms, legs and half a face - dead, rotten with bulging black eyes.

He was up to his armpits in smelly rotten muddy water. Sam wrenched with the awful smell of death. Flesh and mud mingled together. He turned again to his right and waded slowly forward trying desperately to climb out of the hole. His mouth was so dry, it reminded him of the moments before a battle, he pushed his tongue out and tried to swallow, but it was no use, he needed a drink badly. Dragging himself out of the mud and water, slipping and sliding, he feared the worst. He lay still and decided that this was it.

Albert came from nowhere and almost rolled on top of him. They both laughed.

"You frightened the shit out of me, you daft bugger. Thought I was on my own" Sam said.

"Glad you're here, though", Albert said smiling and laughing uncontrollably.

"Me too", Sam retorted.

A tornado of shells began again, suddenly out of the blue, a shell landed in the shell hole next to them, without a thought for his own safely, Albert pushed Sam out of the way, they were both thrown into the air. Sam found himself in the air, all arms and legs. It felt as if he was on a trampoline. He came down with a thud, the wind had been knocked out of his sails. He turned around and looked for Albert, who had taken the full force of the shell and lay mortally injured on the ground a few feet from him.

He crawled over to him and lifted his head a little to make him more comfortable. Both his legs had gone and his lower entrails were sticking out over his belt. Sam pulled what was left of his trench coat over his stomach and held Albert's hand. He was still conscious.

"Sam please do not leave me here waiting to die. Let my wife know I was thinking of her in my last hour and how much I love her and our daughter. God knows how she will manage with a little one on the way".

He looked down at his injuries and smiled at Sam and reached for his rifle.

"Please do not ask me to do this, Albert" Sam turned away still shaking with the after affects of the blast, he was struggling with his hearing and couldn't stop shaking, blood dripping down his arm over his hand, he had been injured by shrapnel in the shoulder, but strangely he felt nothing. He was totally numb and in shock.

"If I was Gracie, you would not hesitate to put a gun to my skull, please Sam, please?", Albert was begging Sam to put him out of his misery. Albert lifted his rifle and put Sam's hand on the trigger. At that moment a soldier rolled into the hole and turned his rifle to shoot Sam.

"It's ok Jack, it's me Sam" he said.

Jack looked at Sam and dropped his rifle, dazed.

"It's bloody bedlam out there Sam, so many have been killed. Are we the only three left?"

Sam, hadn't heard a word.

Jack looked down at Albert and back up at Sam. He shook his head slowly.

Albert asked again,

"Please Sam, do it".

Sam tapped Jack on the shoulder and crawled a little way from Albert.

"He wants me to put him out of his misery, Jack. His legs are gone and he's got it in the gut".

Jack shook his head.

"I can't do it, Sam, please do not ask me to do this".

Jack turned his head, hiding the tears streaming down his face.

"If we both hold the gun together, it will take the blame from you and neither of us will know who pulled the trigger first" Sam said to Jack.

Sam turned away, ashamed at what he had just asked Jack to do. Albert had been a good pal, they had been together six months, he had become part of his extended family on the front line.

Sam crawled up again and looked over the ridge of the crater, a bullet missed his helmet by less than an inch. He lowered himself back down the crater and undid his helmet and looked at it, shaking his head. Even if he could get Albert out of the hole, the shock would kill him, or he would be killed before he crawled a few feet beyond the crater, that's if he managed to get over the top. Sam realised there was no hope of getting a stretcher bearer to take his friend to the First Aid Post, Albert would be dead before he got there. He looked down at Albert, strangely there was hardly any blood present, despite his injuries. Albert's legs had been severed at the hip, they had been literally blown out of his pelvis. Albert was very calm and put his hand on Sam's.

"Please Sam, please, don't leave me here like this"

Sam spoke to him reassuringly.

"Albert you would probably live, if I could get you out of

this bloody hole. Maybe they could save your legs", he smiled gently at Albert.

"Sam, if I can't walk, I do not want to live, please Sam, stop all this nonsense and put me out of my misery."

Sam knew more or less what he was saying, but he could not hear all of the conversation. He looked over at Jack, who was shaking his head and turned away hiding his tears.

Albert grabbed his arm, but passed out before he could speak again.

Sam felt relieved, he was distraught at the thought of shooting his pal. Jack crawled over to Sam and put his hand on Sam's. His hearing was beginning to return.

"We are going to be here for a while, at least until it gets safer out there, if Albert wakes up again he is going to ask us to shoot him. I hope he dies in his sleep", Jack turned his head in shame.

"I feel the same way as you, Jack, but I keep thinking, what if it were me lying their waiting to die"

"Jack took a deep breath,

"Ok, Sam, if he wakes up, we will do this together, but I want to get out of here as soon as possible, so we will take him with us if he does not regain consciousness and if he's still alive, otherwise we will all die in this bloody rat hole, is that agreed?"

Sam smiled at Jack, in his heart he knew this would never happen, but he humoured him, and agreed. He was numb, this man had given is life for him and he was thinking of killing him. Jack lit a cigarette and passed it to Sam, he took a long deep breath.

"Well Sam, I think despite our circumstances, 'God' must be on our side today, we have both survived, despite the odds".

Sam looked over at Albert and wondered why he had survived, and most of all, why had Albert given his life for him. He leaned over and held Albert's wrist gently. Albert was dead. He sighed and thanked God that he would not have to shoot his friend. He emptied his pockets and took his pocket watch out and put his few belongings into his trouser pocket, which was now bulging with personal effects from his mates. He was now the keeper of three soldiers' belongings.

"I will write to Albert's wife when we get back, it's the least I can do, after all he gave his life for me" Sam said.

Jack nodded and smiled coyly. They sat down and lit another fag and smoked it slowly.

"Should be time to move in about an hour Sam, I'm going to try and get a little shut-eye".

Sam couldn't sleep, he just kept thinking of poor Albert. He woke Jack up as soon as the hour passed.

"I'll go first Sam, you follow me, ok".

Sam agreed and stood ready to follow Jack.

Slowly he climbed up the crater and popped his head over the top, peering 'over no mans land'. Sam stood in readiness awaiting the moment he would climb over the top and scurry like a rabbit to freedom and get back to friendly ground. Sam heard a whistle and fell backwards onto the ground. Jack had been killed instantly by a stray bullet. Confused he pushed his friend off him and tried to get up, he was badly winded, finally he was able to get on all fours and turned over and sat down abruptly.

He realised Jack had bought it, again he wondered why had the bullet killed his friend and not him. He felt so very alone, confused and exhausted. He was ready now to throw the towel in and let fate take it's course. He lay back against the wall of the crater, he now shared with his 3 friends and lit his pipe, he had lost all hope of getting out of the tomb alive. He thought of poor Hilda and how she would take his death and, Joe breaking the news to his mother, but who would take the belongings and return them to the families of his fallen comrades. He shut his eyes exhausted, it was all too much. He awoke a little more composed and took Jack's few possessions and put them into his other trouser pocket. Jack looked so peaceful and seemed to be asleep, the bullet had gone straight through his heart. Sam shut his eyes and said a prayer for all the lads. Why I'm doing this is beyond me, he thought!

It had started to rain again and the mud began to slide back down the sides of the crater, which was opening up into a bottomless pit. Sam woke with a start he had begun to slide down further into the pit from hell. Suddenly he felt a hand grab his collar, pulling him upwards, he pushed with his feet desperately trying to get a foothold, the voice called down and told him to try and push upwards if he could. He clambered up with all his might and lay at the top gasping for air. He thought he was dreaming.

The voice spoke again telling him to lie low and crawl back over to the other lads. Sam and the stranger scurried over like march hares and dived into another trench.

Sam spoke to one of the lads,

"What regiment you from".

"Northumberland Fusiliers and Bedford Regiment. Got split up from the other lads", he explained

He smiled and said,

"These last hours have been the longest hours of my life, even worse than in the trenches. There you don't look, you see, you don't listen, you hear, your nose is filled with fumes and death, but here in the dark, alone, all you feel is total desolation and fear".

"I know what your saying, mate", he nodded.

He looked about him and began to smile, Len leaned over and hugged him and they both fell about laughing.

"Sam, I thought you'd had it mate. I was going to marry Hilda meself". Sam pushed him again and they both began to laugh.

"Be quiet you idiots, don't want to be found, do we?"

A voice chirped up from the other side of the trench.

They both looked at each other and shook their heads from side to side, grinning from ear to ear, they put there hands over their mouths to stop any noise coming out. They were too overwhelmed and happy. They were like naughty little boys being told off by their teacher. The laughter was infectious the other lads were giggling with them. The officer just turned his head, he was trying desperately not to join in the moment.

"Glad we left Gracie and Rupert back at the Station", Len said.

"I think they must have known there would be trouble on this latest run, Sam". He nodded to Len.

"I had to kill the two horses left Len, they were in so much pain, the others, what was left of them, went off into the mist. Poor buggers, I hope someone else had the humanity to put them out of their misery".

They both turned away from each other. Tears welled up in Len's eyes, he was fighting the pain and guilt that he felt. He was too big to cry, he thought. He had watched what had happened to the horses and hoped Sam had not seen him hiding away. He knew he couldn't kill them in that way. He felt ashamed leaving Sam to do the dirty work. He tried to change the subject and looked over at Sam.

"Well Sam, fine mess we're in now. Wonder how we'll get out of this bloody mess", he commented.

Sam reached down for his rifle and realised it was back in the shell hole.

"Lost my rifle, Len" he said.

Len crawled over to a dead body a few feet away and pulled the rifle from his hand, he had to pull the fingers back and he heard them crack as he removed the rifle. He shook his head trying not to think of what he was doing. Putting his fingers back out of respect.

'Poor bugger', he thought and crawled back over to Sam.

"Thanks mate, don't suppose you have a piece of rag I can clean it with do you?" Sam asked.

"You're a bloody nuisance Sam Price, where do you think I have a cleaning rag, up my arse by any chance", he retorted.

Len crawled back over what remained of the duck boards and searched the pockets of the dead soldier. He passed Sam a handkerchief.

"That's it mate all I can find", he commented.

It helped Sam to clean the rifle, he undid his trouser buttons, turned away, and pissed on the rifle. Len smiled and did the same. It was the only hot water they had,

"Not worth boiling a Dixie", Sam commented.

They tried to forget what was happening around them. It

only took a few minutes, but they were peaceful minutes. Len watched Sam in amazement and wished he could clean a rifle so meticulously in such a short space of time.

Sam crawled up over the parapet of the trench leaned over and took aim, but before he could shoot, he felt a strong hand on his shoulder.

"Not now lad, trying to remain hidden until we know where the rest of our lads are, they all look the bloody same you know".

Sam, slid back down the trench and put the rifle onto the floor and lit his pipe, making 100% sure it was safe. He leaned back and took a long puff on his pipe and passed it to Len.

"I may take up with a pipe if I ever have the chance of one like this", Len commented, looking at the ivory face carved on the pipe, he passed it back to Sam.

"It's beautiful, Sam" Len said.

A young Officer crawled over to the lads and told them that the Americans' and Australians' were close by and that this was having a tremendous effect on morale, especially in the trenches. They acknowledged what he had said and carried on smoking. The Officer crawled back over the other side of the trench.

"Didn't want to spoil his fun", Len commented.

They had known for some time about the Americans joining the fighting, but did not share the optimism that some soldiers' felt.

A projectile flew over them and ripped a great oak tree out of the ground. They both looked up and thanked god that it was not them that it had hit.

A mule came into view and they both looked out at it. Mules were renown for their proverbial obstinacy. It carried on dragging what was left of the carriage it had been pulling and disappeared out of site.

Len took his Dixie out and made a cuppa.

"Rather this than your piss", he commented.

"Wonder how long we'll be stuck here, Sam?"

Sam shook his head and sipped at the sweet tea in his enamel cup, his hearing was still very muffled, but he was grateful it was coming back. Some poor buggers never got their hearing back at all, he thought!

"Have you seen any of the other guys, Sam", Len asked.

"I have Len, but they're dead. Fred, Jack and George are over there in that crater. I wish we could give them a decent burial and not leave them there like that. Shall we say a prayer for them"? , Sam said.

Len shook his head in disbelief.

""They both had kids, George was from a village close to mine, not sure where Fred came from, I'd hardly spoke to Jack". Len said.

They both shut their eyes and said the Lord's Prayer.

Sam showed Len the picture of George's wife and daughter and popped it back into his pocket.

"If he lived close to you, suppose the best thing is for you to pop over and give this to his wife, when you get home?"

"Will do", Len said.

Len lowered his head and thought: 'that's if I ever get out of this bloody hell hole'.

"You lads, get some sleep, we'll be trying to get back to our lads later", the officer whispered.

"I'll be keeping a watch so take some shut-eye, you must be utterly exhausted". Thank you sir! They both said together.

They tried to get comfortable in the minute space they occupied and Len put his arms around Sam and cuddled up to him.

Sam pushed his arm away from his groin and shuddered.

"Len, I'm desperate, but not that desperate" he said smiling.

Len pulled his arm back and wiped it down his trousers looking somewhat disgusted at Sam.

The officer was not amused.

"Do I have to come over to you silly buggers and throw you out of our trench, or are you going to settle down and get some sleep", he said angrily.

They tried again and huddled up making sure their hands were not anywhere that might cause offence. The lads found it impossible to sleep and just lay quiet trying desperately not to giggle and upset the officer again.

Sam's shoulder had begun to hurt now quite badly, opening his coat to scc thc wound, he shuddered. It had stopped bleeding, he opened his shirt and pulled a piece of shrapnel out of his shoulder and winched. Unfortunately it began to bleed again, but it felt better almost immediately. He put a field bandage over the wound and pressed it down hard into his shoulder. A young lad offered him another pack to put over the wound, Sam leaned popped the dressing into his coat for later.

"You'd best get that looked at when we get out of here", he commented.

One of the soldiers' was staring at Sam, he looked so young and vulnerable.

"How old are you", Sam asked.

The lad blurted out, "I'm 18, why?" almost defensively.

"Just wondered", Sam commented.

"I'm not much older than you myself", Sam smiled reassuringly.

The lad crawled over to them and squeezed in by Sam's side. He thought of Bernard and put his arm around his shoulder. Looking down at him he thought of the times he had cuddled up to Bernard in the past when he had nightmares. His hair was almost the same colour and he touched a curl on the back of his head and turned it through his fingers pulling a lump of dirt out at the same time. He flicked the dirt onto the floor.

Len looked up at him and smiled.

"My brother's a little younger than this lad. I often wonder whether he has joined this stupid regime or stayed at home". He turned his head away, trying not to think of the inevitable. He's not old enough thankfully, he smiled to himself, but neither was I?

"If he's any sense he'll stay at home", Len commented.

Sam looked at the lad and reassured him.

"You'll be ok, just stay close to us" .

The lad went to sleep almost immediately. Sam was so

tired he closed his eyes and fell into a restless sleep. Len curled up in a heap next to Sam and the lad, they were like three peas in a pod.

The flare of a star shell made the trench an easy target and Len awoke startled. He opened his eyes and tried to focus to see what time it was.

Time we were going a voice called out quietly. He shook Sam and the lad and they both sat up, rubbing their eyes, trying to adjust to the night. It had been an eternity this night, and Sam wondered whether he would ever see daylight again.

It was still raining, Sam shuddered with the cold and pulled his collar up around his neck. It was pitch black and smelly, it had become increasingly difficult to get any bearing on what was happening and extremely difficult to concentrate. Sam smiled at Len nervously and tapped the lad's shoulder. The lad looked at Len and fastened the buttons on his trench coat and pulled his collar up, mimicking Sam's actions.

"Remember stay close to us and listen to what we tell you", Sam said to the lad, fastening his coat as he talked to him.

"No heroics, do you hear me, just stay close to us".

He was shaking with cold and fear and nodded. His lips were blue with the cold and his nose was dripping. He wiped it on the sleeve of his coat. He was obviously very distressed and frightened, Len thought. 'Poor kid, what's he doing fighting a war, he should be at home with his father working'. Len shook his head and looked up at Sam.

"On the count of three we'll start crawling over the top. It looks like our lads are over there". The officer pointed to the left.

"They're about 50 yards away, give or take, I think if our information is correct. Looks like there's a lot of our guys out there, thank God. Be careful lads and the best of luck to you all and God Bless". He straightened his uniform and checked his helmet. Turning towards the lads he cautiously climbed the small ladder up over the trench.

The lads started to crawl out after him into 'no mans land' one by one.

Sam and Len decided to take a wide berth and crawl away from the others' and go the long way round. As they parted from the others' a star shell lit up the sky. The lads were like rabbits in headlights. They froze and the Germans commenced firing at them. An eerie scream in the darkness made Len and Sam crawl faster towards friendly ground.

Sam stopped and rolled over onto his back, Len followed him. They pulled their rifles out and turned over onto their bellies. To the far right of them Germans were picking off the other lads. Another shell lit up the sky and they started to fire at the Germans. Sam hit one after the other and Len hit another. The lad clumsily fired his rifle to no avail. Sam patted him on the shoulder.

"Best move before they realise where we are", he said.

They were moving quite fast, when a bullet ricocheted of Len's helmet. He touched his helmet and increased his pace. Within a few seconds they were within feet of the trench where our lads were. Len threw himself into the hole and Sam followed him. They both looked at each other trying to catch their breath.

The lad didn't follow. Sam turned to pull him over the top to safety, but he was a long way from the trench.

The sky lit up again and Sam could see the lad crawling towards them mortally wounded. He was about to go over the top and drag him back when a German bullet hit him in the chest. He reached out his arm looking directly at Sam and went very still, his eyes staring widely at him. Sam turned away and thumped at the mud. The lad was dead.

"The bastards have killed him. What had he done to deserve death at such an early age. I never even asked him his name". He thumped the wall again.

Len pulled him down to the ground.

"Sam it nobody's fault, when your time is up, nothing in this world will save you. It's just the way it is, I'm afraid".

Sam stood up and pulled away from Len, anger overwhelmed him. He climbed to the top of the trench and lay there waiting for the German's next shot. After a few minutes he saw where the gunfire was coming from, he patiently waited, looking through the sight he put his finger on the trigger and squeezed. The sky lit up again with a star shell as he fired.

"Got the bugger, that's the last young man he'll ever shoot", he turned and jumped down into the trench, looking at Len he leaned back against the wall of the trench. He turned his face away, he did not feel shame, just anger. His heart ached at the thought of the lad lying there without a sole in the world caring enough to write home to his mother, who was probably wondering at that very moment, where her son was.

Sam looked about him at the stretchers' with the seriously wounded lying patiently awaiting removal to the field hospitals and the endless stream of walking wounded also, awaiting the tortuous journey to the nearest Dressing Station.

Roll call Lads, a voice shouted. Sam thought how tragic the silences were when the familiar names were unanswered revealing the toll of war's carnage again.

Someone tapped Len on the shoulder and he turned round startled,

"You still here, you ugly bugger", a voice commented.

He turned around, Jim and Arthur had moved from behind him whilst he turned and were now standing in front of him, both covered in dirt and shit, grinning like the cat that had got the cream. They all hugged and patted each other, not talking just elated at the fact that they had survived yet another day on the battlefields from hell. They sat down together on the damp muddy floor, Jim opened his fag tin up and counted his cigs and shook his head. He passed roll-ups around to everyone, leaving himself only half of an already smoked fag. They all burst out laughing again. Sam patted him on the back and commented:

"Next time it's my turn, old fella".

Jim put what was left of the fag into his mouth and it went out. Sam passed him his roll up and he took a long puff and passed it back to Sam.

CHAPTER 16

In spite of the fact that the front line was only a few kilometres from the eastern side of Ypres, hundreds of inhabitants still lived in the historic mediaeval town and it's surrounding villages. Restaurants, cafes and shops were still trading and doing good business with the large influx of Allied soldiers'. The town was bombarded some days from 1000 am to 1230 pm, casualties amongst the inhabitants were regular, but moral was high. British units were billeted in farms a few kilometres to the east of Ypres and they too suffered intermittent shelling from the German artillery.

Sam and Joe walked into the bar in Ypres, six women sat around a large table in the middle of the room, they looked shabby and in need of a good bath, they sat provocatively throwing their hair over their shoulders and enticing the opposite sex. A young women, who looked about 30, pushed her chair away and smiled at your companions, and flaunted herself over towards them. Joe turned his back and kicked Sam, he turned away in the hope that they weren't bothered by her. At the same time a group of soldiers came into the bar, she immediately threw her attentions on her new recruits.

Sam turned to Joe and smiled. Sergeant Ashcroft looked about the bar in astonishment, there was a queue of 20+ young soldiers', of all ages, and officers', each standing on the stairs to the second floor, waiting patiently for his turn to have sex with one of these un-kept maidens. During the time they took to drink their drink, young men were going in, coming out, going in, and so on. The lads on the stairs were smoking and waiting their turn. It reminded Joe of school waiting to go into the classroom for his next lesson. He turned to Joe and then looked around the bar again.

"I couldn't betray my Mary", Joe said.

Sam shook his head,

"Truth is Joe, I've never slept with a women. I'm a little nervous about my first encounter. Do you have any tips for me, I've never told any of my mates. I've killed so many times and never had sex? (He shook his head trying desperately not to show his embarrassment. He took a deep sigh!). I would be the laughing stock of the regiment.", Sam turned away unable to hide his embarrassment.

Sergeant Ashcroft came over to him and smiled. Sam felt safe somehow, he reminded him of his father.

"Lad, no one will take the piss on my watch. You are a man whatever you may be feeling right now. The time will come when you meet the right person. Same happened to me. My mates kept taunting me, it made me feel so insecure and inadequate, then I met my Elsie. We now have four beautiful children and I never look or want any other women in my life. I understand why these soldiers are doing this, it may be their last chance" He went back over to his pint and sipped the glass and turned away again, giving Joe and Sam a little privacy.

Joe hesitated for a moment taking a cursory look around. making sure no-one else was listening. Sergeant Ashcroft moved along the bar and was now talking to a fella from his regiment. He held his glass up to them in acknowledgment and drank the beer down in one gulp. He stamped his glass on the bar causing the bartender to jump.

"Another for myself and whatever these three dirty buggars want, please", he said smiling.

Joe looked at Sam not really knowing what to say:

"I've only ever been with my Mary. We've only made love three times, Sam. All I can say is that it comes naturally.

I dream about our first time, it was in the barn on the old cart".

"Really, Joe. wasn't it a bit uncomfortable",

Sam asked, trying very hard not to laugh or embarrass his brother.

"We didn't have time to think of comfort, Sam. I put my coat down and a little hay and, well! I'm not going to tell you anymore, it's rather private and personal. Young Mary and I grabbed the only moments we had together before her parents took her home. Nancy came in and nearly caught us in the act, fortunately we had almost put our clothes back on. I asked Nancy not to talk about it and she just skipped off smiling. I swear she knew what we'd been up too. We had a blazing row shortly afterwards, I told her I was going to war",

Joe smiled at his little brother.

"I didn't want to know all the details, Joe. I just wondered if you had any tips". Sam said.

"All I can say to you Sam, is treat her gently, take your time and be loyal to her and keep away from places like this one", they both looked at the long queue of soldiers' on the stairs, which had now increased to almost double. The queue had extended to the bar. Sam looked again in absolute surprise, two of their mates were now in the queue. Sam shook his head at them. They pretended not to notice him and turned the other way.

"Joe, I wouldn't give myself to someone like, (he turned around trying not to embarrass the lads), well you know what I mean? These lads are liable to catch something. The girls must be making an absolute fortune. They are having sex probably 5-6 or 10 times an hour. It's no wonder sexual diseases are rife in the armed forces. I don't blame them, though. I suppose if you are going to die, it's probably better to fulfil one desire before the inevitable. It's a bugger though if you live and go home with the clap".

Joe pushed Sam and he fell off the chair.

"Samuel Price you've always been the optimist of the family". He put his arm out to Sam and pulled him up. The bar went silent and everyone was looking at them, thinking it may turn into a good scrap. As soon as they could see that they were obviously larking about the chatter re-commenced.

They drank their drinks and decided to go for a walk around away from temptation, if one could call it that. Joe walked over to Armstrong and offered him some money for the next round. He pushed his arm away.

"Joe, you've been good to my mare over these past months, I owe you an awful lot. I love that old nag, God in heaven knows what's going to happen to her when this bloody war is over. Look after that little brother he deserves some happiness, considering what he's been through" He turned away with tears in his eyes and carried on talking to his mate banging his glass for another beer.

As they walked along the road looking at the devastation around them.

Joe smiled and looked at Sam,

"Look over there, they're even taking in washing", he said.

There was a sign outside one of the few standing establishments

"washing now being done".

Sam looked at the sign and turned to Joe he was very serious.

"I could do with my clothes being washed, I was covered in bugs following my last encounter with that shell hole. My underclothes are due to walk off on there own. He pulled at his crutch and kicked his leg out.

Joe burst out laughing.

"You are so thick little brother, that's another way of telling you, sex is now available. It's illegal to just put a sign out stating "Brothel". Look down , you see those foot prints painted onto the street, they show you where to go".

"Bugger me", Sam said.

"I really thought it meant they were taking in your washing. Good job I never took mine in. What a shocker? I've only got the ones I'm wearing, got to get another uniform as soon as they arrive. It would have been a shock for everyone when I stripped off. I'd have had some explaining to do when Hilda caught hold of me."

The brothers were in stitches. Sam skipped off, he jumped up and kicked his feet together, following the footprints and stood outside the wash house (brothel). A bedraggled young girl came out of the building and asked if she could help Sam, grabbing hold of his arm, she spoke in French. He shrugged his shoulders, she then spoke in broken English. It didn't take long for him to understand her intentions. He took one look at her, pulled his arm out of her grasp, and ran back over to Joe.

They carried on walking briskly and didn't look back, just in case! Finally when they felt the coast was clear, Sam stopped and lit his pipe, Joe took his pipe out of his inside pocket and leaned up against the wall, they both stood their with their one leg against the wall, totally at ease with each other.

"I wonder what it will be like back home. Smoking this "Old Shag" always makes me think of dad. I've been told that it's difficult to communicate with your loved ones after being at the front. Extraordinary bonds are forged with each other and it's difficult to break that bond with the men you serve with. There is a feeling of comradeship, one that cannot be understood, unless you are part of it all. I've found that the barriers between class and social groups makes no difference here at the front". Sam said.

"I know what you mean, Sam. I had the opportunity of going home and I just couldn't do it. I felt a traitor somehow to all my comrades. I want to see this through. God knows why?"

"Hilda has seen too much, she's so brave. At night when the nurses are alone, they talk about their day, exhaustion invariably takes over and they fall asleep, huddled together. She said it helps to forget the suffering, talking, you know? She said the same, that there is a bond between all of them that can never be broken."

"I suppose Hilda and me will have a mutual bond, we know what happened out here and perhaps we'll not have to talk about the horrors of this war, that was supposed to be the war to end all wars?"

"I'm glad you're here with me Joe, without your presence I think I would have gone under by now, just knowing you are only a few miles away makes me feel there's someone watching over me. These meetings mean the world to me, they make everything more bearable somehow".

Joe tapped his pipe.

"Sam, I feel exactly the same. My heart stops when you are out delivering, particularly when you are drafted into the front line. The waiting is unbearable. The weeks before we talk again are like years. I'm just glad we have ways of communication. I think I would go mad if!!"

Sam took over.

"When I was in that crater, the heavy stench of stale blood and death overpowered me, and despite escaping the shells and sheer hell back there, the war has destroyed me in many ways, but at the same time, made a man of me. I suppose what I'm saying is, I love you, Joe"

"I was just a child when I came out here, full of hope and enthusiasm that only a teenager could have, but my hopes and dreams of gallantry faded immediately, shock, despair, fear and total desolation, took over. The realism of how precious life is, the importance of your family and comradeship, this is all that matters at the end of the day. My innocence has been taken from me Joe and I feel far older than my years".

Joe looked at his brother and indeed he looked 10 years older than when he first left England, despite it only being a little over 2 years. Sam carried on talking.

"I've killed so many young men, probably all with the same hopes and dreams of a better world, as I had initially thought. I will never be Samuel Price, the young man who ran away to change of the world again. The death and destruction of this war will haunt me for the rest of my life. I've watched my friends torn apart in front of me. How can any man be at peace with himself following the death and destruction witnessed in this damn war".

"Me too, Sam, me too. The difference being, I haven't actually killed anyone".

Joe hugged Sam and patted him on his back, Sam towered his elder brother.

"Sam you can only do what you are ordered to do, it is the duty of all of us to stop the Germans taking over Europe, if we survive this carnage it will be a miracle. I intend to live every day to the full, when, he hesitated, if, I survive.

Sam changed the subject to avoid Joe seeing the distress he now felt.

"I was told the other day by a veteran, that the Prince of Wales was here on the front line only moments from where we are standing and that he envied the comradeship that we all shared. He also commented that he would like to be a part of the fighting. I've heard he stole a bicycle and tried to get to the front line. They will not allow the poor fellow to fight, he wants to join the Grenadiers. Apparently he said to Kitchener that he had four brothers' and what would it matter if he were to be killed?".

Joe nodded and smiled at Sam, again.

"He should make a good King, Joe."

They carried on smoking and looked about them.

"This war has been going on well over three years now Joe, how much longer do you think it's going to go on for?" Sam asked.

"I really don't know, Sam, I don't think it will be for much longer. Forces from all over the world are now involved".

"Well my little brother, the philosopher, what do we do now"? Joe asked.

"I'm for going back and trying to see Hilda, if I can. Shall we go". Sam said.

"You've really got the bug bad bro. Come on then. Hope Gracie and Rupert are still in the paddock and no bugger has pinched them", Sam said.

"Who would take a stubborn old mare like your Gracie, aye"? Joe retorted.

"Hope the lads had a good time, where we meeting them, Sam"

They walked through the square and market place in almost silence, less than half the buildings were standing, most had outside walls with no interiors. They stood almost in defiance, rather than fall and be beaten totally by their abusers.

They stopped, by what was once the Cloth Market and looked at the absolute devastation. They continued walking into the Cloth Hall, which had been a unique memorial of the thirteenth century.

The build had commenced in 1201 and completed in 1304. A frescoe by Guffens and Swerts, representing the Joyous Entry of Phillip the Bold, Duke of Burgandy and his wife, the last Countess of Flanders, could still be seen on the wall in front of them albeit it was badly damaged.

The south gallery of the Cloth Hall ornamented twelve frescoes by Pauwel's paintings, representing historic scenes of the life of Ypres during the period of it's greatest prosperity.

Joe looked up again, the paintings were barely recognisable. They stood looking for a few moments and walked out in silence, they carried on until they reached what was left of Saint Martin's Cathedral, which had been blown apart.

The smell of fire and putrefaction pervaded the whole place. Her heart had been torn out, her middle stood alone, like Big Ben in London, the corner tower stood precariously, again almost in defiance. The rest of her frescoes and beauty, which had been there since the thirteenth century, were now just a pile of stone and devastation. Her gems of early Gothic could never be reproduced. What was now left was an immense, shapeless brick-field. Brutal destruction was the sole aim of the Germans, the town of Ypres, had no military purpose. The brutality they had shown over the previous occupations was senseless and pointless.

Joe lifted his hand to his mouth in total shock. A poor woman and her children were amid the ruins, she knelt on the floor praying and whimpering. He little boy was pointing out some object he had recognised. She was oblivious to him in her grief.

The Conciergerie and Arcade of the Nieuwerk had also been bombarded, but still stood, this had served as a prison in the old days. All of the buildings had been plundered, their contents sent off to Germany during varying occupations.

"Oh my God", look what those damn Germans have done to this once elegant and noble cathedral". Joe stood aghast at the enormity of it all.

Sam spoke,

"Passchendaele suffered from the same heavy bombardment, Joe. The Germans shelled it until nothing stood. I went to the burial ground of the some of our brave soldiers, in search of a friend of mine, thousands are buried in unmarked graves. Only a few of the crosses have names upon them. I left ashamed at the fact that I was still alive. I said a little prayer for him. It was all I could do to show my respect. He saved my life a few times, I owed him".

He bowed his head in sorrow.

A shell flew over their heads and landed short of where they were standing. They rushed out of the ruins and saw English artillery dragging a large gun through the water. Joe counted ten horses, behind were another convoy of horses and guns. They were trying desperately to get out of the water and onto hard ground.

Sam and Joe ran forward, jumped into the water and took the reigns of the lead horses and tried desperately to guide them up the bank onto dry land. They kept slipping and sliding back down the bank, it was almost impossible for Joe and Sam, let alone the horses to get a foothold. Sam looked at Joe and they both knew what the other was thinking. If they didn't get the horses out pretty quickly they would all be obliterated.

They paused for a few moments and whacked the lead horses with the reigns pushed them up the bank, finally they made a little headway. Another shell narrowly missed and flew over their heads. Joe jumped onto dry ground and heaved with all his might, the shire jumped and almost landed on top of him. He fell to the ground and sprung back up. Sam smiled at him and jumped on the back of the other shire and whacked him again. Finally, after what seemed an eternity the front two pulled the others out of the mud. The other team followed almost immediately.

The officer in charge bowed his head slightly and lifted his crop in acknowledgement and carried on past the cathedral. He stared at it in disbelief shaking his head, he turned around and placed his hand on the horses rump, each man looked up in amazement, all without speaking. The officer shook his head and carried on up the main street, or what was left of it.

"Well thank you both for your valued assistance in not getting us all killed", Joe mimicked and Sam fell about laughing".

"I think there's going to be another big battle here Joe, in the very near future", Sam nodded.

"Suppose this is why all this artillery is moving forward", Sam paused, turned and looked at the total destruction that the Germans had already caused. Tears dripped down his cheeks.

"I never realised that I appreciated the Arts, Joe. When I get home I will be visiting some of England's ancient and cherished grand estates with Hilda and our children, if there are any left that haven't been wiped out."

Joe nodded and put his arm around his little brother and they carried on their journey back to the Field Hospital, where Hilda was waiting.

They had been walking for some time when Sam spoke (he had been thinking about the destruction he had witnessed).

"I would have liked to marry in a grand place like Saint Martin's", he paused for a moment and spoke again,

"Suppose I'll have to make do with our chaplain for now and when I get back home have another ceremony in our local chapel and have a typical Price get together".

Joe smiled and patted him again on his shoulder.

"Can't wait, little brother, lets make it a double celebration, I think the girls would love that, and my little Valerie, if she's walking, can be our chief bridesmaid, not forgetting, of course, Nancy. She would never forgive me if I didn't include her, now would she"

"Go get her big boy, the day is almost past, your late. She will have your "guts for garters and there will be no wedding if you don't hurry".

Sam pulled out his pocket watch and gasped!

CHAPTER 17

Joe fumbled with his gas helmet, he hated wearing it, during drill he always felt sick at the thought of it and rarely managed to get it on in the few seconds allowed. He suddenly felt nauseous and wanted to vomit, he staggered uncontrollably, the floor started to wind like a snake, the sandbags appeared to be floating on air, what was left of the trees, were moving like giants towards him. The noise in his head was unbearable, he sank onto the floor, needles pricking into his flesh, his throat was unbearably dry, he now experienced a terrible pressure and found it difficult to breath. The pungent odour of chlorine was asphyxiating him. Soldiers' everywhere were yelling and stumbling in wild panic in the green sea. Falling, drowning, men guttering, choking and dropping, spewing up yellow fluid, were everywhere.

Panic-stricken, soldiers abandoned their trenches.

The thick yellow smoke had been issued from the German trenches.

Things were now happening in slow motion, Joe raised his head upwards then fell to the ground with a thud.

The effect of the poisonous gases was so virulent it could render the whole line incapable of any action at all.

100's of men were thrown into a state of comatose and dying condition, the gas had been altogether unexpected and the onslaught had been unbelievable.

Albert approached Joe cautiously and knelt down over

him, he took a deep breath, leaning forward he loosened the gas helmet, he felt sick and threw up alongside Joe. Expecting the worse he lifted Joe's head and stroked his forehead. Joe jerked and took a long deep breath, then started coughing and spluttering. He tried to focus around him, rubbing his eyes. He too vomited, choking he curled up on his hands and knees wrenching his guts up. He turned to Albert, not being able to focus properly and threw up again onto his shoes. Albert just looked down at the mess and spoke tenderly to Joe.

"You've been out of it for some time, Joe, best get you to the Advanced Dressing Station. The quicker you act with gas the better, it can damage your lung, if not treated straight away. You were lucky lad, the gas has killed a few in the front line and will probably kill many more before this day is out".

"I can hardly see, Albert. My throat is killing me and my hands are burning. My chest feels as if I've been kicked by a horse, breathing is all but impossible".

He spat blood onto the floor. Joe stared down at the sputum and took a deep sigh.

Albert lifted Joe to his feet and threw water over his face and hands to try to stop the burning. He pointed Joe in the direction of the queue towards the Dressing Station, the injured lads were now awaiting medical treatment.

Barely able to focus Joe nodded and staggered towards the queue, turning backwards he tried to focus on the wanton destruction the gas had on his fellow man. He felt anger and disgust at what he had witnessed.

The lads that could see made their way a little further to the First Aid Dressing Station, whilst the others placed their hand on the shoulder of his predecessor. It was a pitiful sight seeing the lads rendered totally helpless, each relying on the fella in front for support and balance.

Joe could barely see the person in front of him, all he could see was a green and yellow haze and shadowy images. He tried to reassure himself that this was good, he could see, albeit through a hazy cloud. His breathing was laboured, he coughed and wrenched continuously. His head was now so bad he could barely stand the pain, he had a high fever, blisters had started to form on his hands and face. His eyes were almost closed. The pain on the back of his neck felt like hot coals had been pored down his collar, he tried to rub his neck, the skin peeled off onto his hands. He stared at the yellow skin and blood on his fingers and wrenched again doubling up and stumbling to his knees. He had been sick so many times now, he was unable to throw up, just a watery substance came up his throat, he wrenched and wrenched, his eyes felt as if someone had poured vinegar into them. He had never experienced such pain and disorientation.

He thought he was dying. Desperately he tried to focus on young Mary and little Valerie, he took their photograph out of his pocket and clutched it to his chest. For the first time in over an hour he calmed down and felt Mary's presence upon him.

Lads were falling down all around him, the ones who were standing desperately propped themselves up by the wall of the cookhouse, their colour ashen and changing to green and blue, their tongues hanging out, wrenching and frothing. Joe looked at his comrades, afraid he may die before he was reunited with Mary. He forced his swollen tongue out to see if it was frothed up. He tried to moisten it with saliva and sucked desperately on his tongue. A young lad behind him pored water into his eyes and offered Joe the flask.

"It helps", he said.

Joe, thanked him and took the flask, he looked down at his hands, the blisters were now becoming quite big and full of fluid.

Joe held his head back and pored the water into his eyes and over his head. The next bloke took the flask and filled it from the water butt outside the cook house. He followed suit.

Within seconds a young nurse came along the line carrying a bowl of water with bandages in. She carefully wrapped the bandage around the head of the first soldier and so on. When she came to Joe she recognised him and put her arms around him. She held his hand and moved him out of the row towards the Dressing Station. She sat him down on a stump and gently put the wet bandage around his head, she was crying.

"Joe this is going to hurt, but I have to do it"

She pored water over his hands and rubbed the damaged, blistered skin as gentle as possible, Joe looked up into her face barely able to see her and tried to assure her, she rubbed his neck with the wet gauze and shouted for another bowl of water. A young nurse, who must have been all of 19, came over with a galvanized bucket of water. She dabbed his eyelids and cheeks, which were beginning to swell and peel. Despite the pain Joe felt some relief.

"There, Joe, that should help until I get you inside. Bye the way have you got any other clothes with you", he nodded.

"Where are they" she asked.

Joe lifted the bandage from his eyes and pointed to where he had been resting alongside the cookhouse before the attack.

Before the attack he had been waiting, in a queue, to have a shower and change of clothes. He had been chatting and playing a game of cards with his mates in the paddock behind the mobile veterinary hospital, following over 18 hours on duty performing varying operations on the poor Trojans of war. The blood on his clothing stank and he couldn't wait to get out of them. He was sick to the stomach of all the cruelty and destruction of the poor beasts of this bloody stupid war.

She ran over to where he had been sitting before the attack and grabbed his kit bag and ran back to him.

"Take off everything Joe. It is very important. I'm going to get some more water, you must wash your genitals and groin, under your armpits and feet. Please Joe don't be embarrassed, please, please do as I ask. You will thank me one day, I promise". She tried to smile and reassure him everything would be ok.

He took off the bandage from his eyes and dropped it into the bowl of water, then stripped naked. She stood with her back to him and turned when he tapped her on the shoulder. Lily threw the whole bucket of water over his private parts the bandage dropped to the floor, she looked down and kicked it away.

"I'll get another bucket Joe, I wont be too long, I promise."

Joe stood helpless with his hands over his private parts, so many young men were now naked, the nurses were running about throwing water over them and giving them blankets to keep them warm.

Lily returned and threw water over his buttocks, and asked him to lift his arms over his head, again she threw water at him. She gave him a towel and helped him get into his spare trousers and shirt, putting a woollen blanket around his shoulders, she patted him and hugged him.

"That'll have to do, sweetheart, I must go back to the others. You understand don't you?"

He nodded and sat down shivering.

"When Hilda gets back I'll tell her, I promise", she muttered as she hurried over to the queue of injured soldiers.

He watched in amazement as she dragged an unwilling St Bernard out of hiding, a young officer hitched up his cart and forced him forward towards the laundry area. The dog was shivering and looked bewildered. A young nurse and medical orderly patted him and wiped his eyes gently, and tried to reassure the poor thing, before they ran with the dog to get a change of clothing for the men. It was pandemonium.

Large dogs were used for carrying, water, milk and food along the lines. Several were now being organised to take one thing and another to the crippled lads.

Her actions probably saved his life.

Luckily for Joe it had been recognised earlier in the war that water undoubtedly stopped damage to the skin following gas emissions and that quick action actually helped in the long run with the heeling process.

Elsie and Lily came back over to Joe, he thanked them. Lily leaned over and kissed him on his eyelids and smiled.

"Hilda would never forgive me if I let anything happen to

her favourite brother-in-law. She loves you like her own, Joe. I think your skin looks much better now".

She lifted his hands and asked to check his private parts. He looked down at her and opened his flies slowly and dropped his trousers. She leaned over and looked at his penis, moved it to one side and lifted his testicles up.

"Open your legs, Joe, let me look at the skin on your thighs".

He felt like a little boy after a bath. He couldn't help thinking of when he was little, getting out of the tin bath in front of the fire. He was lucky he got in first, all the other siblings followed. They were all inspected in front of the fire before being rubbed vigorously with a big white bath towel, often it was so rough because of drying it indoors. He always fidgeted and quite often got a clip around the ears.

He was still deep in thought, trying desperately to avoid eye contact with Elsie, Lily winked at him trying to break his embarrassed look.

"Well young man, I think I've saved your manhood. Get those trousers back up before I'm accused of soliciting", Elsie smiled and helped him fasten the buttons to his flies due to his swollen fingers which were also bleeding.

Joe tried to laugh but his lips were also covered in blisters. Elsie, put her hand into her pocket and popped Vaseline onto his lips and eyelids. She gave him the tin. Put it onto your fingers Joe and anywhere else that is dry and bleeding. Trust me it will soften the skin for healing. She patted him again reassuringly.

"There now, Joe!"

She held his hands out and kissed the top of his fingers.

She repeated herself nervously,

"There now, told you, didn't I?"

She went back over to the line of bewildered young men to offer her help, she turned and looked back at Joe as she walked away, tears overwhelmed her at the hopelessness of the situation. She wiped her eyes on her handkerchief and commenced walking down the line with the water and bandages. Nurses were now rushing about trying to help the young men, the queue seemed to be getting longer by the minute. She shook her head and looked at Lily, they both puckered their lips together and carried on doing what they could to help these poor soles.

A strong wind had arisen and dispersed the gas, across the land. It had been warmed up by the brilliant sunshine. The cloud of chlorine did not lie as closely on the ground as it would have done on damp ground in the very early hours of the morning, which is when most attacks took place. The gas emissions had not functioned properly, and were not as effective as normal, otherwise, Joe would have been dead with the other poor soles lying directly in the path of the gas.

It was found later in the war, that gas emissions did not function properly for this very reason, prior to the advance.

Joe rubbed his eyelids and desperately tried to focus on the wanton destruction about him. The utterly baron appearance of the war landscape, on the front lines, countryside for miles ahead comparable to a tropical desert, with the broken barbed wire and scorched shrubs looking from a distance like a cactus undergrowth.

Dead animals lay bloated, scattered about, they hadn't had the luxury of a gas mask, even the rats had died. Small mercy, Joe thought.

His mask had leaked very slightly, he had not been quick enough when the first cry was heard.

The RAMC were now busy with the chemical sprayers, spraying the dugouts and low parts of the trenches to dissipate any fumes of the German gas, which may have been lurking along the trenches. So many had been caught out by the alert not being made in time for evasive action.

Only a moments warning had been passed along the line. A new man had been on the periscope.

"There's a sort of greenish, yellow cloud rolling along the ground out in front, it's coming -- ". The lookout was dead.

The lads dropped their rifles and fumbled with their respirators. Pandemonium reigned in the trenches. Soldiers too slow with their respirators sank to the ground, clutching at their throats, spasmodically twisting. It was terrible, not being able to help. A small dog lay on the ground with paws still over his snout. The gas travels quietly, no time can be lost, you only have 20 seconds to adjust your helmets.

Eighteen-pounders' were now bursting in on 'No mans Land' in an effort, by the artillery, to disperse the gas clouds.

An impending attack was now awaited. Normally, after a gas attack the Germans would come in their droves over the parapets. Albert crouched in front of his machine gun raking the German parapets.

Over they came charging, bayonets glistening, in their respirators, with their large snouts sticking out in front of their faces, like some monsters out of a nightmare. The enemy went down in heaps, but new ones just kept taking the place of the fallen. It was a mad rush. Heavy howitzers pounded the landscape.

Dozens of wheeled stretchers were now being brought to the Dressing Station by the Red Cross.

Joe turned to look at the pandemonium that was taking place, he squinted and tried to focus, he could hear what was happening, but could barely see a few feet in front of him, the atmosphere was disquieting. The thick mist of the early dawn persisted; a man ten yards away could not be distinguished. The gunfire, tremendous in its intensity, continued. The earth vibrated almost hysterically.

It was becoming painfully obvious that the Dressing Station would need to be taken back even further. It was too dangerous for the Veterinary Hospital and Dressing Station to remain following the latest German attack. A move backwards had now become critical.

He kept looking about him, he reassured himself that the horses were alright at the back. He wanted reassurance that Gracie was not dead. Sam would never forgive him if something happened to her whilst she was in his keeping.

Sam was on his honeymoon, he managed to get a 48 hour pass. Hilda had decided she was going back to England to practice nursing. Both of them wanted to spend what time they had left on the front line together, neither knowing how long it would be before they were together again.

The wedding had taken place outside the nurses quarters the day before. Hilda had all her friends present. Joe was best man to his little brother. It was a short ceremony, Hilda, had her uniform on, with her mothers' silver Victorian belt buckle gleaming from the hours she had spent cleaning it for the ceremony, her sliver watch pinned to the pocket of her starched apron, presenting a beautiful ornate bow, equally polished. Sam was also dressed in his uniform, Joe had given him their father's pocket watch, which Sam showed off with great pride, for the ceremony. Hilda gave Sam her mother's wedding ring until they could get one back in England. The horses were groomed to show standards. Gracie had red white and blue ribbons sewn into her plaited main and tail. Rupert had been hocked. He looked really grumpy and kept putting his ears back all through the service. Sam couldn't look at him for fear of laughing whilst taking his vows. Rupert kept stamping his feet impatiently.

It had been decided by both of them that this was the best thing, considering Hilda was going home to England, to work. It was getting terribly dangerous for the nurses being so close to the front. Only 2 days previous one of the nurses had been chatting to a young serviceman near to the third trench during her break when a shell dropped and killed them both instantly.

Everyone at the front lived minute by minute, after that it was in the past.

Sam and Hilda had decided to renew their vows in church later in England and hopefully have a double wedding, with Joe and young Mary after the war was over.

Joe had joked that their father hadn't given his permission for the marriage, because he was under 21. Sam threatened him,

"If you dare tell her, I'll"?

"You'll what, little brother"?

They both fell about laughing.

Ironically his little brother was as much a man as their

father. Joe was so proud of what Sam had become. When they walked over to Hilda, he knew that they were doing the right thing, they adored each other.

It was generally thought by all that the war was coming to a close, it was now late 1918, the Germans were falling back and we were finally getting a foothold on the land. The Germans were being halted and the war had now settled into a familiar defensive series of entrenchments. The intervening 4 years had cost hundreds of thousands of lives and horrific losses and the armies were still, quite literally, almost exactly where they had started from.

Someone tapped Joe on the shoulder, it made him jump.

"Gracie and Rupert are ok. Someone had the common sense to lead the horses back into the other paddock. She was very lucky, few feet more and, well it doesn't bear thinking about. I've watered them and put some hay out. How you doing, he asked".

Joe recognised his voice, it was one of the vets, called Harry.

He tried to walk and stumbled to the floor.

"I think this war is over for you Joe", he patted his back, lit his pipe and strolled back towards the paddock.

He looked up into the clouds, it had started to rain, he lifted his collar, to protect himself from the downfall, which was now imminent. The firing had ceased and a calm, with the exception of the wounded moaning, became quite daunting, he wondered if the Germans had any more tricks up their sleeves.

Joe was very ill, he hadn't really absorbed what Harry had told him. He shuddered and pulled his blanket over his shoulders. He huddled against a tree with several other soldiers. He had been standing about for hours. He lit his pipe and passed it along the line. He felt comfort in puffing on the pipe and took Mary's photograph out of his pocket and kissed it. Well my darling looks like I'll be home soon if I survive this damned gas attack, he thought. Then he popped the picture back into his inside pocket and shut his eyes.

A few seconds later someone grabbed his hand and led

him into the Dressing Station. He was handed a garibaldi biscuit and a hot drinking chocolate. It was supposed to be an antidote to the horror of war. However, is gums hurt so bad he was unable to bite the biscuit, he dunked it into the chocolate and ate it gingerly sucking on the chocolate moisture.

He had become almost numb with shock. Staring around the intensity of the injured suddenly hit him.

The Dressing Station was full to bursting point with the injured.

A young nurse came over to him, and asked him is name, rank and number, she wrote it down on a slip of paper and scribbled something else and popped it into his hands.

"Now don't lose this, otherwise you may end up back at the front and not on your way home to England. Good Luck and God Bless you".

Joe tried to read her scribble, but his eyes were still terribly sore. He rubbed them and tried to focus on what was written, but to no avail, his eyes were still painfully sore and he was unable to focus properly close too.

CHAPTER 18

The British Ambulance Train shunted slowly into position, in the nearest siding, ready to take down to the coast a new load of wounded, these were the veritable sweepings of the battlefield; Rejected by the medical board as incapacitated and unable to be patched up for further use by the British Expeditionary Force.

It was a train of great length-seventeen long coaches in all - and they were coloured a pale khaki brown and a deep brown, almost black, with red cross on a white ground coming at frequent intervals on their sides.

Outside the Dressing Station orderlies were lifting the stretchers onto pair wheeled, rubber-tyred makeshift ambulances. Upon these each patient was wheeled by an orderly along the smooth cinder-paths of the camp to the awaiting train siding.

There was much hand shakings, shouting of “Goodbye!” and “Good Luck”. Patients were shaking hands with the orderlies, who had tended them and often dragged them to safety from the front line.

There were surgeons who had friends amongst the patients;

“I want to thank you for all you’ve done for me, sir”

one amputee said to an RAMC officer,

“Oh, that’s alright; don’t speak of it he replied quite cheerily” as he took the hand that reached out from under the coverlet. He shook it sturdily. “Good luck to you lad, and let me know how that leg of yours goes on”. He walked away sadly, thinking what a stupid statement he had just made. He didn’t turn back, just in case the lad realised what he had said.

He wondered to himself how many more young amputees would be going back home to England, without any future when the shock really stepped in, that they were of no use to anyone, not even themselves.

He had hacked off so many arms, legs and sometimes both legs, over the past 12 months, many of his young patients dying of shock due to lack of morphine and quite simple surgical necessities during the operations. He longed to go back on the Ambulance Train, back to his wife and little boy, whom he had only seen for a few days, before he was shipped off to this land of no hope and rid himself of the malodorous smell he had become accustomed to.

The smell of death frightened him, he woke up night after night sweating and panicking, sometimes to his ignominious disgrace, he wet himself. He was still a young man, 32 years of age, came from a good middle classed family. He had been brought up to hold his head high and to be proud of what he had become, until now!

The dream was always the same ~

‘He was being dragged down under the mud, no one was there to pull him out. All the lives he had saved during this God forsaken war and, no one was there to help him, or even wanted to help him. He could see soldiers above him looking down into the pit. He threw his hands up but was unable to reach the top and just slipped down the slimy embankment into the soggy tomb.

The deeper he sank down into the mud he could see amputees staring up at him, with saddened, begging faces, asking him not to cut. He turned his head away unable to answer the pleas of his once patients.

Oh my God, he just wanted his life back. He wished for a little peace from the screams, begging and moans, he had to endure each day and night. Would he ever rid himself of this dreadful nightmare?

He realised he had been day dreaming and turned around guiltily. He composed himself and stood with the other doctors and orderlies and waved, doing his duty to the last. The young surgeon besides him, who had assisted in many operations, nodded and pointed over to *no mans land,*

"We'll be busy tonight Geoff, those are 25 pounders' thundering at the trenches again", they both turned and walked steadily back to their mounts. Geoff turned for one last time and looked at the casualties waiting to be loaded prior to their arduous journey back to England. He wondered how many would perish before they arrived back on England's shores. He shook his head, probably only half will make it, he thought.

The boy who had thanked him for cutting off his leg was now being comforted by an orderly, who tucked his blanket around him, before being finally lifted onto the train for his homeward journey.

The young lad kept chattering incessantly ~

"What he done for me would have cost any 'civvy' a hundred guineas - no less. Took my leg off for nothink, 'e did - for nothink".

Joe opened his eyes for the first time in days, with all the noise and shouting, door slamming, noisy ambulances pulling up and busy orderlies running here there and everywhere.

He could see an genteel senior officer marching along the narrow corridor inside the coach, he stepped onto the step of the train before it had stopped and jumped down, carried on walking along the stretchers and nodded, he had three stars, a captain. You could tell from his appearance that he came from a military family and was probably the grandson of some great general. He tapped his walking stick on the floor and flicked his walrus moustache as he assessed the injured. He reminded Joe of his uncle Bertie.

His assistant fumbled as he came running up behind him. He was a young man, clean shaven and half the age of his superior officer, he was obviously quite nervous in his company. His hair was blond and spikey, it looked as if he had just received an electric shock. The corporal wore heavy rimmed spectacles, he had also fastened his tunic buttons incorrectly and was desperately trying to undo them and put it right.

The officer looked behind in disgust and tapped his stick again tenuously as the young medic finally managed to fasten his tunic correctly. He pulled his jacket down and generally tried to look efficient. The officer coughed and pointed to his flies, turned and walked abruptly along the path with his charge scurrying after him buttoning his flies at the same time. He was like a youngster following a headmaster.

Joe couldn't take his eyes off the pair.

Nevertheless, they both seemed to know what they were doing and made notes about the patients that would be travelling on the train. It reminded him so much of his school days, he was always in trouble for something Sam had done. He rarely told tales on his brother, and often took the punishment for his misdemeanours. Sam didn't get away with it though, after they left school he would box his ears for him. Sam took it on the cheek, so to speak. They rarely went home without joking about the happenings of that day.

Sam had always loved Joe and taunted him throughout their childhood he was always somewhere near to Joe. He smiled to himself and thought of his little brother who was still remaining here in this hopeless place.

Joe realised someone was standing by him and smiled at the assistant and lifted his hand in a gesture. The orderly waved his book at him and wished him well, turned abruptly and carried on assessing the wounded ready to pass them over to the nurses and orderlies who would be travelling back with the patients.

Joe looked about him and felt guilt at the thought of leaving all behind. There were amputees, missing an arm or a leg, some were lucky with severance below the knee and elbow. Hobbling along on their makeshift crutches, or with an empty sleeve tidily pinned onto the front of their tunic. The blind looked even more pitiful being led by a companion. Joe could not take his eyes off the gas victims with the mucous membranes of their noses burnt away by the chlorine gas. He shuddered at the thought of being just a little closer to the line where he had been caught out by the chlorine gas.

He continued to stare at the shell-shocked casualties as they jerked and twitched rolling their eyes uncontrollably. He tried desperately not to stare, but they were too many. He looked the other way at the burn victims, with terrible pink shiny scar tissue over heads and faces, twisted beyond belief. He turned away and looked up at the sky trying to make out what time it was.

The orderlies had put the injured in groups, Joe turned and looked at the lad next to him, who had been gassed, his eyes were shut and his hands were heavily bandaged. Joe turned away again, he knew from experience that he would not make it, his injuries were far worse than his own. He felt panic within him, I may not make it either, he thought! Shaking his head at the thought he tried to move, he wanted to get up and walk back to the vehicles now leaving and go back to duty with his beloved horses, but he could hardly move a muscle, he felt so ill and nauseous. He lay back and patted his pillow and tried to relax, he felt a fake somehow, all these young men with their injuries and he had only caught a whiff of gas. He sighed heavily! Mary came into his thoughts and he relaxed a little and shut his eyes, trying to visualise her lovely face.

'Oh! My darling at last I can see you and cuddle little Valerie, but how can I forget my friends and everyone I will be leaving here on the battlefields. He buried his head in the rough blanket and turned away to hide his shame'.

The coach was an English Railway Coach, of the ordinary corridor type, but divided in the middle of the corridor by a door. At each end of the coach was a little sitting-room and towards the centre were separate compartments, used as a private bed-sitting room for officers and nursing staff.

In all 40-50 male orderlies, cooks, nurses, nursing sisters, were housed at the other end of the train. In the middle of the train were the kitchens and administration coaches. All the other coaches were wards for the wounded and sick. There was one coach which was the isolation ward for infectious cases.

The noise and moaning coming from the patients was unbearable and the smell was even worse, despite all the precautions that had been taken to stop the stench of blood were in vain, the uniforms worn by the injured were still covered in dried blood. The boys had lain in the trenches, with rotting corpses, and filth for so long, short of burning their uniforms and soaking each soldier in a bath of carbolic, this would be the only resolve from this dreadful acrid smell of death. Not only were they filthy but they were also flee infested and despite the gallant efforts of the nurse corps, it was almost impossible to wipe the smell of war from these poor desolate soles.

A lot more people were rushing about now, the train slowly shunted into the siding. The steam of the engine added it's whiteness to the already fullness of the Casualty-clearing Station, as it shunted slowly to an abrupt end cushioning onto buffers.

All the big double doors were thrown open, train orderlies with masses of blankets, pillows, hot water bottles, and cushions were now scurrying along the train leaving little "dumps" of these things at the end of each coach. Other orderlies seized them and began the making up of the beds on the iron-frame bedsteads, that stood three by three, one above another, ship fashion, along the sides of the coaches.

Dozens of RAMC men were attending the sick and wounded carrying them to the area allocated prior to being lifted onto the train. The injured awaited the arduous trip, contributing to even more agony of the already wounded, but without this transportation, the delay with battle casualties from the field hospitals often resulted in high mortality and intensified suffering.

Several Model 'T' automobiles, which had been converted into ambulances, had now arrived and horse drawn wagons. Three or four men lay crossways upon each truck, the orderlies commenced lifting the injured out of the vehicles, they very carefully put the injured onto the floor and waited for the order to load them onto the train.

Many of the lads just sat down on the floor, hunched over holding their heads, other wondered hopelessly, eyes rolling and unaware that they were going home. Many of them barely moved or uttered a word, just followed like sheep to the slaughter.

The young nurses and orderlies led them onto the train if they were able to walk, others were lifted gently by two orderlies. After several hours of loading the train was now ready for it's long journey to the port of departure.

The train steamed slowly away in the half light of the wintry afternoon. It had started to rain again. A sigh of relief to the orderlies though, they had managed to load the injured onto the train dry rather than soaking wet, to be left in sodden uniforms for the rest of the journey resulting in influenza added to their critical condition, would only cause more pain to all.

The guns up the line were booming on a dull and distant note, as the train crawled farther away growing feebler and feebler and, finally to almost fade out. Thus the injured left the war behind at last-it's absence was a relief to all, but there was no cheering or shouting, just quiet disbelief that it was finally over for the soldiers now travelling back home to their loved ones.

A loud bang awoke Joe, he jumped up, banged his head and almost fell off bed. He hung onto the bar above his head, he was confused and totally unaware of his surroundings. He had passed out again when being lifted onto the train. A nurse gently pushed him back into the bed. She wiped his head with a wet cloth and placed another damp cloth over his eyes, gently covering him up with his blanket.

"It's alright, they've just shot one of the horses being taken back to England. We occasionally take them home if they belong to the higher ranks. I understand that this one, in particular, belonged to a Colonel, who is on the train and in a critical condition".

She scurried off to assure another young man, who had also almost fell of his bed.

Joe turned and looked out of the window and was surprised to see the moon shining brightly, it was a full moon and he stared out at the devastation of war. He could just about make out Ypres in the distance. He shut his eyes, they were so sore, he rubbed them and regretted it instantly. He turned onto his back, he lifted the damp cloth up wiped his face and hands and plonked it back over his eyes. At least it was a little relief he thought. He tossed and turned unable to get comfortable.

He was unable to return to sleep, thoughts raced through his head.

'How long have I been asleep. Does Sam know where I am?'

He could hear the horses neighing and snorting in the next carriage. They were obviously frightened and restless and where kicking at the side of the carriage. He sat up again and bumped his head. He was pissed off totally now.

'Bugger it, he muttered to himself' as he rubbed his poor forehead the cloth fell to the floor and he looked over the side to see where it had dropped.

He turned sideways and hung his feet over the bed and dropped down onto the floor with a thud. He landed in a heap and pulled himself up by clinging to the bottom bed. The soldier in the bed just looked at him blankly and turned away. Joe had seen this look so many times over the past few years. It seemed pointless to apologise to the young man because he was now in a world oblivious to the real world and locked in the devastation and destruction he had witnessed too terrible to envisage again.

A young nurse jumped up off her seat and came over to him:

"What the bloody hell are you doing getting out of bed?", she scoured at him.

This was something not allowed, only the nursing staff were allowed to walk along the corridors.

"I can help in there, those stupid buggers don't know what

they're doing, listen to those horses, they'll come through the side of the coach in a minute, they'll be in here if someone doesn't stop that ruckus, and then what are you going to do about your damn rules, aye!".

She pulled a chair over and made him sit down for a moment, then ran up the coach to speak to her superiors.

A young medic came to Joe and asked how he felt. They chatted for a moment. He looked into Joes eyes and checked his wounded hands. Joe's chest wheezed terribly and his blisters were quite painful, but he insisted he could do some good and would feel much better moving about rather than lying on his back worrying about what was happening in the next carriage. The medic re-bandaged his hands and neck and gave Joe a piece of wet gauze for his eyes.

Joe patted his eyes carefully.

"They feel a little better today", he said gingerly, hoping this would be in his favour to allow him to go into the next carriage.

The medic walked off and went through the sliding doors. He seemed to be gone for ages. Joe was starting to think he'd never return. Then the doors slid open and he came through with a gentle smile on his face.

"Right sergeant, you can go in there, the only rule is that if you feel faint, or cannot breath, you bloody well come back in here and lie down. Do I make myself quite clear?"

"Yes sir", Joe retorted.

He winked at the nurse and proceeded to open the doors and go into the carriage, where his beloved Trojans were housed.

As he walked through the doors, a corporal came over to him and opened his mouth, and very quickly closed it.

"Oh my god, Joe. Is it really you?"

The boys patted and hugged each other and another soldier came and jumped up and down and hugged him.

Joe, shouted: "Ouch! Be careful, you silly buggers", they realised he had injuries to his hands and moved back still laughing and welcoming him.

The nurse came rushing through the sliding door to see

what all the commotion was. She had visions of him being knocked out lying on the floor mortally injured. Joe quickly apologised to her.

"Do you realise this young man is supposed to be very poorly and is going home and should be kept quiet at all costs", she said in a very stern voice to the other two soldiers.

The lads both assured her that they would be quiet and look after him. She had a gleam in her eye and wagged her finger at the three of them and winked at Joe.

"I mean it, there are a lot of very poorly and more often critical people, next door, who do not want to hear you lot making such a ruckus".

The boys sat down with a bump and sniggered as she walked out of the carriage.

"We thought you had bought it, Joe, where on earth have you been"

Joe, started to cough and brought up a load of junk and spit into the gauze the medic had given him. He looked down at the blood and folded it up and put it into his pocket. He continued wheezing and coughing and Alf opened the window slightly and gently lifted Joe up and held him whilst he took a deep breath of fresh air. Gradually he stopped coughing and sat down gasping for air.

"I think I've got something might help you Joe", George said.

He scurried off and searched in a large wooden chest in the corner of the carriage and returned with a wooden bowl and some Stockholm Tar. A solution which they used on the horses when they had nasal problems. It had numerous uses, however, and was also put on the frogs of the horses feet to stop mud fever and cracks. It helped with mange too. Joe looked down at the black sticky tar and sighed.

"Oh no you don't", he said

"I'll go get some boiling water, be back in a mo!".

George smiled at Joe and rushed along the make shift stable.

Joe was feeling very poorly and held his head in his hands and rocked his head from side to side. His head was still throbbing and he felt as though he'd been hit over the head with a sledgehammer.

"I got gassed a few days ago, it came right out of the blue. We were well behind the 'safe' zone, that's if there is one? We'd been there for months and nothing had happened for us to fall back. The Dressing Station and Hospital are now being moved. (He had to stop and try to breath in between each sentence). I was slow getting my gas mask on, too bloody slow, but the gas didn't work properly that morning, otherwise it doesn't bear thinking about".

"How long you pair been here?"

"We could have met up and had a drink, if I'd known".

"Our Sam's here too, I found him. He got married last weekend to a lovely young nurse who tended me when I got injured earlier this year. I'm bloody doomed, I tell you, doomed". Joe had to stop talking he could hardly breath and started coughing again.

"After you left for the front Alf and me decided it was far too quiet without you and we volunteered to come out here in the hope of finding you and looking after you until this war was over. Didn't work out though, we got this job moving the horses too and fro for the RVC. We bring the horses from England and take the wounded back occasionally and assist, where possible, not that there are many horses go back home", he turned his head in disgust.

"I get quite sick on the boat though, don't like sailing, but we are doing what we love, working with the animals", George wiped a tear from his cheek. "Sentimental old bugger me" he retorted.

"Oh, George, I'm so happy to see you both after all this time", Joe said.

Alf kicked the door and George jumped up and opened it. He came in with a bowl of boiling water and ordered Joe to get comfortable.

"Undo your jacket, Joe and lean forward", he ordered him in a brisk voice.

"Got some goose grease and whisky mixed here Joe, you'll stink like hell and the flies will love you, but I can assure you that it'll help you to breath a little better. Bugger about good whisky though, but I suppose you're worth it", Alf smiled and winked at his mate and placed the bowl onto the makeshift table.

"My mother always kept a pot of this handy in our kitchen when we were kids, particularly in the winter when we all had colds", Joe smiled.

"Brings back memories this, when we all had colds a few years ago. It was a pitiful sight, all the boys with towels over our heads and mother standing in the middle daring us to move from under them, until we were told too. You didn't argue with her either. Strange though, the girls never caught the cold only us boys." Joe laughed.

"My mom did the same, unfortunately" George reiterated.

Alf nodded and smiled, "Me too".

The lads burst out laughing again. Joe almost choked again coughing.

Alf scooped the goose grease out of the tin, plonked it onto Joes chest and started to rub it in.

"That's done, now bend forward lets put some on your back."

He proceeded to put some into another small jar and screwed the top back on. He wiped his hand on a straw bail and shuddered as he put his hands up to his nose to smell his fingers.

"Stinks like an old whore", he laughed and caused Joe to wrench again.

"I'll keep this pot and you keep that until you get home, ok. I expect your mom will be smothering you with this stuff as soon as you come out of hospital"

Joe smiled and fastened his shirt up.

"Right now for the nasty bit"

He popped some of the tar into the bowl and pored boiling water over it. He grabbed a towel. Joe leaned over the boiling water and Alf popped the towel over his head.

"Right you naughty boy, you stay under there for half hour and I'll go get you a cuppa, now behave or I'll send for the cavalry"

Alf patted him on the back.

George chatted to him relentlessly about what had been going on over the last few years. Joe just nodded from under the towel and lifted his head once and George promptly pushed his head back down.

Joe, came out from under the towel eventually and took a long deep breath. He actually felt a little better. His eyes were watering, but he could actually breath a little better. He coughed and brought up a load of phlegm.

“Oh that feels better lads, you should be in there with the nurses, there's loads of young lads in the same boat as me”,

Joe took a long deep breath and smiled.

Alf told him to lie back, he had an eye dropper with saline in it, he put a few droplets into Joe's eyes.

“You moved, you silly bugger. Have to do it again now. Right you sod, lie down and this time don't move, or else”.

“There, that's better”. He dropped the saline into both his eyes.

“Be sore for a bit Joe, but I've been told that it does help put artificial tears back into your eyes. Here keep this and do it every few hours”.

George opened the double doors and walked along the coach and proceeded to talk to the young nurse who had told them off so sternly.

Alf smiled at Joe and said,

“Not finished yet, Joe, sorry, got more medicine, open wide now”

He grabbed Joe's nose with his thumb and next finger.

“Aah! Yuk! Oh bloody hell, what on earth was that,” Joe said

“One of me mam's remedies, vinegar, butter, sugar and whisky, good for your chest and keeping your feet warm at night”, Alf burst into laughter.

“It's a lovely feeling doing it to someonc clse, rather than having it done to you”, he said tauntingly.

Joe coughed and spluttered and Alf whacked him on the back, almost causing him to fall off the stool.

"What my bloody feet got to do with it, aye!", Joe shouted.

"Don't know really, what me mam used to say, that's all"

Joe stood up still pulling his face following the medicine he'd just swallowed and walked over to the beautiful Bay Gelding he had been watching since he came into the carriage and gently stroked his face. The horse shied and moved back further into his pen.

"Be careful old man, he's a bit skittish", Alf, realised what he had said and quickly changed his tune,

"Forget what I said, Joe, no need to tell you anything about these four legged creatures, is there?".

Joe gently opened the pen and proceeded to walk inside very slowly, not making any fast movements. The horse couldn't go any further backwards and stood quite still. He was shaking and sweating. Joe gently spoke to him and stroked his neck and nose, blowing puffs of air into his nostrils at the same time.

He lowered his hand very gently down his leg and lifted his foot and checked his hoof, he took out his hoof pick and cleaned his foot. Poking it with his fingers to see if there was any foot rot. He proceeded to crawl under his stomach and came out the other side, the horse dropped his head and looked through his legs, whilst Joe checked his other leg and foot. There was hardly room for both of them, he pushed him over a little with his body and spoke to him whilst he moved him. He cleaned his other feet and popped the hoof pick back into his pocket.

"Pass me some of that Stockholm Tar, will you please, Alf", rather he had a little of your medicine too", Joe was laughing.

Joe felt so much better doing something. He moved his hands down his back and stared at an open wound on the horses thigh. He pushed it gently, with his middle fingers, puss oozed out and dribbled down the horses side.

"Well, boy, I can definitely help you with that injury and make your back feel better. Let's see what the lads have in their little box of tricks, shall we?"

The bay seemed to know Joe wanted to help and nuzzled up to him and snorted at Joe, covering him in snot.

"Thanks a bundle, old chap, best get rid of the shit, aye!", Joe patted him on his neck and wiped the snot off his sleeve back onto the horse.

George had come back and was already searching for what Joe wanted.

Joe went back into the pen and gently worked his magic on the bay and proceeded to check out the rest of his body. He had several minor injuries, but fortunately the injury on his back was not too deep and didn't need stitches, but it hadn't been treated, the muck had gotten into the wound. Joe squeezed the puss out again and put iodine on the wound, he talked to him the whole time reassuringly. The horse was quite relaxed now and stopped kicking at the small pen. Joe groomed him and wiped the sweat from under his belly.

"I think he'll need an injection to get rid of the infection, you got anything in that box of tricks, George?".

Joe went into the other two pens and checked the other horses. The one that had been shot was now covered with a blanket. Joe lifted the blanket slightly and sighed.

"She was a lovely looking mare",

He could see her white blaze and two white socks.

"It's a bloody shame and a total waste of good horse stock, but she'd got a suspected star fracture, there was no way of confirming it. Wish I could have helped her, Joe. She was distressed from the moment we bought her aboard." George said, disgusted at himself for having to shoot her.

"Suppose, in a way best now, rather than later, putting her through the stress of travelling, stopping and starting at each Casualty pick up and the journey home. They're not going to be too happy with us, she belongs to the Colonel's cousin he was killed in action. Apparently it was the last thing he asked the Colonel to do, to have her brought home. Within seconds the Colonel himself was hit and hence! Well you know the rest, Joe. He's on the train".

"As I said, Joe, she had damaged her fetlock, poor thing, all the kicking and jumping about had caused even more damage to her leg. I thought it was the kindest thing for her, rather than let her suffer any more. It was also causing the others to become restless. When one starts, they all start".

George stood looking at her shaking his head in disgrace.

"I've had to slaughter hundreds, if not thousands, like her over the past few years, it's a wonder there's any left at all in England. Don't knock yourself out, you did what had to be done",

Joe turned away, his thoughts were also of remorse for the pure waste of good horse stock. They both looked down and sighed together.

George changed the subject and turned away from the dead animal.

"Well, Joe, I've heard they were using camels and elephants back in England to get the crops in and pull the trees out for the wood to build the trenches". George smiled and sipped at his tea, which was now cold.

"Elephants and camels you say" Joe retorted.

"Definitely, they've come over from Egypt and India".

"Well, when I get home I'm going to buy an elephant for myself, always fancied a ride on one of those big buggers", Joe said.

They all fell about laughing again. Alf put his hand on his lips and said

"Sssh, you'll have grumpy drawers back".

It only made things worse. They giggled like naughty little school boys.

Joe burst out coughing again and brought up another load of junk and blood, he spit it onto the straw on the floor and rubbed his boot over it, scuffing a little straw over the phlegm.

George looked down at it and asked him what would happen about his lung. Joe shook his head and looked out of the window.

"My uncle Bertie is a big Surgeon in London, I'm going to wait until I get an opinion from him first. I trust him. My mother will very quickly be intervening when she knows I'm back. Bet she's onto it right now if she got the telegram sent recently. I've been told my eyes will recover, its just surface damage at the moment, still bloody sore though".

Joe looked out of the window and stared at the distant flashes and thought of Sam. He had been assured by the nurses that he would get the message about him going back to England. Joe was still wondering about Sam when the door slid open again and to his amazement Hilda walked in with a big grin on her face.

"I thought it might be you making all the noise. Might have known".

Joe stood up and flung his arms around her.

"Well to have all of you here with me makes me feel on top of the world. Let me introduce you to my oldest and dearest friends, next to you, of course, Hilda. Joe started to cough again and turned away spitting out the junk back onto the floor. He dragged some straw over it avoiding Hilda's stare.

"Alf, George, meet Sam's new wife now my dearest sister-in-law, Hilda"

They all shook hands smiling and laughing.

"What are you doing here, Hilda" Joe asked.

Hilda proceeded to explain in great detail.

"Well, whilst you were unconscious, these past few days, I looked after you. You were out of it totally. Sam had already returned to his unit when I got back and realised you'd been injured, I turned and ran out after him but he had long since gone. I had already requested to return to England, as you know, and after a further request to go on this next evacuation, luckily I was given permission to leave. Had to pull a few strings though. I felt a bit guilty leaving all the other girls behind, but Sally and Monica are also on the train".

Sam now knows why I left so abruptly and sends
'God Speed' and 'Good Luck'.

"I got a letter yesterday from the lads bringing supplies to the Clearing Station, another few hours and I would have missed them. At least you'll be out of this war for good, Joe. I only hope that it is coming to an end and I can start a new life with Sam." She wiped her nose and tried not to cry.

She bent down and kissed Joe tenderly on his forehead.

"I feel better now, seeing you here with these damn horses, I should have known it wouldn't be long before you were back amongst them.

George snorted and rubbed his foot on the wooden floor and made a very bad impression of a horse. Hilda smiled and offered him some hay, stroking him across the shoulder at the same time.

Joe sweetheart, I'm terribly sorry, all joking aside, I must go unfortunately I am expected to work during this trip. Oh! whilst I think about it and, before I forget, when you are asked, probably by an RAMC orderly on the ship, to what part of the "blighty" do you belong, every effort will be made for you to be hospitalised as near to your home town as is possible.

She shook his hand and hugged him again,

"Oh! Sam sent your Hunter watch back and thanked you from the bottom of his heart".

She gave him a letter from his brother and another for his mother. He looked down at them and took them from her. He popped them into his inside pocket.

"I will see you before embarkation and probably during the journey Joe, you be good or else you'll have me to contend with" She pointed her finger at him and the other lads and tried very hard to remain stern, but to no avail.

Hilda shook hands with Alf and George and asked them to look after her big brother and shut the double doors behind her and, to please be quiet if at all possible. She winked at Joe and closed the doors behind her.

The lads realised Joe needed time to himself and quietly went over to the horses and tried to look busy.

Joe sat quietly thinking about Sam. He blinked several times to adjust his sore eyes and popped another couple of drops into them. He took his glasses from his pocket and wiped the fluid from down his cheeks, blew on onto the glasses and wiped the lenses. He also wiped his eyes on the other piece of clean gauze, focusing a little better now he could see the writing on the envelope, he slid his thumb along the top of the envelope and took the letter out and began to read:

10 December 1918

My dearest brother Joe,

Firstly and most importantly, look after my Hilda for me. I love her more than life itself. I know you will keep her safe, whatever happens?

God knows who will look after me now?
I still have my Gracie, though ~ ha! ha!
What will my life be like without our meetings?

Joe wiped the tears from his eyes and looked out of the window into the cold winter's night, the drizzle pattered onto the coach windows and the star shells lit up the sky at intervening intervals. He looked up at the two small windows above him and pulled them shut, shuddered with the cold and sat back down. The effort of closing the windows had taken his strength away, making him feel lethargic. He sighed and took a deep breath,

'Such a small task and I feel like shit' he thought to himself.

He tried to continue to read Sam's letter, but had to wipe his eyes again on the gauze, before he could focus on his writing.

Joe, Hilda has told me about your injuries and assures me that you will survive them, albeit you may not come out without breathing problems for the rest of your life, or wear glasses, but that would enhance your looks slightly, wouldn't it, aye! At least you will have a life with young Mary and little Valerie. Maybe you will get a War Pension?

Joe tried desperately to compose himself, it was so difficult reading Sam's letter, knowing this might be the last news of his brother. He took out his photograph of Mary and little

Valerie. It helped him to think positively. He touched Valerie's face and continued to read the letter.

Heard about you stripping off in front of those young nurses. Naughty! Naughty! Think I'd rather concede to my injuries than be nude in front of all those beauties ~ You were always a bit of a poser! Was old Bertha watching?

Joking aside ~ I love you Joe and God speed to you. I hope you got father's hunter watch from Hilda. Didn't want to damage it. I know how much it means to you both.

The other envelope is for mother, I do miss her so. Don't miss that bloody broom though. Wonder if she's still got it? When I get home I'm going to buy her a push along cleaner. Heard that they are quite good.

Your Little Brother, Samuel, Harry, Price xxxx
(One for you, Hilda, Valerie and mother).

Joe folded the letter and put his photograph with it back into the envelope.

'I will see you again little brother, that is my oath and promise to you. So until then Samuel Price, be safe until we meet again', he muttered as he looked out of the window into the night.

He had become exhausted again, he curled up into a ball and fell into a deep sleep.

CHAPTER 19

Elsie screamed, grabbed her knees with both hands and pushed with all her might.

"Oh! My god, ooooooh!" she shouted out.

She had now been in labour for almost 18 hours, the birth seemed to be taking far too long. She was hot, sweaty and generally worn out, from all the pushing and most of all from the midwife poking and prodding her.

Young Mary kneeled down by the side of the brass bed and held her friend's hand, trying to give her moral support. She had been by her side, without sleep, for the whole 18 hours and was herself exhausted, but she would not leave her best friend in her hour of need. She patted her hand.

"Not much longer now luv, this part is always the worst, I promise. Once the crowning is over, the rest happens very quickly, then all the pain disappears, your just so overwhelmed with the wonder of your child. In a few days you'll not even remember today and all this pain, just the joy of your child".

Young Mary looked at her friend reassuringly.

"Really, Elsie cried out in a high pitched voice, you could have fooled me. Never again, she shouted, never again, oh, oooooh! "

She gripped her knees again and pushed, her face looked as if she had turned into a giant bullfrog, you couldn't see Elsie's eyes now, they were constantly squeezed shut.

Young Mary wiped Elsie's forehead and tried to be positive

for her friends sake. Remembering the birth of Valerie she looked away from Elsie trying desperately not to lose control of her fear that Elsie may die in childbirth. She, herself, had a very difficult birth and almost lost Valerie. She said a little prayer for Elsie and bowed her head.

"Please Lord, don't let anything happen to her or her unborn child. Amen"

Elsie dragged her back to reality and screamed at her again.

"If you have any other stupid comments to make Mary, soon to be Price, keep them to your bloody self, ok!"

Poor Mary nodded like one of those laughing clowns at the circus unable to utter another word of encouragement for fear of upsetting Elsie even more. She turned and looked at her friend.

Elsie gritted her teeth, trying to control the excruciating pain she was in.

"Ok! Elsie, I'm sorry" young Mary blurted out.

Young Mary turned around looking for reassurance from the midwife and Mary, she felt a little stupid, following her comments to Elsie and her outburst.

Elsie gripped her hand so hard at the next contraction her nails stuck into the back of her hand. She turned back in shock and stared down at her hand, trying not to let Elsie know how much she was hurting her. She gently prized Elsie's hand away and moved her fingers about, they'd gone numb. She looked at the deep nail marks and wiped the blood off her hand onto her apron and then quickly sat on her hands avoiding looking at Elsie.

The midwife came over to Elsie, lifted the sheet for the 100th time and, looked to see what was happening, if anything. Again, she put her fingers inside Elsie's vagina causing her to cringe and hold onto the brass bedstead. Elsie took a big deep breath and looked up at the ceiling. The midwife leaned further over the bed and continued to poke about, without any comment to Elsie or consideration to her pain, or feelings.

Elsie had had enough, she couldn't put up with her fumbling anymore.

"Take your grubby smelly fingers out of my fanny, right now" she shouted and promptly shut her legs, and forced her bottom into the air, causing the midwife to fall backwards, lose her balance and fall in a heap on the floor at the bottom of the bed.

Elsie and young Mary found this quite funny and burst out laughing at the sight of the midwife on the bedroom floor, curled in a ball trying to get up like some drunk in the street. Young Mary was so tempted to kick her up the backside, but she restrained the urge. Mary shook her fingers at them, but could not help laugh herself.

They both turned away and giggled, it helped relax Elsie a little, thinking of something else for a few moments.

The midwife finally got to her feet, straightened her long black skirt and petticoats, looking daggers at the two girls the whole time. She indicated to Mary to go over to the bedroom door on the other side of the room.

"She's not opening up, I'm a bit worried about whether she is strong enough to go through this without some help, she's a bit young for childbirth. I think it may be a big child? Don't know whether we should get Dr Bern Quinn in to see her? It wouldn't take long for Harry to fetch him?"

Mary turned and looked at the door and then back at the midwife.

"I've had 10 children and each birth has been different. My labours' have varied from a few hours to 24+ hours. My first was also the worst, it was very similar to this birth".

She paused for a moment and fiddled with her apron nervously, looked over at Elsie, who was shaking her head. Elsie had heard every word. She didn't want any intervention by doctor's at this stage causing her daughter more embarrassment and worst of all questions about the father. Mary turned back and spoke to Gert.

"My pelvis just suddenly opens and the baby pops out. Perhaps Elsie will be the same, she's got a very prominent pelvis bone. Lets give her a little more time, aye" she said trying to reassure herself that things would be ok.

Elsie smiled at her mother and then gripped her knees and

pushed again with all her might at her next contraction. She dropped her legs and sobbed into the pillow.

'Oh! My poor baby' Mary thought looking over at her daughter. There was nothing she could do but stand and watch and give her moral support.

She tried again to reassure Gert and, also herself, that this would be the right thing to do. Mary couldn't help wondering whether she had made the right decision, but wouldn't admit it to Gert, or in fact to herself.

"Ok, but I'm not too happy about it", Gert muttered averting Mary's stare.

"I'll give her another hour or so and then we fetch the doctor, ok?" Gert was now asserting her own authority on Mary now.

Mary and Elsie both nodded at the same time.

The midwife wiped her sweaty hands on her apron and went back across the bedroom. Shaking her head with disgust, looking back at Mary, before lifting the sheet up again and peering between Elsie's legs, pushing her legs open even wider as she put her fingers inside Elsie to see if there was any further progress. Elsie groaned and lay her head sideways on the pillow avoiding her mother's sympathy and the pain she was enduring.

Gert wasn't Mary's choice of a midwife. Her life longstanding friend Nellie was delivering another sole into the world in the next village. So many women were having babies with no one to support them, their husbands' having been killed in the war.

Gert was small about 4'8" or thereabouts, very fat, with piercing beady little tiny dark blue, bloodshot eyes, her face was full of wrinkles and her cheeks were covered in dark blue broken veins. She had extremely large feet, (Size 9 at least Mary thought), too big for any woman and her legs were short, with folds of fat, just like the rest of her.

She also had crusted lumps of dark brown flesh on the

back of her heals, where the shoes had rubbed her. Her backside was enormous, when she walked, it seemed to have a life of it's own and wobbled from side to side, it bounced like her drooping breasts. She had rotten teeth, her nails were very long and she had very long fingers, but the worst thing of all, she smelt of stale booze, her breath was unbearable. If she got up close you had no alternative but to turn your head away from her. It was like something had died inside her.

Mary couldn't help but giggle when she went through a door, her hips spread across the gap and touched both sides of the doorframe. She had to turn sideways before she could encounter the space of the door.

Gert knew she was being ridiculed and frumped around the bedroom looking back at Elsie to see if she was laughing at her. She plonked herself down on the nursing chair by the window muttering under her breath.

Mary looked at her beloved chair as she dropped down onto it.

Mary tore away from her thoughts of Gert, breaking her chair and asked young Mary to go and make a nice cup of strong tea.

Gert only needed an excuse to get out of the bedroom and quickly followed young Mary downstairs. The stairs shook as she stepped down each step. Young Mary felt overwhelmed at the thought of being crushed by this troll from the underworld. She rushed into the kitchen and breathed a sigh of relief when she saw Harry by the fire.

"Wont be long luv, I promise", she went over to Harry and kissed his forehead.

"Lot of noise up there, is everything going to plan?" Harry asked as he puffed on his pipe.

He had stopped awake with the family too from the beginning of labour. He rubbed his eyes and looked up at the grandfather clock on the opposite side of the room to see what time it was. He stood up, went over to the clock, opened the glass door and pulled the chain down gently, adjusted the minute finger and closed the door, turned the key and popped it back into his trouser pocket. He went back to his seat in front of the fire and sat down again.

In the bedroom, Mary pulled the nursing chair over to the side of the bed, checking it first before sitting on it, to see if it had been damaged by fat Gert. She tried not to look too worried and fidgeted with her apron. She patted Elsie's hand gently and wiped her forehead, pulled up the sheet and generally tidied the bed up, chatting away about this and that. Then she became very serious and looked down at her daughter.

"Elsie, now listen to me. You'll have to work harder if this little sole is to come into this world naturally, without the help of doctor Bern Quinn. I know it's difficult, God knows I've had 10 and believe me, it gets no easier. She patted her stomach, this little bugger will be here soon enough and she'll need a playmate. The first is always the worst, it's a known fact"

She said reassuringly, trying to convince herself, at the same time.

"How do you know it's a girl, mom" Elsie quizzed with interest.

"Well I don't, but your dad seems to think so, I just humour him"

She looked down at her swollen stomach and then over at the oak cheval mirror. She hated to see herself so fat again. She had spent most of the past 20 odd years pregnant.

"No more", she muttered to herself, "no more".

She was so carried away looking at herself that she had forgotten Elsie. She grabbed her mothers hand, arched her back, then grabbed her knees and pushed with all her might and screamed out again.

"Oh! Bloody hell mother, I'm being torn apart, oooooooh!"

The baby's head came out and it's eyes opened immediately. Mary was surprised at how alert the baby seemed, particularly in view of how long Elsie had been in labour. She focused her attention back onto Elsie supporting the babies head at the same time.

"Now young lady, hold still and don't push for a little while, must check everything's ok".

Mary, wiped her forehead on her apron as she balanced the child in her other hand and took a long deep breath. She was in a lot of pain and didn't want her daughter to know. She paused for a moment.

"Everything looks ok to me luv, now I want you to push again as hard as you can with the next contraction",

Mary felt as if she was giving birth herself.

Elsie shut her eyes and took a big deep breath and pushed with all her might.

"Oh! Bloody hell, mother" she screamed again.

The baby slipped out onto the towel and started crying almost immediately. Mary gently held the baby in her hands and looked down lovingly at the child.

"There, I told you". Mary smiled, relieved it was finally all over.

Elsie lifted herself up on her elbows and tried to look down at her baby and fell back immediately too exhausted to even care.

Gert and young Mary came running up the stairs and tried to push through the bedroom door together. Gert just forced her way into the room and left young Mary out on the landing fuming, she turned as she deliberately shut the door in her face. Defiantly, young Mary clipped the iron latch up on the latch and brace door and stamped in almost knocking Gert to the floor as she past her.

"You're just a fat old bully", she said, pulling her tongue out at her. She pushed her and rushed across the bedroom to her friend, turned and scowled at Gert again, daring her to say, or do anything.

"She's like me, told you". Mary winked at Elsie and young Mary.

"Get some hot water will you and pass us the scissors".

Gert ordered, looking sternly at young Mary, trying to show her authority.

Young Mary looked at Elsie and giggled. She passed the scissors, towel and bowl to Gert, clicked her feet, saluted, threw her right arm in the air and proceeded to fetch some more water from the kitchen.

'Oh! Bugger she thought, didn't look see what it was', as she ran down the stairs.

Gert looked disgusted at young Mary as she went out of the bedroom and stamped over to Elsie and her baby, her breasts banged up and down, almost hitting her knees. Elsie couldn't help but giggle at the sight.

"What's so funny, Elsie" she asked abruptly.

She couldn't look at her for fear of bursting out in fits of giggles and turned to look at her mother, who was also in tears at the sight of her big tits and wobbling fat arse.

"Well lets have a look at what the Good Lord has provided for you",

Gert grunted, without conveying any sympathy to Elsie whatsoever for the difficult birth she had just gone through.

"Don't agree with this business, having children out of wedlock",

She muttered, clamping and cutting the cord at the same time.

Mary looked at her in disgust and Gert turned her face away, knowing she had said too much. She bit her lip in anticipation of the bollocking she was about to get.

"I'll speak to you later, Gert, keep your comments to yourself, or else", Mary scorned, not finishing the sentence on purpose.

"My Elsie has enough to put up with, without your bigotry!"

She glared at her again sternly. (If looks could kill, Gert would surely now be dead).

Gert quickly scurried across the bedroom and sat down after checking everything was as it should be with the cord.

She was a known coward, with a bloody big mouth. She wiped her forehead on her apron and sipped at her cold tea.

'The Sooner I get out of this madhouse the better, she thought to herself'.

Mary looked down at the little bundle and kissed his brow.

"My you're a big bonny boy", she lifted him up by his arms and studied his weight. The baby wriggled, pulled his face, but didn't cry.

"Got to be 10lbs, if he's an ounce", she smiled and walked over to her daughter, cuddling the naked child in her arms.

"He's almost as big as Sam was, doesn't look like him though, it's any wonder you had a difficult birth, our Elsie".

She shut up and realised she might have offended her daughter.

Elsie, lifted the sheet back slightly and smiled up at her mother and then at the baby. Young Mary came running back into the room and nearly dropped the boiling kettle over Elsie as she tripped over the rag rug they had all happily made in the evenings.

"Ups a daisy" She jested as she gathered herself back up.

"What is it, Elsie", she asked.

"A Boy, it's a little boy. I knew I was having a boy, all along,"

She wiped the tears from her eyes on the coarse starched white bed sheet.

They both cuddled up on the bed and looked at him together. The baby was now lying tummy down on his mother. He was trying to lift his head almost immediately and seemed to be looking around the room.

"He's been here before", Mary said looking at him lovingly. She patted his little bottom as she spoke to her daughter.

"Well what are we going to call this Big Bundle then", Mary asked.

"Charles, his name is ~ Charles, William, Harry, Price",

Elsie looked down at her son and started to cry again.

Mary took the child off her, washed him in the bowl of water and put him into a beautiful white cotton nightgown, which she had sat a night making, crochcting the lace around the wrists and neck. The bottom of the nightgown had taken her almost a month to complete. She popped a nappy onto him, put the pin through the middle of the nappy, placing her fingers at the back to avoid pricking the child, then lifted him into the air. She looked at him proudly, then popped him into the wooden crib, that had been used for all the Price children.

Elsie protested, but knew it was a waste of time, you didn't argue with mother on any account.

"Now Elsie, just another big push left to get rid of the afterbirth, then you can cuddle your little son all you want".

Mary stood by Elsie patting her hand reassuringly willing her to give a last push.

Elsie waited and waited, but nothing happened. She looked up at her mother appealing to her knowledge. Mary sat down with a bump and sighed.

"Well young lady, only one thing for it, you'll have to breast feed this little one and hopefully your womb will contract and cause you to push the afterbirth out".

Mary walked over to the crib, picked up Charles, who was sucking at his thumb.

"Bad habit that young man", she said, as she gently took his thumb out of his little mouth.

She settled him onto Elsie's breast and sat down again. She was totally exhausted and felt quite faint. She looked down at her belly and stroked it gently, looking at her daughter as she breathed heavily. She took several deep breaths trying to remain calm.

Elsie started to feed Charles, he suckled her greedily, holding onto her breast with his little hand. She looked down lovingly at the child. Then she threw her head back onto the pillow.

"Oh! Shit", she shouted and gave a big push, the afterbirth came out and slithered onto the towel. The baby didn't even stop suckling. Young Mary and Elsie smiled at the newborn.

"Well I'll be buggered" Elsie said to young Mary.

"There told you", Mary was quite chuffed with her observations.

"Got to get you cleaned up now Elsie.

She tried to pull Charles off his mother's nipple, but he clung on gallantly for a few moments, his little lips puckered up and he started to cry pitifully. "None of that young man, I do not do moods, sooner you learn the better. Charles you are now going to give your mother a little peace and quiet. I'll take you to meet!",

The child looked up at her and stopped crying, his little lips quivered for a moment, then he promptly stuck his thumb into his mouth again and started sucking.

Mary paused for a while, pondering on her next words, looking down at her grandson. She hadn't got the heart to take his thumb out of his mouth.

"Well to meet your step-brothers' and sisters'. No, no, that doesn't sound right somehow, does it young man - your brothers' and sisters'! Right, that's sorted" she kissed Charles on the forehead again and smiled at Elsie.

"From this day forward Charles will be known as brother to all 10 of my children and, if anyone says any different, they'll get a boxed ear from me. That includes you Gert, do you hear me. There that's it, settled".

She quickly popped Charles back into his crib, she had a sharp pain in her stomach and almost dropped him, as she crouched up. Elsie saw her first and tried to get out of bed. Young Mary rushed to her side and lifted her upright very gently.

"Don't fuss, I'm ok, just a twinge". She patted her stomach and pushed young Mary out of the way.

She looked sternly at the midwife and winked at young Mary and went back over to the bed and continued to wash and care for her daughter, changing her nightie and the bed linen, with the help of young Mary.

Gert turned away muttering again, but she knew better than cross Mary, they had crossed swords in the past and, she didn't win that argument either. Mary had punched her in the mouth and chased her with her notorious broom. Gert had been horrible to her friend Nellie after the birth of her twins. She had suggested she go to the Workhouse, because her husband would not be coming back to look after them.

Nellie had stayed at Mary's after she received the telegram informing her of the death of Albert, her husband of only a year. She had now moved in with her brother and sister in law.

"Well at least Nellie had a husband" Mary shouted at Gert, who to everyone's knowledge had never even had a fella in her whole life. She appeared in the village one day and no one knew from where she had come from. She lived in lodgings above the butcher's shop in town.

Harry came up the stairs, knocked and opened the door, poked his head in and asked for permission enter. He limped across the bedroom to his daughter, kissed her, before going over to the crib. He popped his stick on the end of the bed, but it fell onto the floor. He kicked it so that no one would fall over it.

"My he's a bonnie baby, typical Price too, not going to be dark haired though, blonde I'd say", as he looked over at Mary. He turned and smiled at his daughter and kissed the little one on his tiny fingers. Mary came over and looked into his eyes.

"Looks like a little China man, Elsie. Are you sure the father is of English origin", she said jokingly.

Elsie burst into tears again.

"Oh! Luv, I'm sorry, he's absolutely adorable, he really is".

Mary looked at Harry and lovingly he stroked Charles's still wet curls.

"Normally it's me who jumps in with both feet" he said nervously laughing out loud. 'Too loud really, he thought to himself'.

Elsie composed herself, she sniffed and wiped her nose on her clean nightgown. She tried to smile at her father and tears continued dropping down her cheeks. Young Mary took out her handkerchief and gently wiped the tears from her red face. Harry smiled lovingly at his eldest daughter.

"Got to take him to meet his brothers' and sisters' now, so see you in a little while".

He winked at Mary and Elsie, but gave Gert a stern look of antipathy, then proceeded out of the door with Charles. He very carefully stepped down each step, checking before he took the next one, he was not too good going down stairs. His leg caused him that much grief, he tried hard not to let Mary know how painful it had become over the past few months.

'Must send Nancy up for my stick', he thought, as he opened the door at the bottom of the stairs.

Nancy was first to hold Charles, she sat down in the rocker and cuddled him close.

"Oh! Dad isn't he a lovely little chap".

Phyliss had no interest in him whatsoever, just looked at him from across the room and walked off out of the cottage muttering to herself. She was still such a baby, but she would have to move over now for Charles now and even worse for the new baby soon to be born.

"He's your new brother, you arrogant little shit", Harry shouted after her.

Harry stamped his foot and regretted it instantly, the pain shot up his leg, but she completely ignored him turning round defiantly as she walked out of the kitchen door.

He lit his pipe in frustration. One of these days I'll have to sort that girl out, he muttered to himself. Phyliss had always been a grumpy and a spiteful child. 'Not at all like my little Ena', he thought!

His thoughts went back to his childhood and Ena skipping along the bridleway with Henry chasing after her.

'None of my girls have beautiful auburn hair with shades of autumn leaves or green eyes like the sea in the sunlight' he thought guiltily looking over at Nancy.

Bernard, David and Leonard, poked their heads through the door and asked their father, if by any chance thcy would be wetting the babies head later. Harry tapped his pipe on the oak shelf and smiled at the lads.

"Wouldn't hurt, I suppose. Mom wouldn't be too pleased though. Lets say we celebrate when Elsie feels up to it, aye".

The lads turned away and went over to the barn.

"Typical that", Leonard said.

"If it was one of his, I'm sure he would be opening the home brew right now?"

"You had better not let him hear you say that Len" Bernard turned around guiltily, making sure his father was nowhere near.

"He's not my brother, I will not accept him as such", Len said defiantly, David nodded in agreement.

They all sat down on the bails of straw, picking at it and popping a strand into their mouths almost together.

"I've got a secret stash of booze" David said, smiling like a Cheshire cat.

"Got it out of the house when mother wasn't looking the other week".

"You hadn't better let mother know you stole it David, otherwise it will be curtains for you, or the broom". Bernard didn't agree with him stealing the wine.

The three boys passed the bottle around.

"Parsnip wine, my favourite" Len said,

"Mine too David mimicked",

Bernard just sipped it and passed it back to Len without comment.

Inside the cottage, Nancy was loving holding her new brother. She was in her element. She didn't care who his father or mother was. He's a baby and needs our love, she thought.

'Don't care if Phyliss sulks forever or the boys, I'll always love you Charles, you can come and talk to me anytime", she said lovingly and kissed him on the forehead. The child was fast asleep.

Harry wondered why his children were so different, he looked lovingly at Nancy cuddling Charles. He was still day dreaming about his childhood, 'I wish I had a brother or sister now' he shook his head and his thoughts moved onto his own children and their futures.

Susie had now left home and was in Service in Gloucester, courting a fine young man of means. Marriage was in the pipeline. Susie was quite small, blond, with blue eyes and extremely stern features. She had no intentions of having children and just wanted security and a nice house. Susie was like Mary's side of the family and tried to be above others. She snubbed her family and rarely came home. Her intended had never been to the family home. Elsie was the spy who told all about her sister to her mother who in turn told Harry late at night when they went to bed.

Dolly lived in lodgings in Birmingham, she had managed to secure a post as a seamstress, meeting up with Elsie on her odd days off. They used to go to the local Lyons tea shop and enjoy a scone and a nice cup of tea. She was not happy working for other people and wanted to start her own business as a milliner and hopefully one day open her own shop in the town centre. The mistress of the house encouraged her to sew and could see her potential. She had a business brain and reminded Harry of his beloved Mary.

Bernard's life was already planned out, he had become a brilliant horseman and stable manager and hoped to be put in charge of the stud farm, if Joe didn't take the post up again. He had already commented that another yard was interested in him should Joe return to his old job when he came out of the army.

He was like Joe in many ways, tall, handsome and of a gentle nature. He too had an admirer in the village, young Betty. They had attended the same school together and was one of Mary's closest friend's daughter. A fine match Harry smiled to himself.

David, was short, very mischievous and somewhat of a dreamer. He could mix with anyone and had a funny sense of humour, was afraid of nothing, not even his mother. Harry couldn't make up his mind who he was like. Harry shook his head at the thought of David, never making anything of his life, too much of a rebel, he thought.

Leonard was a different kettle of fish, he had big ideas about his future. He was tall, slim, confident, with black curly hair and prominent high cheekbones and dark ebony eyes. His ears stood out too much though, he deliberately combed his hair forward to hide them. He spent a lot of his life in the toilet looking at them, pushing them back against his skull. His ears didn't seem to bother the young girls in the village though, they gathered around him like moths to the flame.

He wanted to design and build better houses and employ people to do the work for him. He would talk about when the war was over, people would be rebuilding their life's, needing new homes. He was quite sure that the country would need skilled carpenters' and builders'. He talked of taking an apprenticeship with Hickman's Builder's Merchants in Wolverhampton and hopefully attending night classes in architecture. He had already sent his c.v. to prominent construction companies, with the help from his school mistress. She had always felt that Len was a natural in design and had encouraged his raw talent in art. He had ideas way beyond his station, but Harry hoped he would achieve his young dreams.

Leonard was a brilliant artist and spent hours designing houses and drawing old buildings and churches. He would go off for hours riding through villages looking at different buildings. He preferred Tudor style rather than Victorian, he had commented to his father cheerfully recently.

Harry had taken a few of his drawings to Wolverhampton and left them with an old friend of his, who was now in the family building industry. He had lost his only son, who would have taken over the family construction business. They had been in the Army together, unfortunately, he had been badly wounded on the Somme and had to retire from the forces. He promised to meet Len and discuss his future as soon as he was able to organise a mutually convenient meeting. Len still had another year to do at school before he was able to venture out into the world. Every available moment he had a pencil in his hand and his artist book.

Nancy wanted to be was a dancer and travel the world. Initially she wanted to be a midwife, but changed her mind following the births she had witnessed during her young years. She was such a pretty slim child, with beautiful black hair and dark green eyes. He looked back over at his daughter and smiled, few years before I lose her, so no need to worry myself on that score, he thought.

Phyliss, well it would be a long time before that one has to make any decisions, he thought. Probably end up a school teacher, bossing every one about. He chuckled to himself.

Dolly was expected at any moment, she eagerly awaited the birth of her niece or nephew and visited her now every four weeks. She loved her big sister, who was the only member of the family she bothered with. She had a bob on herself. Too good for her big family. Only commoners' had so many children she had shouted at her mother during their last outbreak. Mary had ordered her out of her home, unless she apologised. Dolly reluctantly and quite sheepishly apologised. Mary was unforgiving following this fracas, the love and trust between mother and daughter, were now destroyed. She rarely spoke to Dolly anymore and just acknowledged her when she came to visit. There was no love lost between them. Tolerance was the only thing they now had in common.

God knows what I would do if she became pregnant, he thought, bad enough taking on Charles.

He was still miles away in thought when a knock came upon the door. Harry walked over the kitchen to answer it. He couldn't understand why Dolly had not just come in as she always did rather than knock. He opened the door expecting to see his daughter with gifts in her hand for her new nephew and stood in shock as he looked at the postman.

"Got a telegram for you Harry. Hope it's not bad news regarding one of your boys".

The postman stood in the doorway with his postbag thrown over his shoulders awaiting a response from Harry.

"Do you want to come in and have a cup of tea Fred before you go", Harry said looking for moral support.

"No got a few more of these to deliver today, he patted the bag on his shoulder. I'll pass thank you, Harry".

Fred made it a habit not to go into the premises, following delivery of a telegram, whoever the recipient was. He felt guilty enough delivering these dreadful telegrams, but someone had to do it. Jobs were becoming more scarce lately that one could hold onto once the war was over.

He'd lost his boy a little over a year ago and couldn't bear the thought of being present when the telegrams were opened. He now knew how it felt to receive such terrible news 'that your son had been killed in action'.

Fred's wife rarely spoke to him nowadays. He had another son, just 19 years of age, who was fighting somewhere in Belgium. His only daughter was nursing in a convalescent home in London, she was still but a child, robbed of her youth. She wouldn't speak of the atrocities she had witnessed, after nursing the injured, following their return from the front line. Each day he cautiously turned the telegrams over one by one, thoughts going through his head, that the next one was for his own residence.

Before the war they had been such a happy family, the whole world in front of them, plans for a better life were now shattered completely. Nowadays, it was all sadness and dismay, his wife invariably asked who had had received a telegram and then would go very quiet and continue with her chores, making the tea for the two of them, as if nothing had been said. Gwen sometimes didn't speak again till the following evening, asking the same question over and over again. Fred had learnt to survive on a daily basis, saying as little as possible and keeping his fears to himself. All he really wanted was for his life to go back to some sort of normality.

"Hope it's not!", he paused and guiltily smiled at Harry.

What could he say that wasn't being thought by Harry already. He threw his post bag over his shoulder and briskly walked off.

'Me and my big mouth, he thought!'

Harry stood at the door for some time staring and wondering How Mary would react to the telegram. The boys had disappeared into the barn and he could hear them laughing and wondered whether he should destroy their fun. Nancy was wrapped up with the new baby. He looked up at the ceiling where Elsie had given birth and shuddered;

'One in, one out'! He shook his head in despair.

"Please God don't take my boys from me", he said aloud.

Nancy turned and looked at him, he smiled pathetically.

He took a deep breath, turned and walked back across the room and poked the fire, hiding his despair from Nancy. She was still wrapped up with Charles, she hadn't noticed her father's mood.

"Thank you for small mercies" he said mockingly looking over at Nancy.

Mary had heard the knock on the door and watched everything out of the bedroom window unbeknown to Harry. She dreaded the content of the telegram, this moment had been at the back of her mind for over two years.

Only two days before, she had sat in the kitchen of her friend Gladys, when the dreaded telegram had arrived, informing her that her only son had been killed in action. He had never ventured out of the village prior to the war and had been in Belgium for a little over a month. He hadn't reached his 19th birthday. Her husband had been taken two years earlier. She had begged her lad not to go, but he said it was 'his duty'. So many young men thought this way, dying before they reached manhood. He had attended the same school as Joe and Sam.

Mary put her fingers over her quivering lips and dared not

turn around and look at Elsie. She looked down at her stomach and stroked it gently.

She wanted to scream out:

'Oh, my God, please, please, not my boys', she restrained herself and turned to look at Elsie and young Mary who had fallen asleep in each other's arms.

"Gert, I can manage now, thank you. How much do I owe you for your services" she asked.

"Five bob, thanks Mary. You can pay me later, if you want", she had also seen Fred deliver the telegram. Gert tried to avert Mary's tormented eyes.

"No, I'll get your money for you, wouldn't want you talking about me, would I?", Mary said sarcastically, taking out her anger on poor Gert.

She took the money off Mary and rushed out of the bedroom door, looking back at Elsie and young Mary for a brief moment. She clambered down the stairs, threw the door open, looked at Harry without speaking, grabbed her belongings and scurried across the kitchen like a bat out of hell. She took a last look around her to make sure she had left nothing behind picked up her portmanteau.

"Well Harry! Don't know what to say!" She stood looking at Nancy for a few moments awaiting the opportunity to run away from this madhouse.

"Bye Harry, hope it's not bad news", she said guiltily, then she was gone.

She almost fell off her bicycle as she peddled over the bumpy courtyard. The boys fell about laughing at her, David mocked her by waddling around in the yard. He had messed with her bicycle chain and waited eagerly for her to fall off the bike.

Bernard had seen the postman, he was too busy thinking to be amused by David's antics, then suddenly he realised that this wasn't the normal time for the post. He turned to the boys, the penny seemed to drop for them all at the same time, they looked towards Gert, who was peddling off down the lane. David thumped his side.

Mary came down the stairs very slowly and into the kitchen, holding her stomach, she looked over at Harry who was poking the fire. She wanted to run over to him, but she composed herself, looked at Nancy and sighed.

"Have to get some more wood in luv" he muttered as he turned around looking at her trying to avert her eyes. He was breaking apart.

Mary knew how close he was to breaking down. Joe was his oldest, he was closest to him. Joe was Harry's shadow throughout his childhood. Wherever Harry was Joe would be by his side even up until he joined the RAVC. Joe was so much like his father. He shared his love of farming and horsemanship. Oh! he loved Samuel too, but the bond he had formed with Joe outweighed any he had with his other children. Mary's heart was breaking, she didn't want to take the telegram from Harry.

"Nancy, could you just go upstairs sweetheart for a little while and take Charles with you please", Mary smiled at her daughter fondly.

Nancy had also realised that the telegram that had been delivered might be bad news. She walked very slowly across the kitchen, staring backwards at her parents. She started to cry as she climbed the stairs, hugging baby Charles to her chest tightly.

As soon as the kitchen was empty Mary put her hand out to Harry for the telegram. He took it out of his pocket and passed it over to her. He was shaking as he handed it her.

"He may be injured luv", not knowing which of his boys names was on the telegram.

Leonard and Bernard came running into the kitchen at that moment, David fell over the mat almost knocking all three of them over. He got up and kicked Len and dead legged him. Mary was too involved in the telegram, she shook her head in disgust.

"Mom, mom, mom they all said together"

"Sit down boys and call Nancy back down the stairs, we might as well get this over with as a family, I'll talk to Elsie and young Mary afterwards."

Mary sat down on her ladies Victorian rocking chair, leaned over and knocked the lock off, she felt better rocking to and fro. Nancy came down into the kitchen without Charles. She stood in front of her mother. She stopped rocking in her chair, Nancy sat down on the arm of the chair, Mary put her arms around her and comforted her.

"Have you said anything to the girls" Mary asked Nancy.

"No I haven't, honest mom, I haven't",

Nancy was shaking her head guiltily, as if she had something to hide. She looked over at Bernard for reassurance.

The girls had realised something was wrong and squeezed it out of her. Young Mary was now sitting at the bottom of the stairs too afraid to come into the kitchen in case the telegram was about Joe.

Mary was just about to speak to the family when the kitchen door opened and Dolly walked in, she went over to her mother and gently kissed her on the cheek, then perched herself on the bench opposite the boys. She had already spoken to Leonard outside.

"Shall I fetch young Mary down" Dolly asked?

"After we", Mary paused for a moment, "No not now, later when we know what the telegram entails", Mary said coyly looking around at her family.

It had all been too much for Mary, she began to cry gently at first and broke down sobbing into her apron. Nancy gave her an handkerchief. She could feel the baby moving and stroked her stomach. She knew the stress was causing problems with the baby, she had been uncomfortable ever since Elsie first went into labour. Nancy looked lovingly at her mother begging for reassurance. She wiped a tear from her mother's cheek with her middle finger and buried her head deep into Mary's shoulder again.

Leonard put the kettle onto the range and sat down on the bench opposite Dolly, pushing Bernard up the bench at the same time, David shuffled up and almost fell off the end. He gave Len a filthy look and pushed himself back onto the bench, kicking Bernard at the same time, who promptly kicked him back harder.

Mary saw everything and blew up at David.

"For God sake, can't you behave for one second, I'll kill you, if!", She stopped and stared down at the telegram too afraid to open it.

Harry walked across to David and slapped him across the ear hole. David put his hand up onto his ear, but didn't dare move, he lowered his eyes too afraid to be insolent to his father. He knew he'd gone too far, again. His father was man in this house and no one argued with him, expect Mary, of course.

"Shall I open it mom", Bernard asked, looking up at his father and then over at Len and David, daring them to utter a word.

He got up and walked over to his mother and put his hand out trying desperately to be brave. He kissed her on the cheek very gently. Mary gave the telegram to him and turned away burying her head in Nancy's arm, waiting for the shock of what she was about to hear, about one of her beloved sons.

Harry turned and walked over to Mary, lovingly putting his arm around her shoulder. He knelt down beside her, despite the pain he felt in his leg as he kneeled. Nancy looked at her father and smiled. He touched her young face tenderly and bit his lip to stop him from breaking down.

"It'll be alright daddy, Joe and Sam are too stubborn to! Oh! What am I saying", Nancy broke down in tears.

Mary patted her and tried to console her daughter, who was now distraught. Dolly stood up and went over to her and held her hand, looked into her face sympathetically and wiped her tears away. Dolly knelt by her side and then patted her lap, Nancy sat on her lap and cuddled up to your big sister like a little child.

Bernard opened the telegram and sat himself back on the bench, pushing the other two again. He felt somewhat safer with his younger brothers, despite them always fighting over one thing or another. Leonard tried to read the telegram over Bernard's shoulder, he turned sharply and gave Len a dirty look.

"It's our Joe, he's!", he never finished the sentence.

Mary jumped up, keeled over and fell onto the floor. Harry, Dolly and Nancy jumped up at the same time. Dolly tried to lift her mother up off the floor and young Mary came running into the kitchen. She stood looking at the pandemonium on the floor.

Harry stood over Mary and asked her what he should do. He was hopeless when it came to childbirth.

"My waters have broken, Harry", she looked up at him sadly, not knowing what else to say.

Nancy quickly jumped into action, fetched a towel out of the airing cupboard, order Dolly to go upstairs and fetch a sheet to cover her mother.

The lads stood up off the bench all together and rallied round as their father gave them instructions as to what to do.

Mary shouted to Bernard, who was about to go upstairs to sort the other bed out for his mother. He turned around and looked down at the telegram and then at his mother.

"Tell me, what about our Joe" she clung to Harry's hand, waiting for the bombshell.

Young Mary was being awfully brave, she stood staring over at Bernard, waiting for the dreadful news to be announced. Len put his arm around her and held her gently.

"He's been injured mom, he's coming home", Bernard jumped up and down and the lads shouted "Thank God" all at the same time. Len kissed young Mary and hugged her, lifting her off her feet and swinging her around. He put her down too quickly, they lost their balance and fell on top of each other. Young Mary, jumped up, took a deep breath, smiled and jumped up and down with the boys, completely forgetting about Mary on the floor.

Mary grabbed her stomach and screamed.

"Oh! My God, please, please, not now, ooooooooooh".

There was now a pool of blood and watery liquid on the floor, Mary's dress and apron were sodden. Nancy quickly put the towel over the stain and proceeded to clean the mess off the floor. Harry looked down at his wife and gently lifted Mary up into his arms, she put her hands around his neck and buried her head in his shoulder. Bernard held the door open for his father whilst he carried her up the stairs. Nancy ran up in front of him. It took all of his strength, as Harry climbed the stairs cautiously one at a time, afraid he would fall and drop Mary. His leg had been dreadfully painful the past few months, with the constant downpours of rain and winter setting in. He didn't want Mary to worry, each step was shear agony for him, as he climbed the stairs he counted them in his head, so that he did not miss his footing. He leaned against the landing wall at the top of the stairs and looked down. He was relieved he had made the climb. 'Only a few more steps' he thought to himself. He kissed Mary and took her into the bedroom.

Harry gently placed his wife onto the bed, Nancy assisted her mother in changing and helped to wash her, then covered her up, carefully folding the top of the sheet back. She tucked the sides under, as her mother had taught her. She looked around the bed to make sure that the ends were all tucked under correctly. Mary smiled at how meticulous her daughter had become and how proud she was of her.

The boys waited eagerly downstairs, whilst Nancy washed and changed their mother, they came bounding into the bedroom, like two bull elephants, then came to an abrupt standstill at the bottom of the bed. Nancy gave them an evil look. They were both frightened and concerned about their mother, they stood awaiting instructions like soldiers' on the parade ground. Nancy came around the bed and held onto David's hand, she had forgiven him immediately for his stupidity. She smiled at Len, he put his arm around her shoulder and hugged her gently.

Elsie heard all the commotion from the other room and got up from her sick bed, walked very slowly in to see her mother, who promptly told her to get back into bed, or she'd bleed too much, getting up so early. Elsie stood looking at her mother, whom she loved more than life itself.

"Charles has suckled off me mom for ages, I feel a little stronger now, the bleeding has slowed down. What can I do?" she said bravely.

Elsie sat onto the old oak nursing chair and held her mother's hands, too afraid to tell her how weak and lethargic she felt. She patted her hands, as she had patted hers, just a short while ago. Elsie looked at her mother's worn out hands and then up at her face and smiled.

"Well, well, your turn now mom",

Elsie grinned as she wiped her mother's brow with a damp flannel.

"Joe's coming home, where's young Mary", Mary said happily.

"She's making a cuppa", Harry said reassuringly.

"I'll go down and have a word with her as soon as I know you're comfortable, my angel, never been very good in this department. Only good at sewing the seed, so to speak, besides with your girls and boys handy what good is an old cripple like me going to be".

Harry winked at Mary, kissed her tenderly on her lips and, proceeded to walk out of the bedroom.

"You coward, Harry Price", she screamed as her next contraction started. Harry turned to look at his wife and took a long deep sigh.

"Best get things organised downstairs, this is woman's work" he said worriedly, as he disappeared through the door.

As he stepped over the top step, he tripped on a rugged piece of carpet, his knee gave way and he slipped down the whole length of the stairs on his back. Young Mary had just opened the door at the bottom of the stairs and he came to an abrupt end on top of her. They both landed in a heap on the kitchen floor, the tray with the tea pot and cups and saucers flew in the opposite direction thankfully.

Leonard and Bernard came running down stairs, picked their dad up together, then carried him over to his chair by the fire.

Young Mary got up, dusted herself off. She looked down at the broken china and was glad she only used the day-to-day cups, rather than the best Royal Albert fine bone china. Luckily, the tea pot was enamel, it came out of the fall unscathed. She mopped the tea off the floor and proceeded to make yet another cuppa for her mother and father in law.

"Don't tell your mother, do you hear me", Harry shouted at the boys, pointing his finger at then scornfully, as if it was all their fault.

He looked down at his twisted leg and grabbed his knee. The pain was unbearable. He realised instantly that his knee was dislocated and grabbed Bernard's arm.

"You'll have to fetch the doctor, both for me and your mother. Go tack the grey up and be quick about it".

Bernard was out of the kitchen and over to the barn within seconds, tacked up and gone.

Leonard asked his father if he could help.

"Well you can fetch my stick from my bedroom first, Len", he said.

Len ran up the stairs and into his parents bedroom, he looked to see whether Elsie was in bed. He saw the stick, darted over to the bed, picked it up and ran back down the stairs to his father.

Mary screamed out again. Harry put his hands over his ears and rocked to and fro, trying to take the pain in his leg.

Dolly came running down the stairs, threw the door open and stood in front of her father with her hands on her hips scowling.

"Mother's struggling with the birth, I don't know what to do", she stamped her foot and looked about her. She finally sat down on the rocking chair and rocked to and fro noisily patting her lap and staring blankly into the fire. Harry just looked at her in disgrace. He shook his head from side to side.

Young Mary went over to Harry and gave him his cuppa and patted him on the shoulder. She too could not believe how Dolly was behaving, unable to contain her emotions for a moment longer she put her foot down firmly on the rocker, Dolly jumped up and stormed over the other side of the kitchen and continued to tap her fingers on the work surface.

Young Mary gave Dolly a look of contempt and went back over to Harry.

"I think it might help if I put a poultice on that knee, dad. I've boiled the kettle, there's enough bread and milk for later, if I have to make another one after the doctor's been. Mother swears on milk and bread poultices for breaks and bruises, she also uses whisky and goose grease, but we have none, so for now, I'll just make do with what we have available. Doc may not want to be bothered with old fashioned remedies, so we best wait till he's gone, before I administer my witch's secret components". Harry agreed with her.

She pored the boiling water over the towel and left it in the bowl for a little while, she untied his laces, took his socks off, then pulled his boot, nearly falling into the fire, as it came off into her hands. She quickly rolled his trousers up over his knee and stared at his badly scared leg and injured knee. It was the first time she had ever seen his injuries.

She looked up at Harry gently smiling trying to hide her shock, he smiled reassuringly back and, then turned to look into the fire. Mary pulled at his leg as hard as she was able and turned it at the same time, he winched with the pain and grabbed hold of the sides of the chair. He wanted to shout out and swear, but he withheld all his emotions. It took all his strength to remain comparatively calm. He pulled his handkerchief from his waistcoat and wiped his forehead and popped it back into his pocket.

"Well dad I think your knee is straighter than it was. Please, try to keep your leg like this until the doctor comes, he'll probably twist it again, but I believe it's not too far out of line now" Young Mary kissed him on his sweaty forehead.

She looked down at the kindling lying on the hearth and picked up a straight piece of dried wood, then wrapped the hot towel around Harry's injured knee tightly, putting the stick into the towel close to the leg. She ran over to the kitchen drawer and took out a cotton tea towel and ripped it in half and then tied it together. She pulled it tight, checking it would not come apart, then she looked at the length. Confident it was long enough she returned to where Harry was still seated. She tied the tea towel around the wooden splint tightly. Standing back and looking at her handiwork she tapped Harry gently on the arm.

'That'll manage until the doctor arrives', she said to herself.

Harry hardly noticed how hot the towel was, the pain was too extreme, he tried desperately not to show his pain. He continued looking into the fire and, tried to think of other things.

Young Mary held Harry's injured leg rigid, too afraid to let go, she wanted to keep it stretched out exactly as it was until the doctor arrived. She looked about the kitchen for a stool.

"Could you pass me the foot stool Dolly, please" she said angrily, too frustrated to be nice.

Dolly stood up and dragged the footstool over to her father and promptly went back to the other side of the kitchen. Mary shouted at her and asked her to put a cushion onto the stool, like immediately and not tomorrow. Dolly stamped across the kitchen again and threw the cushion onto the stool and stormed out of the kitchen. Young Mary pushed the stool nearer with her foot and gently lifted Harry's injured leg gingerly onto the stool. She turned and gave Dolly the filthiest of looks, who had decided to come back into the kitchen and annoy everyone again. She turned to face Harry again.

"Right, now don't move dad please, stay like this until the doctor arrives, otherwise you might end up with even more complications. Don't want that do we? I think the knee is quite straight now, the heat should help a little, and I've got my fingers crossed that the splint should hold your leg straight, but I can't be sure. I've seen father do it with an injured lamb once and, it did recover for a while".

Harry looked lovingly at her awaiting the rest of the tale.

Mary looked down at him wondering what Harry's bemused look was for and realised.

"Oh! " she smiled tenderly at Harry and continued with her story

"We ate it later that year, it tasted lovely". Young Mary licked her lips and giggled.

Harry roared with laughter and whacked young Mary on the bottom.

Young Mary reassured Harry and, more importantly herself, that her handiwork should work, and in fact should be beneficial.

Harry looked up at her teasingly;

"You've already given me the instructions about not moving once Mary",

She looked down at him not knowing what to say.

"Lost your tongue now have you, young lady" Harry said jokingly.

Panic over, she was now on the verge of bursting into tears. All she wanted to do was sit on his lap and cuddle up to him and fall asleep in his strong arms, like she had done throughout her childhood. Harry had been her second father, she had spent more time at the Price's, than at home and hated seeing him in so much pain.

Harry could see how distraught she was.

"Our Joe is going to have to watch out when he comes home, aye! You're a bossy little madam, aren't you?"

Harry held her hand, patting it with his other hand, he smiled at young Mary, trying desperately not to show her how worried he was for the welfare of his eldest son. After all, he had witnessed the carnage of this damn war first hand, he knew that Joe must be badly injured to be shipped back home to England.

Mary realised she was trembling and quickly put her hands by her side. She looked around her, wanting to run away and hide, far away from this terrible place, but knew she had other duties awaiting her upstairs. She composed herself, messed with her apron and tried to look positive.

"Well suppose I'd better go up there and see what I can do, two babies in one day", she said smiling.

Young Mary, opened the door at the bottom of the stairs, taking a last look over at Harry, she climbed up the first step turned and closed the door quietly, then sat down on the second step. It was all too much for her, she started to cry. Only now had she allowed herself to finally let go.

'Oh! My darling, you're coming home to me', she cried into her clenched fists, as she rocked backwards and forwards.

"Please God, let my Joe be in one piece and not torn apart like!"

She looked up the stairs to the bedroom and took a big deep breath.

'I cant think about it now', she muttered under her breath,

'Elsie needs me'.

Young Mary wiped her eyes on her apron, stood up and climbed the stairs very slowly, ready to face her next challenge.

'I'll not think of it, I'll not', she said defiantly to herself.

CHAPTER 20

As young Mary walked into the bedroom, she could see Elsie standing at the bottom of her mother's bed holding onto the brass bedstead in a pool of blood. Elsie shook her head at her friend and looked back over at her mother, who was now deep into labour and, obviously very distressed. Blood was poring down Elsie's legs onto her feet and then the floor.

David walked over to Elsie staring at the pool of blood, he tugged at her dressing gown, then pointed down at the blood. He looked up into her eyes beckoning her to speak.

She looked down at David shaking her head in despair, her secret was out, in shear frustration she smacked him around the head and immediately felt sorry for taking it out on him.

"You've always got to open your bloody big gob, our David", she blurted out.

David grabbed his injured ear and plonked himself down on the chair sulking.

"Bloody fed up of being smacked today",

He pouted and looked up at Elsie, who was now feeling extremely sorry for lashing out at him.

'What did I say wrong'

He muttered to himself, without looking up at his sister and not being able to take his eyes off the blood on the floor. He gritted his teeth in defiance and stamped his feet on the bedroom floor almost falling over backwards on the chair.

Elsie looked down at David again and then over to her mother. She apologised to them both.

"I'm not going to be able to stay mom, I'm afraid I'm going to be sick",

She looked to young Mary for moral support and turned, away sadly. David jumped up and tucked his head under Elsie's arm, he had forgotten his boxed ear, and would not let go of her, they squeezed through the bedroom door together. Elsie looked down at him fondly and kissed his head and also apologised for hitting him so hard. David looked up at her with tears in his eyes;

"You can hit me any time sis", he said proudly.

Elsie dropped down on the side of the bed. She was exhausted and white as a sheet. She could hardly speak and knew she was on the border of passing out. She held onto David's arm swaying as she spoke.

"Go downstairs and see if you can find two thick heavy pieces of wood and put them under the end of the bed to lift it up to tilt it, please", she said to Leonard, who had followed them into the bedroom. He too loved Elsie dearly and was concerned at the loss of blood and how ill his big sister looked.

David and Leonard both clambered down the stairs, looking at their father as they ran out of the kitchen. They came clambering back into the kitchen, with the wood, Harry asked them what on earth they were doing making so much bloody noise.

Leonard quickly explained what was happening to Elsie. Harry quickly gave them orders.

"Right, after you've tilted the bed, lie Elsie back and put a pillow under her bottom".

The lads looked at each other blankly.

"You must get the bottom of her body as high as you can to stop the bleeding. Take some towels upstairs with you and bed linen".

They nodded in unison

" Do you both understand what you have to do?"

"Yes father, we do understand". Leonard patted David and pointed to the stairs.

Harry was besides himself, he desperately tried to lift himself up out off the chair, but sat down with a thump.

"Bloody leg", he thumped his upper leg and instantly regretted it. Pain shot down his leg. He grimaced, straightened his leg with extreme care and put his leg back onto the foot stool.

The lads looked down at his heavily padded knee, then asked if there was anything they could do for him, after they had finished upstairs. Harry shook his head.

David and Len ran upstairs pushing and shoving each other, each trying to be first into the bedroom. Len almost fell down the stairs as he turned left to look in on his mother first. He kicked David on the shin.

"Get out of my way, you idiot", he ranted.

Len popped his head through the door, and pushed David out of the way. He looked at young Mary and Nancy, who were now sitting with his mother, reassuring her that everything would be alright. Nancy waved at him light heartedly, he turned, shut the door and went into Elsie.

David was now sitting on the bed next to his big sister, eagerly awaiting Leonard's return and his instructions. He promptly dropped the dirty wood onto the white sheet. Len hissed at him and he picked it up moments before he got yet another slap around the ear~hole.

The boys helped Elsie into the nursing chair, went back over to the bed, lifted it up, David couldn't hold the weight and dropped his side to Len's annoyance. Eventually after several attempts they both managed to place the wooden blocks under the two legs at the bottom of the bed. Len stood back from the bed, stared in disbelief, then went over to David and punched him in the stomach.

"You silly sod, that block isn't the same as mine", he continued to shout at him.

David, pushed him back and Len almost fell over Elsie.

"I'm bloody sick of everyone having a go at me today, it's your's that's not as big as mine" he scorned.

Elsie smiled at David, patted the chair she was sat on and, David stamped over to her, sulking again, he punched his upper leg then sat down by her on the floor, resting his head carefully on her knee, avoiding her blood stained nightie. He thought twice about where he was resting his head and moved over to the other side of the chair. He leant against the nursing chair trying hard not to offend Elsie.

The bed was obviously unsafe with the uneven blocks, so Len kicked the wood out from under the end of the bed and came back over to Elsie. He looked at the two pieces of wood, lifted them up looking at them carefully, trying to decide which one would be most suitable for the job.

"It'll be alright sis, I promise, better take both with me so that I get it right this time", he said juggling the wood about.

David held his sister's hand and looked up at her lovingly.

"Sorry I never get anything right" he said worryingly.

Leonard rushed back downstairs, he sounded like a wide elephant as he clambered down the steps. Harry just gave him a harsh look as he shoved the door open and jumped down onto the flagstone floor. He shrugged his shoulders and ran over to the barn to get two blocks of wood the same size. He picked about 10 pieces up before he finally got two the same. He looked at the barn floor which was now littered with the wood offcuts. He muttered to himself.

' I'd better come over afterwards and pick up this mess, otherwise it will be me who gets the boxed ear. Can't blame our David for this bloody carnage'.

He turned and darted back into the kitchen, fell over the mat and the wooden blocks went flying over the kitchen floor. He stood up, looked down at his grazed knees, knocking the dust off them, then he stared across at Dolly in disbelief. They had never got on, he basically couldn't stand the site of her.

'Waste of bloody time you are', he muttered to himself.

He gathered the wooden blocks up, looked back over at his father, who was also shaking his head at Dolly. He then ran over to the stair door, nodded at his father, then ran back up the stairs.

Harry looked at the door at the bottom of the stairs, then lifted himself up slightly, got his pipe and lighter out of his pocket, then lit his beloved pipe. He patted the tobacco down with his finger and burnt it. He shook his hand and then sucked his finger and blew on it.

"Bugger, he said angrily, absolutely nothing is going right for me today". He popped his finger into his mouth again, then sucked it in between smoking his pipe. Harry looked at his finger a large blister had now appeared.

Dolly was still rocking on her mother's chair with her head in her hands. Phyliss had come in from playing and sat by the side of her father looking up at him not knowing what to say or do. She jumped up and kissed his finger gently. Harry couldn't help but feel sorry for her. He patted her on the head and she sat down again by his side.

"Dolly, put the kettle on and get the bowl, scissors, towels and twine, ready for the birth, like now, please and put the boiler on for the soiled sheets".

Harry could have strangled her, if only he was able to get over to her to do the task. Phyliss stood up eager to assist her big sister.

"I shouldn't have to ask you to do these jobs" he said angrily.

She got up, casually walked over to the sink, without a care in the world, filled the kettle, put some wood into the range and sat down again waiting for the kettle to boil.

Harry was fuming. Dolly daren't even look at her father, she knew she had pushed him too far. Leg or no leg, if she even looked at him defiantly he would be out of the chair and over the kitchen in a flash. She lowered her eyes and tried to busy herself with the boiler and clean bed linen.

Meantime upstairs, the boys managed to tilt the bed evenly. Len stood and looked at the bed, nodded at David and, then over at Elsie, who was bent over like a little old women, barely able to move. Both of her lower legs were now covered in blood.

He turned around and looked out of the window, tapping his fingers softly on the pain of glass. Len turned and smiled at his big sister.

"Elsie could you just sit there for a little while longer, can't have you lying in that can we",

He tried to make light of the situation, but deep down he was afraid Elsie would bleed to death.

David pulled over another chair, took her hand in his. He looked down at his sister's hand and measured it against his. Elsie looked at him lovingly and then over at the door where Len was standing. She wanted to get back into bed and knew if it wasn't soon she would be flat on the floor unconscious.

Leonard felt sick, he couldn't stand the sight of blood, he turned his head the other way trying hard not to wrench and throw up. David couldn't even look at Elsie's face, he just looked down at the floor staring at the rag rug they had all made.

Elsie nudged David and pointed over to the blanket box.

"Over there in that box".

Len was first to go over to the blanket box across the bedroom. He pulled out two white sheets, a bolster case and two pillow slips. Len shouted into his sister in the other bedroom.

Nancy came running in and protested instantly that her mother needed her at this moment. She then realised that Elsie needed her as well.

"Won't take me long to sort you out Elsie, then it's back to mother I'm afraid".

Nancy quickly washed and changed Elsie, whilst the boys changed the bedclothes. All three of them very carefully put Elsie back into the tilted bed.

Nancy rolled the soiled linen into a ball and threw it down the stairs for soaking and washing later, with all the other dirty linen accumulated during the day, which was piled up in the kitchen. She stared down at the soiled sheets, wondering when she would be able to put them into the boiler. It was raining again and there was already a load hanging on the line in the barn, waiting to come into the kitchen by the fire, later that night. She came back to earth when Len spoke to Elsie.

"Dad said to put a pillow under your bum", he averted David's eyes.

"Elsie, lift your bum up, please" Leonard carefully assisted his sister up and shuffled her up the bed, he patted the pillow under her backside and stroked her forehead.

"Well is there anything more you want My Lady", he said jokingly.

David bowed and waved his hand in the air.

"At your service also Madam", he jested.

Elsie was too ill to notice, or in fact answer her brothers. Len knew how poorly she was and sent Nancy downstairs to get a flannel soaked in cold water to place onto her forehead. He realised she had a fever. He stood looking at her from the bottom of the bed, but didn't know whether to pull the bedclothes back off her, to bring her temperature down. He pondered for a few more moments, then thought twice about it, he left her with a little dignity. He tucked her into bed like a small child. The roles were now reversed somewhat, it had always been Elsie who had tucked Len in over the years.

He placed the flannel onto her forehead and wiped the sweat away. He went over to the washstand and pored water into the bowl, then placed the flannel back into the cold water and squeezed the flannel out into the Victorian flow blue bowl. He then folded it and placed it back onto Elsie's head.

Leonard was composed and totally in charge now, he sent Nancy back into the other room and ordered David to stay by Elsie's side in case there was any change.

David knew better than move. He took his shoes and jumper off, lay on the bed beside Elsie, patted the pillows and, promptly went to sleep on top of the bedclothes.

Elsie smiled and shortly followed him and fell asleep cuddled up to her favourite little brother.

Nancy sat with her mother, becoming increasingly concerned

about the impending birth. She went out of the bedroom seeking Len, he was sorting the soiled linen out at the bottom of the stairs. She crept down the stairs and whispered to him and asked him to come back into the bedroom with her because she thought the birth might become too complicated. Her voice was quivering, she was so afraid, he could see it in her young eyes. He didn't want to go into the room with his mother either and tried to wriggle out of it.

Nancy pleaded with him and pulled at his jumper

"Please Len, I am so afraid, this is not a normal birth. There is something not quite right, I know it". She sat on the stairs and hid her head in in hands.

He reluctantly went back upstairs and into his mother's bedroom. He sat down on the nursing chair and held her hand. She smiled at him and asked him to fetch young Mary, who was downstairs with Harry.

He was so relieved, he jumped up, opened the bedroom door, slamming it as he went out of the bedroom. He almost fell down the stairs like his father and managed to stop himself falling by grabbing the stair rail. He looked down at the ragged piece of carpet below his foot and kicked it, swearing out loud, he turned around suspiciously in case someone was behind him. He sighed to himself, relieved no one was there. His father had warned him on several occasions that he would wash his mouth out with carbolic soap, if he caught him swearing again.

Young Mary brought the boiling water and towels up to the bedroom and put them down on the marble topped washstand. Len popped the small basket containing other items for the birth next to the bowl.

Mary felt something was wrong and asked young Mary to have a look to see what was happening. Len stood over by the door looking for an excuse to retreat downstairs to the kitchen with his father, but knew better than leave without consent. He tapped his leg eagerly awaiting his exit.

"I can't see anything", young Mary said cautiously, as she forced Mary to open her legs wider.

"Oh! Hang on a minute, I can see the babies head", she

wiped her forehead on the sheet and took a deep breath, it was stifling in the bedroom with the open fire blazing, she was so tired after being up with Elsie and now Mary for over 28 hours none stop.

Mary screamed and pushed at the same time, which startled Young Mary, it made her jump, causing her to fall backwards over the rug at the bottom of the bed. She very quickly gathered herself up and lifted the sheet again, peering between Mary's legs she gasped.

"Oh dear, dear! dear! the cord is wrapped around the babies neck".

Young Mary gasped and stood with her hands to her mouth not knowing what to do, desperately she looked to Mary for help.

"Oh! Mother the baby is blue, oh! Dear me, I don't think he's breathing", young Mary instinctively held the baby‘s head supporting it.

There was no one else who could take over, she realised how important it was to remain as calm as possible. She looked over at Nancy and smiled gently then at Leonard and finally back at Mary. She knew she had to be brave for everyone's sake, she looked down pitifully at child.

Mary punched the bed with both her fists, she was unable to move for fear of causing more damage to the child, then she spoke to Leonard.

"We don't have much time son. Both of you do exactly as you are told, otherwise this little sole will die, do you hear me", she was distraught and unable to help in any way, other than verbally.

"Len, you hold the babies head. Mary, try to get the cord from around the babies neck. We don't have much time".

Young Mary tried to take the cord from around the babies neck, but it was solid. The child was now blue and lifeless.

"Nancy, you try, your hands are so much smaller than Mary's", she said waving at her daughter to move quickly to the bottom of the bed.

"Ok mother", Nancy sprinted across the bedroom and

wiggled in between Len and Young Mary. Nancy tried to take the cord from around the babies neck, but to no avail.

"Oh! Mother, it seems to be tighter now than when I first tried to move it". She looked up to her mother for reassurance.

"We'll just have to cut the cord if you can't get it from around the neck, is everything ready, she looked up at the ceiling ~ Oh! Wait a minute. I remember something I saw when I was present during my friend Ann's delivery. Nancy you be ready with the scissors and twine". Nancy looked at Len and then at young Mary and smiled, she felt totally inadequate. She had doubts now of becoming a midwife, she felt absolutely useless.

Mary threw off the bedclothes and lay there with her nightie up over her tummy. Leonard looked down at his mother's swollen stomach. He couldn't take his eyes off her. He had never seen a naked women before, let alone his own mother.

"Right Len, are you listening to me", she said sternly. He nodded without taking his eyes off her naked body.

"Gently flex the babies head back against my thigh. When my next contraction comes keep the baby against my thigh, do not release your grip and hopefully the baby will somersault out". Len stared in awe at the child coming out of his mother's vagina. He could not take his eyes off her dark mass of public hair.

"Did you get all that Leonard", Mary shouted to him. Len nodded and tried to remember what she had said to him only moments before.

Mary could feel another contraction coming on.

"You ready Len" she shouted gritting her teeth.

He looked up at his mother, nodded, still unable to take his eyes off her private parts.

"Young Mary, you get ready now for when the baby turns, ok".

She too nodded. Len, Nancy and young Mary all looked at each other together, they all nodded simultaneously.

Mary pushed with all her might, she screamed out, "Oh! Dear God".

Len kept the babies head pushed up against his mother's thigh, as he'd been ordered. He was petrified and turned his head away, biting down hard on his lip.

"Please, please God, let this little one be ok", he said out loudly.

The baby somersaulted exactly as Mary had predicted, but almost fell onto the floor, if young Mary hadn't jumped to the rescue. The head was now up by Mary's perineum, the body and legs were resting in young Mary's arms.

"What now, mother" Len asked, as he held the babies head, shaking like a leaf. Young Mary moved over slightly giving Len full control of the baby.

No longer did he stare at his mother's tummy and bloody pubic hairs. His attention was now on the swollen and bloody fanny, with the multi-coloured cord hanging down between her legs and onto the bed. He couldn't believe a baby could come out of such a small hole.

He had fondled and put his hands down Agnes's and Polly's knickers, behind the toilets, but this. All the tales that he had heard at school, about a women's private parts and, how beautiful they were to touch, seemed ridiculous, nothing had prepared him for this. He literally shuddered at the thought of how he could caress, or make love to any woman in the future.

Mary shouted at him and he immediately came back to earth.

He looked down at the lifeless child now in his shaking hands. Mary was now bleeding profusely. Len looked at young Mary sadly begging her to step in and do something. He then lifted his eyes and looked at his mother not knowing what to do.

Nancy took over and cut, then tied the cord off. She had seen her mother and midwives do this many times during various births around the village. She stood for a moment in case she had forgotten something and went through the procedure in her head. She was quite satisfied and nodded to herself.

The baby was blue and not breathing. Young Mary took

the child off Len and placed it onto the bed tenderly, ran across the bedroom for another towel and promptly put it between Mary's legs to stem the bleed.

"Mother close your legs tightly onto the towel", please she said.

Mary lifted herself up looking down at the lifeless child. Mary shook her head with despair.

"I've never lost a baby yet and I'm certainly not going to lose this one", she shouted adamantly.

"Hold him up by his feet Len, over the bed, in case you drop him. Now smack his bottom as hard as you can". She ordered.

Len looked at his mother, then at the child, who was long and lifeless, and reminded Len of a skinned rabbit. He shut his eyes, lifted the child as high as he could, then whacked the babies bottom as hard as he could, as he had been ordered to do by his mother. No sound came out of the babies mouth. He shook him from side to side, in the hope that something might happen, this he had seen his father do when they had problems with stillborn pups. Tears were beginning to fall down his young face.

"Bring the child to me", Mary shouted.

Len passed the baby to his mother.

"It's a little boy", he said pointing to his little penis.

"Not got time for what gender it is Len, got to do something, or else!" She paused for a moment and looked up at her son, unable to go any further with sentence.

Mary turned the child onto his stomach and lifted his head up and proceeded to put her little finger into his mouth, she gently turned him over and breathed into his little mouth, which was now dark blue. Again, she moved her finger around inside his mouth. She wrenched herself and felt physically sick thinking of what she was doing to your son. Black mucous came out of his mouth and onto the sheet, she thought he'd moved slightly. She looked back at Len, who hadn't taken his eyes of her for a moment.

"Len, this time hit him harder, it's life or death son, do

you hear me? If you don't get this right he'll suffer from hypoxia".

Len didn't really no what that meant but, nevertheless, he did exactly what his mother had ordered him to do. He held him high above his shoulder, even higher this time, holding his little feet quite firmly, then he whacked him as hard as he could straight across his buttocks. The baby squealed, he sounded like a new born piglet, the shock caused Len to almost drop him again. Red and blue weal marks were now showing across the child's bottom. Len looked at them and was shocked at how quickly they had appeared. He felt ashamed and terribly upset at the sight of the marks.

Len passed the infant to his mother, who promptly put him to her breast. The baby started to suckle on her nipple, then threw up instantly a load of black mucous all over her nightie. She looked at Nancy.

"Sorry luv, another thing for you to wash".

Nancy came to the side of the bed and looked at her new brother.

"He's a fighter mom, isn't he, aye" she said proudly.

"Get me a blanket Len, we must keep him warm. He's very small, only 3-4lbs in weight, I think. She was cleaning the child's face with the corner of the towel when she realised she was about to have another contraction.

"Oh! My God", she screamed as she brought her legs up and pushed again.

"I think there's two, she shouted at Len. Take him down stairs and ask your father to keep him by the fire and on his stomach, until the doctor gets here". She passed the child to Len.

He was a poor looking little sole, Len thought as he tenderly looked down at his new brother. He pulled the blanket around him tightly and carried him downstairs to his father carefully watching each step to avoid a fall.

Harry took the child off Leonard and lay him on his lap face down as instructed by Mary. He gently moved his uninjured leg up and down comforting the child, as he had done to all his other babies. The child threw up again, brown liquid trickled down his trouser leg.

"That's it young man, start as you mean to go on".

He smiled as he looked down at his soiled trousers, patting the child on his back at the same time.

"He's full of mucous dad, the cord was wrapped around his little neck and he's swallowed the shit from the birth". Len, just let it all out to his father.

"It looks like we're going to have another birth father, where is that bloody doctor."

Len looked over at the door willing Bernard and the doctor to walk through it. He stamped his foot in frustration.

Harry lifted the child into his arms and put him over his shoulder, he tried to stand again, but his leg gave way, he almost dropped the child, as the pain shot up his twisted leg. Len managed to stop him falling onto the floor and steadied him.

"Mother wouldn't be very happy if we killed him father after all the hard work we've just gone through to bring him back to life",

Len jested to his father.

"Shall I go and see what's going on father". He looked to his father for reassurance, turned and stared at Dolly in disgust. She got up from the chair and took Phyliss over to the barn. She never even spoke to her father or Len, just walked solemnly and slowly out of the kitchen, not offering, or asking if she could help in any way.

"Go upstairs and see how your mother is and, ask if you'll be needed before you go to find Bernard",

Harry patted his son on the shoulder.

"Good work lad, sure you don't want to be a doctor",

Len frowned at his father. He didn't want children after what he had witnessed that day. The vision of his mother lying helpless with her legs wide open, screaming, would live with him forever.

Len climbed the stairs again two at a time, however, this time he felt different somehow. He had become a man, from this day forward, I will be my own person, he thought confidently.

'If I can deliver a baby, I can do anything I want to do'

He walked into his mother's bedroom, with his head held high, until he saw another baby being born.

"It's ok son, this time the birth is quite normal", his mother smiled at him as the baby popped out into young Mary's loving hands.

"Three in a day mother, that will beat the "Guinness Book of Records", I do belief". Len said as he looked down at his newborn sister.

They all laughed together, relieved that the babies were now in the world of the living.

Young Mary went downstairs and popped the kettle on and put the soiled sheets to soak in the boiler. She went across the kitchen to have a look at the baby now sleeping on his father's lap.

"How's my Mary", he said crying, as he looked down at his newborn son.

"Well father, you now have a little girl, who is absolutely beautiful. Your wonderful wife is sitting up breast feeding the child".

She patted him on the shoulder and went over to the range enabling Harry to compose himself.

"Fancy a cuppa daddy", she said smiling back at him.

Leonard came down the stairs with the other little bundle and took her over to meet her father. Harry looked in disbelief at the twins.

"I've got the honour of naming my siblings", Len said proudly.

He gave Harry the little girl, then picked up his little brother.

"I hereby name you Bertram William Harry Price, Bertie for short, after uncle Bertie". He passed the child back to his father and picked his little sister up.

"And, you my little beauty, I name you, Joan Mary, after Joan of Arc and my dear mother, who in my opinion is a Saint".

He winked at his father, passed him the child and promptly went over to the pantry, bought a bottle of home brew over to the table and opened it, gave his father a glass, taking Bertie from him at the same time, to enable him to lift up the glass, Len gulped his wine down in one go, then burped. Harry burst out laughing.

"You deserve it son, I'm very proud of what you've achieved today, but don't make a habit of helping yourself to my home brew. This wine should be sipped and drunk very slowly, nurturing the flavour. It's an art, son". Harry looked lovingly at his son.

"Rather drink it down father, and have another one. It's wasting time sipping, don't you think?"

Harry looked at him smiling and wondering whether he was the culprit who stole his bottle of parsnip wine. He felt guilty instantly after what Len had just been through.

'No, it's not him, I know who it is. It's just proving it' he thought to himself.

"If I find out who took the other bottle of parsnip wine, which incidentally was for Christmas, they'll get my belt. That's a promise and not a threat".

Len, looked up at the bedroom, where David now slept and, smiled to himself. He started to talk to the baby, Len lifted his eyes very slowly, to see his fathers' face, in the hopes that this latest question would be forgotten.

Len lifted Bertie up into the air and smiled at him tenderly, kissed him on the forehead and, looked down at him lovingly.

"Well young man, suppose I'd best get used to having another little brother about. Hope you're not a nuisance like our David".

Len cradled him to his chest. He felt totally different about this little sole, he swore there and then, that he would look and, watch over him, for the rest of his natural life. The child looked back at him blankly. Len looked at the back door and then up at the ceiling, where his mother lay in her bed, he desperately tried not to cry, biting his lip until it hurt.

David came clambering down the stairs, walked through

the kitchen and promptly asked for a glass of home brew. He looked at his new siblings, not even bothering to pick them up or, ask there names, drank the parsnip wine down in one gulp, then burped. He licked his lips and looked around the kitchen to see if there was anything to eat.

Harry asked him if he'd taken the bottle of parsnip wine out of the pantry holding his gaze at his rebellious young son. David looked at his father and then at Len, daring him to say a word.

"How come, I'm always the guilty one, aye!" He gritted his teeth and stamped his foot for the umpteenth time today, but felt confident he was not going to get a boxed ear, because of his father's injured knee. Harry surprised him by laughing out loud.

"Well son, because there's no other person in this household, who is stupid enough, or brave enough, to steal from mother. This time young man, I'll let it go, but if you touch it again, it'll be my belt. Do I make myself quite clear? I know every bottle brewed and also what stock is in the pantry".

Harry pointed at the pantry and continued to stare at him.

David didn't push his luck, he screwed his mouth up and chewed at the side of his cheek, then sat down on the bench averting his father's glare.

'Phew that was a close shave!' He thought to himself, as he licked his lips. He felt a little tipsy after consuming almost half of the first bottle of wine in the barn earlier and the glass he'd just guzzled down. Len smiled at him, knowing exactly what was going through his cunning sly devious mind. He shook his head and wished he had a little of the Dutch courage his little brother portrayed when confronted.

'He would defy the Lord if he came down to earth and accused him'

Mary would often say.

On one particular occasion, she knew it was David who had

pierced a hole in the cork of her slow gin, which she had brewed for last Christmas. She stood over him and stared him in the eyes and he just stood there brazen as ever denying the fact that he had been in the barn collecting wood for the fire. She even smelt his breath and couldn't make up her mind whether or not he had been drinking. He just looked at her and said, 'it's a pear drop Len had given him'. Poor Len caught the belt that day. The boys never told tales on each other that was a sworn oath. Their differences were always sorted out behind the barn when mother was not about.

A few seconds later the doctor and Bernard came into the kitchen. The doctor looked over at Harry, who now had both children in his arms.

"We had problems with the birth of the boy. The cord was stuck around his neck and he wouldn't breath, at first". Leonard blurted out, taking him from his father, as he walked across the kitchen and over to Bernard

"How's Mary", the doctor asked, without responding to Leonard.

"Young Mary and Nancy are up there with her", Len retorted, still trying to attract the attention of the doctor.

"Well who do you want me to tend to first", the doctor said jokingly to Harry. He looked up at the bedroom above him.

"Elsie had a difficult birth doctor, she's lost a lot of blood" Harry explained to the doctor.

"Well suppose I'd best go and see what's going on", he said looking over at Harry who was still holding Joan.

The doctor climbed the stairs slowly, then stood on the landing looking left into the bedroom, where Mary lay. He twiddled with his moustache, then went right into Elsie's room first. The bleeding had now subsided and her colour had begun to return to normal. He stood at the side of the bed.

"Well young lady, I think it's total bed rest for you for a few weeks and, then only moderate duties for a month, or so. Do

I make myself quite clear. Keep the bed tilted for another day or so, ok?", Elsie nodded and smiled at the doctor.

"Now let's have a look at your son".

The doctor checked Charles over thoroughly and passed him back to Elsie.

"He may have a slight rupture Elsie, you'll have to put a penny on his naval and pop a bandage around his stomach for 7/10 days, that should stop it protruding. If that doesn't help, bring him back to me at the surgery. Ok, young lady? Also, pop some Sanfrazan onto his belly button, twice a day, it'll help the cord to dry up quicker".

He smiled at her gently and patted her on the shoulder.

He knew of Elsie's predicament and sympathized. There had been talk at the Surgery only a few days earlier. He had asked his staff to keep their gossip mongering until after they left work. He felt Elsie would be best far away from the whole bloody Monckton family. The doctor touched Charles gently with his middle finger, popping his curl off his face and out of his eyes. The baby jumped startled at the touch of the doctor and started to cry. Elsie gently rocked him to and fro.

"Hasn't he got a good head of hair Elsie?", he asked.

"I need to examine you Elsie, shall I pop Charles into the crib for a moment?" Elsie passed the baby to the doctor and he gently popped him into the pine crib.

He gently pressed her stomach and checked her internally. Elsie breathed in and looked up at the ceiling, too afraid to look at the doctor. She was so embarrassed.

"Well Elsie, what can I say to you that your mother hasn't already said. I'm quite happy with everything. You're a very lucky young lady to go through this on your own without the assistance of a doctor?"

He looked about the poorly furnished bedroom and shook his head. Elsie recognised the look on the doctor's face as he looked around the bedroom, she had to put up with this all the time from the neighbours.

"I wasn't on my own doctor, mother delivered Charles. That stupid midwife Gertie, is a complete and utter waste of time and space. She shouldn't be aloud within a 100 miles of a newborn".

Elsie found inner strength, she was defensive, where her mother was concerned. She looked back at the doctor clenching her fists, daring him to utter another word. The doctor realised he was stepping on thin ice and, really didn't want to upset her any more than she already was. She'd had a rough deal all around, he admired her young spirit.

He changed the subject.

"I understand your mother has produced twins today, a boy and girl. It's 12 now isn't it", he asked, as he looked at Elsie.

"12 it is doctor, and we're very proud of our large family, we are that!" she said.

"Thank you very much, doctor".

Elsie retorted with arrogance, realising the doctor's contempt at large families, in particular the Price clan. The doctor realised he'd gone too far and made a hasty retreat into Mary's room.

"Good day Elsie, you know where I am if you need me", He smiled turned and was gone.

Elsie punched the bed and shouted Nancy.

The doctor asked Nancy and young Mary to leave the bedroom before going over to examine Mary. Nancy didn't want to leave her mother, she could hear Elsie shouting her. Young Mary grabbed her hand and, almost dragged her out of the bedroom. Nancy muttered and cursed, as she stamped across the stairs into Elsie's room. She forgot her paddy instantly when she stopped and looked at Charles.

She picked him up and passed him to Elsie.

"I'll make you a drink and bring it back up when I've checked the twins".

She went out of the bedroom and put her ear against the door in her mother's bedroom.

"How are you Mrs Price", the doctor asked, very professionally.

Nancy shrugged and went downstairs muttering to herself.

The doctor checked Mary thoroughly, pressing her tummy and internally, which Mary thought was unnecessary. He ordered her to stay in bed for at least a week and then do only light duties for a month.

He looked into Mary's pale eyes and then at her gums.

"Your quite anaemic, Mary" he said worryingly, as he looked tenderly into those once beautiful green bright eyes.

Mary looked up at him, reading his thoughts, she assured him that she had no intention of doing anything at all for a while, other than feed her two babies and eat plenty of meat and vegetables. They both felt uncomfortable being in the bedroom alone.

The doctor smiled and looked at her coyly. He wanted to lift her up into his arms and whisk her away from this madhouse. He patted her hands gently, turned and walked across the bedroom, he took a final look at her, as he opened the bedroom door, and then closed it quietly. Mary finally broke down and cried bitterly into the starched rough sheet.

The doctor stood outside the bedroom door, he could hear Mary breaking her heart, he wanted to go back inside the bedroom and carry her away into a home full of modern conveniences and servants. He shut his eyes, fiddled with his tie and looked down at his wedding ring, as he turned to go down the stairs, he stumbled on the stair carpet.

'That bloody carpet has been like that for donkeys years' he thought to himself, looking down again at the threadbare runner.

The babies had been put into a drawer each and were now sleeping contentedly in front of the fire. The doctor looked down at the twins in disbelief. They had been put into two pine drawers, he looked around the kitchen and over at the 2 up and six under, chest of drawers, on the far side of the kitchen, which was now minus the two top drawers. He looked back down at the children.

Harry smiled proudly,

"Didn't expect two doc, had to improvise. I'll have to carve them new cribs, our Elsie will need ours for Charles for a while. Good job there're so tiny, they fit into the drawers, just fine. I'll get on to it as soon as I can stand?"

The doctor was not amused, he pulled a chair over to where Harry was seated and proceeded to examine his injured knee.

"Harry, let's have a look at that knee of yours",

The doctor took the poultice off and turned Harry's leg straight towards him. Harry put his hands onto the chair and gripped the cushion with both hands, trying hard not to shout out.

"Hospital for you Harry, I'm afraid you'll have to have that put back and supported by a brace for some considerable time. Do you still have your brace from the original injury?"

Harry nodded and pointed over to the pantry.

"Don't think it'll ever be any good to you. If I were you I'd have it took off and be done with it",

The doctor dropped his leg onto the cushion and stood up abruptly. Harry was still gritting his teeth and looked at the doctor in disgust, daring him to say another word. If Harry could have stood up he would have punched him right on the nose. He breathed deeply and responded to the doctor's suggestion.

"Well your not me are you doc? The legs stopping on, thank you very much". It took all Harry's strength and reserve not to punch him on the nose. Harry could feel the resentment and hate the doctor felt for him.

"Ok, it's your leg, not mine, which hospital do you want to go into, I'll arrange it as soon as I get back to the surgery. In the meantime, put your old brace on, at least it will give your leg some support. Can you organise the transport?", the doctor awaited a response from Harry, tapping his foot on the hearth, as he looked down at him.

"I'll have a word with Mary's uncle Bertie first, if you don't mind, doc", Harry replied.

"Do you want me to telephone him for you from my surgery

and have a word with him". He continued to tap his foot on the grate, knowing full well he was annoying Harry.

"Would that be possible please Dr Quinn, I'm unable to get to the telephone at the present" Harry said looking down at the doctor's tapping feet.

"Ok, Harry, have it your way. I'll see if I can get hold of him. The last I heard, he was working at Hollymoor Hospital in Birmingham. He's a very busy surgeon, you know?. Might be too busy to see you",

He looked down at Harry with contempt, as if he had just wiped shit off his shoe. He twiddled with his moustache and sniffed, took out his pipe and lit it, throwing the match deliberately short of the fire, Nancy jumped up and picked the lighted match up from by her father's leg and promptly popped it into the fire. She sat down on the brass fender stool and checked the babies. She popped her tongue out at the doctor, Harry shook his fist at her, but smiled at her at the same time. The doctor was looking the other way at the time. Her father continued his stern look, but Nancy was having none of it. Harry turned and spoke to the doctor.

"Thank you doctor, but if you don't mind, I'd prefer you kept your comments to yourself, the children have enough to worry about at the moment with Joe being injured and on his way home and not forgetting the birth of the twins. Uncle Bertie is family after all? I'm sure he will help us. Could you ask him to call and see Mary, she wants him to find out where our Joe will be hospitalised".

Harry looked up at the doctor and tried to smile, but it was very difficult. Joan started to cry and broke the silence.

The rivalry between the two men had been going on for over 20 years during which time they had crossed swords on numerous occasions.

Doctor Bern Quinn had been one of Mary's beaus, when she lived with her parents at the Manor house. He had loved her since childhood, it was all he ever wanted, to be married to Mary. He had made no secret of the way he felt.

He never understood why she preferred a stable hand, rather than be with him, wanting for nothing and living a life of luxury, in his family's retreat in the country.

Despite all the children and, years past, he still loved Mary deeply and would open his arms to her at a moments notice. His own marriage had been loveless, the children at home were spoilt brats. He slept in the spare room, unable to stand being in the same room as his wife. She had been having a sordid affair with his associate. It was the loudest whisper, but divorce was not an option. They lived together, for the sake of the family name. His eldest son had just been posted to the front line. At least with Lionel at home he had someone to talk to, but now there was nothing but an uncomfortable silence between him and his wife.

He looked over at Len and smiled.

He knew how bright Leonard was and his dreams for the future. He admired the lad and could not help but envy the bond Harry had with him and in fact all of his boys. He hated his own youngest son, he was lazy, arrogant and opted to hide behind his mother's apron strings, which ultimately kept him away from the battlefields. His wife had pulled a few strings with her influential father who owned a gun barrel manufacturing company.

He shouted goodbye to Mary, as he was about to leave, then turned and spoke to Harry, almost as an after thought.

"You'll have to see a Paediatrician with the boy, in case he's sustained brain damage, due to lack of oxygen to his brain during the birth. He doesn't seem to be responding as he should, Harry?" He didn't wait for a response and walked over to the back door. He closed the door abruptly behind him and walked over to his carriage.

Bernard followed him out of the house, he looked over to his father sadly as he walked out of the kitchen.

Bernard took the rug off Dr Quinn's horse and held the reins, patting the horse on the neck gently, whispering assurances to her. The doctor climbed up onto the buggy and yanked the reins off Bernard, who was staring into oblivion shocked at what he had heard the doctor say about Bertie. The doctor looked down at him and apologised for pulling the reins off him. He instantly felt guilty and sighed loudly.

Bernard turned and walked over to the barn slowly, shaking his head in disgust, kicking at the floor with hands firmly in his pockets. The grey gelding he had quickly put away, neighed and kicked at the stable door impatiently. Bernard forgot the doctor for a moment, who was still sitting on his buggy outside the cottage, he patted Murphy on the rump and took his saddle off. He popped it onto the stable door, he patted him on the nose and took his bridle and martingale off, then dropped the bit into a bucket of clean water. He fed the horse the sugar beet he had soaked earlier that day. The horse dribbled down his clean shirt. Bernard smiled and wiped it back onto Murphy's nose. He patted him on the neck and put his hay in the hay net, then sat down on a bale of straw, not wanting to go back into the kitchen. He started to cry and turned to face the back of the barn in case someone came in and saw him.

Dr Bern Quinn looked up at the bedroom, where Mary still lay in her bed, a tear rolled down his cheek. He quickly looked about him and wiped it away on his woollen glove.

'Oh! My Darling, why do you punish your body so!' He said, as he shook the reins and, slapped the gelding on his rump with his whip, he turned the carriage around, then put the horse into a fast trot immediately across the courtyard. The doctor turned around and had one last look at the bedroom window before disappearing around the corner.

Bernard watched him from the barn, he shook his head at the way he treated his horse.

Bernard muttered under his breath.

'Bloody idiot, people like that shouldn't be allowed to own such a beautiful piece of horseflesh".

Bernard felt angry and sensed his father's concern of the

possibility of Bertie being brain damaged. He thumped the bale of straw, he felt guilty and, wondered if he'd been quicker, whether Bertie would have been perfect, like Joan. He knew he would live with this guilt for the rest of his life.

Back in the house Harry looked down at Nancy as she poked the fire.

"Pass Bertie to me lass, please".

She jumped up quickly and dropped the poker almost burning herself on the foot.

"Be careful, Nancy don't want you immobilised. What would we do without you"? Harry smiled at his daughter and held out his hands waiting for the child.

He looked closely at Bertie, he hadn't responded to Nancy picking him up, or in fact to being passed over to him. There was no response whatsoever as Harry moved his fingers in front of his dormant eyes. He then moved his hand away from the child's head slightly, it immediately dropped backwards. The child made no attempt to stop his head from dropping. His little hands lifted slightly.

Nancy, Len, and young Mary, all waited nervously. Dolly turned her head as she put the kettle on.

"Pass me Joan please, Nancy",

He handed Bertie back to Len.

Len looked down sadly at the child, he rocked him tenderly in his arms, turning away from his father, as he openly started to cry.

"Whatever, Bertie, I'll always love you and look after you", Len whispered into his ear. He kissed him on the forehead and looked over at Nancy, wiping away the tears on the child's blanket. Nancy didn't speak to Leonard she just acknowledged the fear that poor Bertie was indeed brain damaged. Leonard bit his lip and looked up at his mother's bedroom, wondering who was going to tell her the bad news.

Nancy lifted Joan and passed her to her father, she watched him as he did the same test on Joan. She immediately started to cry as Harry moved his hand away from her head, she lifted her head and almost supported herself, despite being so young. Harry popped his little finger into her mouth and she suckled quite happily.

Harry put her over his shoulder and hid his face, averting Nancy's inquisitive stare. He realised that their was indeed something very wrong with his son, Bertie.

He held Joan out in front of him.

'Well, Harry, she's not going to be auburn, like Ena', he thought to himself.

'If only I could have one girl, just one, to replace!!'

He realised how wicked it was to think in this way. He knew he should be happy with what the good Lord had given him and, not go wishing for something he would never have.

CHAPTER 21

Elsie stood up, pulled the leather strap up and the window dropped suddenly causing her to jump backwards. She put her head out of the window, only to be covered in smoke and steam from the train. She pulled her head back in and pushed her hair out of her eyes. She looked back out of the window, the cold air caused a shiver throughout her body, the train pulled into Rubery Station, Northfield, Birmingham, slowly at first then came to an abrupt standstill. The porter jumped off the train and announced Rubery Station to all the passengers' disembarking the train. Doors slammed along the train one by one as the people scurried across the platform.

Young Mary patted her friend on the shoulder, Charles was crying, the noise and sudden cold had frightened him. Young Mary picked him up from the seat and rocked him gently. Elsie looked down at her son bewildered, she undid her coat and was about to unbutton her blouse, then stopped. A well dressed women, who had travelled in the same coach, stared distastefully at her, then turned to her husband punching him in the ribs. He was obviously embarrassed more by the way his wife was behaving than Elsie trying to settle her child. The woman shrugged and pushed her husband forward, he lowered his head and continued to disembark from the train. He turned sympathetically and smiled at Elsie, his wife dug him in the ribs again, he turned and obeyed her, like a small puppy would his master.

Elsie shrugged, shook her head, then hurriedly tidied herself up and reached up for her portmanteau from the luggage rack. Young Mary in the meantime collected bits and pieces from around her, they seemed to be everywhere. Charles had now settled, he looked about him. Young Mary pointed to Elsie.

"I swear he's been here before. Look at him".

The girls giggled at the funny look Charles had on his face.

Elsie stumbled on her shoe and fell backwards against the table.

"Bloody hell, we'll never get off the train this way", she muttered.

A young soldier stopped her falling and gently lifted her up.

"Ups a daisy", he said smiling at her.

Elsie smiled and thanked him coyly.

"I'll get that for you", he said as he lifted the portmanteau from the luggage rack.

"What you got in here, the crown jewels", he said as he popped it onto the table.

Elsie picked the bag up and young Mary lifted Charles.

Young Mary pushed forward through the train door and rushed off towards the toilet. Elsie was so busy watching Mary she fell again as she tried to step down the steps from the train. The same young soldier stopped her from falling flat on her face.

"Hang on a minute, there's a young lady on the floor here", he shouted turning back to look at the other passengers in the coach.

He lifted Elsie up and helped her onto a bench nearby. He went back and picked up her portmanteau and checked there was nothing lying on the platform. People were rushing and pushing past him. He stood up and exclaimed in a loud voice.

"Is this what I've been bloody fighting for".

No one even noticed he was there. The passengers just walked around him and stared down at him. He stood up angrily and looked about him wondering what the world was coming to. Looking over at the young woman he had helped twice he suddenly felt humbled by her.

He walked over to where Elsie was now sitting. She was looking down at her poor scraped knees, dabbing them with her hankie. Her stockings had big ladders down the front of both legs. She dropped her skirt down hurriedly when she realised the young soldier was standing in front of her staring.

"I've got a pair of perfectly good stockings in my kit bag, if you'll allow me to give them to you. Bought them for me mam, don't think she'd mind helping a damsel in distress". He smiled at Elsie then plonked himself down onto the bench and continued to rummage through his belongings.

"Ah! There they are, little blighters". He smiled at Elsie, who was quietly wishing he'd just bugger off.

Young Mary was surprised to see Elsie looking so bedraggled and uncomfortable, she had missed the fall. She had been so desperate for a pee that she rushed off without giving Elsie a second thought. She walked back over to her friend with Charles cradled to her breast oblivious to Elsie's dilemma She stood looking at Elsie, who was quite bewildered at the attention this young man was giving her. She looked up at Young Mary hoping to be rescued from the soldier's impromptu advances.

Realising he had a captive audience, he jumped up and gave Elsie the stockings.

"Sorry ladies you must think I'm an ignorant sod, my name is Billy! Billy Palmer", he smiled at Elsie and put his hand out to shake her hand. She put her hand out, looking up at young Mary for support, shook his hand. Young Mary looked down at her friend not knowing what to say or do.

"You in town long", he looked at young Mary and then Elsie.

"No, not really", she answered shyly.

"Well if you are ever in this vicinity again and, you want to have a drink, my parents run the only decent pub and hotel around here. That's if those bloody Germans haven't bombed it. 'Man on the Moon' it's called. Redditch Road between

Redhill Road, West Heath". He couldn't take his eyes off Elsie he was besotted with her big eyes and slim figure.

"Do you know where that it, lovey?", he retorted with a big smile.

Elsie nodded her head slowly, wishing he would just bugger off.

"Well I must be away, my transport will be here soon", He checked his pocket watch, tipped his cap and left. He marched swiftly along the station, whistling chirpily, he turned to wave as he handed his ticket to the Inspector in the doorway. He was quietly wishing Elsie had been more responsive towards him.

'What a beauty she is' he thought to himself, 'if I ever see her again she will not escape me, that's a promise, lad'. He stood for a little while looking back at the exit wishing she would walk out and share his cab.

'No such bloody luck. Daydreaming will not get you anywhere Bill', he said chuckling to himself quietly.

He whistled for a cab.

"I think that young man fancied you, Elsie" young Mary jested.

Elsie looked at Charles and then back at Mary and turned away.

"There's only one man for me Mary", she stood up and proceeded to make her way to the toilets to change her stockings.

"I'm sorry luv, didn't mean anything by what I said back there", young Mary said as she talked to Elsie through the toilet door.

Elsie came out looked at her face in the mirror, pinched her cheeks and combed her hair.

"There that's it. If they don't like it, they can bloody well lump it" She stamped her foot on the ground, lifted her skirt to show Mary her knew stockings.

"I know you didn't mean it luv, it's ok. I just!". She broke off the conversation and took young Charles off her friend and cuddled him. His little lips puckered again ready for another feed. Elsie sat down on the bench in the toilets and fed her son for the umpteenth time that day.

"He's a greedy little tyke, my Charles is". Elsie kissed him on the forehead.

She gently pulled him off her nipple and passed him over to young Mary. She tidied herself up again. Charles made a big burp and the girls both fell about laughing.

"I'm so glad you came with me today, I'm dreading meeting those bloody Solicitors' again. It's strange they want me to bring the baby, don't you think?" Mary shook her head not knowing what to say to her best friend.

Young Mary lifted Charles up and smelt his nappy

"I swear it goes in one end and out the other. Better change him, I suppose, don't want the Solicitors thinking he's not looked after. Do we, aye?" She promptly sat down again and fumbled in the portmanteau for a clean nappy and Vaseline. She looked at the dirty nappy she had just taken off Charles and promptly popped it into the waste bin.

"Can't carry that with us all day, can we?. Wouldn't like to be the cleaner who empties that bin", young Mary jested to Elsie, who had become very serious.

Elsie checked the time as they walked out of the toilets. The Smiths clock showed 1230pm.

"We've got 2 hours to get there Mary, we'll have a little time to spare. We should just about be able to squeeze a cuppa in my favourite tea-house. Charles and I used to meet there on my Sundays off. Actually it's not far from that pub Billy mentioned. Perhaps when we come out of the Solicitor's we can go there for a quick shandy before we catch the 6.00pm train back home".

"Good idea", young Mary hooked her arm into her friends and they whistled for a buggy together.

Arriving near to the restaurant young Mary climbed down first, took the portmanteau from her friend, placed it onto the floor and held out her hands for Charles. She looked down at him and kissed him gently on the forehead.

Elsie paid the driver, she looked over the road at the Patent Hob Nail & Rivet Company in Station Road, memories came flooding back of the first day she had met Charles on that very spot. A tear trickled down her cheek.

"This Industry is declining rapidly Mary. Charles used to talk about the nail industry in this area. He reckoned most of the Nailer's Workshops would be non-existent within the next two decades".

Young Mary, bit down on her lip and acknowledged what her friend had just told her not knowing what to say.

"Joe, loves horses so much, I don't think he'll ever settle doing anything else but work with his beloved Trojans. Your dad reckons that the horses, in the workforce, will no longer be needed in the coming years, due to the motorcar and new rail networks". Young Mary sighed.

"Our Joe will have to change Mary, he'll have too. The whole world will change when this damn war is over. There's so much to be done. The destruction to England is immense". Elsie smiled at her friend.

"Didn't mean to upset you, luv. Charles spent hours talking to me about the 'new world' as he called it. I'm beginning to sound like him, aren't I, aye?"

Young Mary pulled Elsie towards her.

"It's cold today, luv", young Mary shivered and pulled her friends colour up. They carried on walking up Station Road to the tea parlour.

"Here let me have him for a while Elsie, we'll swop over again when we reach the Solicitors", Mary wrapped her coat around the child, it had started to rain slightly.

"Not long now, just up past Hollymoor Hospital and round the corner and we're there".

Elsie sat on a bench overlooking the canal and took a deep breath.

"It didn't seem this far when Charles and I walked this way", Elsie sighed deeply. She was exhausted. She had not given herself much rest following the birth of her son despite the constant nagging of her mother. She rocked gently backwards and forwards, pushing her legs tightly together.

"I'll have to find a toilet luv, I think I may have started bleeding again. There should be one at the corner of this street. Come on before I have an accident". Elsie stood up and took a deep breath and carried on walking.

Young Mary had carried Charles most of the way up Station Road and now offered to carry the portmanteau as well as Charles. Elsie shook her head and carried on walking.

Finally they arrived at the Solicitor's with only minutes to spare.

Elsie looked up at the sign above the door. 'Springthorpe, Holcart and Bishop. She turned to young Mary and smiled.

"Well, here we are at last. Mr Richards is the guy we've come to see. Best get it over with, aye!"

Elsie had never felt this nervous in her life. Even the day she stood up to Charles's father had nothing on the way she felt now. Somehow deep inside she knew what the meeting was to be about. She shook her head trying to wipe out the fear from her mind.

The reception was on the first floor, the girls climbed the stairs gingerly. The Secretary asked them to sit down and promptly ran up another flight of stairs to notify Mr Richards that his next appointment was waiting downstairs in the waiting room.

Elsie looked around the reception and remembered the last time she had come here.

"Could you wait here for a little while, Mr Richards is still waiting for Mr Charles", she didn't finish her sentence and politely apologised and went back to her desk and sat down. She looked over at the girls and smiled sympathetically.

Elsie stood up when Charles's father arrived, she could feel herself shaking all over. He walked over to her and shook her hand and then walked over to look at the baby. He stood with both his hands behind his back, tapping his walking stick on the side of his leg. Elsie held her hands out to Young Mary for the child to passed to her. Young Mary passed Charles over and sat down quickly.

"Elsie, you'll have to excuse me for a little while there are a number of things I need to discuss before", he hesitated for a few moments. Elsie nodded to him and continued to unwrap Charles from inside his shawl. He looked down at the crocheted shawl and smiled.

"Did you do this, Elsie", he asked.

"Yes, I did. It took me almost 6 months to finish. Mother lost her temper several times with me, whilst she taught me the 'shell pattern'. It was not easy to make, but I did enjoy the end result", she said proudly.

He was being very sympathetic towards her. It aroused a feeling of unrest in her. Elsie wanted to run away and take her son, never to come back to these meetings, but she knew it was in Charles's best interest. She tried desperately not to show fear to this man.

"Well, my dear, it shouldn't take long. Do you girls want a cup of tea", he asked almost as an after thought.

"Oh! Yes please. Mine is one sugar please, young Mary piped up". Elsie nudged her with her knee.

"I'll have one without please, if you don't mind, sir". Elsie said very indignantly.

He walked over to the reception and asked the Secretary to have tea and biscuits bought over for the girls. She looked at them and smiled cautiously. He turned, smiled and carried on up the flight of stairs.

Elsie took a deep breath and fumbled with her buttons.

"He always makes me feel insecure", she remarked to young Mary.

"Bugger him, Elsie, he's just flesh and blood the same as us" Mary retorted.

The girls sat in silence, drinking their tea and dunking their Rich Tea biscuits in the tea. The receptionist watched with interest.

Over an hour passed. Elsie was dying to use the toilet and couldn't wait another second.

"Where's the toilet, please" She asked the receptionist.

The girl pointed to a door at the back of the building, it's on the left, down those stairs and outside the back of the building.

"Customer's aren't allowed to use the Staff toilets", she remarked. At that moment Mr Bishop, the Senior Partner, came into the Reception.

"Elsie, I'll show you where the toilets are. Please bring the child with you, I'm afraid your friend will have to stay here". He put his hand out and held her gently under the elbow. He turned and gave the Secretary a glare that would frighten even the bravest sole.

They climbed the stairs and turned right into his office.

"Give the child to me for a while to enable you to visit the w.c." Mr Bishop held his hands out to her and smiled gracefully. Elsie passed him over without hesitation, strangely she trusted this man, they had met twice, and he had always treated her with respect and kindness.

"The toilet is over there, Elsie". He pointed to the door opposite.

She turned and proceeded to go through the door. Her body was folding under her. All sorts of things raced through her mind.

When she got into the toilet, she was unable to pee. Her fear had got the better of her. She leaned forward and turned the cold water tap on in the small sink opposite the toilet. She tapped her feet in anticipation and looked up at the cobwebs in the corner of the toilet. After what seemed an eternity she peed. With a sigh of relief she got up, pulled her pants up and straightened her petticoat, checked her hair and pinched her cheeks. She looked down at her shoes and rubbed them on the back of her skirt. She stood looking at herself in the mirror for a few moments longer and then popped her hands on her hips and spoke to herself in the mirror.

"Well Elsie, you have to stand up for yourself, there's no one else here apart from Mary and she's downstairs. No surrender, My girl". She muttered to herself, stamped her foot and proceeded to walk across the landing into the office where the three gentlemen were staring down at Charles. He was enjoying all the attention and seemed totally at ease with his situation.

"He has his eyes." David commented, not realising Elsie had entered the room.

The room went quiet and Elsie could feel the tension arising.

Mr Bishop bid her good day and walked out of the office, smiling at Elsie as he shut the door.

It was David Richards, who spoke first.

"Sit down over here by Charles". He held his hand out and pointed to the chaise adjacent to his desk. Elsie stood in front of the desk and did not sit down. She felt better standing, it gave her courage somehow.

David admired her tenacity.

"My dear, I have some bad news for you. I think you should sit down". He walked over to her and gently assisted her into the high backed leather smoking chair, which he regularly sat in to read notes. Elsie stared at the chaise opposite her, wishing she had taken that option. The chair was cold and smelt of tobacco. It reminded her of the tobacco Charles smoked.

He looked over to Charles Senior for assurance. He nodded to him to proceed.

"Charles was killed on the battlefield, my dear". He stopped for a moment awaiting a response from Elsie.

"We have bought you here to discuss the terms of our agreement and offer you our sincere apologies for all the grief you have had to endure not knowing what was happening over the past months".

"Charles wrote to you". He tapped the letter on the desk.

"Unfortunately, he died shortly after he gave this to a AVC Sergeant. We have tried to contact this young man. William, Charles's brother, is not far from Ypres and is going to the Emergency Station again, where he died, to see if he can find out any further information as to what happened following the battle. We understand that the whole regiment was wiped out. Charles survived, but his injuries were too severe, he died hours after being taken to the Emergency Station.

I feel sure that we will soon know who the young man was who sat with Charles and visited him in hospital. He posted these letters to us. We have pieced together a little of the puzzle from other Hussars who were there and nursed at this station.

A young sister, who attended Charles, was unavailable, unfortunately she was returning to England, with the injured on the HMS Glenart Castle. We are hopeful that she will visit us and give us details of how Charles died. We have written to her superiors and hopefully she will remember him".

He paused for a moment and wiped the sweat from his brow. He turned and poked the fire, looking up at Charles's senior he turned and looked at Elsie wanting desperately to go over to her and hold her close to him. He knew he could not because it was not the done thing. He hated the stiff upper lip that he had to endure in his clients. David had been lucky with his upbringing. His parents and family were kindly and showed their affection.

Elsie was numb. She looked about the room and stood up. She walked calmly over to the desk, where the men stood and put out her hand for the letter Charles had sent to her. David lifted it from his desk and passed it to her. He lowered his eyes.

"Elsie, I'm very sorry, but there are other things to discuss with you, other than the death of Charles. Are you up to it, or would you prefer to be booked into a hotel for the night and come back tomorrow and go over the formalities of Charles's estate". She hadn't heard a word of what had been said.

David came around the desk and knelt down by the side of the chair. He went back to the chaise and bought the baby over to her.

"I'll arrange for you and your friend to stay at the 'Man on the Moon', it's a lovely place and run by the most wonderful family. If you'll allow me to do that dear". She looked up at him and nodded.

"I'll arrange for the Rolls to take you both and we'll meet here tomorrow morning at 10.30a.m. I'll send the transport to pick you up at 10.00am".

Charles came over to her and kneeled down. He was devastated at the death of his youngest son. He put his hand to his mouth as he knelt before Elsie. I'll get some nappies sent over for you from the hall and anything else you may need for your stay, if that's alright with you, Elsie". He had become very humble and seemed genuinely concerned for her welfare.

"May I hold the little one for a few moments", he asked.

Elsie passed him over to Charles Snr, she folded her hands on her lap.

"We have a perambulator back at home, it's not used anymore. Williams little ones are walking about now quite well. Do you have one Elsie?" He waited for an answer.

"No I'm sorry, it's been the least of my worries, Sir. My mother lets me use the one that has been used for all of my brothers and sisters". She looked at him sternly, her courage had returned.

"I will accept your offer though, carrying Charles around is very difficult, and the nappies will help too. I didn't expect to be staying". She went to get up and fell backwards.

The two gents were standing over her when she came around. David offered her a glass of water. Elsie rubbed her eyes and quickly tidied her skirt and looked up at them, oblivious to what had happened a few moments earlier.

"Elsie, if you'll allow me, I'll sort everything out for you. Please feel comfortable here whilst I sort out your accommodation and arrange transport. I've also sent for the family's physician. He pointed to the carpet. A stain of dried blood had appeared".

Elsie felt so embarrassed. She looked at David and apologised and offered to clear it up. He would have none of it.

"Elsie you are a very brave young lady and someone to be proud of. I will have this sorted and I want you to just stay there or lie on the chaise until you feel fit to travel, and that's an order, young lady". He tapped her on the shoulder gently.

David turned and looked at Charles who was lighting a

cigar and standing in front of the fire. He gestured to him to follow him to the other side of the room.

The two men quickly talked and Charles left. David rushed down the stairs and asked Young Mary to sit with her friend for a little while. Mary jumped up and pushed David out of the way.

"If you've harmed her, Sir, I promise you will have me to contend with". She took the stairs two at a time and burst into the office where Elsie was sitting on the chaise staring at her baby.

She ran across the room and knelt down in front of her friend. Elsie took a deep sigh.

"He's dead Mary, he's dead" She cried out.

Young Mary took Charles from her and looked about the room. The child was sleeping blissfully. She walked over to the desk and promptly took out the bottom drawer and threw everything onto the top of the desk. She returned to Elsie and took the baby away from her and promptly put him in the drawer in front of the fire and returned to her friend.

"Bugger them, if they don't like it, bugger them", she repeated.

Elsie was in no mood to smile and just broke down sobbing into Mary's shoulder. She rocked her like a small child. The sobbing eventually subsided and Mary asked her what was happening.

Elsie sobbed and sniffed and pointed over at the stain on the carpet.

Young Mary gasped!.

"You shouldn't be walking Elsie you need to get yourself to bed and your legs lifted high". Mary promptly put a cushion under her legs.

"They're arranging accommodation for us tonight and transport. Charles Senior has gone to fetch a perambulator for the baby and clothing. We're to wait here until they return. He's also getting a doctor". She blew her nose and wiped the tears from her bloodshot eyes.

Someone knocked at the door and Mary walked over and opened it, ready for anyone who dared scorn her for emptying the drawer. The secretary from downstairs was standing in the doorway.

"Would you ladies like another cuppa while you wait for Mr Richards to come back?" She waited for an answer.

"Yes please", young Mary answered without looking at Elsie.

"Do you have anything sweet for Elsie, she's feeling a little faint?".

I'll get the junior to pop over the cake shop and see if there's any rock cakes left, they're lovely". She smiled at young Mary, turned and rushed down the stairs. Ten minutes later she returned with the rock cakes and another pot of tea.

"Mr Richards shouldn't be too long. I'm so sorry about the young master, he was a perfect gentleman". She walked over to Elsie and patted her on the arm.

"May I look at the child".

Elsie nodded and smiled back at her.

She walked across the room and kneeled on the floor to have a good look at the baby, who was oblivious to the world. He had his silver Victorian rattle in his little hand. Charles had given it to her. It was his and he wanted his first child to have it. She touched him gently and turned to speak to Elsie.

"My he's a bonnie baby. What have you called him?"

Elsie sat up proudly.

"He's called Charles, Harry", she hesitated for a moment "Price". She looked at young Mary and she winked at her.

"Well Elsie, you take no notice of this bureaucracy, it's just bullshit. Charles loved you with all his heart. I hope they live with this guilt for the rest of their natural lives. He didn't have to fight, he didn't have to die. He left because he couldn't face life without you". She stood up and turned to look at Elsie.

"We used to talk when he came to visit his father. He always kept him waiting downstairs. I knew about you both, I actually used to lie for him when Charles and David were after him. We kept it our little secret. Well it's out now, and I'm glad".

"I stay because David relies on me and, besides I've nothing to go home to my Danny was killed in a battle near Candit Troere Farm on the road to Ypres. He was just left on the side of the road. I have nowhere to take him flowers or visit to talk to him". She broke off.

"Oh dear, I'm so sorry for burdening you at this terrible hour of your own grief". She wiped her nose and eyes. Young Mary walked across to her.

"My Joe has been injured and is returning as we speak. He's been injured and I have no idea how badly". The girls hugged.

"If you are ever near Kidderminster please come and see us and there's no need to write before you come, just turn up, you'll be welcome." Young Mary took a sheet of writing paper and proceeded to write Elsie's address down.

"No need to write my address, I spend more time with Elsie than at my own house".

"My name is Ethel" She put her hand out to young Mary and shook her by the hand. She walked over to Elsie.

"I already know who you are, my dear. I'm so pleased to meet you at long last".

There was a bond formed that day with the three girls. They promised they would keep in touch, if only by letter.

"Must go back downstairs, otherwise I'm in for a bollocking", she winked at the girls.

"I'm sorry for the frosty reception earlier, believe me it was nothing personal. I have to play a part when the 'Powers that Be' are about, if you know what I mean". She promptly walked out of the door and back down the stairs to the reception. Looking up at the ceiling where the girls were she smiled to herself.

'Charles was right in what he said 'she's not beautiful, but she has a strength in her that is very rare'.

"I promised you, and I intend to keep my promise, Charles. I will watch your son grow into a man and I will always be there for them. God Bless and Keep You my lost friend".

Elsie was oblivious to the next few days. There had been no meeting the following day. The family doctor had ordered total bed rest for a week minimum. Elsie had become quite anaemic and incoherent. He had stated in no uncertain terms that she must not be burdened further with things that could wait. The doctor had been a close friend to Charles Snr for many years and had delivered young Charles just 20 years earlier. He did not agree with the stigma that poor Elsie had been forced to endure because of the family's name. Charles had argued with his friend and insisted he had not been responsible for Elsie being so ill, but deep down he felt the weight of guilt that his own son had died needlessly and his young grandson would never bear the family's name. Doctor Harris had been very angry with Charles Snr, he was totally on Elsie's side and offered her assistance whenever she needed it, even if it meant upsetting the friendship he had with the family for almost 30 years.

Young Mary handed Elsie a cup of tea. They had been staying at the 'Man in the Moon' since that dreadful meeting at the Solicitor's. Billie Palmer had waited on them all hand and foot since their arrival and had become a welcome visitor to their room.

Billie knocked the door.

"Can I come in ladies, got some coal for the fire. Don't want you lovely young soles to get cold, do we?"

"Come in" young Mary answered, smiling at Elsie.

Billie was home on a month's leave, following being injured on the battlefield. He was somewhat of a hero, Elsie had been told by his mother, who was very proud of her only son.

He had dragged several of his mates out of a deep crater, one by one, back to friendly ground, despite shrapnel being embedded in his shoulder and being shot in the leg, whilst under enemy fire. His shoulder had finally begun to heal, but he made light of his injuries. The shrapnel had narrowly missed his lung. He was due that morning to attend a medical board to see if he was fit to return to the front. Billie had volunteered to go back, he could have been discharged on medical grounds, but he wouldn't hear of it. A Casualty Form for Active Service would need to bc completed before he was allowed to go back in the field. Billie had spent a lot of time thinking since his encounter with Elsie, whether he had made the right decision to go back to the front?

"Well just thought I'd check on you all before I go to Hollymoor Hospital to see if I'm fit for work. Hope they send me to the right part of the hospital, don't want to end up permanently in the Lunatic Asylum. Must be mad thinking of going back, need to have me head looked at, not me bloody shoulder and leg". He turned and stared into the fire. 'Shouldn't have said that Billie me lad', he muttered quietly. 'Well Billie it's now or never - don't know what comes over me when I'm near to her, I give talk a load of old bunk'.

He took a long deep breath of air turned around quickly, stepped forward kissed young Charles on the forehead and promptly kissed Elsie before she had time to realise what had happened. Before she could comment he marched out of the room, as he opened the door he turned again and smiled.

"See you later, I hope". He bid them farewell at a tilt of his cap and left. He walked out of the door turned slightly and looked at Elsie then smiled. She returned his smile, and placed her hand on her cheek where he had kissed her.

He shut the door and left whistling as he went down the stairs.

'Well she didn't smack you in the gob, did she?' he muttered again to himself. 'Must stop this silly one to one, namely myself, gabber, before I ends up in that bloody hospital'. He turned around at the bottom of the stairs to make sure no-one was listening to him making a fool of himself. Millie retreated into the kitchen cautiously and held her hand over her mouth to stop herself from giggling. Billie turned around again to see if there was anyone about. He peered up the corridor and smiled. 'She's a nosy old bugger, my mother' he said so that she could hear his comments.

Millicent, Billie's mother had also befriended the girls. She had taken young Charles on long walks in his new pram and had fallen deeply in love with the child. She had no grandchildren of her own and had so much love to offer. Millie, as she liked to be called, was a well built women, with very kind dark blue eyes and lovely blond hair with grey streaks, which complimented her rather than aged her, she kept it immaculate and tied back in plats.

She fitted well into the profession of publican/landlady, her raucous laughter infected everyone who came into contact with her. Her family had lived in the area all their lives, her father had been in the Nail Industry from a very early age. The Nail Industry was the most notable industry during the 19th century within the area.

The Industry was now in steady decline and the only Company in operation now was Patent Hob Nail & Rivet Company, where her husband had served his apprenticeship. Jim had left the industry at the beginning of the war to help in the family business, following the death of Millie's father, who had become a publican during the latter part of his life. His wife died within a few months of his death from a broken heart, Millie would tell everyone, when asked how she became landlady of The Man on the Moon pub.

Jim, Millie's husband, was painfully thin, extremely short and an insignificant sort of bloke. Millie overpowered him, but nevertheless, they were devoted to each other. Their first child died at the age of 5, at the turn of the century, from consumption. Billie survived the dreaded disease, but was left with a weakness. He suffered throughout his life from a cough and would constantly come down with colds. Millie would tell everyone that Billie should not have gone to war due to his heart condition. She was constantly moaning about his condition to her customers. When Billie was present he would look at her with daggers in his eyes. She would turn away too ashamed to finish the sentence she had started. In her mind she had lost one child, she certainly did not want to lose another?

Elsie had begun to trust Billie and spent many hours talking to him over the past few days, opening up her heart to him about what had happened when Charles had told his father of his wish to marry her. Billie had listened intently as she started to trust and confide in him. He felt terribly sad at the way she had been treated by the Monckton family.

Billie had been there as a confidant when she needed to talk and release herself from this terrible burden she carried of her poor Charles dying in some God forsaken place in the middle of nowhere. He had vowed to her that he would be there for the rest of her life and that when he went back to Belgium he would do his utmost to trace Charles's steps from the battle he had fought to the time he had spent at the Ambulance Station, prior to his death. He realised that he may never learn the complete truth, but he had promised he would try to piece together a picture of this young man's last hours. He thought it may put to rest the hurt and guilt that she felt and given time that she may learn to love him.

Billie had fallen completely and totally in love with Elsie since their chance meeting on the train. She was the one he wanted to spend the rest of his life with. He was not the bubbly person he had portrayed on their first meeting. He was quiet, loving and very sensitive. Elsie had learnt to trust this young man and had been welcomed into his family without fingers being pointed.

David Richards had been terrific. He bought the perambulator and loads of clothes for Charles. He still hadn't been tucked and the gowns that were sent were family heirlooms. The initial 'C' had been embroidered on the Victorian gowns and the tiny socks. They had beautiful hand crochet on the cuffs and hems of the gowns. The little socks and gloves had been lovingly knitted in 2 ply pure cotton, numerous hand knitted cardigans were all packed in the trunk.

Young Mary stood in ore at the intricate work on the garments and kissed the letter 'C' on one of the gowns. 'My darling you must have worn this gown when you were just a baby'. She wiped her eyes on the corner of the gown and took a deep breath.

A trunk full of clothes and blankets had been given to Elsie. Mr Richard's wife, Anne, had sent the clothes for Elsie and baby and was now a daily visitor to the pub. Discussions had taken place with Anne regarding Charles's future and what Elsie was going to do. She had no intention of being bullied into anything that she did not want to do.

Anne had offered to try and find a small cottage and nursemaid for the child, so that Elsie could follow her dream and open a haberdashery shop nearby.

Charles Snr had only been to see Elsie once, he did not want to become too involved with her or the child, but he was finding it more and more difficult not too. He had admiration for this strong minded young woman and could understand why his son had fallen so deeply in love with her.

David Richards reported to him daily of her progress. It had been decided that the intricacies of the estate and young Charles's inheritance would be discussed as soon as Elsie was well enough to visit the Solicitor's. However, Anne had suggested that they help this young women set up a business without her being aware of the involvement of Charles Snr, who was totally in agreement. He instructed David and Anne to do everything in their power to help set up a small business for Elsie. He wanted to be able to see his grandson grow and keep in the background for his future. Charles regretted the way he had treated Elsie and knew that if he had not acted in the way he did, his son would still be alive, albeit married to a commoner.

Elsie kept Charles's letter close to her heart. The envelope had traces of blood across it, she could see a fingerprint on the back where it had been sealed. She stared down at it, she had slept with it under her pillow since that terrible day and refused to open it for fear of it's content.

She had dreams of the young Sergeant posting the letter to her.

Young Mary sat down and patted Elsie on the hands.

"What is it luv?", she asked.

"Well there are questions going through my head all the time. Our Joe is in the AVC, I wonder if he knows anything about what happened out there and the mysterious Sister who nursed him. Our Sam has married a nurse and I believe she is on her way back to England as we speak. Wouldn't it be strange if Joe was the young man who sat and comforted my Charles?" Elsie looked out of the window as she thought of those terrible last moments of Charles suffering alone and dying from his injuries.

"Yes it would be a strange" young Mary answered.

"Elsie, I want to go back home tomorrow and check when my Joe is coming home, if you don't mind. I've spoken to Jim and he is willing to take me to the Station. Will you be coming with me?"

Elsie paused for a moment.

"Yes, I think I am well enough to travel now".

"Bloody hell, how on earth are we going to pack all this stuff and get home". She looked around the room and sighed.

"Suppose I can leave a lot of it here as I will be coming back to look for a place to live and little shop. You know Mary, I think, for the first time in a long long time I feel optimistic about my future".

The girls hugged.

"Tomorrow it is then", young Mary said as she hugged her friend.

CHAPTER 21

The Rolls Royce 40/50 hp Silver Ghost, six cylinder, giant pulled gracefully into the courtyard. Len dropped his pitch fork, turned, walked towards the entrance of the barn, his mouth wide open. Bernard came over to see what he was looking at, he gently shut Len's mouth with his middle finger. David crawled over on the floor and pushed through the middle of the boys legs to see what was so interesting.

The Silver Ghost's body balanced huge over a silky smooth, transverse leaf spring and a drive-train, powered by a huge, but silent 7ltr six cylinder inline block.

Len looked to Bernard then proceeded with a statement that absolutely amazed him:

"That car has broken the world endurance and mileage records, it has a 4 speed manual transmission and a top speed of 34mph. It's impassable on any road, particularly on the roads in Europe, which includes Switzerland.

Bernard smiled,

"I've studied Geography as well Len".

He carried on with his lesson on the Rolls Royce motor car, regardless of Bernard's comments:

It has Oxblood leather interior trim and kerosene coach

lamps on the front and one on the back. Only Royalty and Lawrence of Arabia drive them".

Leonard raised his head and puckered his lips, biting on the side of his cheek, proud of remembering the details of this beautiful automobile. He took a deep breath.

Bernard just looked at Len, but was unable to stop his next comment coming out of his big mouth.

"Bullshit", Bernard pushed Len sideways.

"How do you know all that, Len" he asked.

"Uncle Bertie told me, we spent a long time chatting last time I visited him with mom. He promised he would take me for a spin as soon as the war was over and, what's more he's promised to give me a driving lesson. He's also promised me, dependant upon how good I am with my exams, he will ask a few of his friends about suitable employment for me. He turned back and looked out of the doorway.

Len continued his lesson on the subject:

"Rolls-Royce now make engines for aircraft, but they've had to stop manufacturing this masterpiece due to this damn war". Len puckered his lips again and looked up to the skies.

"This bloody war, wish it was over". He cussed aloud and kicked the floor causing a cloud of dust to rise.

Bernard wiped his face and patted his trousers,

"Len, I wish you'd watch your temper, these are clean trousers".

Bernard continued to brush his clothes off.

"I'm going to own one of those 'Rolls Royce motorcars', one day, Bernard. I've promised myself" He smiled at Bernard, but David spoilt the moment, he sniggered and started pulling faces at Len.

Mocking him aloud, he proceeded to annoy Len.

"I'm going to.........,

Too late - Len kicked David in the shin and knocked him sideways.

"Piss of you runt", Len screamed at him.

He was just about to kick him again, when Bernard grabbed his shirt and pulled him backwards.

"One day you prick, you'll push me too far" Len growled.

"You're a bloody bully, Len. I'm going to kill you one day".

David retorted, as he legged it towards the house, pulling his tongue out and pulling his ears at the same time. Finally, realising he was too far for Len to catch him, he mocked Len again.

"I'm going to own one of those ROLLS ROYCE MOTOR CARS one day", he smirked mockingly, daring Len to cross the yard. Bernard held Len's arm.

"He's not worth it Len. We're supposed to be young adults, you know". Bernard put his arm around Len's shoulders.

David disappeared into the doorway of the cottage, fell over the mat, then sprawled along the floor. He came to a sudden halt in front of his father's chair. Harry, whacked him across the head with his paper and scowled at him. David picked himself up from the floor, not daring to look back up at his father, he ran off upstairs and slammed the door behind him. He stamped up the stairs tears streaming down his cheeks.

Harry took his pipe out of his pocket and lit it.

"He's a bloody nuisance, our David is. One of these days he'll push Len too far and I won't interfere, that's for sure".

Harry shook his paper trying to remember where he was before being interrupted.

Len had quietened down and decided to let his nuisance of a brother go. He didn't want Uncle Bertie to see him being drawn into a petty argument with his shit of brother.

"Better stay here for a while Bernard until our Joe has gone into the house, don't want to crowd him too much", Len patted Bernard on the shoulder and they both sat down on a bail of hay. Bernard pulled a stork out from the bail and promptly popped it into his mouth, Len copied him.

"Tell me more about the car", Bernard asked.

Len was miles away and didn't hear a word that his brother had said.

"I'm glad he's back" Len said to Bernard.

He nodded and wiped the tears away from his eyes. Bernard gave him his handkerchief, but Len declined, for obvious reasons. They both burst out laughing as Len showed Bernard a big bogy sticking to his handkerchief.

"Oh yuk!" They both laughed raucously.

Mary looked out of the kitchen window in amazement. She wiped her hands on her apron and patted her heart with her hand. She turned to look at Harry, she was finding it terribly difficult not to burst into tears. She walked across the kitchen and put her arms around Harry's neck, she could not hold her tears, not for one moment longer. Harry pulled himself up, threw his paper on the chair, and hugged his wife, who was falling apart in his arms. Harry held her at arms rest and lifted her chin up.

"My darling, Sam will be home soon, I'm sure of that. He's stronger than our Joe, and he too has so much to live for now".

He tried desperately hard not to cry, but he was overcome with relief that his boy was home. He sobbed relentlessly on Mary's shoulder and the heartache he had endured over the past few years suddenly became too much to bear.

"Can't let our eldest see us like this, can we, Harry?" Mary retorted.

Harry smiled at Mary and wiped his eyes on his sleeve. Mary looked at him lovingly, then she spit on her handkerchief and proceeded to wipe his face.

"I'm not one of the kids", he said as he pretended to wipe the spit off his face.

"You might as well be one of the kids" Mary joked.

"I have to do everything, but wipe your arse!" , she jumped out of his reach but he caught her right across her backside with a good slap.

"You missed that one girl", Harry smiled as he looked down at his hand.

"Ouch! That bloody hurt", she smirked at him.

"I'll get you for that one, Harry Price" she jested to her husband lovingly.

She shouted upstairs to the girls, who had been in the bedroom tidying up and making the beds.

"Young Mary, there's someone here to see you" she shouted up the stairs.

Elsie and Mary were sat on the bed together holding hands.

"How on earth has uncle Bertie managed to find our Joe?" she asked Harry.

"I don't know Mary, but I know one thing, our Joe would not be outside today if it hadn't been for all his efforts. We are so lucky to have him in our corner. I'm so glad he stuck with us all these years". Mary turned around and walked back over to Harry, who hugged her again, then gently pushed her forward towards the door.

"Go my darling, your boy is home", he said.

The Batman opened the door and walked around to the side of the Rolls. He opened the door and popped the seat up. Bertie climbed out of the car and tapped his leg with his Malacca walking shaft, he looked down at the carved ivory head admiringly. He had inherited the shaft from his father and coveted it.

The Batman offered him his cap, but he declined to take it, turning he smiled at Joe. Twiddling with his moustache, he acknowledged Len and Bernard by lifting his stick in the air.

Len was ecstatic, he waved and smiled back at him. He nudged Bernard. The boys sat down simultaneously on the bail of hay, not knowing what to do next, whether to go and help Joe, or leave it to young Mary. They shrugged shoulders and picked up another piece of hay and sat waiting for young Mary and their mother to go over to the Rolls.

Young Mary came running down the stairs, almost falling down the bottom step, she fell into the kitchen and then composed herself, looked at Harry and then at Mary and promptly walked elegantly towards the door. She stood still on the porch outside the cottage, crying freely now, she flung her arms out and ran towards the Rolls.

Joe was out of the car now, he smiled at her and stood still awaiting her embrace. She flung herself into his arms almost knocking him off his feet.

Mary came out of the cottage with Valerie in her arms, she cried into the child's cardigan, as she watched them kiss and embrace. Harry had managed to get to the door and put his arm around his wife balancing on one leg with his crutch under his other arm.

"Well my darling, that's a sight, I've waited a long long time to see".

He kissed her tenderly on the forehead.

Mary put Valerie down onto the floor, checking first that Harry had support, she stepped down the steps and let her go. Her little arms went into the air for balance and she cautiously wobbled towards her parents, who were now watching anxiously, for their daughter to reach them.

Valerie fell on her knees smiling the whole time, then crawled a few paces, she climbed back up onto her feet. She walked precariously towards her parents looking back at her grandma chuckling. Young Mary couldn't stand it another second, she ran over to her daughter and picked her up in her arms, gleaming she smiled at Harry and Mary, then turned and took her over to Joe.

He was balanced up against the car, exhausted following the long journey he had endured over the past few weeks. This was the moment he had dreamt about for almost 2 years. Bertie gently put his arm around him and lifted him slightly for balance. The Batman proceeded to thc back of the car and bought out a wheelchair. Joe turned around and shook his head. The poor Batman was embarrassed and looked at Bertie for advice. He shook his head also.

Bertie continued to support Joe, and asked him if he

could manage to walk across the yard, Joe smiled looking into Bertie's green eyes.

"I could do with a little help please, Bertie".

Young Mary realised it had all been too much for Joe and ran across to her mother in law and gave her Valerie, she turned and scurried across the yard to support Joe. She smiled at Bertie and thanked him.

It took a lot of effort to get Joe back into the cottage and also to help Harry back to his chair in front of the fire. Mary pulled her rocker opposite Harry for Joe to sit down.

Finally, after moving the furniture about, everyone was chatting and asking questions. Joe was exhausted, he fell asleep almost immediately in his mother's rocker. Young Mary gently lifted Valerie from his arms, she had also fallen asleep on her father‘s lap, she crept back upstairs trying hard not to wake her sleeping daughter. She gently put her into her crib and rocked it sideways. Elsie sat on the bed looking at her friend not talking.

"Suppose I'd best show my face and let our Joe know he's an uncle and Uncle Bertie a great uncle". Elsie took a deep sigh.

Mary walked over the bedroom to Elsie and hugged her friend.

"You're the sister I never had, Elsie, whatever happens down there, you'll always have Joe's and my support. I love you Elsie and always will".

Young Mary hugged her friend.

Elsie picked Charles up off the bed and crossed her fingers, as she closed the braced pine door. It was dark on the landing, she climbed down the stairs quite gingerly. At the bottom of the stairs she took a deep breath and opened the door and walked into the kitchen with Charles cradled in her arms.

Len took Charles off her and sat down by the window. He gently lifted his knee up and down. The child seemed quite happy with all the attention he was getting from Bernard and Len.

Elsie walked over to uncle Bertie and shook his hand cautiously.

Bertie looked down at his niece sympathetically.

"Elsie my dear, I know you've had it hard these past months and I haven't been over too much, but I want you to know that I will help as much as I can. Your mother tells me you want to open up a shop in Northfield. Well young lady, it's never too early to start a business. Things will change once this war is over and people will want to be cheered up by buying the latest fashion. If you want help with moving give me some notice and I'll try and arrange transport for you. Also, I have that other matter in hand regarding the demise of your young man".

Uncle Bertie looked over at Mary, he tapped his leg with his cane as he looked out of the kitchen window.

Elsie thanked her uncle, smiled then walked over to Len. She took her baby out of his arms and proceeded to go out into the yard. Len and Bernard followed her. David reluctantly followed them outside, after his mother had clipped him around the ears and pointed to the doorway. David reluctantly opened the door and stepped down the steps and cautiously walked towards the barn.

Len snarled at David.

"You'd best keep your distance from me, or else".

David ran over towards Elsie and stuck to her like a limpit.

He poked his tongue out at Len, Elsie saw what he had done and clipped him around the ear again.

"You ask for all you get our David, honestly all I've said, and you still keep pushing Len's buttons".

David walked away from everyone and skulked off down the driveway towards the fields. He turned and looked at his siblings and shrugged his shoulders. He climbed onto the wall and started throwing stones into the field.

'Don't need any of you', he muttered to himself.

"I'll show you arseholes, I have my own drcams too!"

CHAPTER 22

Elsie and Joe looked up at the sign above the door, Springthorpe, Holcart and Bishop, Joe grabbed her hand and climbed cautiously up the steps, holding the cast ornate handrail tightly with his other hand. Elsie smiled at him sympathetically, realising how difficult it must be for him to climb the stairs.

She had asked him to come along with her. Joe turned and looked at the Rolls Royce as he climbed the last step, he lifted is hand and waved at them. Bertie was sat in the front seat. He nodded his head in acknowledgment, then tapped his Batman to proceed, but changed his mind. He opened the door of the Rolls before it came to an abrupt standstill. He instructed his driver to go and take Mary and Len to the Tea Room up the road and pick the family up at 12.30p.m. sharp. The driver walked around the Rolls and checked that the door was closed.

Mary nodded at Bertie, relieved that Bertie would be present at this important meeting. He briskly marched across the road to the Solicitor's, tapping his leg with his stick and fumbling with his moustache, as he always did. Mary smiled to herself turning her head slightly she looked down at Leonard, who was staring out the window at his uncle, who he obviously adored. Mary turned the blanket down from around young Bertie's head, he didn't move his eyes stared blankly back at her, she slowly lifted it back up. Len smiled at her and held her hand.

"It'll be alright mom, you wait and see", he said optimistically.

"Are you two ready then", the driver asked.

Mary nodded and smiled at Len.

"Special treat for you today young man, scon and jam with fresh cream finished off with a nice cuppa"

Len licked his lips.

"Can't wait to tell our David" he smirked.

"One day Len, you will realise how important it is to have brothers' and sisters'. When they're gone it's too late".

Mary turned her head towards the window to hide the tears that were beginning to fall down her cheek. She pulled her hankie out of her portmanteau and wiped away the tears.

Len looked the other way and thought to himself 'me and my big trap, I wish I didn't hate him so much'.

The Rolls pulled up outside the Tea Room, Mary and Len climbed out of the car. Mary leaned in to get young Bertie, but Harold smiled at her.

"You two go and enjoy yourself, here's ten bob the master asked me to give it to you. I'll take the baby, I'll be parked just across the road. I'm going to watch the fishermen in the river Rea, I was bought up not far from here. Me and my father often came here when he finished work at the Nail Factory. He's dead now, 'God rest his poor sole' and me mam. Go on now, the lad will be alright with me, I promise.

Mary hooked her arm into Len's and chirpily walked into the Tea Shop. As they walked into the shop the door bell rang. Len looked up at it in amazement.

Mary sat down at the table nearest to the window and sent Len over to the counter to order the tea and scons. Len's eyes almost popped out when he saw the cakes on the counter, he turned and looked back at his mother and then back down at the cakes.

Joe sat down in the Reception and held Elsie's hand. He was surprised when Bertie popped his head around the corner.

"Here for the moral high ground lad. No one will bully Elsie, not whilst I'm about. Elsie shut her eyes and thanked God that he was going to be with her at this meeting. She put her hand in her pocket and held the letter she had received from Charles tightly.

David Richards waited eagerly for them to get comfortable and popped his head around the door and held his hand out to shake Joe's hand.

"David Richards, please to meet you at last, Joe" he shook his hand vigorously.

Elsie smiled at David.

"This is my uncle Bertie, he's here for moral support and to make sure that there's no more bullying or intimidation". She took a deep breath and smiled at uncle Bertie.

David held his hand out and shook Bertie's hand.

"Very pleased to meet you Sir".

Bertie shook his hand and coughed slightly and stepped back and sat down.

"I hope we're not going to be kept waiting for long, I've got a very important meeting to attend", he blurted out.

"We're ready for your now, please follow me. We're using the Board Room on this floor due to Joe's breathing problems and the stairs".

David turned to the Receptionist.

"Tea and biscuits for 5 please, in the Board Room in ten minutes. Thank you".

She jumped up and scurried off to the back of the building.

The Rolls pulled up outside the Solicitor's, Elsie shook hands with Bertie and thanked him for all his help and kindness.

"I'll be staying at the 'Man on the Moon' for a couple of nights until I've sorted the details about the shop. If there's any problem with Charles you can telephone me, mother".

Elsie handed her mother a note with the address and telephone number of the Man on the Moon.

"I'll be back home on the first train on Thursday. Mother please listen to what is said about little Bertie".

She hugged Bertie and thanked him and then held Joe. I love you Joe with all my heart. I'm so glad you are back."

Joe felt humbled by his sister and kissed her on the cheek.

"I love you too Elsie".

Joe fumbled in his grey coat for his handkerchief. He wiped the tears off Elsie's face, then proceeded to blow his nose. They both laughed and hugged each other again.

"Thank you for everything you've done today, I'll never forget it. Hope everything goes alright for you in West Heath. Me and Mary will be over on Sunday. I understand that you can stroll over the Lickie Hills when you start to feel better. I've been told by Billie that the altitude is good for the lungs. Look after yourself luv. Perhaps one of these visits, when he gets back from the front line, I'll bring him over to meet you. I'll watch over Mary for you, I promise!"

Bertie instructed his driver to drive to West Heath, where Joe got out. Before he could speak a plump nurse pushed a wheel chair out to the car and promptly pushed him into it.

"Your late, Mr Price" she scowled at him. Before he could thank everyone she wheeled him towards the hospital.

Bertie smiled at Mary,

"Don't worry about him, I'll be back tomorrow and will find out about visiting and anything else that needs to be sorted. He's in a good hospital that specialise in pulmonary problems".

Bertie tapped the driver and told him to drive to Southern General Hospital, Selly Oak. The driver nodded and turned the Rolls around full circle, Joe waved as the Rolls continued back down the long driveway.

On arrival at Selly Oak, Bertie walked around to the door and opened it for Mary to climb out.

"Pass the little one to me", he held his arms out for Mary to pass the child to him.

Mary and Len both climbed out of the car. Mary tidied her skirt and straightened her hair and popped her hat on. Bertie smiled,

"That's a grand hat you're wearing, Mary".

"Our Elsie made it for me, just for today" she said proudly.

Bertie nodded and looked down at the baby.

"Well it's your turn now young man. Lets see if we can" - he stopped and looked at Mary.

Bertie walked up the stairs holding baby Bertie in his arms firmly. Mary and Len followed him quietly.

At the top of the stairs Bertie pushed the double glass doors with his side and walked over to the Reception and spoke to the receptionist. He turned and indicated to Mary to follow him.

Bertie stopped for a moment and spoke to his niece and Len.

"Now when we get to the Paediatrics, I will be seeing my Associate first and calling you in afterwards. He has agreed to see the child as a favour to me. He's a very busy man. I know you would rather be in there with me, but I think I know what is best for the child". Bertie looked to Len to take care of his mother.

A tall thin balding man came out of the room and walked over to Bertie.

"Ah! Vincent" Bertie acknowledged his associate.

"I'm sorry I've kept you waiting", Bertie shook hands with his left hand as he was holding the child in his right hand.

A nurse came out and took the child into the Consultation Room and popped him into an iron cot.

Bertie walked in with his friend whom he had known for many years.

The young nurse came out of the room and went out to see Mary.

"Do you want a cuppa luv, they'll be ages in there"

Mary smiled and thanked her.

"Two teas and sugar in both, please" she looked down at Len as she ordered the tea. He was looking very worried.

"He's in the best place Len, we must do what is best for

our little one", Mary put her arms around him and sat him down on the bench. Len bit on his nails in frustration and kept looking at the Smiths Clock above the doorway to the wards.

After what seemed a lifetime, Bertie came out of the Consultation Room, without Vincent. Mary jumped up and hurried over to him.

"He will be staying here for tests Mary. I don't want any arguing from you. Believe me if anything can be done, Vincent is the one to find a way of helping your son. Now I want you to both go in and say goodbye. Now promise me you'll leave him here and not try to take the lad home. If you can't do that, I'm afraid I will have to stop you going in there". Bertie looked down at Len in particular as he spoke.

Len walked into the Room, where the boy was and, slowly walked over to his cot. He was shaking and emotional.

"Well Bertie lad, as soon as you come home, I'll", - Len stopped and started to cry quite openly, he turned and ran out into the arms of his uncle. Bertie put his arms around him and sat him down on the bench.

"Lad, you've got to be brave for your mother. Your brother will not be coming home again and you have to understand that there is nothing in this world that can help him. You have to throw all that love in the direction of your little sister, Joan. Now I want you to go back in there and say goodbye and be supportive and brave for your mother's sake".

Bertie lifted him up and wiped the tears from his cheeks.

Mary was now in the Consultation Room and had young Bertie in her arms, she was rocking him from side to side. Len walked in with his shoulders drooped and his arms tightly down his side. He breathed deeply and cuddled up to his mother. She lowered her arms for Len to kiss Bertie. Len's heart was breaking, He looked up at his mother and puckered his lips trying desperately not to break down, but burst into tears.

She gently popped her son into the crib and lifted the blankets up to his chin, leaning over she kissed him gently on his forehead.

"Goodbye and God Bless, my little one, till we meet again".

She turned to Len,

"Say Goodbye Len", she patted him on his shoulder and gently encouraged him closer to the cot.

"Goodbye my brave little soldier. I will love you forever and will play with you when I come to Heaven, when you will be whole and laughing and tormenting me, just like our David. You will always and forever be my favourite brother".

He pulled the blanket back and picked him up for one last time. Len looked up at his mother and then down at Bertie, who was oblivious to them both.

"I am so sorry mother", he passed the child back to his mother and ran back out into the corridor and into Bertie's arms again. Mary kissed her son again on his forehead and gently placed him back into the cot. She pulled his blankets up and tucked him in. She followed Len out of the consultation room, she had become quite composed. Walking over to Len she put her arms around Len and cuddled him until his crying subsided.

"Len you have nothing to be sorry for. You delivered that boy and your little sister. Most midwifes would have panicked, but you did everything humanly possible to bring those babies into this world. You not only saved Joan's life, but also mine. I am so proud of you, son".

She rocked him like a baby.

Bertie put his arms around both of them and gently guided them back towards the car.

"Right, you two. I've got a surprise for both of you, now get into the car otherwise it will be too late".

Mary stood for a few moments looking at the hospital and whispered 'goodbye my little one' then climbed into the Rolls with Len.

"Hollymoor, Tessalls Lane, Northfield, please now and put your foot down or we'll be too late".

Bertie ordered his driver.

On arrival at Hollymoor, Bertie quickly told Mary that this was one of 4 asylums, together with an annex to Hollymoor, and that they had treated in the region of over 9,000 patients, who were casualties of war.

"Now wait here for a little while", he patted Mary's hand and marched off towards the hospital steps. He jumped up them two at a time. He tipped his cap with his stick at a young officer and then disappeared into the hospital.

After nearly an hour, Bertie came out with a young nurse. He held her arm on his and walked proudly towards the Rolls, they chatted as they came nearer to the car.

She wore a scarlet tippet edged with red and had two stripes on her sleeve. She wore a blue-grey cotton dress and a long white apron with a red cross on it. On her head she wore a white veil. She was dressed immaculately, her black shoes shone and her black stockings were just visible below her apron she held her head high as she walked briskly with Bertie. Her hair was clipped back neatly behind the white veil. She smiled broadly at Mary and Len and held out her arms to greet them as she approached them.

"I'm Hilda, Sam's wife. I've heard so much about you all. I feel as if I already know you, and who is this young man, let me guess! You must be Len, Sam told me about those big ears".

She gently wiggled his ear, as she jested.

He pulled back and then put his hands over his ears and then laughing he put his hand out eagerly to his new sister in law. He began to smile and looked up at Bertie who was beaming from ear to ear. Leonard diverted his attention back to Hilda.

"Very pleased to meet you, Hilda", he said smiling.

Mary just stood in amazement looking at Hilda. She walked over to her slowly and put her arms around her.

"Well our Sam has certainly found himself a lovely bride. It doesn't seem five minutes since I chased him around the garden with my sweeping brush". They both burst out laughing.

"Sam told me to beware of that brush, I hope you've left it at home", Hilda jested.

"I've only got a short while, but I am off this weekend, I can catch the train and come over to see you Saturday if you wish". She said, eagerly awaiting Mary's answer.

"I'll phone our Elsie and she can bring you back with her, she's staying at the Man on the Moon for a few days. If that's alright with you. I know she wants to ask about her beau, a young cavalry officer you looked after for a day or so before his untimely death". Mary took a deep breath and sighed.

"He was so very young to die before he saw his son", she turned her head for a moment trying not to burst into tears.

"How is our Sam", Mary asked changing the subject.

"I haven't heard from him since leaving the Clearing Station, my nursing friends are eagerly awaiting news of him. Everything happened so quickly, I didn't even know about Joe being on the train until I went into the carriage to see what all the noise was about. As soon as Sam turns up I will be told. He didn't know the details of my return when he left for Ypres.

So many people have been so kind to me. Uncle Bertie in particular. I feel as if I've known him forever".

Mary looked at Bertie and smiled lovingly.

He's got influence, I'm sure we will hear something any day soon". Mary patted her on the shoulder and put her arms around her lovingly.

Hilda started to cry. It was all too much.

Bertie put his big arms around both of them.

"Our Sam is strong as an ox and as stubborn too. He'll get through this damn war safe. I've got a job lined up for him when he gets home".

He winked at Leonard.

"I'm going into manufacturing brushes".

They all smiled and then burst out laughing.

CHAPTER 23

"I'm glad I left Gracie behind, she never goes lame, must know something I don't know" Sam whispered to Len.

"I'm thinking the same thing, Sam" Len muttered back looking around him nervously.

"Sooner we get these bloody wagons back to the First Aid Station the better" Sam retorted.

'Len nodded', he turned around again.

Sam stared down along the road at the dead bodies strewn along the ground on both sides of the road. He breathed a sigh of relief, at least most of the bodies were Germans and not those of our own lads he thought to himself.

"Len if you turn around again, I swear I'll make you walk back to the First Aid Station, you're making me and, what's more, look at Rupert's ears, he's as nervous as you are. Now pack it up, do you hear me, pack it bloody up!", Sam turned around himself and Len pushed him.

"Alright for you to turn round though, isn't it?" Len jested.

They were all nervous. It was dusk and it was becoming dark, the mist was making it difficult to see too far. Sam hated to be out with the wagons at this late hour. They'd been stuck in a crater and it had taken the strength of 6 to pull the horses out of the mud and get them back on course. They had to shoot a young mare and it upset them that they had to kill her, but she was too exhausted to move.

Silhouettes were forming in the distance against the last traces of the sunset.

"I'll never become accustomed to this time of night" Len muttered again to Sam.

He looked in front of him at the mangled war-rolled roads, flanked with shell-snapped trees and field telephone wires strewn everywhere. It was becoming increasingly more difficult to drive forward along the road there was so much debris.

Sam smiled at his mate and tried hard not to show his own fear.

"I bet this is beautiful farming land, or was beautiful land", Sam sighed and thought of his own land and green fields.

"It will take donkeys years to get it back to normal, that's if it is ever normal again", Sam shook his head as he looked across the landscape.

Sam looked over at the barbed wire entanglements, it seemed to have suddenly gone horribly dark, the stillness of the night was broken by the croaking of frogs in the distant water. There was a boom of guns in the distant south. A shudder went through his whole body. He felt like a rabbit caught in the headlights of a trap.

"We'd best get a move one lads, only another 2 miles or so, before we get there". Sam turned as he whispered to his men. He lifted his reigns and ordered Rupert and Merlin to walk on. The horses were jumpy and started to bolt. Sam pulled them back into line.

"Easy lads, sign our Gracie's not here to calm you buggers down". He tried to make light of the situation and turned to reassure Len, who was equally as skittish as the horses. He shrugged his shoulders at Len trying to make light of a bad situation.

"I swear next time we get a convoy I'll change and put you at the back so that I don't have to listen to your damn wining". Sam said angrily to Len.

They advanced slowly and cautiously along the road, each wagon trying not to make a sound. There were 4 wagons in the convoy, each carrying vital hospital first aid accessories and other necessary equipment for the First Aid Post. The wagons were adequately marked with a red cross. Each turn of the wheel seemed to last an eternity. Sam leaned over the side of the wagon and peered at the back wheel.

"That wheel is going to come off, I think! I just hope it lasts another couple of miles, or at least until we are nearer to our own guys". Sam lifted himself back into the seat and turned to look at Len.

"This buggers the same Sam". Len almost fell off the wagon as they went over a bad bump. Sam just caught his arm, otherwise he'd probably have ended up under the back wheels of the cart.

Len shook himself and moved closer to Sam. They both smiled and pushed on.

"I wish now, we'd waited for the full convoy tomorrow, rather than be martyrs and try to get through tonight", Sam took a deep breath as he spoke to Len.

"They're so short of supplies" Len answered.

"Suppose so, wish I could light my pipe, I always feel safe when I've got me 'diddy' in". Sam looked about him for something to put into his mouth and chew.

"Don't suppose it would hurt just to put my pipe in my mouth and dream about the Old Shag coming out of my pipe". He breathed in pretending to smell the aroma of his pipe.

Len burst out laughing and pushed Sam sideways. They both started to laugh raucously. Alan in the next wagon asked what the bloody hell they were laughing about.

He was always serious and rarely laughed. Every word that came out of his mouth was a moan or groan about this and that.

Len pulled a sad face and they both giggled together, putting their hands over their mouths to stop Alan hearing them, they were acting like small children. Sam mocked Alan, which made them both start giggling again.

You're like a couple of bloody school kids" Alan muttered to them as he turned around listening for the enemy. He pushed his horses on. Alan was as nervous as Len. He took a deep breath and puffed as he looked at Arthur, and shook his head sideways.

"They're a pair of stupid idiots", he muttered to Arthur, cautious not to let Sam or Len hear what he was saying.

Arthur nodded and continued to scan the land nervously.

The wagons were practically within whispering distance of each other. They advanced slowly and quietly for about 400 yards past the remains of a row of willow trees, a stream ran the other side of the trees, which was almost dry. Tiny noises magnified a hundredfold, a rabbit jumped out from behind the trees and caused the horses to jump. They continued along the road, Sam turned again to make sure every one was still following, he was weary and trying hard for the sounds not to get on his nerves. He could just about see Fred and Tom at the back of the convoy, they had stopped. Tom was leaning up against his shire lifting his front leg. Sam, passed the reigns to Len and jumped down from the wagon.

"Carry on Len, slowly, I'll be back in a few minutes when I find out what the bloody hell is going on back there". Sam patted Rupert on his rump, he had become quite jumpy and started to snort and stamp his feet. Sam sensed danger and looked about him, he patted Rupert again then gently crept around his breast and stroked his nose.

"I'll be back lad in a few minutes, promise" Sam reassured the horse patting him on his shoulder as he disappeared into the darkness. Rupert turned his head and watched as Sam disappeared. He continued to snort and jig about. He knew something was going to happen and just wanted to get the hell away from this part of the road.

Within seconds of walking along the convoy a flare rose above them.

Sam's heart missed a beat, he held his breath and looked up towards the flare. He thought that the enemy could surely hear his heart beating, it felt like it was about to burst out of it's socket. He pushed past the other 2 wagons telling each of them to go on and get the bloody hell out of this place.

"I'll catch up, now go". He hit the lead horse of the second wagon hard on the rump.

Another flare rose in the sky, Sam looked into the field, there were dead cattle and bits of equipment strewn everywhere, which had been left from previous battles.

Sam saw red and white flares shoot up into the sky at short intervals. He waved his arms to the wagons again. The air tasted sour and he felt edgy. He lost his footing and tripped, he rolled down into a crater at the side of the road. He staggered up onto his feet dazed, he quickly started to pull himself up, but there was too much mud, he just kept losing his footing and sliding back down into crater. Sam felt an induced sense of desolation, everything around him seemed to be in slow motion. He crawled up to the lip of the crater and looked around him and was sickened at the carnage.

Sam peered across the field trying to make out what was lurking in the darkness. He could see gas clouds rising, he knew they were to far to affect them, but he could hear the soldiers' coughing and spitting, and screams and then quiet and moans. He was totally alone, the three wagons had moved forward. He strained his eyes to see if he could see the last wagon. He lost his footing and slipped down to the bottom of the crater.

The 3rd battle of Ypres had taken place earlier that month and the Germans were supposed to be retreating, a turn of the tide, the general census among the soldiers' was discussed daily.

It was late September 1918 and things were beginning to change, but not quickly enough for Sam.

Again, he found himself stuck in one of these damn holes unable to get out. He remembered the last time and shut his eyes trying not to think of that terrible day.

He now suffered from nightmares, which were always the

same, he was being sucked down deeper and deeper until he could breath no more, as the thick mud engulfed him covering his head slowly and finally being suffocated in the mud and stench of the black abyss.

He took a deep breath and clawed at the mud. He pushed his hands into the mud and felt something soggy. He lifted it in the air and threw it behind him trying not to look, a lump of rotten black stinking flesh remained in his hand. He tried to rub it off in the mud. It was the remains of someone. He could see the mud moving and a large rat, followed by others, came up from under the mud and ran up his arm and down his back. He shuddered and reached for his revolver, but decided against shooting them and moved over slightly enabling the others to pass without confrontation. He continued to crawl up of the crater nervously looking for more vermin.

These pits presented appalling difficulties to man and beast alike, they were always filled with smelling rotten corpses, rats and water. They engulfed whoever came into there path.

A brilliant, irradiating glare of the enemy's light producing projectiles lit up the sky and then there was a battery of howitzers firing towards the road. Sam could see the reddened sky as the flares lit up the distant village.

Sam's eyes scanned the land around him, the tragic significance of the scene surrounding him made him feel totally alone and ashamed at what man could do.

He finally managed to climb out of the crater and back onto the road, he crept on all fours towards the wagon, a rat stopped and reared up onto his back legs and stared at him menacingly and then decided to jump up over his head and down his back and along his leg. It stopped on his shoe and reared up again looking back towards him, whiskers twitching as it smelled the air, turning it jumped down onto the ground and scurried off into the darkness. Sam shuddered and sat on the ground, he hugged himself, shutting his eyes as he shook his body. He opened his eyes after a few moments and continued to crawl along the road.

"I bloody hate rats", he muttered to himself.

"That one was as big as a cat", he shuddered again and, carried on crawling on all fours along the road. Black shadows silhouetted against a sombre sky going towards the front trenches. Then darkness came again. Sam looked at his watch, it was almost 8.00pm. Everywhere seemed to be covered in a mist, it had begun to rain, making it more difficult for him to focus.

"I wish it was bloody light, I'd just jump up and take me bloody chance, he muttered to himself, but I can hardly see 3ft in front of me", he wiped his eyes on his sleeve.

Looking about him he could see the trees stripped bear of their branches by the shell fire. Then he heard a horse snorting, it hobbled passed him on three legs, it fell head first into a shell hole and rolled down onto it's back. It desperately tried to get up, but it was no use. Sam turned back and dropped back into the crater, he crept to where the horse had landed. He looked about and gently stroked the horse, trying to reassure him, he knew the horse well and cried openly as he took his pistol out, rapped the end of the barrel in his handkerchief to muffle the sound, he gently found the spot to kill, then put the gun to the horses head and fired. He jumped backwards and threw himself onto the floor throwing the gun down. He hated putting a horse down. He wiped the spattered blood off his face with his sleeve, he looked around him to see where he had chucked the revolver. He reached and put it back in his belt.

Sam looked about him, expecting trouble any second but, no-one appeared and nothing happened. Wiping away his tears he set about getting back out of the crater, he crawled back up the crater and cautiously looked about him in case some German was hiding in the shadows waiting to ambush him, but to Sam's surprise no-one was out there. He jumped up and ran towards the wagons turning and looking backwards as he ran.

He stopped and almost fell over, he could see the carnage caused by the howitzer shell. He shuddered from the cold, his uniform was now soaking wet, he was cold, exhausted and in shock, steam rose from his stinking uniform. Sam could hardly breath, he became frantic to find Len. The wagons had been blown apart, the dead horses were strewn about, entrails from Alan's lower body were on the road in front of him, the drivers' from the wagons were all dead, their bodies lay still on the sodden earth all around him. He called out to Len quietly.

"Len, where are you?", he waited eagerly for an answer from his friend.

No answer came, so he walked solemnly through the carnage looking for his friend.

The back wagon had been blown apart, it had taken a direct hit, the horses lay motionless. He turned his head unable to look. Everything had been blown apart. He was relieved that he wouldn't need to shoot another trojan warrior and continued to look for survivors. In a way it was a blessing in disguise he thought to himself, at least they were out of their misery and wouldn't be forced to pull heavy wagons anymore over treacherous roads. He hated the way these creatures were treated. At the end of their usefulness they were shot and sometimes eaten, it was all so senseless and inhumane.

No-one thought about horses, only what they could do, thousands upon thousands had died from both sides needlessly. It sickened him to think about the way they were treated.

The horse he had just killed was the lead horse from the second wagon. The other horse was lying on the ground lifting his head and dropping it back down, to exhausted to get up, he kept trying to lift himself up. He was tangled up in the chains from the shaft of the wagon. Sam kneeled down and stroked him gently, he pulled at the chains trying to unravel the mess. The horse was fighting him all the way. Everyone appeared to be dead, his friends had been blown apart, he turned and looked up at the sky.

"Can't think about this now", he muttered to himself.

He spoke to the horse tenderly, as he took out his revolver and, gently put it to his head, his hand was shaking. He took the gun away and looked up to the sky again and took a big deep breath. He didn't want to shoot him, but he couldn't release him from the mangled chains, he had no choice.

"Oh! God why do you punish these beautiful beasts so", he shouted out in frustration.

He breathed deeply and put the revolver barrel against the horses head, hands shaking, he was desperate and alone. At that very moment a hand reached over his and gently pulled it away.

"Don't want to shoot just yet Sam, let see if we can get him back on his legs first aye" Len leaned against Sam for support and plonked himself down by his side. He had a grimaced smile on his face.

Len was injured badly, he had crawled over to where Sam was. He began pulling at the chains trying to get the horse free holding his side as he battled with the chains.

"I thought I was a goner", he said to Sam still holding his hand over his stomach.

Sam was so relieved to see his mate. He turned and hugged him. They were both covered in mud and stinking as they lay in the quagmire happy to see each other.

"Ouch! Ouch!, put me down. Ouch!", Len cried out.

"Oh! Len, I'll never shout at you again, I'm so glad to see you" Sam puckered his lips and tried not to cry. He bit so hard on his lip that it bled, he licked the blood off his lip.

"You soppy old bugger", Len jested.

"Let's get this boy free and get the hell out of here, shall we?". Len patted Sam on the shoulder. He was as relieved to see his mate as Sam was to see him.

Len struggled to release the chain, he was in so much pain from his stomach wound.

Sam stopped and popped a dressing inside Len's jacket.

"One dressing left and then that's it, must have been waiting for you, Len" he put pressure on the wound as Len fastened his jacket.

"Thanks mate, I'm sure that will help stem the bleeding", Len shut his eyes as he fastened up his jacket. The pain was as much as he could bear.

Sam pulled at the broken shaft and felt a little movement in the chain, he carried on pulling and tucking and eventually he untangled the horses back legs. They were buried in deep water almost up to Rupert's girth. The poor thing just lay there with his head in the mud too exhausted to move.

After a few minutes the chains finally became untangled, the horse put both his front feet forward, and pushed his back legs, trying desperately to get a foothold, then finally after what seemed an eternity he lifted himself up onto his four legs again. He shook himself and pricked his ears up and then looked down at Sam and Len, they were now covered all over with the mud off the horse, but neither minded, they were so relieved that he was out and on his four legs.

The poor thing was shaking all over, he was petrified.

Sam pulled himself up out of the mud and checked the horse out, he was amazed that he only had a few cuts on his body, but otherwise he was fine. Len pulled a piece of the shaft from his shoulder and put pressure onto the wound.

"I don't think the wound is too serious", he said to Sam.

"When I first saw this horse, I thought he was a gonner and look at him now. I nearly shot him, Len". Bugger me! Sam said happily.

Len tried to stand up, but sat back down with a bump. He was in terrible pain and clutched at his stomach, he checked to see if the bleeding had stopped.

"Got some shaft in me belly", he said to Sam.

"Well if I can get you up onto the horse we've got some transport to get back to the Dressing Station". Sam said, as he looked at Len's wound.

"We'd best leave the broken shaft in the wound, it may help stop the bleeding. Hilda has instructed me on this sort of injury" Sam took off his belt and gently put it around Len, popping his last dressing into his coat, as he pulled the belt through the buckle Len winched. He turned his head trying not to let his friend see the tears in his eyes.

"Is Rupert ok, Merlin copped it, I had to put him out of his misery". Sam said sniffing.

"I think Rupert's ok,". Len pointed in the direction where he was standing, the poor thing was shaking and too frightened to move.

Sam lifted his mate up and pushed him up onto the gelding's back and led him to where Rupert stood. He stroked him gently on the head and down his legs, he walked around him checking for injuries. The horses nudged noses, obviously relieved at seeing each other.

Sam was amazed that Rupert had come out of the carnage without a scratch. He lifted off his colour and chains and what was left of the shaft and threw them on the side of the road. He grabbed a clump of main and lifted himself up onto his back, then grabbed his withers and turned him around towards Len gently kicking him to turn.

Len was smiling.

"Takes more than a German shell to kill this boy", he patted the gelding he was on and put his head down on his neck, leaning forward he put both his arms around the horses neck.

Sam nodded and smiled and patted Rupert.

"Bet you can't wait to see Gracie and tell her about this story, can you lad", Sam whispered in Rupert's ears. Rupert took a few steps forward eager to get out of the carnage. He was becoming increasingly restless again, he snorted and turned around eagerly.

The next few seconds happened so quickly, the sky lit up and, at that moment a shell came over and lit up the skies. Sam watched the following moments in disbelief.

Len and his mount took the full force of the shell. One moment Sam looked at his pal smiling and patting his mount, and the next second he was being blown into pieces. The blast missed him and Rupert totally, but the noise was deafening and the shock of the blast stunned Sam.

Len's leg flew through the air and smashed down on Rupert's head, blood and debris were thrown everywhere. Rupert jumped in the air and fly bucked, then bolted down the remains of the corduroy wooden roughly made tracks towards the Dressing Station. Sam pulled and pulled at him with all his might to stop him, but with only a make-shift bridle and no bit, it was impossible to gain control of him, he was out of control. Rupert had no intention of stopping, galloping relentlessly in panic stumbling and tripping. Sam leaned down onto the horses withers and talked to him gently,

"It's alright Rupert, it's alright, now slow down before we end up in a crater, or worse. I'm here lad, I won't let anyone hurt you".

Sam was crying and worried that Rupert might be hurt. He looked down his side, he was covered in blood.

"Come on Rupert, slow down. Let me see if you're hurt. There's a good lad".

The horse began listening to him and started to slow down. Then came to an abrupt halt, snorting and panting. It came as a bit of a shock as Sam flew over his head and landed on his bum on the road. He bounced to an abrupt standstill, groaning as he sat on the floor absolutely covered in mud and shit.

'Didn't expect that he muttered to himself. Glad my dad isn't here' he muttered to himself, trying to make light of the event.

He still had the make-shift reigns in his hands as they slipped over Rupert's head. He looked up at Rupert, who was still shaking and covered in blood.

"Please God do not let this horse die needlessly" he prayed aloud.

The horse came over to him cautiously and tickled his face with his whiskers. Sam smiled and turned over and lifted himself up slowly, then he patted him as he got up.

"Well lad, it's just you and me now". He patted him hard on the neck as he looked at his belly. He gently felt along his belly and crawled under the horse carefully checking him out and then ran his hands down his legs. He popped his head out of the horses legs, Rupert almost bolted again. Sam pulled his head back quickly and jumped out from underneath him.

Sam realised that the blood was that of his friend and the

other horse. He looked back up the road to where his friend had been blown apart, knowing full well that it was no use going back. He sighed heavily and embedded his head in Rupert's neck and cried like a new born baby.

"I'll look after you my friend, I promise you" he whispered as he wiped the tears from his face.

Rupert seemed to know what Sam was saying, he snorted and pushed Sam sideways. Sam looked into the horse's wall eyes and smiled.

"You are a beauty, it's any wonder we fell in love with you. Look at your feathers, they need washing and you need a good groom and a bath.

First thing when I get back to the First Aid Post I'm going to bath you and see to those cuts and that's a promise Rupert. You and me deserve a break after this."

Sam looked about him, every tree and shrub in the vicinity was withered, following the incessant shelling, craters' were all around them, dark shadows and distant shelling, were present in the distance.

Sam grabbed a hand full of withers and lifted himself back onto Rupert's back and pushed him forward.

"Come on lad, if we get out of this shit-hole alive, I'll never let you travel these treacherous roads again. I'll make some excuse to keep you out of service. You can rest with my Gracie, I'll desert with you both if I have too".

Sam leaned down onto his neck and kicked him on, he turned for one last time and wished farewell to his lost friend.

CHAPTER 24

The Silver Ghost Rolls Royce stopped at the church, the driver climbed out and walked around the car, he lifted a wheel chair out of the boot, then opened the door for Mary, she climbed out, straightened her clothing and popped her gloves on. She looked down at her ankles and felt conscious of the flesh exposed and pulled her skirt to hide the new look, which she new would be shunned by her mother. She turned around and put her hand out to help Harry climb out of the Rolls. He smiled at his wife and willingly accepted the help she offered him.

Bertie checked inside the Rolls before rushing around to assist Harry, who grabbed the handle and the side of the door and with the support from Bertie and Mary, he manoeuvred himself into the wheelchair, the driver stood behind the chair and dropped the foot rests down for him. Mary stood back and smiled at Harry, she took the blanket off Bertie and wrapped it around Harry's legs.

"There my darling" she said lovingly.

He pushed it off in disgust.

"I'm not a total invalid Mary" he retorted angrily.

Mary insisted.

"You've just had surgery Harry, do you want to undo everything that Bertie has done for you?"

He knew better than argue with her and reluctantly

accepted the blanket. Bertie smiled and patted him on the shoulder.

"I learnt a long time ago not to argue with a woman, particularly a Wakelam women".

Harry nodded and smiled sarcastically at Mary.

She turned away and smiled into her gloved hand.

Another Rolls Royce pulled up behind them, Leonard climbed out, then Bernard and Nancy came running around the car and stood the other side of Leonard. Elsie and young Mary climbed out and checked that the children were organised, David held Elsie's hand. He was not allowed to move away from her side, this was the condition given to him that morning.

He had been allowed to attend the funeral only if he stayed by his sister's side. Susie and Dolly were not present, they could not get away, they had sent a bunch of white roses.

The children walked over to their parents to await the arrival of the hearse.

The Model T arrived within a few moments. The tiny coffin was covered in roses, it looked lost in the back of the Model T.

The driver lifted the coffin out and walked solemnly towards Leonard, who was now waiting nervously.

"Are you sure about this, Len" he asked as he looked over at Bertie.

Leonard nodded.

The driver returned to the Model T and gathered the flowers up with the help of Nancy, they carried the flowers into the church.

Elsie and Mary assisted Leonard, they walked either side of him giving him the support he needed to carry out this daunting task.

Bernard followed closely behind.

David carried a small bunch of flowers, he had been warned before he moved from Elsie's side, that if he put a step wrong he would be punished with his father's belt. David knew that today was not a time to play up, he too was deeply upset at the loss of his little brother. He wiped the tears from his face and tried not to let his siblings know he was crying.

Elsie put her arm around him and smiled lovingly, he buried his head in her long black skirt. Elsie too was crying openly, young Mary took out her handkerchief and offered it to David. He accepted it and wiped his tears away and offered it back to young Mary. She declined his offer and gently pushed his hand away. David popped the handkerchief into his trouser pocket.

They continued into the church.

Mary was about to follow Leonard, when another Rolls Royce Silver Shadow pulled up. Mary stood in amazement, she held onto the wheelchair shaking.

Her mother climbed out of the Rolls Royce with Dr Vincent, he held her arm courteously as he escorted her towards her daughter.

She was impeccably dressed, in black with a jet necklace around her neck. She had black gloves on and a fur coat down to her ankles. She held her head proudly and walked over to Mary and Harry and put her hand out to shake Harry's hand. She quietly said how sorry she was at the death of young Bertie, then stood back looking nervous as to her next move.

Bertie gently nudged Mary towards her mother, she stepped forward under duress and gave Bertie a look that would kill. She was shaking and felt very emotional, but at the same time didn't want her mother to know how overwhelmed she felt that she had decided to attend her little boy's funeral.

Mary cupped her hand into Bertie's. He smiled at her and then turned to Mary's mother's and offered her his other arm.

Harry looked up at his wife and mother-in-law, both standing in front of him now, too proud to speak to each other. He wanted to bang their bloody heads together, all these years and even now at this very sad time they hardly said a word to each other.

'It beggars belief' he said under his breath.

He shook his head and looked up at the chauffer, who had just spoken to him.

Mary looked down at her husband and shrugged her shoulders, making sure her mother didn't see her reaction to her husband.

Bertie released himself from Mary's hand and put it into her mother's hand and took charge of the wheelchair and continued into the church.

Bertie pushed Harry through the church and placed him by the side of the aisle on the front row and sat down besides him.

Mary and her mother followed with Dr Vincent closely behind. Neither party said a word. They both looked at the leaded glass windows together. The light that now shone down into the church reminded her of when she was a little girl holding her father's hand. She took a deep breath and carried on walking down the isle, the church was adorned with beautiful flowers, the aroma of the roses filled the air. They both sat down on the front row. Mary passed her money a hymn sheet, she thanked her and looked down at the hymn that had been chosen.

Leonard walked very carefully towards the church holding out the coffin, Bernard followed him, Nancy held his hand. Elsie, David and young Mary followed, the other children had been left with young Mary's mother, they were too young to attend the church.

Joe came last, he carefully climbed out of the front seat of the Rolls, assisted by the driver. He refused a wheelchair and clumsily walked into the church with a little help from Bertie's Batman. He sat down on the opposite side to his parents. It was a relief to sit down. He burst out coughing almost immediately. Young Mary sat down next to him and held his hand, she passed him her handkerchief. Joe declined it and lifted out his own handkerchief and smiled at her. Realising Joe needed to get rid of the phlegm she turned her head away so that Joe could spit into his handkerchief. She patted him on his back gently and asked if he was alright. He nodded.

Elsie, Nancy and Bernard sat down on the next row. David

pushed past everyone and sat at the end of the second row treading on Elsie's foot in the process. She looked at him and pushed him along the row. He lowered his head and carefully made sure he did not stand on anyone else's foot.

Leonard put the small coffin onto the platform in front of the vicar. He turned and walked to his brothers'. His arms ached, he had pins and needles in both hands. Joe smiled at him proudly and then burst out coughing again. He took his handkerchief out of his pocket again and screwed it up in his hand. He looked down at it and hid it in his pocket feeling totally embarrassed and moreover worried. It was covered in phlegm and blood.

Mary sat opposite her children, she was heartbroken. She sobbed openly. Her mother put her arms around her and gently rocked her. Harry held her hand and patted it with his other hand. He leaned forward to see if Leonard was alright.

Joe acknowledged his father and moved up to sit next to Leonard. He put his arms around his shoulders, he was crying bitterly, Joe hugged him gently until the crying subsided.

Leonard didn't hear a word the vicar said, he continued sobbing and sniffing throughout the service. Nancy cried into Bernard's arms, he remained quite composed and subdued, he put his arms around both his siblings. Leaning forward slightly he asked if Joe was alright. He nodded and Bernard sat back against the pew.

Joe stared at the tiny white coffin with it's ornate brass handles. He'd seen too much death over the past years. His thoughts were with Sam back in Belgium and all the soldiers', who had died needlessly, left without being properly buried on the battleground or some side road leading to nowhere.

Joe was overwhelmed at being home with his family, but felt totally detached from this world and young Mary. He was finding it difficult to communicate with anyone, other than his father and his uncle Bertie, who had seen war and it's total destruction first hand. Joe felt betrayal to his fellow comrades being home and safe, despite his injuries. He was worried sick about Sam, he'd heard nothing from him for weeks.

The vicar opened his bible and started to sing
"all things bright and beautiful"
everyone stood up and commenced singing.

Leonard nudged Joe after the service had finished to get up, Joe came back to his senses and got up holding onto the bench. Bernard walked around the two of them and offered his hand to Joe. He smiled at his brother and leaned on him for support.

Bernard had grown so much, Joe couldn't believe how tall he had become and how Leonard had changed. He put his arms around both of them and walked along the isle with his young brothers'. He felt so proud at how they had turned out and relieved that they would not be going to serve in the war.

The service had been quite short, the vicar prayed for all the soldiers' that had been lost in the war and for all the families who had lost their loved ones.

Following the service the coffin was laid to rest next to Mary's brother.

The family plot had been opened, uncle Bertie had seen to it that the child was buried in the family grave.

He had argued with his brother bitterly about where the child should be buried and it was Mary's mother who suggested that the child be buried next to her only son. She had insisted that it was only fitting that little Bertie should be put to rest in the family plot. She argued bitterly with her husband and threw it at him that the child had his own blood running through his little veins.

They argued for days, until reluctantly Mary's father agreed that the child be buried in the family plot, but he vowed that he would not, under any circumstances, attend the child's funeral, or be buried in the plot himself.

He walked out of the room and drank himself into oblivion. Mary's mother had not seen her husband for days and quite frankly didn't give a damn if he drank himself to death. He was just a bitterly twisted old sod who had become embroiled in his own hatred.

Mary's mother hugged her daughter sheepishly, as they

stood looking at the tiny coffin and shook Harry's hand. She also shook hands with the boys and young Nancy, then the girls. She returned to the Rolls Royce, pulling her coat together, then popping her gloves back on. She felt suddenly quite cold and more importantly, guilty.

Dr Vincent shook hands with Harry, Mary and Leonard and offered his deepest condolences at the sad loss of their son. He asked if Joan was alright. Mary shook her head trying not to cry again.

"You must bring her to my next surgery so that I can examine her more closely and keep an eye on her".

"She's fine doctor, I will bring her across next week, if that's still the plan".

"Best we check her out Mary, just to make sure that she has no!", he stopped himself and gently kissed her on the cheek.

"See you next week, Mary" he said, looking at Bertie for moral support.

Bertie stood next to Mary and held her hand.

"Don't worry Mary, I'll get you picked up and take Joe back at the same time", he nodded at Joe and young Mary.

Dr Vincent walked over to the Rolls Royce, embarrassed and annoyed, at the behaviour of both mother and daughter.

He also felt deep guilt over the baby. He knew from the very first moment that he held the baby in his hands that there was nothing he could do to help the child.

In those days, the kindest thing to do was to let the child die and not assist them in any way.

He turned and smiled at Mary and Harry and climbed into the Rolls.

The Rolls Royce pulled away, Mary's mother rolled the window down and waved tearfully to Mary and Harry. The hearse followed shortly afterwards. She sat back into her seat, looked at Dr Vincent, took her handkerchief out, and wiped her tears away and blew her nose.

"Home please driver" she ordered as she played with her gloves in her lap.

Dr Vincent bit his lip and looked out of the window, he

wanted to say something, but felt it was none of his business. They continued the journey in complete silence.

Vincent knew of the family feud and wanted to bang all their heads together. He had lost his two sons in the war and had no grave to visit, they were left where they had dropped on the Somme. His wife had become withdrawn, she rarely got out of bed nowadays. And, here was a family in grief, obviously needing each other and, no-one willing to bend. He lit his pipe and tapped his foot on the floor of the Rolls, frustrated at the whole damn scenario.

Mary's mother was obviously annoyed at the way Vincent was behaving and moved over to the other window and opened it. She turned and looked at him lifting her head high. She lifted her hand to her mouth and then coughed feebly, realising it was useless, she looked out of the window again at the beautiful landscape.

Vincent closed the other window and sat down abruptly, making sure that she knew exactly how he felt, and puffed his pipe deliberately to annoy her.

Of course, she wanted to talk to her daughter, but didn't know how to. Well over 20 years had passed, without a word being spoken, with the exception of the heated argument at the hospital, when her son died.

She had felt so guilty at her husband's insistence that they kept "Mickey", who had died tragically of colic some months after the death of her son. She swore that if the horse had been given to Mary it would still be grazing in a field somewhere. The horse was buried on their land with other loved livestock.

She wanted to hug the children, but she knew her husband would never accept the family. It was no use going behind his back, it would never work. She had defied him coming to the funeral. She was obviously going to return to yet another family argument about her wayward daughter, but she was glad that she had attended the funeral. Her husband had turned into a bitterly twisted man and drank himself into oblivion daily to hide all the pain of losing both his children.

He had turned into a lonely recluse and had no love left to give.

She desperately wanted to chat to Leonard, she had heard so much about him from Bertie. He was full of pride when he talked about him to her in private.

He had told her that he was a typical Wakelam, tall, intelligent, proud and extremely sensitive, with lovely thick dark brown hair and big green eyes. They laughed as he said that Leonard adorned the big ears and was regularly teased about them. Bertie talked about him incessantly and of his ambitions for Len's future whenever they were alone.

Bertie loved Leonard as he would his own son, he also felt a strong responsibility for Joe and Sam.

Mary's boys were all he would want his own sons to be, sadly this would never happen now. He chose his career before family values. Sadly he had watched his brother turn his back on his own child years before and had watched the love of his life die of consumption. He could not help Daisie, he watched her frail life end after suffering for months. He promised himself following her death that this would never happen again to anyone he loved. So he threw himself into becoming a surgeon, little did he know at the time that fate would bring him full circle to save the lives of both Harry and Joe.

He had no regrets, other than having no children of his own. Mary's boys filled in that void and he had to be content with this.

Mary's mother had heard about all of the children from Bertie and desperately wished that things had been different and that she could be a proper grandparent to Mary's children and not someone who heard everything second hand.

She knew in her heart that her husband felt the same, but he was just too pig headed to admit it.

Thank goodness for Bertie, he would keep an eye on them all for her. She hadn't even a photograph of her grandchildren, just memories of today and pictures that Bertie had embedded into her memory of Joe and Sam in Belgium and how proud he was of them.

She read the obituaries every week in private and drew a sigh of relief when their names were not on the list.

Deep in thought she continued the journey back home in total silence.

Back at the churchyard the children each dropped a white rose into the plot and said a chosen few words.

Leonard and Bernard threw their roses together, turned and walked back over to the Rolls.

Young Mary and Joe, stood and looked at the plot for some time, then threw their roses in. Joe kissed young Mary on the cheek and put his arm around her waist, she helped her husband back to the car.

Mary and Harry were the last two at the plot.

The Batman stood over on the path near to the church waiting instructions.

Mary turned away from Harry and walked over to her brother's grave and placed a single rose on his marble head stone.

She asked him to put his arms around her little one and look after him until the day came that they could be together again as brother and sister as they had been as children. She kissed her hand and placed the kiss on his grave, then turned to go back to Harry.

Realising Mary had put her rose on her brother's grave he gave her the rose he was holding. They threw the rose into the plot together.

"Goodbye my son", she said quietly.

Harry was too emotional to say a word.

Mary turned the wheelchair and pushed Harry towards the Rolls. The Batman came over to her and took over pushing Harry to the car.

Uncle Bertie made sure that the children were all settled and returned to his own Rolls. After checking everyone was seated he instructed the driver to take the family home.

Bertie turned and looked over at the plot and sighed.

"One day I will join you boys and girls and we will all be together again, one big family, as it should have been in this world".

He tapped his hand on the side of his leg and jumped into the Rolls.

CHAPTER 25

It was 11th November, 1918, a little after 11.00am, Armistice Day, the war had finally ended.

Sam leaned over the paddock stroking Gracie, she nuzzled up close to him and smeared a mixture of hay and food all down his clean uniform as she chomped on the apple he had just given her. Rupert barged forward in an attempt to get Sam's attention and the rest of the apple, Gracie bit him on the neck, he turned and fly bucked across the paddock.

Sam laughed out loud and wiped the muck of his arm, he turned to face Bertie, who in turn patted him on the back. Both popped their pipes into their mouths and puffed smoke out of the side of their mouths. They laughed as they did it simultaneously.

"Well my lad you survived the War, and it's time we got you home to that gorgeous nurse back in England, and what are we going to do about those two fleabags".

Bertie patted his pipe on the paddock gate making sure that the ash was not alight, He took a deep breath.

"I just hope they behave a little better on the boat", Bertie looked across the paddock, both of them were now happily side by side eating what little grass there was on the frosty ground.

"Leave it to me Sam, I'll have to pull a few strings. Most of the horses are going to auction for meat and even worse a life down the pits. Only the chosen few are going home, mainly officers' horses. It's a crying shame that so many of these Trojans are being disposed of, despite their gallant efforts throughout the war. Bravery awards should be awarded to the surviving few, not the bullet or sent to some abattoir, or worse, worked to death down the pits". Bertie looked out at the carnage in front of him and sighed deeply.

"So many have died during the past years, not a family in the land have come through this unscathed, and for what?" Bertie thumped the gate angrily.

"Thank you Bertie for getting me posted onto the ship. Transporting the horses back to England will be so rewarding, seeing our four legged friends go home, where they belong. Shame our Joe couldn't be here at this moment".

Sam stared out across the devastation in front of him. They both stood still remembering.

Bertie broke the silence and spoke first,

"Joe is recovering nicely in the hospital, the fresh air will do his lungs a world of good, he was so lucky, the damage is minimal, thank God for Hilda's quick thinking. He should be able to live with the left lower lobe of his lung collapsed, quite well. He will always have congestion and suffer with his breathing and pain, but he's alive and should be able to work again. The work our nurses are doing is exceptional, these young men are being spoilt rotten, they don't want to go home at the end of their convalescence",

Bertie stopped for a moment and looked about him.

So many have died from this warfare Sam, on both sides. It's a terrible way to die.

Bertie was thinking now of the young soldiers' that had come to him for surgery and help and died in their hundreds.

I'm not sure if he will ride again, though, Sam?"

Sam smiled and nodded.

"If I know our Joe he'll be back in the saddle before I get home".

Bertie twisted his moustache and sighed out loud.

"You're probably right, Sam"

They turned and started walking back towards the Dressing Station.

"Got to get you back to Hilda, she's so looking forward to your return. I've had my orders from her for your prompt and safe return. She's quite bossy isn't she, Sam".

He smiled at Bertie and remembered how caring she had been when he first came into the Dressing Station. How she had cared for Joe and other wounded soldiers', and how he had watched her whilst she attended to his brother.

He was away in another world thinking of his love and returning home with his beloved horses and seeing his family again.

He sat down on a bail of hay and looked out at what was left of the burnt trees and wire entanglements and desolation of what must have been a beautiful landscape before the war.

Bertie sat down next to him and kicked the soil from under his feet. He too was thinking of what the land must have been like before the bombs and barbed wire and death of so many young men.

The firing had finally ceased, however, up until a few minutes ago, the shelling had been quite heavy, it seemed that every battery was trying to burn it's guns. Finally, their was an abrupt silence.

There had been no celebration, just quiet between both sides.

Sam could only think of the crude little crosses that marked the graves of the dead. Bewilderment, and the shock of peace, consumed his ever minute. He had waited so long for this moment and now it was here he could not comprehend that it was all over and that he had survived the carnage of war.

Sam looked at Bertie with tears in his eyes.

"What was it all for Bertie, so many sons will not return to their mothers', and husbands to their wives'. I will never be the same again, I have witnessed too much death and cruelty for one lifetime".

Sam turned his head away hiding his tears.

Bertie put his arm on his shoulder and comforted him. Sam cried bitterly as he held him close.

"I witnessed death and destruction in the Boer War, Sam. I never thought I would ever forgive, or forget, but time is a great healer. The horror never goes away, but it gets easier, I promise you Sam, the nightmares fade as the years pass by, they become a distant memory almost as if you've dreamed it all. Bertie took out his pipe and banged it against the tree stump behind him. He filled his pipe and lit it, taking a deep puff and blowing the smoke out of the corner of his mouth.

"Never will I forget this wanton destruction and killing, My friends and comrades were all killed here, I'm the last one. I feel guilty that I survived. I can never forget, neither do I want to forget them"

Sam turned his head and wiped his face on his sleeve.

Bertie leaned forward and wiped some hay from his face and smiled gently at his nephew.

"Sam, you must believe me, that the only way forward is to live your life and thank God every day that you survived and live for your comrades and loved ones", Bertie patted him lovingly.

Bertie had become so close to his nephews over the past few years. He loved them as his own and was proud of them. He put his hands out and held Sam, taking a deep breath of air, trying desperately not to cry. He felt so emotional and knew how Sam felt.

"I feel ashamed Bertie. Will this guilt ever leave me".

Sam waited for Bertie's answer.

"My boy, I cannot answer all your questions. I do not have the answers. The only advice I have for you is to go home, turn your horses out, put your arms around that lovely wife and thank God that you did survive and are not buried somewhere out there in a nameless grave, as so many other brave soles are".

Bertie pointed out at "no man's land".

"Live for your friends, Sam. They would have wanted you to have a life, I am sure of that".

Bertie walked back over to the paddock and patted Gracie and passed her some hay.

"Well girl, you'll not feel guilty, I'm sure. There's a lovely field waiting for you and Rupert, and if your dad tires of you, I'm sure I can find a nice home for you on my land".

Gracie nuzzled up to him and paid him the same compliment by slobbering down the front of his No. 1's.

He turned and smiled at Sam.

"Well that's gratitude for you".

He brushed the slobber off with his handkerchief. Smiling as Gracie walked away from him.

"Come on lad, lets get something to eat and see about the transportation of these two hero's and see my friend the Colonel".

CHAPTER 26

Elsie smiled at young Mary as she passed her a cup of tea. The girls sat down around the table in the shop, each with a rock cake in their hand, giggling like little children.

"Shall we eat these before the others come, Elsie, or shall we put them back in the bag and share them".

Young Mary licked her lips and waited for Elsie's answer patiently.

"That's a difficult one. The kids are finally asleep and we've worked hard on the window display, I think we deserve to eat them right now" Elsie paused with her mouth inches from the bun and was just about to take a bite when the door bell went.

"Bugger", she said aloud and dropped the cake back into the paper bag.

Hilda shouted "hello", then poked her head into the kitchen.

"Caught you, going to eat that lovely rock cake before I came, were you, aye?".

Elsie looked guiltily at young Mary and smiled coyly.

"Well it's a good job I bought another two for us then, isn't it" Hilda shook her bag of goodies and dropped them on the table.

Within seconds the bell rang again, and in popped David Richards and his wife. They came into the kitchen and sat down around the table.

"Put the kettle on Mary and let's make this an opening party, shall we?" David said, smiling at his wife.

The bell rang out again and in came Mary with baby Joan in her arms.

Elsie jumped up and took the child from her mother and popped the baby into the pram with Charles and little Valerie.

"Room for more" Elsie said, as she looked at her mother smiling.

"Some party this is, thought you might like a few rock cakes", Mary dropped the cakes on the table.

They all burst out laughing. Just one person missing now and that's our Nancy. Elsie joked.

Then the bell went again and in walked Nancy with a loaf of bread and some cheese and butter in greaseproof paper.

Well this is going to be a lovely party Mary jested and plonked herself down at the head of the table.

"Get the carving knife out, Elsie, lets have some cheese and crunchy bread before we devour those rock cakes".

"Mother I haven't got a carving knife", Elsie said worryingly.

"I'll have to do it the old way then", as she tore at the bread and broke off big pieces and passed them around the table. She managed to cut the cheese and left it to the individuals to butter their own bread.

"Nothing like having bread and cheese this way", she said to everyone as she devoured her crusty bread and popped a lump of cheese into her mouth.

They were all chatting, eating and drinking tea, when the bell range again and in walked Millie and Ethel.

"Thought you'd have a party, without us, did you?". Millie jested and plonked some more rock cakes on the table, opened her coat and bought out a bottle of brandy and port, and promptly put the bottles down onto the table.

"We'll have to use cups, Millie, we haven't got any glasses here"

Mary smiled, we haven't even got a carving knife for the

bread", she pushed Millie in a friendly way and plonked herself back down on the chair.

Elsie held the port high and kissed the bottle. Young Mary quickly washed the cups that they had previously been drinking tea from.

"Hurry up then you lot and drink your tea and get some of this lovely port down your necks", Millie shouted above all the chatter.

They tipped what tea was in the cups down the sink and held them out for the port.

"Here's to our Billie, Joe, Sam, Harry and our loved ones", Millie banged her cup against Elsie's and then young Mary's. Everyone turned and said cheers and drank down the port.

The kitchen was so full they moved into shop.

"Time for another tipple, Millie filled up the cups and held her cup high in the air.

"Here's to Elsie's success in her new business".

"To Elsie" the cups banged together again.

They had a lovely time chatting about the end of the war and the family coming home.

Elsie was ecstatic with happiness and talked to David about not only selling hats, but also the latest 'drawers, shoes, and brassieres'. He felt a little embarrassed and outnumbered by all the women present. He lifted his coat and wife's off the hanger and popped it over her shoulders.

"Time to go, my love, I think this party can do without us two outsiders".

They bid everyone good day, shaking hands as they exited from the shop.

Elsie got her drawings out and showed her mother her latest designs in hats, dresses and the new drawers and chemises that she would be making. She fetched and opened a shoe box with the latest high-buttoned, high heeled shoes, having dark leather black foot and a contrasting upper top. Mary lifted them out of the box and hiccupped, she was too far gone to appreciate what her daughter was talking about. She nodded and said "nicccccccccce" and slumped back on the chair.

"I'll make you some silk nickers, mom, you can be my first customer, but don't wear them when dad's about, don't want anymore little Price's do we, 11 is enough for any family". Elsie said looking into the pram at the sleeping babies.

"I've also written to a hosiery company in Sutton in Ashfield, Nottinghamshire, about ladies stockings, which will be on the market in the coming months". Elsie was full of enthusiasm.

Mary looked at her daughter's drawings in awe, but they quickly became duplicated, she wiped her eyes and looked again. Mary was very inebriated. She wondered to herself where all the talent her daughter had inherited had come from. She waddled about the shop and looked at all the beautiful hats she had made. Young Mary tapped her on the shoulder. She turned quickly and fell down, young Mary lifted her back up. They both staggered backwards falling against the counter.

"Hasn't Elsie done well", young Mary. She said staggering back into the kitchen.

"She has a talent, that's for sure. I am sure that this business is going to thrive and her ideas, regarding hats and drawers, will be welcome after the country being at war for all these years. I'm just wondering whether the ladies who are currently in mourning will appreciate such fashion". Mary tried one of the hats on and staggered back into the kitchen holding it in case it fell off. She had it on back to front. Elsie popped it on correctly and made her mother sit down before she fell down.

Elsie had drunk so much port and brandy she could barely stand and dropped down on the seat next to her mother.

Everyone was so happy the war was over and that their loved ones would be coming home. Even Nancy had too much to drink, she was fast asleep on a chair with her head slumped on the table.

Millie had started on the brandy and couldn't understand why everyone was staggering about.

Bertie's driver came into the shop, looked around and

promptly sat down, wondering how he could get this mob back home, without someone being sick in Bertie's car.

Mary could barely stand, young Mary fell on her bottom, and Elsie tried desperately to pick her up. Nancy was totally out of it. They giggled like little children. Mary put her hand out to be lifted up and promptly fell back down onto her bottom and hiccupped, giggled and said "pardon"!

"Good job the kids are all asleep. Don't know why, with all this noise going on", he muttered to himself.

Millie smiled and patted him on his shoulder, almost knocking him over.

"You take our Elsie and I'll get Nancy, we'll get young Mary on the next trip, then the kids. I'll lock up and away we go", she went to pat him again and he moved out of the way.

Finally after what seemed like hours, Millie checked the shop looked about and closed the door and locked it.

'I'll bring my cleaners tomorrow and sort this lot out' she muttered to herself, Elsie will be in no fit state tomorrow to do anything, let alone look after Charles. She smiled and thought of the child and how well Billie and Elsie were getting along.

'Wont be long now' she said rubbing her hands together.

Harry was due home soon, Sam in the following weeks, and arrangements were being made for Joe to be picked up by Bertie's driver from the convalescent home, for another party.

Mary had been planning her welcome home party for weeks and was just waiting for Sam's return, so that her Boys could be together again for the first time in over 4 years.

CHAPTER 27

The Homecoming of Mary's Boys

Harry, Joe and Sam, all climbed out of the Rolls Royce, Sam and Joe were in full military uniform. Harry had tweed trousers and a khaki jumper and tweed jacket on.

Hilda, young Mary, and Elsie, arrived shortly afterwards, together with Billie Palmer, also in full uniform and Millie. Baby Charles was fast asleep in Billie's arms. The driver went to the boot and started unloading the food for the party. Millie walked around to the boot and checked that the Port and Brandy were handled carefully. She stood watching the driver making sure everything went into the cottage. He had still not forgot the party at Elsie's shop.

Bernard, Len, Nancy and David, all came running out of the cottage and flanked poor Sam. Phyliss followed unable to catch up to her siblings.

Mary stood on the porch looking at her sons' alone and bewildered. She was shaking with emotion and excitement, she put her hand to her mouth unable to believe that Sam was finally home and safe.

Harry walked clumsily across the yard on his sticks, climbed the two steps and stood by her side.

"Well old gal! he's home". He said lovingly, putting his arms around her waste.

Sam stared nervously back across the yard at his mother. He had dreamt of this moment throughout the war. She hadn't changed a bit. The broom she had clobbered him with was still in the same place by the back door. He smiled and looked up to the sky trying desperately not to cry.

He walked quickly across the yard to her, she ran into his arms. Sam lifted her in the air and twirled her around.

"You'll make me giddy Sam, put me down". She said as she looked down into those lovely green eyes of his. She took his beret off and looked at him, not believing that he was finally home and safe.

"My you've grown", she said, feeling giddy with love for the son she thought she would never see again.

Sam plonked her down on the floor.

"Well mother, I think you may have shrunk" he said jokingly.

Despite travelling with his father and talking to him in the car he threw his arms around him. He smelt the pipe tobacco on his clothes and breathed the smell into his nostrils. It was so welcoming. He had thought about this moment during the long lonely nights on the front. He never thought this moment would come.

Sam smoked the same OLD SHAG tobacco, it reminded him of his father and Bertie.

Harry put his arms around his son and forgot his leg for a moment. He almost fell over. Sam managed to stop him falling and carefully steadied him. Mary sent Bernard for a chair to sit him down before he damaged his knee again.

Harry reluctantly sat down.

"Stop fussing woman, you're like a mother hen, always cackling about me". He smiled at her and conceded to sit down, as he had been ordered.

"When are the horses arriving", Mary asked Sam.

"They should be here any time now, uncle Bertie is following in his Model T, he's organised a convoy in case the horses are hijacked."

Sam winked at his father, who in turn winked back, they both looked at Mary's expression.

"Always, the joker", Mary jested, as Sam plonked himself on the arm of his father's chair.

"Had you for a moment though, didn't I, mother?" Sam looked up at his mother admiringly.

"The horses didn't eat during the crossing, the sea was very rough and the cradle lifting them on board upset Gracie. She had a bit of colic during the journey. I mixed her a bran mix and stayed with her all night. Rupert took it in his stride, but she was terribly afraid. Gracie neighed and swayed backwards and forwards, I thought I might have to shoot her, but she seemed to calm down when I lay in her pen with her.

She'd had a rough time before me and a mate found her up to her withers in mud and shit. They were going to shoot her until we stepped in. Ever since that day she's always been a one man horse", Sam said.

He began to worry about why it was taking so long for the transport to arrive.

He paced the yard wishing he'd travelled the last few miles with his beloved Gracie.

"I should have travelled with her and changed clothes when I got here", he said guiltily.

He had began to chew at his nails. Hilda came across to him and put her arms around him. She looked over at Harry and smiled.

The horses finally arrived over an hour late. Uncle Bertie jumped out of the cab and apologised for the delay, then stood on the outside of the paddock waiting for the horses to be set free, after their long arduous journey.

Gracie came storming down the ramp, snorting and stamping. Sam caught her lead rope, then patted her on the nose and led her to the paddock. She quietened down when he took hold of her. She had already kicked the two privates who were in charge of her, who came limping across to the paddock.

"She's been stamping and kicking in the back, and look at her now", the driver said to Bertie.

"Little madam", the private said quietly, so nobody could hear him.

The driver put his hands on his hips and marvelled at the rapport between them. Gracie trusted her master totally.

"Well suppose I'd best get the other bugger out before he comes out of the side of your automobile, Sir!", the driver saluted Bertie. He ran back up the ramp. He forgot himself for a moment, remembering he was still in the army and that Bertie was his Senior Officer. He waited for a moment, leaning against the inside of the truck, to see if he was in trouble, then breathed a sigh of relief.

He popped Rupert's bridle on, because he'd snapped his head collar earlier. He pushed on his chest to force him around. Rupert was having none of it, he turned quickly and dragged the private out with him, who just about managed to hold onto the reins.

Rupert came bombing down the ramp, snorting and bucking, until he saw Sam and flew across the yard to him, dragging the poor private with him. He jumped up and dusted himself off, embarrassed at not being able to handle the horse.

"He's a bit excitable, this one, isn't he, sir!" he jested as he stood to attention.

"No need to salute me" Sam said angrily.

Sam quickly grabbed Rupert's reins and made sure he was alright. He checked his legs and under his girth. He looked daggers at the private. Then he proceeded to put Rupert in the paddock with Gracie.

The children came out from behind Joe and jumped up on the rails of the paddock.

The horses both came across to Joe, almost as if they remembered him and nuzzled up against him. He had carrots hidden in his pocket and caused a commotion when he tried to give Rupert one before Gracie. She bit him on the neck and kicked him full in the chest with both her front feet.

"Good job we took their shoes off" Sam said to Joe.

"I think you may have to separate them, Sam, just in case

one of the kids gets in the way". Joe scratched his head as he looked at them.

"We'll see, Joe, lets just let them settle in, after all they've been travelling for days, they're bound to be a bit techic".

Sam and Bernard jumped over the paddock gate and strolled over towards them.

"As soon as we put them to the plough and work them for a while, I'm sure they should settle down", Bernard said, patting Gracie on the neck.

"She's a beauty Sam. What is she? 17hh, or thereabouts. My measuring stick is at the stables, I'll bring it Monday, and we can see exactly how big she is. Wall eyes, they're beautiful. Unusual you have two", Bernard said looking at her and checking her over.

"I think she is more like 17hh 3. She's as comfortable as an armchair to ride and not at all skittish. We can take them out in a couple of days and you can see what she's made of, if you wish".

Sam put his arm around his brother and they casually walked back towards the others. The horses followed nudging them in the back as they walked.

"I'd like that, Sam", Bernard answered turning round to see who was head butting him.

It was Rupert, he'd took a shine to Bernard.

The girls all gathered together, and put their arms around each other laughing and skipping like young children.

"Well you lot we've got a party to organise, so we'll see you boys later". Hilda shouted over the fence at Sam.

They walked, skipped and then ran into the cottage. Mary joined them, she looked back over her shoulder at her son as she disappeared into the kitchen to give the girls a hand. She popped her head back out of the kitchen door and gave her husband instructions:

"Harry you're in charge of the children today, so don't take any nonsense from them, particularly our David", she pointed to him and he lowered his eyes knowing he was still walking a very fine line with his parents, after being caught red handed in the parsnip wine for the umpteenth time.

"This was going to be a Christmas to remember" Mary said, as she looked around the kitchen at the girls all busily cooking and organising.

"I'm glad I decided to raise a turkey this year, I didn't really want to kill her though, so I decided it was a man's job to deliver the final blow. Took our Bernard and Len over an hour arguing in the barn, I thought I may have to go in and do it for myself, but I think they drew straws eventually as to who was going to deliver the final blow. Last year we had a small chicken and, it ran around the yard headless for over 5 minutes, our David chased it, it frightened the young ones, they wouldn't eat any meat that year", Mary said as she took the turkey out of the oven.

Bertie stood by the paddock smoking his pipe. He was rather pleased with himself getting the horses back, but it had cost him. A matter which he would not be discussing with anyone soon. He watched the children playing. He took a deep breath and walked across to the barn to chat to the boys who were all sitting on bails of hay chatting.

Later that day, with the party in full swing, young Mary, Joe and Sam stood outside the barn. Elsie and Billie joined them, with Hilda in tow.

"I think it's the barn for us tonight", Joe said to Sam.

He specifically looked over at young Mary. She new why he was winking at her. Valerie had been conceived in this very barn the night before Joe went off to the war. She bit her lip and winked back at Joe and chuckled. Elsie watched with interest, she new exactly what was going on between them.

Billie asked unwittingly what 'was the secret', Elsie popped her finger onto her lip and turned around guiltily.

"I'll tell you later, big mouth" she said, as she pushed him. He walked away from her wondering what on earth he had done, again! Unfortunately he felt a little pushed out. He plonked himself down on a bail of straw and looked over at the paddock wondering what to do next.

Sam and Joe ran into the barn and left the girls and Billie wondering what was going on. They in turn quickly followed not wanting to miss out on anything.

"First come, first served", Joe said laughing.

Sam and Joe, fell on the floor laughing. They threw hay at each other and all hell broke lose. Everyone joined in.

After the hay fight Joe and Sam decided where they would sleep.

The boys were so happy, their loved ones finally in their arms.

Sam started to sing 'Jerusalem' and they all joined in, singing and staggering back into the party.

That evening, following the party, two babies were conceived in the barn.

Mary looked out of the bedroom window towards the barn it was a beautiful night and a full moon. Bernard, Leonard and David, were running across the yard, each with a bottle of parsnip wine in their hands. David turned quickly and checked that no-one was following him. He sat down and pulled the cork out of the bottle with his teeth and spit it out. He quickly guzzled a mouthful of the wine out of the bottle and ran after his brothers.

Mary, turned and looked at Harry.

"They will regret taking that wine tomorrow, it's not ready for human consumption, I moved the good stuff under the stairs last night".

Harry turned his wife away from the window and held her in his arms.

"My love, I couldn't care less what the little buggers are up to tonight, I'm so happy. I love you so much, it hurts".

He kissed her on the lips and held her tightly. She felt his manhood pressing into her groom and breathed heavily.

He pulled away and looked down.

She smiled and pulled him back towards her. She hadn't a care in the world other than tonight and being with her husband, finally after so many months of waiting.

"What if you!", Mary put her hand onto his lips and smiled.

"So what if we have another, what's one more", he chuckled and dropped his bracers off his shoulders.

"Harry Price, I've always said that "once those bracers drop" another baby Price can be expected". She nudged him lovingly and undid the top button of his trousers.

He kissed her again, this time with more passion and started undoing the buttons of her dress.

It was a beautiful dress, in ivory and cream, the hemline was above her ankles. The dress was layered, the material chiffon from London. She looked elegant with her new fashionable shoes, which she bought from Elsie, on the never! Never!

Elsie had made the dress for her, especially for the party.

Harry held her away from him and looked at her admiringly. He took the ivory comb out of her hair and let her beautiful hair drop over her shoulders. He ran his fingers through her curls, then he put his hands on her waist.

Even now after 11 children she still had the figure of a 20 year old.

He kissed her breasts and continued to undo her dress button by button slowly tantalising her.

She could hardly breath. He always had this effect on her.

"Harry you still take my breath away when I am near you, I love you now as I did that very first day you kissed me all those years ago in the meadow. Do you remember, my love?", she said as she kissed him tenderly.

"Of course, I remember my darling, how could I forget that day. It was the beginning of our life together". Harry kissed her again and again on the lips teasing her with his tongue.

Mary climbed out of her dress and stood there in her new low neck chemise and bloomers, which were above her knee.

He smiled looked her up and down, adoringly, and said:

"Suppose our Elsie, made them too",

Mary smiled and undid the string on her drawers, which fell to the floor, she carefully stepped out of them, picked them up and popped them onto the chair.

"They're very hot being silk, I still prefer cotton" she looked at them, feeling a little embarrassed being almost naked.

She turned to look at her husband, who was fully clothed.

"This is a little unfair, Harry", she said as she put her hands down to his flies and undid his buttons one by one. He watched her intently. She popped her hand inside his long-johns and commenced playing with his manhood. Harry let his trousers drop to the floor and eagerly climbed out of them. He took off his vest and threw it onto the chair by the window. Naked and sweating he looked down at his penis, which was hard and throbbing, wanting to enter that forbidden place.

Mary was also now totally naked, standing opposite the man she had always loved. He pulled her to him and kissed her tenderly.

"Better do this carefully, my dear, I do not want to injure my knee again. It would be hard to explain to the kids, that we injured it whilst in a passionate embrace".

"I want to lift you in the air and throw you down and ravage you, but I cant".

He took her by her hand and led her to the bed and gently pushed her down onto the feather mattress.

She lay there naked and wanton. Harry stood looking at her, penis erect. He lowered himself onto her and kissed her again and again. He moved down her body kissing her neck and then those beautiful breasts. Her nipples stood out like organ stops. He teased them with his tongue.

Mary lay their not wanting to move and spoil this special moment, she could hardly breath.

She wanted him. Needed him. God how she wanted him.

She pulled him onto her and rolled him over onto his back and started kissing him from his chest down his body, teasing for her seductive moves. She looked at his erect penis and put it into her mouth and moved up and down, slowly at first then more urgently. Harry moved and lifted her head.

“My darling!, you carry on like that and it will be all over and you will be left unfulfilled”. He kissed her and rolled her onto her back.

She lay still waiting for him to mount her, but his knee wouldn’t let him. He rolled back onto his back and smiled at her.

“This bloody knee is a damn nuisance”.

She climbed on top of him and began to move up and down, he breasts bounced as she moved. Harry lifted up and took her left breast in his hand kissing and licking her nipple, he looked into her eyes. She had the devil in her tonight.

She moved quicker and quicker, until he was spent. She rolled over onto the bed and puffed.

“Well my darling, that’s a baby if ever we’ve made one”. Harry smacked her on the bottom as she got out of bed to wash herself.

She carefully walked across the room trying not to awaken the babies, she put her housecoat on, crossed the landing and looked in on the children in the next room.

Joan was in the top drawer of the pine chest of drawers, Charles was cuddled up in the crib, Nancy had Phyliss were huddled together in the double bed. She smiled and closed the door softly.

She tiptoed downstairs to get a drink. She opened the door very carefully. Bernard, Len and David, were unconscious on the window benches, empty bottles by their sides. They sounded like pigs nuzzling the ground for food. She smiled at them. Then continued to tiptoe across the kitchen to the sink and made herself a nice cup of tea. She sipped at the tea and looked up at the bedroom where Harry lay.

“Well Mary Price, you’ve only got yourself to blame if you have another child growing in your belly”. She looked down at her body and shrugged her shoulders.

"What will be, will be", she said out loud. She looked over at the barn smiling and then proceeded back to the door at the bottom of the stairs.

She climbed the stairs and crept back into bed. Harry stirred and kissed her passionately on the lips.

"I haven't finished with you yet, young lady", Harry rolled her on top of him and gently, put his hand down to his erect penis and put it into Mary's warm inner self.

They made love even more passionately than before.

Another child was conceived on that evening, a baby daughter was born on 25th September, 1920. They called Ena Victoria, weighing in at 8lb 7oz. Exactly 9 months to the day of the homecoming party.

Harry held Ena high and cried. He pulled her to his chest and kissed her little head.

She was beautiful, with auburn hair and big eyes. She also had freckles on her little nose, just like his little sister Ena.

At last he had the daughter he had dreamed about for so long, little Ena Victoria, after his lost sister and Victoria after the old Queen and the victorious battle that had been won.

ABOUT THE AUTHOR

Sandra Shakespeare was born in a 2-bed council house in Wolverhampton, England, in June 1946.

She was educated at a Secondary Modern Girls school and left without any qulifications at 14 ½ years of age.

A rebel of the 1960's.

This is her first novel with 2 more in the pipeline to complete the trilogy.

She now lives in a small village in Staffordshire and owns a Longere (a long building) in Brittany, France, that has been painstakingly renovated over a 10 year period, where she now relaxes and writes.

Lightning Source UK Ltd.
Milton Keynes UK
UKOW042055100513

210513UK00002B/74/P

9 781481 788687

Lightning Source UK Ltd.
Milton Keynes UK
UKOW042055100513

210513UK00002B/74/P

9 781481 788687